Blood Bound

THE GUARDIANS OF THE WELDAFIRE STONE

TRINITY CUNNINGHAM

◆ FriesenPress

One Printers Way
Altona, MB R0G 0B0
Canada

www.friesenpress.com

Copyright © 2023 by Trinity Cunningham
First Edition — 2023

All rights reserved.

No part of this publication may be reproduced in any form, or by any means, electronic or mechanical, including photocopying, recording, or any information browsing, storage, or retrieval system, without permission in writing from FriesenPress.

ISBN
978-1-03-916937-1 (Hardcover)
978-1-03-916936-4 (Paperback)
978-1-03-916938-8 (eBook)

1. FICTION, FANTASY, ACTION & ADVENTURE

Distributed to the trade by The Ingram Book Company

Dedication

For my family.

Acknowledgements

TO START: THIS BOOK WOULD NOT EXIST IF NOT FOR MY GOD WHO HAS blessed me with imagination, and has opened doors to make publication possible. I am grateful to Colin, my husband, for all his patience and encouragement. My children—Genesis, Cillian, and Declan—I hope you find something that you become just as passionate about one day that you love and are able to do always. You've all been so patient with me and I can't thank you enough for that.

I'd also like to thank my mom and dad, Auntie Sharon and my niece Brooklyn; your alpha reading and listening to me rant on and on about fictional people and places has allowed this story to come to life in written form (smiling and nodding counts as listening).

Nicole at Whisler Edits, your work editing has improved this story significantly, and I am grateful that I've had the privilege to work with you and get to know you.

Friesenpress, for helping me see this through to completion, and Daniel for the beautiful map.

Thank you to all my beta readers who took the time to read and offer feedback. And I'd like to make a special thank you to a teacher from my elementary school days, Mervin Haines, who put a book in my hands at a difficult time in my life, and created in me a love of reading. If I didn't have that, this book might never have been written. In his words: "I have always believed that if you have a book or a poem in your pocket, you are never alone."

Thank you.

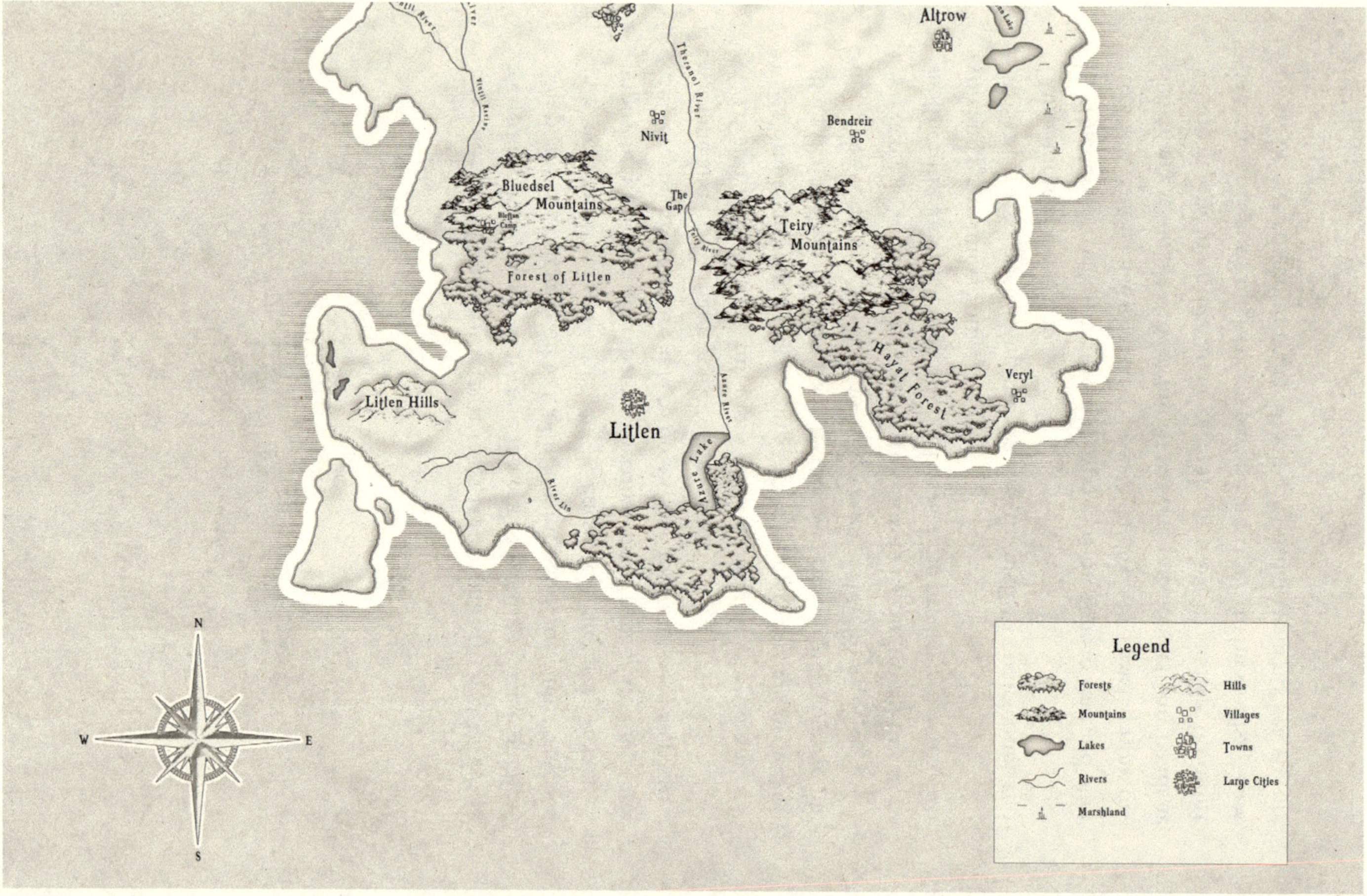
Altrow
Nivit
Bendreir
Bluedsel Mountains
The Gap
Teiry Mountains
Forest of Litlen
Theranol River
Virgil Ravine
Teiry River
Azure River
Hayat Forest
Veryl
Litlen Hills
Litlen
Azure Lake
River Lin
N
W
E
S
Legend
Forests
Mountains
Lakes
Rivers
Marshland
Hills
Villages
Towns
Large Cities

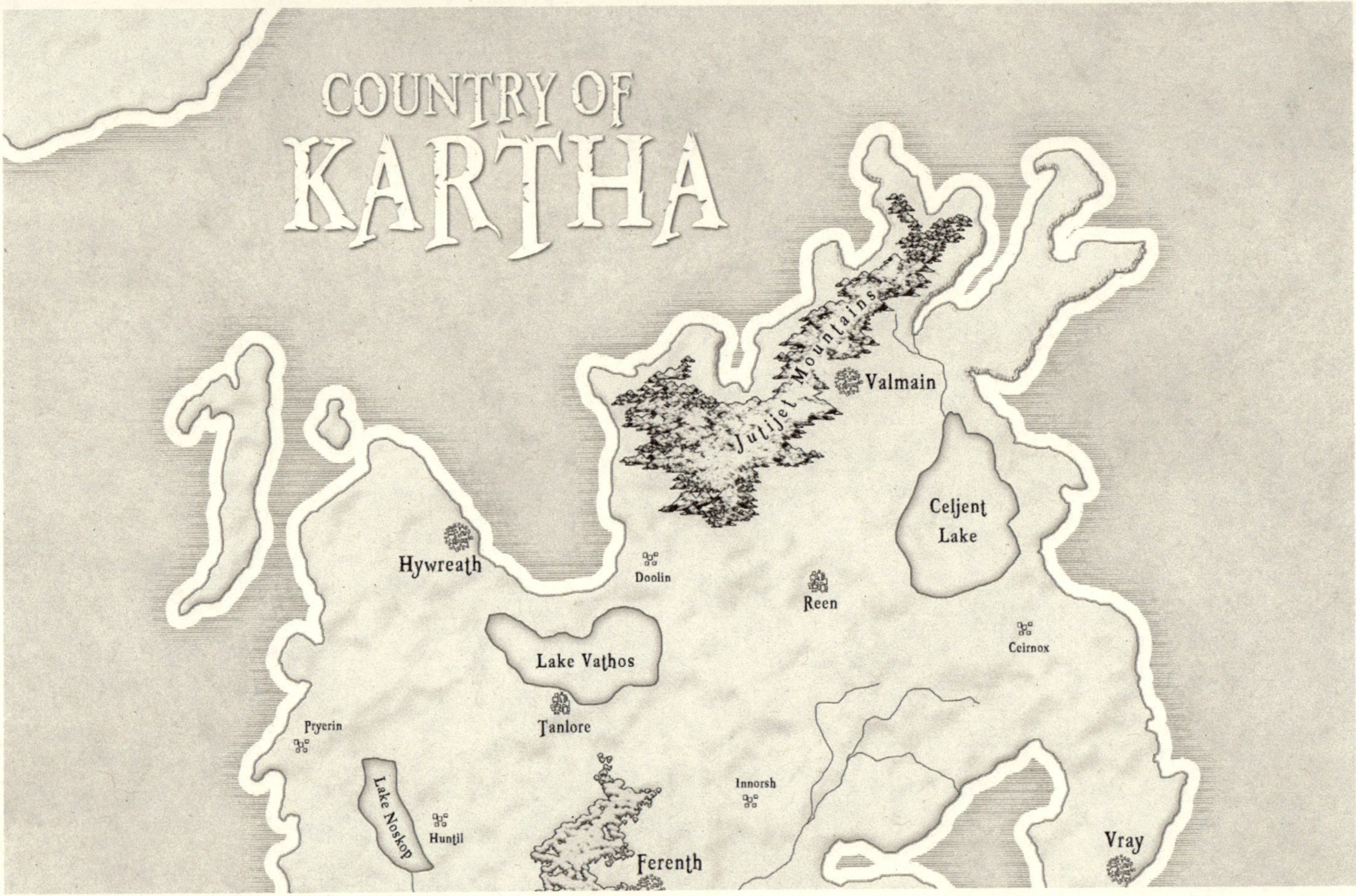
COUNTRY OF
KARTHA
Jutijet Mountains
Valmain
Celjent Lake
Hywreath
Doolin
Reen
Lake Vathos
Ceirnox
Pryerin
Tanlore
Innorsh
Lake Noskop
Huntil
Ferenth
Vray

Chapter 1

Giggling broke the quiet of the morning. Raidan stared with unfocused eyes at the blanket in his hand, barely aware of his son's gleeful sounds.

Upright on the bed beside him, Ida tickled Cassian's tummy, setting him off into another burst of laughter. Cassian's baby feet kicked at the air as he squealed and wriggled. The warmth of Ida's hand on Raidan's bare shoulder brought him back to the moment.

"Raidan?"

He focused his bleary gaze on her. Dark circles blurred under Ida's eyes, shadows that likely matched his own. She brushed a lock of his hair from his forehead, then cupped his cheek in her dainty hand.

"Did you sleep?" she asked.

He shook his head. Unlike her, it hadn't been Cassian that had kept him up, but Ida knew that. She dipped her chin. "Another nightmare?"

Raidan nodded. When was it ever anything else?

Ida's blond curls fell gently over her shoulder. She removed her hand from his face to sweep them back. "Was it any different this time?" she asked.

"It was the same. I'll get over it." It would take a few minutes to shake the image of Adrik from his head. The actual memory of meeting the man twenty-some years ago was vague. But the nightmares had stayed with him since. Adrik's copper skin in the night, his wild, unkempt hair, his eyes rolled back into his head, and then the crazed look he'd given Raidan when they returned to normal—the look of a madman. This was the image that stuck with him most.

"I think your son wants you to play," Ida said, drawing his thoughts from the nightmare. She gestured to Cass. Raidan sensed Cassian's expectant gaze on him. He turned his head down to meet deep-set brown eyes. Raidan and his twin, Dimitri, had inherited those eyes from their father, and their father had inherited them from his. A distinguished trait of the Dairner's, as their mother used to say.

Cassian's toothless smile filled his whole face. Blanket in hand, Raidan raised it up to cover his face. After a moment, he pulled it down, his eyes crossed.

"Peek-a-boo!"

Cassian burst into another fit. Raidan's smile stretched his cheek muscles. He bent over and kissed his son's forehead.

The sun poked in through the square window in their bedroom, a gentle reminder to get on with the day. He laid the blanket over Cassian, covering all of him. Cassian's hands flailed up and down until he got a hold of the blanket's edge and continued to wave his arms with the blanket in hand. Raidan got to his feet and stretched. His trousers lay on the floor by his bedside. He bent over to pick them up, then slipped his legs in and fastened the buttons.

"Rees has been on me constantly, asking about his cabinet."

"Rees from Ferenth?" Ida frowned. "You only started that job three weeks ago. Surely it takes more time?"

"Not always, but in his case, it does. The detail in the carving takes time. If he wants it done well, that is."

"So just tell him it'll be a while longer."

"I have. Several times. And he's understanding. Until another few days pass, and I receive more letters about it."

Cassian rolled over and almost fell over the edge of the bed. Raidan jumped and caught him. He lifted him into his arms. Cassian must have thought this was funny because he hiccupped a laugh and his eyes twinkled up at Raidan.

Ida's dimples showed when she smiled up at the two of them. Then her eyes flickered, losing their sparkle. "We need to talk about yesterday's announcement."

The reminder of what was coming brought the weight of their circumstance down on Raidan. He walked around the bed to Ida, set Cassian in her lap, and bent down to brush his lips against hers. "There's nothing to talk about. I'm not going anywhere." He said it like he meant it, but his words felt empty. Who was he to stop The Order from drafting him into their army? The Order took what they wanted and that was that.

"You can't pretend they're not coming, Raidan."

Raidan kissed her again and held his lips to hers for longer. When she was about to pull out of the kiss, he leaned in and deepened it, breathing in her scent.

Ida freed her lips to speak. "I know what you're up to." She grinned.

"Oh? Am I up to something?" Raidan smiled and looked her in the eye. "And here I thought I was just giving my wife a kiss."

Cassian got ahold of Ida's hair as it draped down near his face. She gently grasped his fingers and pulled herself free.

"We need to have this conversation." She took Raidan's chin and squared his face to hers. "We can't just sit here and wait for them to come and take you away."

Raidan clenched his jaw. This was not how he wanted to start his morning. "Now you sound like Dimitri."

"Dimitri's not wrong. What does Kingston need more men for anyway? He has an army." Ida's voice went up an octave. "I can't do this without you, Raidan."

Raidan scanned the bedroom floor, searching for his shirt. He spotted it by the wall, right where he'd thrown it the night before. "I've got to get to work. We can talk about it later." He pecked Cassian on top of the head and Cassian's whole body squirmed.

Standing, Ida rested Cassian against her body. "This conversation isn't over. We'll continue when you get home."

Raidan picked up his shirt, shook it out, and threw it over his head. The sleeves fell loosely over his arms. He tucked the bottom hem into his work trousers and cinched his tool belt in place at his waist, then removed his cloak from the hook on the wall and threw it around his shoulders.

Not wanting to make any promises, he simply nodded and gave Ida a quick last kiss before turning to go. "I love you."

The hardness in her eyes softened. "Love you. Get that cabinet finished already."

The lightened tension made it easier to leave, but it would be hard to focus today.

Raidan left the house and was immediately hit with the cool autumn breeze. He kept his head tucked as he walked along the dirt road on his way to work and glanced up briefly. Stalks of corn rose high in the field to his left. Sunflowers lined the opposite field and hid those tending the land from view. Everyone in the little village of Veryl knew what was coming, and he and Ida weren't alone in dreading the day the Valca Order arrived. The Order was not to be opposed. The Great Battle at Reen had shown just what came of those who revolted. Raidan's own father had charged into battle, knowing full well they lacked the numbers to defeat Kingston Valca and his army. He'd left his wife widowed, alone in raising two sons.

No. Raidan wasn't going to make the same mistakes as his father and chance not being there to raise Cassian. But being conscripted into the Valca Army had a similar outcome, nonetheless.

He shook his head and put it from his mind. He had time. There was still time.

Chapter 2

Raidan's workbench took up the wall opposite from the door. A row of tools and chisels were mounted to the wall above the bench, and the high window to the right of it let in a sliver of the afternoon light. The clock on the wall indicated it was nearly seven o'clock. Raidan had gotten carried away in his work. He wasn't entirely discouraged that he'd be getting back late today, not when he knew Ida would be home waiting to finish their discussion.

Rees's cabinet stood upright on the floor under the window, four feet tall and made from junjen wood. Rees himself had made the arrangements for the light, tan, exotic hardwood to be transported from Xihngrahv, one of the eight countries of Ecstein and of the wealthier class in Zareff Continent. All that was missing on the cabinet now were the last touches of the carvings of Moss Rose engraved along the outer edges of the doors.

Out of habit, Raidan scrutinized his work, then covered it for the night. He left his workshop and secured the door with a padlock. Crime was not high in Veryl, but he couldn't risk anything happening to Rees's cabinet. If he wanted to make a reputation for himself and his intricate carvings, he needed to build a rapport with Rees.

The days were growing shorter. The sun hung low to the west, just over the roofs of the shops across the street. Raidan's workshop was a simple wooden structure that he'd built himself. It sat perched between a line of timber-framed buildings.

Jogging over from across the road, Dimitri made his way toward Raidan, attempting to flatten his dishevelled hair as he neared. "Good," he said, sounding out of breath. "I caught you in time." He stopped just short of Raidan and put his hands on his hips, then held up a finger.

"Thought you were supposed to be in Altrow?" Raidan said while Dimitri caught his breath. As the village leader, Dimitri had gone two days ago on a trade business trip to the nearest town.

Dimitri nodded. He sucked in one long breath and straightened up. "I was," he said. "Let's take a walk." He indicated the opposite direction to Raidan's home.

"Ida's expecting me back. We can talk on the way to my place."

Dimitri made no move to go with Raidan. "I've got to show you something. It's important." His underlying hint of a smile meant this was something he was excited about. That could be anything for Dimitri.

Raidan sighed. It wasn't as though he didn't believe his twin. It was just that whenever Dimitri had something *important* to talk about, it usually pointed to one topic.

"If this is about what I think it's about, save it. I haven't changed my mind since the last time we—"

"It's not like that," Dimitri interrupted. "This is something else."

"Then what is it?"

"Come with me. I'll show you." Dimitri had a way of baiting Raidan. It was something Raidan had grown used to, not that it made it any less irritating. The thought of not going home now to finish the conversation with Ida appealed to him. On the other hand, going with Dimitri didn't necessarily mean he'd be avoiding that same conversation.

Raidan hung his head, too tired to argue and not exactly eager to get home just yet. He relented. "All right." He gestured for Dimitri to lead the way. "Show me."

The grocer, Ash Grange, approached from the next shop over. Under Ash's eyes were dark, puffy shadows. Ash ignored Raidan and made a beeline for Dimitri.

"Is it true?" he asked. "Is The Order really on their way?"

Dimitri gave a solemn nod. "We have around two weeks until Ilan Valca arrives. You don't look too good, Ash. Go home to be with your family."

Ash grabbed Dimitri's arm with his two hands. Tears filled his eyes. "But my boys. You've got to do something."

Raidan recalled Ash's three sons. Unlike frail Ash, his boys were all built strong. All over seventeen years in age, they would be eligible for the conscription.

Dimitri placed a reassuring hand over Ash's. "I understand you're afraid. Right now, the best you can do is be there for your boys. Remain strong for them. I'm doing what I can."

Raidan envied Dimitri's confidence, ability to make quick decisions, and way with the people. As a relatively young leader—not yet with any silver in his hair—he'd earned his place countless times.

The blacksmith, Jarvis Urik, joined them from his forge across the street. Jarvis acknowledged Raidan and Ash, then turned to Dimitri. "I have that order for you, should you require it." Jarvis winked.

Dimitri gave Raidan a sideways glance.

"Thank you, Jarvis, that won't be necessary. Not yet anyway. I'll keep you posted."

Jarvis nodded, then made his way back to his forge. Raidan thought he might have had an idea of what that was about. He didn't ask, but somehow, he suspected he was about to find out.

Chapter 3

Dimitri led Raidan west of Veryl toward the outer perimeter of the Hayat Forest. With every step farther from home, Raidan wanted to turn back. This forest stirred memories he wanted to forget.

Leaves crunched under their feet, and the tall trees in the dense wood stretched high above them. Many had yet to shed their bright red and yellowy leaves. It wouldn't be long before all the branches were bare.

When the abandoned cabin came into sight, Raidan stopped walking. The two of them used to sneak off to the cabin as children until it became the place Raidan swore he'd never return to. In the fading light, he could barely make out the derelict structure of the cabin. Its timber walls leaned dangerously low to the ground; the sunken roof had a gaping hole, exposing the outside elements.

From several steps ahead, Dimitri cocked his head at Raidan. "Why'd you stop?"

The sun was sinking lower and the canopy of leaves overhead blocked the remaining daylight. It was cold enough now that Raidan could see his breath. He drew his cloak closer to himself.

"What is this, Dimitri? What do you want to show me?"

"I've got a plan to help us with The Order."

"I thought you said this was about something different."

"It is. I'm not talking about a revolution. I had something else in mind. Something better."

"And you thought here was the best place to tell me?"

"It's on the way," Dimitri said. He always had a flair for dramatics.

"On the way where?"

Dimitri paused, then lowered his voice as if he were afraid they might be overheard. "To magic."

Neither spoke for a minute. Raidan debated whether Dimitri was joking.

"This is not a game, Dimitri. It's not like how we used to play when we were kids."

"I'm being serious. It's real, I've seen it."

Raidan didn't doubt the reality of magic. He just didn't want to mess with it again.

"Right," Raidan said, indulging his brother. "Say we go with that. Where are *you* going to get magic?"

"Adrik." Dimitri raised his eyebrows and grinned.

Anxiety stirred in Raidan. He'd seen Adrik's magic before—if it could be called that.

As a boy, he'd heard the stories. The ones in which Adrik found and tricked unsuspecting, grieving children. Raidan himself was a victim of his deception. Adrik had told him magic was real. Made him believe he could wield it too.

Twenty years ago, the day their mother died, Raidan had come to this very cabin to grieve. He'd stayed out until after dark. Adrik had found him that night, claiming it was Raidan's sorrow that drew him there. Seeing him had sparked wonder in fifteen-year-old Raidan. Adrik had offered a drink from his canteen and Raidan had thoughtlessly accepted.

After he'd drunk from the canteen and taken Adrik's hand, his head pounded so intensely he'd gotten sick. Adrik had convulsed; his wild bug-eyes had gone white. His voice had turned harsh and demanding.

Raidan hadn't stuck around after that to find out what would have happened next. He had run from there, but he'd never managed to escape the nightmares that tormented him.

"He's real, Raidan," Dimitri said. "All the stories we thought were made up—real!"

"I know," Raidan told him, but Dimitri carried on without any indication he'd heard.

"He came to me, showed me his magic. He made a blue light appear from nothing. He could shape it and move it. It was amazing! Told me he'd show me more when you were with me. He even said he can give *us* magic! Said that with it, we could defeat The Order and restore Kartha to its former glory. This is what we've been waiting for! This is what's going to tip the scales in our favour!"

Whatever Dimitri thought Adrik could do, Raidan didn't want any part in it.

"No," Raidan said. "He's a liar. He tricks people. That's all it is—tricks. And tricks are not going to tip any scales in our favour."

"It's not tricks. I'm telling you this is it. He wants us to meet him at a cave in the Teiry Mountains. He told me how—"

"Dimitri," Raidan cut in. "I want The Order gone as much as you, but this isn't the way to do it." Despite the cold air, Raidan wiped sweat from his brow. He did not miss the reference to *us*.

Dimitri's smile dropped and his shoulders sunk. "I don't understand. Why not?"

"Ilan is on his way as we speak. Looking for magic in the night is not going to help us figure out our problem."

Dimitri held out his hands. "Then tell me what else to do, because so far, you've come up with nothing. When The Order comes for our men, what will we have left? For all you know, you or I will get conscripted, and where will that leave Ida and Cass? Our whole village is barely standing on two legs and it's more than we can take."

All of that on top of the taxes and contributing a quarter of their harvest to the Valca Order. Raidan wasn't about to bring that up now, though.

"I know," he said. "I know." He closed his eyes. There had to be something else. *Anything* else. Raidan didn't care what, so long as it wasn't this.

He opened his eyes. "Maybe Ilan will see reason," he said. "You can talk to him—explain the situation. You represent the people; he has to listen to you. He might be nothing like his father." Though from the reports, Raidan doubted that. As did Dimitri, judging by his scrunched nose and raised brow.

"Look," Dimitri said. "The cave isn't far from here. The trail is a little rough, but if we go now, we can be back by morning to prepare for Ilan's coming."

"And do what? What then?"

"We'll figure it out, but by then, we'll have magic."

Raidan rolled his eyes. "*I'll* talk to Ilan. Let me do it. We have to at least try!"

Dimitri ran a hand through his hair and shook his head. "Raidan, what's with you?"

Raidan looked away. As the evening grew darker, a chill ran down his spine. Traversing a mountain trail they'd never been down before... in the dark... to a *cave* to meet with Adrik?

Anything but Adrik.

He didn't think he could bear new nightmares. Raidan couldn't be sure if the maniacal laughter that resonated in his memory was a figment of his imagination, but that didn't matter. He puffed out his chest and straightened his stance. "I'm not going, Dimitri."

Dimitri shrugged, letting his hands hang by his sides. "I told him we'd be there. Please come. I don't want to do this alone."

"You shouldn't have told him we'd come."

Dimitri was silent. He looked at Raidan with the saddest eyes. He really did believe this was the answer.

Dimitri had a way of persuading Raidan to do things he didn't want to do. Always, when they were growing up, he'd made Raidan think it would be fun or that they wouldn't get in trouble or that he'd take the blame if something went wrong. Usually there was some trouble to be had, but they were some of his greatest memories and adventures. Raidan never regretted those times.

This time was different, though. To go would mean facing one of his biggest fears, second to losing Cass.

But Dimitri was right: The Order did need to be stopped. Raidan just wasn't sure this was the way to do it.

"Don't give me that look," Raidan said. "You didn't even talk to me first before you agreed for me."

"I didn't think I had to. I thought we both wanted this."

"We do. Just—not *him*." Raidan did not want to accidentally summon Adrik out of the dark shadows.

"You don't have to do anything. Just come and listen to what Adrik has to offer. You can't know what he might say if you don't go."

Raidan considered the idea. He was about to refuse again when Dimitri spoke.

"Do it for Cass."

His words gave Raidan pause. His thoughts turned to his son. Not yet a full year and totally innocent of the conflict around him—of the kind of world he'd been born into.

His unfinished conversation with Ida nagged at him. What would she say to Dimitri's proposition? If meeting with Adrik had the potential to stop The Order from taking him away, she'd encourage him to at least listen to what was being said. He didn't want to fall back into his usual pattern of being talked into something he didn't want to do, but it might be good for him to face his fear.

"I'll go," he said, "but not now while it's this late. And not in a cave." Seeing Adrik again was enough. This time it would be on his terms.

Dimitri shook his head. "Can't wait. He's already there waiting for us." He started toward the mountains. "Think of it this way," he called over his shoulder. "The sooner we do this, the sooner we can go home and come up with a plan."

Raidan's mind searched for another excuse. It was getting harder to see in the dark; Dimitri was just a shadow moving in the night.

"Dimitri, wait!" Raidan scrambled to catch up to him. "We're not prepared for a journey into the mountains. How are we supposed to see anything?"

Dimitri paused and put a hand to his chin. "Right. I'm getting ahead of myself. The shed behind the cabin had some old lamps in it the last time I was here. Think there's any oil lying around?"

"No, I don't." Raidan hoped there wasn't.

Dimitri trudged through the fallen leaves, making a ruckus in the stillness of the forest. He disappeared inside the shed, which looked just as precarious as the cabin. After a moment, firelight flickered inside the open doorway, flashing once. The dull orange glow illuminated Dimitri's face as he reappeared with a lit lantern. He grinned. "Good to go."

Raidan grimaced. "That thing is useless."

"It'll have to do." Dimitri went on his way again, bringing the light with him and leaving Raidan in the dark.

Raidan took cautious steps, hardly able to see his feet. "We're only going to hear him out," he said as he caught up. "And the only reason I'm agreeing to come is because someone has to keep you out of trouble."

Dimitri gave a crooked smile. "It'll be worth it, I promise." He turned and headed toward the mountains. Raidan followed close behind, mentally preparing what he might say to Adrik for the first time in twenty years.

It was going to be a long night.

Chapter 4

Raidan weaved his way along the uneven ground in Dimitri's wake. *The path was a little rough,* Dimitri had said. That was an understatement. The lantern offered little light, and Raidan kept tripping over many jutting rocks and boulders.

The Teiry Mountains marked the edge of the Hayat Forest. Before them, a wall of solid rock towered above. The only way forward into the mountains was through a narrow passageway of stone.

Without hesitating, Dimitri led on. Raidan stumbled along in the darkness, dragging his feet. As they ascended at a gentle incline, the passage ended, revealing the expanse of the night sky and the surrounding mountain range. The crescent moon hung low over the snow-capped peaks above, casting shadows in the valleys. Between the higher elevation and his distress of paying Adrik a visit, Raidan had to stop briefly to catch his breath.

Dimitri stopped with him and shivered. He adjusted his cloak to cover the back of his neck. "Probably could have dressed a little warmer."

Raidan estimated they'd been walking for close to two hours. "It's not too late to turn back."

Dimitri waved his hand. "We're getting close."

"How do you know?"

Dimitri handed Raidan the lantern. "Hold this." He reached into his cloak to take something out of an interior pocket, then hunched his shoulders to block the wind as he showed the object to Raidan.

"Because of this," he said. In Dimitri's hand was a white five-petalled flower that was just small enough to fit in his cradled palm. Hues of blue spread outward from its centre, not quite reaching the tips.

"What is that?" Raidan asked.

"It's called bethrail. It grows as two flowers on one stem. Adrik said it would lead us to where we need to go. He gave me this one, and he has its inverse pair. I keep it close to my heart and can feel its warmth on my skin. The closer I get to its other half, the warmer it gets. Then somehow, I just . . . know which way to go."

Raidan stared at the magic plant. His stomach knotted. Why were they meeting in a cave?

He thought to voice his question aloud, but instead he asked, "How did you come to meet him anyway?"

"Adrik?" Dimitri put the flower back in his cloak, reclaimed the lantern, and walked on. Raidan could only presume the flower would lead them true. He followed in step. "He approached me while I was in Altrow," Dimitri said, veering from the trodden path and continuing up an incline. He lost his footing and backed into Raidan, who pushed Dimitri's weight forward until he'd regained his balance.

"Thanks," Dimitri said, then kept hiking upward.

The way ahead was no longer a part of the path. Their dim light flickered and faded as Dimitri moved farther away from Raidan. He wasn't stopping or slowing down, so Raidan picked up his pace.

"He knew who you were?" Raidan asked when he was almost to Dimitri.

Dimitri looked back and smiled. "Does that surprise you?"

It didn't. Not really. Dimitri knew a lot of people. Whether it was perks of the job or stemmed more from his personality, Raidan didn't know. He supposed it was a bit of both.

Dimitri went on. "Gunther—Altrow's appointed official—invited me to join him with a few others to dine. When I returned to the inn late that night, Adrik came across my path." He paused for a breath before continuing. "I couldn't believe it was really him when he told me who he was. I was never sure what to make of the stories about his magic, but if you saw how he manipulated and shaped his light, you would have been amazed. The stories are true."

Raidan kept his head down. He watched his steps so as not to fall but also to avoid his brother's eye. From the sound of it, Dimitri's experience with Adrik differed greatly from his own. His suspicions grew.

"So what did he want?" Raidan asked. "Why did he go to you?"

"He told me I could have magic if I wanted it and that he'd show me what we could do with it." Dimitri cocked his head at Raidan and smiled slyly. "I wasn't about to say no to that."

"Why didn't he give it to you right then?"

"He said it was for both of us," Dimitri said. "You and me. And what kind of brother would I be to deny you getting your own magic?"

"I wouldn't have thought any less of you."

Dimitri chuckled as he continued uphill. "Besides, I'm glad you're with me."

That makes one of us, Raidan refrained from saying aloud. Dimitri meant well. It wasn't his fault he couldn't grasp Raidan's reluctance. Ida had dealt with years of calming him down after his nightmares. But out of embarrassment or denial—he wasn't sure which—Raidan never told Dimitri about his encounter with Adrik. How could he now expect his brother to understand?

"Did he—" Raidan stopped short. He wanted to ask why Adrik wanted both of them without sounding too paranoid. Because he *was* paranoid. "Did he say anything more?"

"What do you mean?"

"I mean, did he say anything about why he wanted to give us magic?"

Dimitri shrugged. "You can ask when we get there."

They reached the peak of the mountain and looked down into the shallow basin on the opposite side. Dimitri closed his eyes and put a hand over his heart near the bethrail. After a moment, he opened his eyes and pointed to the bottom of the basin.

"Down there."

Moonlight reflected off the snow peaks, producing natural light in the sky. Even so, Raidan had to squint to make out the basin's contents. He estimated the way down was half a mile. The tall rock face on the opposite mountain rose straight up in a vertical wall. The peak on which they stood appeared to be the only way down.

Dimitri, in typical Dimitri fashion, gave Raidan a mischievous grin. "Isn't this great?" he said, then stepped down into the basin without waiting for Raidan.

Raidan opened his mouth but had no response. *Great* was not the word that sprang to mind.

Twenty minutes later, they stood at the bottom of the basin. The light of the lantern revealed an opening in the face of the mountain. Dimitri stepped closer and peered inside.

Raidan stayed back a few paces. "This doesn't alarm you at all?" he asked. "No big warning bells, nothing like that?"

Dimitri straightened. "I would hardly expect someone like Adrik to behave in a way that's considered normal. He's supposed to be a myth, or *creature of the shadows*, as they say. This seems fitting."

A breeze blew from the opening and extinguished the lantern's flame, leaving them in darkness.

Come, it said.

Raidan's chest tightened. The voice came from inside his mind.

His legs trembled. He looked at Dimitri, backlit by the starry sky. The inside of Dimitri's cloak lit up in a soft white glow. Raidan pointed, and Dimitri glanced down at himself. He withdrew the bethrail from his cloak. It glowed bright, reflecting off Dimitri's face and his broad smile.

"That's useful," Dimitri said, then edged into the dark opening. The flower's light glowed brighter. Dimitri's broad shoulders made the space seem tight. He circled in place as if to convey there was nothing to be scared of, then extended a hand to his brother.

Raidan licked dry lips.

Do it for Cass. It was manipulation, certainly, but that didn't take away from the truth of the words.

Heart racing, Raidan pushed aside his doubt and fear. He accepted his brother's hand and stepped into the tunnel.

Chapter 5

It was not as tight through the opening as he'd imagined it would be, but the tunnel itself was narrow. If Raidan raised his arms up, he could touch his hands flat to the ceiling.

He breathed in.

For Cass, he told himself while exhaling, then followed Dimitri. The length of the tunnel stretched out before them. It seemed like a long time before they arrived at their first fork in the path. Dimitri paused to sense the flower's leading, then veered left. A few tight turns later, Raidan had lost track of where they had entered. Even if he changed his mind, he didn't think he could turn back now. He'd never find his way out.

The light of the glowing flower in Dimitri's palm dimmed, then died. The silence in the blackness around them was unlike any other silence Raidan had ever known. To orient himself, he felt for the walls around him. He closed his eyes and it somehow made the darkness less frightening.

"Do you hear that?" Dimitri asked.

All Raidan could hear was his own raspy breathing. He strained his ears. A trickling sound came from deeper within the cave, though it was hard to tell how far away it was. "Water," Raidan said, eyes still closed.

"There!" Dimitri said.

Raidan opened his eyes and searched the darkness. A dim blue glow shone from ahead. A few more turns, Raidan thought, and they'd find its source. Dimitri walked toward the light, and Raidan had no qualms about following him if it meant he didn't have to stand there, blind in the dark.

Around a couple more bends, the light got brighter. Raidan swallowed past a hard lump in his throat and wet his lips. Dimitri had said Adrik's magic light was blue, hadn't he?

A scent lingered around them—woodsy with a hint of something foul, mixed with the earthy smell of the underground. It had a strange effect on him, like there was a heaviness in the air, weighing him down. He shook his head to try to remove the fogginess. He needed his wits about him.

One more turn to the right, and they came to an opening like a doorway, leading into an open chamber. The first thing Raidan took any notice of was the dark figure of the man, standing in the centre of the room.

Adrik. Raidan's heart skipped a beat.

His trimmed hair and beard didn't take away from the look of the madman that haunted Raidan's nightmares.

Adrik looked first to Dimitri, then settled his gaze on Raidan. His eyes looked different from the last time they'd met. Where once they had a sadness in them, they now held a fire and determination. It was that sadness when they'd first met that Raidan thought had mirrored his own, and was why he'd decided to trust him then. He wouldn't be so naive this time.

A blue spherical light on the ceiling hovered above Adrik and lit the chamber. The source of the sound that Dimitri had heard was revealed in a steady flow of water that poured from a curved stalactite in the ceiling. It flowed into a pool on the ground. The stone pool was circular, and its ledge was almost as high as Raidan's knees. The outside of the stone ledge was marked by carvings of trees and forests, mountains and rivers. The pool was filled to the brim with dark water, yet even with the constant flow of water, it did not spill over.

Encircling Adrik, who stood beside the pool, were six smooth stone chairs that faced each other. The chairs appeared to have been carved from single chunks of rock rather than pieced together from multiple stones. The backs of each of them stretched abnormally long, extending as high as Adrik's chest. Each chair had armrests on either side of its seat and a stone table at its side, level with the armrests. On one of them, incense burned. Beside it lay a blue flower, similar to Dimitri's white one. Its colours were the same but reversed, with white in the inner centre extending out onto the blue.

Adrik extended his arms out in welcome. "Dimitri and Raidan Dairner. Come. Sit. There is much to talk about." He gestured to the chairs. His accent, though it was subtle, had the underlying fluctuations of a Reij dialect.

Dimitri stepped toward one of the chairs, then stopped when Raidan made no attempt to move.

"What do you want?" Raidan said.

Adrik lowered his arms and linked his fingers in front of himself. "Ah, Raidan. I see you have not recovered since we last met. Believe me when I say that if I had known who you were then, things would have gone very differently."

Dimitri's eyes widened, and he looked at Raidan. "You've met?"

Raidan blinked. *If he had known who he was?*

Dimitri shook his head and returned his attention to Adrik. "Wait, what do you mean by that?"

Adrik stepped toward them. Raidan backed up, and Adrik paused in front of one of the six chairs. His eyes never left Raidan.

"Tell me, what do either of you know about the Elderace?"

Raidan clenched his fists. He was about to repeat his question, demanding Adrik tell them what he wanted, but Dimitri cut in first.

"They were killed by The Order in the war a hundred years ago. Their territory was destroyed and is now the cursed lands, an entire city in ruins, where nothing grows."

Adrik's eyes betrayed a hint of sadness, but only for a moment before the determination was back. "Litlen. Yes," he said. "And what else?"

"They had magic," Raidan said. He was not in the mood for games. "What about them?"

"The Elderace were my people," Adrik said, "and yes, they had magic. There was great discord between us and the mayanon—that is, the non-Elderace. One man, a mayanon, was adopted as one of our own. My father had taken him in and given him an important responsibility. He was granted the greatest magic there is and was entrusted with a power like no other: the power of the Weldafire Stone."

"We didn't come for a history lesson," Raidan snapped. As interesting as the story was, Adrik standing there, looking so calm and collected, overwhelmed Raidan with renewed hate. He was reminded of every night he'd woken up in a cold sweat. His stomach churned and he thought he might be sick. "Just tell us why we're here."

Adrik squinted at Raidan. "To understand what I am going to tell you, you need to understand the history," Adrik said. "Otherwise, you will not know how important you are—how important you both are—and what your being here could mean for all of Kartha."

Raidan's mouth went dry. What did he and Dimitri have to do with all of Kartha? Whatever Adrik was up to, he wanted nothing to do with it.

Spots danced across Raidan's vision in his peripherals. It was that smell. It was so strong. Adrik followed Raidan's line of sight to the incense. "If you relax, it will not bother you."

The only thing that would make Raidan relax right now was to leave this place.

Dimitri paid no attention to Adrik's remark. "What made the mayanon so special that he was accepted by the Elderace?"

Adrik turned to Dimitri, continuing his story. "Your desire to revolt against The Order seems to run in your family. Your ancestors have been known for their acts against The Order. But that was not why this particular man was chosen. It was, however, how he came to be raised by an Elderace couple." Adrik's eyes went distant for a moment. He gave a slight shake of his head and continued, "The six delegates"—he indicated the six chairs—"gave him the magic of the Weldafire Stone . . . a sacred magic that exists in a single stone . . . the very life of Kartha. When the war came to Litlen, the stone was at risk of being taken. It could only be bound to someone in blood by the six delegates, united together in agreement. One of our own people had intended to take it for himself. It was believed that he had the potential to succeed, and it became imperative that it become bound to someone else before that could happen. And so, here in this room is where they bound the magic to the man called Sermarc, who would become the Guardian of the Weldafire Stone. The Guardian's bloodline would carry out the honour for generations to come. Before I met you, Raidan, I believed his bloodline had ended. Now, there is hope again for magic to be returned and Litlen restored."

Raidan recognized the name Sermarc. It sounded like the word Adrik had shouted out to him when they had first met. But Raidan had already been running home by then.

Dimitri's mouth hung open, and his wide-eyed expression was that of a child's. "But *you* have magic?"

"Mine is limited." Adrik pointed up toward the blue light hovering above them. "Light is my magic. Until Litlen is restored and the curse is broken, it will remain that way."

The corner of Dimitri's lip turned up in a crooked smile. He glanced at Raidan, a hopeful gleam in his eye.

Adrik took another step toward Raidan, but Raidan put up a hand. Adrik stayed put. He lifted his own hands up in a show of surrender.

"After the curse and Sermarc's death, the stone went missing," he continued. "I searched, and when I did not find it, I gave up. Until I discovered Sermarc had a child. To my shame, I never sought out his wife after the war ended—if you could say it ever truly ended. Landon Valca raided the city for years following its destruction, determined to exterminate us. I assumed Sermarc's wife, like my father and Sermarc, had died." Adrik looked at Raidan. "But it was you that opened my eyes that night. When I discovered you were Sermarc's heir, I went looking for the stone. It took me many years to find it, but sometimes, that is the way of magic: it reveals itself when the timing is right."

He reached into a little leather pouch strapped to his side and extracted a small blue-green gemstone.

"And now I have the Weldafire Stone—and the brothers whose blood is intertwined in its power."

Chapter 6

Raidan retreated to the outskirts of the room. Next to the circle of chairs, water still babbled in the pool in the centre. If he weren't so worried about getting lost in the maze of tunnels, he'd have left already. Dimitri was an arm's length away, while Adrik stood by the chair nearest to them, holding up the Weldafire Stone.

"So, what does that mean?" Dimitri asked. "For us."

Adrik replaced the stone in its pouch. He smiled for the first time since they'd arrived. "By activating the power of the stone in your blood, you'll provide the key to restoring magic in the land. You two are to uphold the task given to Sermarc."

"Task? What task?"

"It doesn't matter," Raidan said. "We're not a part of this. This has nothing to do with us."

Adrik turned to Raidan. "On the contrary. It has everything to do with you."

Movement above caught Raidan's attention. He looked up. Vines stuck to the ceiling *slithered*. They moved like snakes jumbled up in a ball, curling on top of one another. Without looking where he was going, Raidan took a small step backward. He stumbled and used the wall to steady himself. On the floor by his feet, vines wriggled and spread, circling around the edges of the room.

Dimitri took a step closer to Adrik, apparently unaware of the vines. "How do we activate the power?"

Coming here had been a mistake. Raidan moved away from the vines nearest him, which brought him closer to Adrik. "Dimitri, we're not—"

"Irony is a funny thing," Adrik said, his menacing eyes fixed on Raidan, taunting him. "You are to drink from the Pool of Sovereignty and become bound to the stone in blood."

Heat flushed in Raidan's cheeks. He'd heard enough. He would not be accepting any drink offered from Adrik. He wasn't about to make the same mistake twice.

"Right," he said. "We came, we heard, and now we're done. Dimitri, time to go."

Dimitri gawked at Raidan. "Didn't you hear? He's going to give us magic so we can stand a chance against The Order."

Raidan was trembling all over. The heavy feeling from earlier hadn't worn off. In fact, it had worsened. The air was hard to breathe. That smell! He wanted to throw the incense across the room or into the pool in the centre. The Pool of Sovereignty, that was what Adrik had called it. The same water in Adrik's canteen Raidan had drunk from all those years ago.

Magic or not, Raidan didn't trust Adrik.

"We'll find another way, Dimitri. Let's go." He turned on his heel to exit and almost walked into a wall of vines. The thick branches weaved within the threshold, blocking the only way out.

Raidan stumbled backward. "What is this?"

Dimitri gaped at the vines.

Raidan ground his teeth. He imagined his face looked as contorted as it felt when he turned to face Adrik. "Get this out of my way!"

Adrik tilted his head. "You are not hearing me."

"I hear you," Raidan countered. "I'm just done listening. Get rid of the vines."

"Raidan," Dimitri said, glancing at the vine wall. "What's gotten into you?"

Raidan's vision blurred; his head spun. He looked at the ground, wishing he were anywhere but here, cornered. A new level of hate toward Adrik took root in him. He pointed an accusing finger.

"Adrik—" he began but stopped short. Tiny pieces of rocks from the ceiling floated in front of his face. "Move the vines. I'm leaving."

Adrik slanted his head and lifted a hand as if to command silence. Only the steady flow of water pouring into the pool resounded in the room.

"You cannot leave," Adrik said. At a wave of his hand, the vines slithered closer to Raidan. "Not without becoming bound to the stone."

Dimitri took wide steps over the vines toward Adrik. "This way, Raidan," he urged.

Raidan lifted his feet high, one at a time to keep from getting tangled. His back bumped into the wall of vines at the threshold. They wrapped around his body and pulled him further into the wall, twisting around his arms and legs. Panic swelled inside him and he flexed his biceps, fighting against the hold the vines had on him.

"This does not work," Adrik said, "without the both of you." Raidan didn't care for the hardness in his stare.

"Why not?" Dimitri asked.

Raidan groaned, straining to break his limbs free.

Adrik didn't blink. "If only one of you does this, it is recognized as half. You are two halves of a whole."

The vines cut into Raidan's skin. Every time he pulled, they squeezed tighter.

"That doesn't make any sense," Dimitri said. "We're two people."

Adrik bowed his head. "Twins share a different bond from that of ordinary brothers. Truly, I wish it were not so, but this is the way it must be."

Raidan shook his head. "No. No! I'm not doing this again." He thrust himself forward and bent his knees to gain leverage, backing himself further into the wall, hoping to push through to the other side. But the vines held his arms stretched out on either side of his body. They twisted around his legs and lifted his feet off the ground. He dangled within the threshold as if he were a part of the wall.

Weary from struggling, he stilled. He needed to conserve his strength. "Dimitri, you can't trust him. He's a liar. Whatever he's told you or showed you with his magic, believe me, you don't want it."

"Raidan, please." Dimitri looked on the verge of tears. "You don't have to fight. What do you think is going to happen? Why are you so against this?"

Raidan could not remember a time in his life when Dimitri hadn't talked him into doing what he wanted. But he refused to go through it all again. The visions, the head-pounding pain, the nausea. And the nightmares that only worsened over time.

"Look at me!" Raidan shouted. If his current dilemma wasn't enough to make Dimitri understand, he didn't know what would. "Tell me you know this isn't right."

Whether Dimitri knew it or not, he didn't attempt to help him. He met Raidan's eye, then cast his gaze down. Raidan's eyes burned as he held back tears. He lashed out against the vines with all his strength, gasping as the pressure around his chest increased. He couldn't get enough air into his lungs.

"The Anguivina will only squeeze tighter the more you struggle," Adrik said. He waved a hand and the tension around Raidan's torso loosened. Not much but enough that he could breathe.

"Please, Dimitri," Raidan said, panting. "I know you think this is the only way to fight The Order, but I'm begging you, don't. Don't let him trick you like he tricked me."

Adrik raised his chin. "You did not unders—"

"I'm talking to my brother!" Raidan shouted, his voice strong. Adrik shut his mouth and narrowed his eyes.

Something tickled the back of Raidan's head and the nape of his neck. A vine wound its way around his face and over his mouth. It tasted like grass and dirt. He tried to talk, but his words were incomprehensible. In a sudden rage, he thrashed and screamed until his throat was raw. When he ran out of breath, he hung limp and breathed heavily through his nose.

The muscles in Dimitri's jaw tensed. "It's going to be okay, Raidan. You don't have to be afraid." He turned to Adrik. "You won't hurt him, will you?"

Tears coursed down Raidan's cheeks. Dimitri still believed Adrik was trying to help them. *How could he?*

Adrik stepped over vines to get to Raidan. He stood face-to-face with him and sighed. "Raidan is too strong-willed to be persuaded—stubborn would be a better word. He does not yet realize the importance of this legacy." He looked at Dimitri. "Your legacy. Both of you." His voice grew quieter. "He will, though, and he will thank me one day."

Something wet trickled under Raidan's nose.

Adrik pulled a handkerchief from his pocket and gently wiped away the blood there. "He is doing this to himself," he told Dimitri. He stuffed away the handkerchief, unstrapped his canteen from his side belt, and filled it from the Pool of Sovereignty.

Then he approached Raidan, whose last encounter was at the forefront of his mind. It was Adrik's touch, combined with drinking the water, that had brought about the visions and the shaky feeling the last time. Raidan twisted his head this way and that as if it would do any good. Adrik removed the vine from Raidan's mouth and put his hand around the back of his neck.

At Adrik's touch, Raidan's heart jolted. He could feel every pulse of blood pumping through his body. He became aware of every sound, every tiny flicker of the blue light, every breath. Bright flashes blurred in his vision. Adrik grabbed his hair, yanked his head back, and poured the liquid down his throat.

Chapter 7

Instinctively, Raidan tried to pull his head away. He coughed and sputtered as the water poured down his chin.

Adrik tightened his grip in Raidan's hair while holding the canteen to his lips. The steady flow of water made Raidan choke. He gasped and swallowed some of it.

When Adrik finally took his hand away, Raidan's heightened awareness let up, but his head felt like it might split open. He coughed and sucked in as much air as his lungs would allow while suppressing the urge to retch.

Adrik handed Dimitri the canteen. As he accepted it, Dimitri glanced at Raidan. Frowning, he lowered his eyes, then drank. While he did that, Adrik unsheathed a knife from his belt. He removed the Weldafire Stone from its leather pouch and resumed his place in front of Raidan.

Raidan hung his head. Trying to get away was no use. He held his breath, awaiting what came next.

"Everything is going to be better," Adrik said. "Trust me." He pressed the blade against Raidan's upper arm, tore through the fabric of his shirt, and made a small cut. Raidan flinched. Blood trickled from his arm. Adrik placed the stone against Raidan's skin and allowed the blood to drip over it, then headed toward Dimitri, who held out a hand for the knife.

Raidan tensed his muscles. Something was different, as if whatever Adrik had just done had given him new strength. He felt like if he tried to break these vines now, he could tear them to pieces. This new strength—it terrified him. But he'd use it.

With all the force he could gather, he wrenched his arms inward. The vines didn't break right away, but he kept pulling. The grip around his arms loosened, not much but enough to give him hope. He screamed and doubled his efforts.

The room trembled. Adrik turned to Raidan, his eyes round and worried. A pebble fell from the ceiling and hit his hand and he jumped. The knife dropped to the floor, but he didn't pick it up. Adrik yelled something, but over the sound of his own screaming and the rumbling of the mountain, Raidan couldn't make out his words.

The rumbling deepened, and the ground shook. Adrik bent down and covered his head. Dimitri grabbed hold of the nearest chair and protected his head with his arm.

The vines keeping Raidan restrained snapped and he fell, landing on his hands and knees. The vines writhed back and slunk away, back to the edges of the room, where they lay still, in a heap. Raidan was out of breath from screaming. Rocks the size of his fist fell among the smaller ones. At the Pool of Sovereignty, the water bubbled and rose. It spilled over the outside of the pool and onto the cave floor.

Raidan got to his feet, unsteadily at first, but he found his balance and set his gaze on Adrik. He strode over and grabbed him by the throat, directing all his fury into his grasp as he squeezed. Adrik's eyes bulged, and his hands clawed at Raidan's.

"Raidan!" Dimitri shouted.

Raidan kept his eyes on Adrik's satisfying look of horror. The roar of the cave grew greater still, like a warning of more danger to come. Water sloshed as the Pool of Sovereignty spread across the floor.

A heavy force slammed against Raidan and he lost his hold on Adrik. He thought he'd been hit by a falling boulder, but when he turned over on the ground, Dimitri was there. Adrik moved away, clutching his throat and making horrible choking sounds.

Water poured down from the walls all around. It now covered the whole floor of the room and was spreading into the cave's tunnels. A boulder fell into the water an inch from Raidan, drenching him.

We need to go, Raidan thought as he stood.

Adrik was on his hands and knees, coughing. His blue light flickered and dimmed above them all. Soon it would go out completely and they'd be left in the dark while the cave collapsed and crushed them. The threshold was open and clear, the vines no longer blocking them from leaving. The raining boulders were their biggest concern now.

Adrik gasped and groped around in the water. "No!" he exclaimed. "No-no-no-no-no, where is it?"

Raidan helped Dimitri to his feet. Dimitri sprung up and shoved past him, rushing over to Adrik. He grabbed his arm and tried to pull him up. "We have to leave this place!" he yelled. Adrik swatted Dimitri away and kept up his panicked search. Raidan had a pretty good idea of what he'd lost.

They didn't have time for this. Raidan grabbed Dimitri's shirt at his shoulder and yanked him along. Dimitri stumbled as he backed away from Adrik but followed without a fight. Raidan took a last look back at Adrik, whose teeth were clenched and eyes crazed as he searched the water. Raidan nearly expected him to summon the vines to try and stop them.

Raidan used his newfound strength to tow Dimitri into the tunnel after him. Together, they sloshed through the water, rounding bend after bend on their way out of the cave.

When Adrik's magic blue light was too far away, Raidan stretched an arm out beside him to feel his way along the tunnel. Rocks pelted him with every step. Something heavy whacked into his shoulder and he grunted.

"Dimitri, I can't see anything."

"I can't either." Dimitri's voice was close. "We need light."

"Where are we going to get light? We don't have time."

A half-second's pause. "You. You can make light!"

The ground beneath their feet shook. "I can't!"

"Raidan, we can't see where we're going. You can—"

"No! You do it."

"I don't have magic."

"You were there! You drank the water too."

Dimitri said nothing. Something collapsed from somewhere behind them, back toward Adrik.

"Raidan!" Dimitri shouted over the noise. "Make a light!"

"I don't know how!"

"Try. Something—*anything*."

The water at their feet lapped at their ankles. Raidan snapped his fingers a few times in a quick motion. He unclenched a fist, imagining a light would appear in his hand.

Nothing.

He lowered the hand that was protecting his head and rubbed his hands together. Still nothing.

"I can't!" he said as he clapped his hands together. A spark of blue flashed and was gone.

"You did it, Raidan! Do it again."

Raidan clapped again, but nothing happened.

"I don't know what I did. It's not working!" He tried snapping again. This time a blue light appeared and hovered over his hand. Raidan stared with a combination of disgust and awe.

A boulder fell from the ceiling and splashed into the water at their feet. The blue light hovered over Raidan's hand, illuminating the tunnel. Dimitri charged ahead, and Raidan followed. Another few turns, and another chunk of the cave came down. It landed so close; Raidan threw his hands up in surprise. The light went out, and the sudden darkness halted him.

The current pushed against the back of Raidan's knees. He planted his feet while he snapped and clapped, trying to get the light back.

"There!" Dimitri shouted. "Light ahead. We're almost out. Come on, Raidan, run!"

Raidan bounded after him toward the faint sliver of light ahead. The ceiling and walls were coming down in bigger segments now. He pushed through the resistance of the water, which continued to rise.

Two more bends, and fresh air hit Raidan full force, cooling his sweaty forehead as he emerged from the cave into open territory. The sun had not yet risen, but the sky lightened in the nearing dawn. Raidan glanced back at the mouth of the cave in time to see a pile of boulders crumble down, blocking the entrance entirely. The ground continued to shake as Raidan hiked up a steep slope after Dimitri, away from it all.

Before they'd gone ten paces, the shaking settled and the air was still.

Chapter 8

Raidan jogged a little further up the slope to stay out of the rising water. He fell to his knees, unable to stand any longer on his shaky legs. Dimitri was doubled over and breathing heavily.

In the early morning light of the sky, a purple haze hovered over the mountain. A feeling of foreboding overwhelmed Raidan as if things were different now—not just for him, but for Kartha. Whatever Adrik had done, something had changed.

He held his hands out in front of himself. They looked normal. But only moments ago, they had done something impossible: Making light appear from nothing?

He dropped his hands and looked elsewhere. The cut on his arm stung. The dried blood stained his white sleeve, and his skin was already beginning to scab over.

Water gushed halfway up the heap of boulders that blocked the cave's opening. More water flowed down the vertical mountain face.

Raidan rose and straightened his back. His muscles were tight, and his knees wobbled. He kept his eyes on the boulders at the cave entrance, expecting Adrik to emerge, not that he thought it would be possible for him to get through now. He didn't know the extent of Adrik's magic and what he was capable of, but he had to consider the possibility that Adrik had survived.

He breathed in the clean morning air and stared at the spot while the world brightened around them, then let out a full breath, assured that Adrik wasn't coming.

Dimitri stood tall. He extended an arm toward the barricaded entrance. "Adrik didn't get out."

"Good," Raidan said.

"And the stone," Dimitri went on, ignoring Raidan. He vocalized his thoughts as if Raidan cared to hear them. "It looked like he'd dropped it."

Raidan shifted his balance from one leg to another, testing his stability. He needed to get away from this place and figure out what he was going to do now. He wouldn't be sticking around to become more of an accessory in any plans after he'd made his objections clear.

Whatever Adrik had done to him, something was different. He sensed a power in himself, sitting like a heavy burden. He was intensely aware of his blood pumping in his veins. A tingling pricked just beneath the thin outer layer of his skin, and a headache lingered at the back of his skull.

How could he have been so foolish to have agreed to go to the cave with Dimitri?

"What happens now?" Dimitri asked. "If the stone is missing . . . and Adrik, well . . . gone, where does that leave us?"

"Not *us*, Dimitri. You. Not me. I told you I don't want to be a part of any of this! You do what you want. It's what you always do anyway. I'll have no part in it. I'm leaving."

"Leaving?" Dimitri said. "Leaving where?"

"Away. And you stay away from me. Don't come anywhere near me and my family."

The rising water continued to fill the basin and had almost reached their feet. Confident he could walk now, Raidan started back up the way they had initially come from only a few hours ago.

"Away from where?" Dimitri asked. "You can't leave now, not at a time like this. What about The Order?"

Raidan turned back to face his brother and threw up his hands. "What about them? I told you we'd figure something else out and you didn't listen. You allowed Adrik to do whatever he wanted, and now it's too late."

"What would you have had me do?"

"Anything!" Raidan shouted. Water came in rushed spurts down the vertical mountain, pouring into the basin.

Dimitri stepped forward, away from the edge of the developing lake, closer to Raidan.

"I don't care what," Raidan said. "It would have been good to know you had my back."

Dimitri stood with his mouth hanging open.

At this point, it didn't matter what he might say: Raidan had made up his mind. He was leaving Kartha. With The Order on their way through the country and soon to reach Veryl, the worry over whether he'd be conscripted and the events from inside the cave . . .

He needed to clear his head, to get away from it all and figure out what it meant for him and his family.

"Where will you go?" Dimitri asked at last.

Raidan wasn't sure what to say. Leaving Kartha was drastic, but this seemed a perfect time for drastic action. Dimitri's betrayal hurt. It made Raidan want to hurt him back. Taking his family somewhere far away would certainly do just that.

"I'm leaving Kartha," Raidan said.

"Leaving Kartha? You can't go. I need you here."

"You should have thought about that before you let Adrik perform his little ceremony on me." Raidan turned his back on Dimitri and headed up the mountain on his own.

The sun appeared above the lower peaks of the mountain range. He and Dimitri had been out all night, and Ida would be wondering where he was. Now more than ever, he needed to get back to his family.

"Raidan, wait! Hey, wait up." Dimitri ran after him.

"No!" Raidan turned on his heel with his hand extended out toward Dimitri. Dimitri fell backward and hit the ground hard. Raidan retracted his hand and tucked it close to his body. Not only was he overwhelmed with anger, but sorrow filled his heart. This power in him was strong and dangerous. What was Ida going to think? Would she be frightened by him? He wouldn't blame her if she were.

The purple haze was fading in the morning light as mist disappears in the sunshine.

"Don't follow me," Raidan told Dimitri. He left him where he'd fallen.

The best thing for Raidan to do now was to go home to Ida and stay out of the way of The Order. As much as he wanted change, this wasn't what he'd had in mind. And now there was no going back. He would never be the same again. Nothing would be.

Chapter 9

THE BLUE-ORANGE FLOWERS STANK LIKE SEAWEED IN THE TIGHT SPACE of Laila's cavern room. A piece of her fiery mane of hair came loose from its long plait and fell in her face and in her way. She swept it aside, adding it to the rest of the tangled mess on her head.

Laila deposited the flowers into a vase. The vase was one she'd retrieved from her old home in Litlen. She'd acquired it long ago during one of her many ventures outside the mines. Placing the bouquet on the little desk, she carefully arranged the eshuair flowers. While they were not her favourite, her mother loved them. They were not the easiest to get her hands on. They grew low to the ground, typically among the poisonous xhinelet bushes. Laila had been careful while retrieving them for her mother, but her pinky finger burned where she'd accidentally touched one of the many broad leaves of the xhinelets. It was starting to blister a little. Laila grimaced at the look of it. There was salve in the medic's corner. She'd go there after she was done here.

The door swung open and Laila nearly knocked the vase over in her surprise. "Royl!" she said with too much force. "You scared me!" She straightened the vase and adjusted the flowers. Apart from her mother, whom she shared the room with, her older brother, Royl, was the only person who entered without knocking.

Royl opened his mouth but stopped short when he saw the flowers. "Where did you get those?"

Laila didn't think that was what he'd come here to ask her. She rolled her eyes. "You know where I got them."

Royl checked over his shoulder, then entered the room fully and closed the door. Lowering his voice, he said, "You went out again? Laila, how many times do I have to say it? You can't keep going outside."

"So you keep saying." Laila grinned. "But what's going to happen? What are you so afraid of?"

Royl stared intently at her. He looked good for a hundred and sixty-nine years old—not yet even in his middle years.

She herself was considered quite young in Elderace years at a hundred and fourteen.

He broke eye contact and shook his head. "Did anyone see you go?"

Laila hesitated. He was protective, but he'd not yet crossed the line of *overly* protective.

"Yes."

"Who?" Royl didn't sound angry, just resigned.

Laila bit her lip. If she didn't tell him, he'd just go and question each of the sentries at the main-way.

The sentries watched the comings and goings in and out of the mines, which used to be abandoned but had served as their home for almost a century now.

"Bailey," Laila said, adding quickly. "Don't speak to him. Please."

"Why not?"

"Because he's the only one who doesn't give me a hard time when I go. And telling him not to let me pass won't stop me. There are other ways out, you know."

Royl raised his eyebrows. "You mean through the tunnels you're not supposed to be wandering around in?"

"Exactly. I know my way around down there better than anyone. Speaking to Bailey won't stop me from going out. It'll only mean I'll have to be sneakier about it."

Going out was forbidden unless you had a job that required being outside. Laila argued for one such job many times, but Royl, as an apprenticing elder, managed to dissuade the others. According to him, it was too risky. But he was not oblivious to her regular adventures outside on her own. And while he disapproved of her frequent outings, he had a twinkle in his eye as he held her gaze. They both knew the dangers were much less than what they had been decades ago. There was nothing left in Litlen. Between Landon's war a hundred years ago that destroyed every structure and monument and the curse that destroyed every living thing, the city remained abandoned and dead. The war was one thing, but the curse over Litlen was a mystery. It only touched the city of Litlen itself and not the surrounding areas, which allowed Laila's people to dwell inside the hills west of the city.

"You've seen it out there, Royl. No one ever comes this way. Yet we're still living down here, fearing for our lives." It wasn't as if Litlen offered a better life, but at least, they wouldn't be underground.

"It's not my decision. It's up to the elders."

"Then speak to them. Make them understand we could leave this place and—"

"I *have* spoken to them, and I understand why they choose to wait. I also get why you go out, but I don't approve of it. I worry about you, *tsarioc*."

After watching her flit in and out, never truly settling in one place, Royl had taken to calling her little bird. *Tsarioc*. But only in private. The image of Laila flitting in and out of the mines as she pleased was not something either of them wanted widely known.

Royl took a breath, about to say more, but the sound of humming stopped him. He cocked his head to listen, as did Laila. The hum carried out a tune, rather like a lullaby, and then a woman's voice sang, low and melodic. Her song carried around the room.

"Do you hear it too?" Royl asked.

Rather than answer, Laila pushed past him, opened the door to her room, and stepped out into the tunnel beyond. The song resounded just as clearly there. Laila felt it inside herself. The tune was familiar—how did she know it?

Royl followed her out, his gait casual. That was Royl, though: never in a hurry.

In the hall, they shared a look and listened.

Royl's forehead creased and his lips parted, but nothing could wipe the smile from Laila's face. The song felt like magic—something her people had been without ever since the war and the curse on Litlen.

Laila strode down the hall, where torches in sconces lit the carved stone on either side of them. Most of the halls were solid stone, except in some places where the walls and ceilings were the packed soil of the hills, dug out and contained by wooden braces spaced evenly apart. Many of the carved-out rooms had been added after the citizens of Litlen had lived there for a decade.

Laila's mother's artwork adorned the walls to give the mines some feeling of homeliness. It did no such thing for Laila. Although she did enjoy seeing scenes from Litlen scattered throughout the place, the mines would never be home.

Laila passed the drawing on the wall of the pavilion that remained standing at the southern cliffs in Litlen. It hasn't looked anything like that image since the war. Royl followed in his laid-back way, though she was sure he was in just as much of a hurry as she was to discover the source of the song.

Through the halls, Laila walked and listened, noticing the lack of chatter and noise. The place was silent save for the song. Laila could make out the words in the Eldrace tongue, still commonly spoken among her people. The language was something they valued and held onto, even as a dying race.

The song spoke of the one who would mend the tear.

Laila had heard about such a person before. The one called *thei Theranol*. The Healer. Vix, the head elder, used to talk about *thei Theranol*. He believed the healing was not literal but more about uniting the people of Kartha. Thus, *thei Theranol* was more a reconciler than an actual healer. The Elderace and the mayanon had a sad history of tumult. It was the reason her people had never reached out to the surrounding villages for help when they most needed it. Their pride and stubbornness wouldn't let the past be the past. Laila never understood the discord and why it was necessary for someone in particular to bring them together. Or why her people couldn't get over their differences and unite with the mayanon without the help of a so-called healer.

But it didn't matter. It was all in the past. The song was what mattered now.

She and Royl neared the assembly room, an open chamber where the community gathered from time to time. Usually, they used it for announcements and meetings, but today, the people who gathered in the assembly chamber were quiet. Almost half the population was already inside. And each one of them—men and women and the younger ones who weren't much younger than Laila—listened in silence to the song. Mouths gaping, some shot questioning looks at their neighbours, while others stared at the ceiling as if they'd find answers there.

It was something new. That in itself made Laila's skin tingle with excitement . . . or perhaps it was magic.

To be sure, Laila whispered, "*Vint*," and tried to make a ball of light with her hand. Nothing happened. She lowered her eyes but wasn't surprised. That would have been too easy. Royl saw her gesture and raised a brow.

She shrugged. "It was worth a shot." Hardly able to contain herself, she backed away from the assembly hall, toward the mine's exit.

Royl put a hand around her wrist. "Laila, you're not seriously thinking of going out right now, are you?" He knew her too well.

She pulled her wrist free and matched his low volume. "Of course, I am."

The song's notes shifted from mournful tone to joyous tones, like the music was nearing its end in a hopeful finale. Soon, the people would erupt in chatter over it, trying to explain its significance. Laila had no interest in discussing it. She wanted to explore and find out where it had come from.

She backed away from Royl, who followed her. "Laila, it could be dangerous. We don't know what this means."

"That's why I'm going to find out. If you're so worried, come with me."

He hesitated and glanced around, probably to find the elders, who would likely expect him to take part in their private meeting to talk about it. He was taking too long to decide.

Laila kept moving. "Are you coming or not?"

He relented with a sigh. "I'll come, but you have to listen to me out there."

"Of course!" She smiled at her victory. "Whatever you say, Royl."

Chapter 10

A WOMAN'S VOICE ECHOED IN THE BREEZE. IT CARRIED THROUGH THE air and seemed to come from every direction. Ilan tugged on the reins of his horse and slowed to a stop. He raised a fist to halt the nearly eight hundred men following him. They were only a small portion of his personal army, enough to make sure the people of Kartha complied with his father's orders and didn't attempt to defy him.

The woman's tones were melodic and beautiful. In sad minor notes, she sang of war and bloodshed, a broken land and a curse.

"*Biltim. Biltim.*"

War. War.

The Eldrace language had only ever been spoken by the Elderace people. Since their existence was no more, the language was long forgotten. But Ilan had been educated in such things—not by any of the tutors his father had hired for him. That would have been the day. Kingston hated the very idea of magic and Elderace. Ilan never understood what his father had against them. It wasn't like they'd ever done anything to *him*.

Perry, the captain of Ilan's army, approached. He held his head high, which made the dragon tattoo on his neck fully visible, as he pulled his horse up beside Ilan's. The tail of the tattoo wrapped around the circumference of his neck and rested at the dragon's hind leg, near Perry's collar-bone. He'd gotten it during his days of being a slaver in the country of Ectarin. And if that wasn't enough to intimidate, the muscles on his body bulged, as if they were constantly flexed. Ilan liked having him around.

Ilan's narrow chin and smaller frame made it almost comical that Perry was his man rather than the other way around. It wasn't as though Ilan was small, but Perry was just that much bigger. Between Ilan's family name and Perry's look, they made a frightening pair.

"What do you think?" Perry asked.

Ilan scanned his surroundings. He wanted to hear the rest of the song before speaking.

The streets of Ferenth were quiet for the typical bustling crossroads town in the middle of Kartha. It had been the same in Vray when they had been there the week before. Ilan had expected this response from each village and town they'd pass through. The Valca name struck fear into people's hearts. His father made sure of that.

The few villagers who were outside had stopped to hear the voice of the woman singing. It must have been confusing to hear a foreign tongue and not understand its meaning.

It was Ilan's great-grandfather's war that had wiped out the entire race a hundred years ago. He hadn't stopped in his pursuit until every last Elderace man and woman was gone.

Except for one man.

The Elderace man that dwelt in the dungeon of the Valca Keep was a well-kept secret from the rest of the world. Ilan himself wasn't meant to know about him. His father had never told him, nor did Ilan think he ever would. But that didn't matter. Ilan had found out about him all on his own. He'd spent years visiting him without his father's knowing. The prisoner had taught Ilan much about the Elderace and their culture. Their language, the people, the land. Their magic. Ilan wanted to know more. He wanted to know everything.

The song faded to an end on a joyous note, referring to a healer of the land—one who would mend the tear and break the curse.

Hearing the woman's voice stirred an emotion within Ilan, a bubbling well of feelings and music. It made him feel light, like if he'd have allowed himself to listen more intently, the music might well have carried him away. But he had no time for that. He needed to know where the song had come from.

Ilan raised an eyebrow at Perry. "I think it's time I picked up where I last left off."

"What about your father?"

"What about him? He's not here; I am."

"So what are your orders?"

Ilan glanced back at his army. It wouldn't be ideal to bring them on this quest, but he had no time to take them back to Valmain.

Litlen—the cursed land—was on the opposite end of the country, and they were halfway there. If that song came from anywhere, it had to be in the land that was once home to the Elderace. According to his father's prisoner, it had once been a place full of vivid colour and incomparable beauty—the most striking city in all the countries of Ecstein.

"I'll send Regan with half the army to Hywreath to collect the men for my father's army from the villages along the way," Ilan said. "That should appease him. You and I will take the rest to the village that lies to the east of the Teiry Mountains. You'll take charge there while I go to Litlen to see what I can find."

"You think you'll find it this time?" Perry asked.

Perry knew all about Ilan's search for the Weldafire Stone. Years ago, when Ilan had gone to the place where it was said to be last—in the delegates' cave—he had witnessed the war-torn streets and ruins of the city of Litlen. Still, he'd never found any bright-coloured stones of significance, or anything colourful for that matter. The city was destroyed, courtesy of Landon Valca. And for good measure, Kingston had kept up the regular patrols through there to ensure it stayed that way.

Ilan stared off into the distance toward the mountains.

"It's worth checking into," he said. "Let's get a move on."

He nudged his horse and led his army straight through Ferenth. The people they passed scurried indoors, keeping their heads low. Perry let himself fall behind so he could inform Regan of his task.

Kingston would still get his army. It'd just be slower going than expected. This was the kind of thing Ilan had been waiting for, what he'd spent years hoping for—something magical and new . . . something mysterious and exciting.

The Weldafire Stone, which he'd spent so much time seeking years ago, was said to hold great power unlike any other. That wasn't what drew Ilan to it, though. It was the promise of something more. The stone's sacred role in Elderace history was more than enough to inspire pursuit.

After four years of lost hope, now he faced the perfect opportunity to resume his former quest. The song gave him a new confidence in pursuing this path.

Did he think he'd find the stone this time? That was difficult to say. But that song—it meant something. He just didn't know what yet.

Chapter 11

THE WALK HOME FROM THE CAVE SEEMED QUICKER TO RAIDAN THAN their trip the night before. The sun had risen, and the morning air was cold.

The journey back gave him time to calm down some. He didn't know if it was his hatred toward Adrik, his anger toward Dimitri, or the magic forced upon him that was making him feel so strange.

He walked through the open gates of Veryl.

His fingers tingled, and though the heaviness he'd felt in the cave was gone, he was still lightheaded. Perhaps sleep deprivation was to blame, but he had no way of knowing if it wasn't the magic making him feel that way.

As Raidan walked up the road through the village square, he didn't hear the usual clanging of steel hitting the anvil at Jarvis's forge, nor the chatter of villagers out and about, starting their day. It was odd that the village was so quiet at this hour.

Raidan passed his workshop. A wave of guilt flooded him as he thought of Rees's cabinet. He had every intention of leaving Veryl. Leaving would mean not finishing that project.

Lothaire, Dimitri's long-time mentor and friend, exited the administrative house on the opposite side of the grocer's. How would he take Dimitri's news when he returned? They shared common interests. Maybe Lothaire would get on board and the two could scheme together.

Lothaire spotted Raidan and set his white-grey eyes on him. Raidan always got the impression that Lothaire could peer right through his soul. When Lothaire had come into their lives, Raidan had been coping with the death of his father. In his heart, he knew Lothaire only meant to help, but while Dimitri embraced this new father figure, Raidan had distanced himself.

Raidan slowed his pace as Lothaire came his way.

"Raidan, have you seen Dimitri?" Lothaire's voice sounded higher than normal. "I must speak to him right away. I've received word that Ilan is on his way here from Ferenth."

Raidan came to a full stop. "What? He's on his way here now?" Did he know about the cave and the magic? Could he have known about Dimitri's scheming against The Order? "Where did you hear that?" Raidan asked.

"My contact in Ferenth sent a letter by vohrsit. Word travels fast."

Raidan looked up in the sky as though he might spot the bright orange-headed bird flying overhead. They were big and ugly. A few clouds floated above, but no vulture-sized carrier birds soared.

"Where is your brother?" Lothaire asked.

"I don't know."

Lothaire's bushy eyebrows furrowed. "You were with him, were you not? And how in the world did you get so filthy? Where did you go?"

Raidan glanced down at himself. His clothes were covered in a layer of dirt from the cave. "Dimitri and I parted ways a while ago," he said. "I have to go, Lothaire." Raidan stepped past him and continued down the road, past the shops, toward home. If Ilan was on his way there now, he needed to flee Veryl before it was too late.

"Raidan!"

Raidan ignored Lothaire. His brisk walk turned into a jog as he neared his home.

Entering his house, he called for Ida.

"In here," she said from the bedroom.

Raidan found her propped up on an elbow, lying on the bed next to Cassian. He wobbled in his sitting position. Ida's hand hovered nearby to steady him in case he toppled over. When she looked Raidan's way, her eyes widened. She lifted Cassian and went to Raidan.

Aware of how he must look to her, Raidan raised a hand to his head. Pebbles and dust crumbled between his fingers at his scalp.

"Raidan," she said. "What's happened?" Ida brushed a hand across his forehead. He winced at her gentle touch. She pulled her hand away and adjusted Cassian in her arms to rest in her opposite arm. His wispy light curls stuck straight out from his head. Cassian reached for Raidan and she handed their son over for him to hold. As soon as Raidan had him, he started to cry. Raidan tried rocking him, but Cassian's cries only grew louder.

Ida took Cassian back and cradled him close until he'd settled. "You're worked up about something and he can sense it. What's going on?" Her forehead creased. "Where were you last night? Why didn't you come home?"

"I was with Dimitri. Ida, I need you to pack some things. We're leaving."

"Leaving? Where?"

"I'll tell you about it on the way."

"On the way—Raidan, we can't just leave."

"We have to! We can't stay here!" The ground trembled. A cup on the side table fell, and water spilled on the floor. Cassian began crying again and Ida gently swayed him until he was calm.

Raidan held his breath as he waited for Ida's reaction to the tremors. He hadn't meant to do that.

Her eyes searched him. "That was like what I felt last night," she said. "A shaking but not so strong. It woke Cassian up. There was a song too. At first, I thought it was coming from outside, but when I listened closely, it seemed to come from everywhere. Did you hear it too?"

Raidan didn't know what song she was talking about. He shook his head.

Ida glanced at his arm where the fabric was torn from Adrik's cut. Dried blood stained the edge of his sleeve. "What is that?"

Raidan glanced where she pointed, then scooted around her. "It's a long story." He removed a fresh shirt from the dresser and changed out of the one he was wearing to don the fresh one. "Let's go to your cousin's in Altrow."

"What, now?"

"Yes, why not?"

Ida chuckled. "All right, who are you and what have you done with my husband?"

"I'm being serious, Ida."

Her smile disappeared. "I'm sorry, love. I just . . . knowing how Esef feels about you . . . something must have really shaken you." She paused, probably hoping he'd clarify. When he said nothing, she sighed. "Why don't we take a walk for now? You can tell me what's bothering you, and then we can decide if now is the right time to take a journey." She adjusted her hold on Cassian, stepped closer to Raidan, and put a hand to his cheek. "Whatever it is, we'll get through it together."

Cassian wriggled. Ida held him out toward Raidan, who hesitated, not wanting to upset him again. His son looked at him and his whole face smiled. Relenting, Raidan took him and cradled him in his arm. Cassian grabbed Raidan's fingers and tried to put them in his mouth.

"Ilan is coming here," Raidan told Ida.

"We already knew that."

"Yes, but he's coming here *now*."

Ida's head flinched back. "Why? Out of all of Kartha, why come to Veryl before the larger towns?"

Raidan bowed his head. He didn't know, but he feared it had to do with him, Dimitri, Adrik, and all that happened in the night. Ever since he'd been—what had Adrik said?—"*bound to the stone*," there had been a change in the air, a feeling of something to come, though what, Raidan couldn't say. He only knew he wanted to get his family far away from whatever *it* was.

Cassian squawked when Raidan didn't let him have his fingers to chew. Ida found his rattle and put it in his grasp to soothe his gums. Such a simple thing, yet it contented.

"Raidan," Ida said. "What's going on with you? What's happened?"

Raidan sat on the bed, weary from the night's events. Beside his legs was the night table where the water had spilled. He gestured to the cup on the floor.

"I did that," he said. "And the shaking you felt in the night, that was me too."

Ida looked at the cup. "What do you mean?"

"It's because of Adrik."

"Adrik? I don't understand."

She sank beside him, and Raidan told her everything. He owed it to her to explain his rush to leave. Cassian dozed off in his arms while he spoke. It seemed he didn't feel the jittering that Raidan felt beneath his skin.

When Raidan finished, Ida was quiet. She stared at the floor for too long. Raidan had no idea what she was thinking. "Would you say something, please?"

She looked at him, then averted her eyes.

"What? What is it?" he asked.

"Does it hurt? To use the magic? What can you do? Apart from make the ground quake, I mean. Can you show me?" Unlike Dimitri, she didn't show the same excitement about seeing a bit of magic.

"No. I can't. I can't control it." Not that he would try anyway. The sooner he found a way to rid himself of it, the better.

There was a knock at the door, followed by Dimitri's voice. Raidan stood abruptly, and in doing so, he jolted Cassian awake. He'd only just gotten him to settle. Cassian fussed and Raidan adjusted him in his arms, swaying him gently, encouraging him to go back to sleep.

"Raidan!" Dimitri called. "I need to talk to you." He knocked again. "Please open up."

Ida tugged Raidan's elbow, stopping him before he could go to the door. She stood. "I'll handle this. You stay with Cass." She stuck a hand in his face to silence his protest. "You just said yourself that you can't control the magic. It's better if I speak to him."

She made a good point. Raidan consented, listening from the bedroom door as she left.

"Ida, is Raidan here? I need to speak to him."

"You need to go, Dimitri," Ida said. "Now's not a good time."

"Please I just need to see him. We have to talk about—"

"You need to give him time," Ida cut in, her words sharp. "You're only making it worse for yourself."

A pause. "He told you?"

"He did. We're going away for a while. Surely you understand his desire to distance himself from you."

Cass had fallen asleep again. Raidan leaned against the bedroom doorframe, where he could see both Dimitri and Ida in the small landing. Dimitri looked at him.

"Raidan, can we talk?"

Ida stood by the door as mediator. She waited for Raidan to respond.

"We've talked enough," Raidan said. "When I want to do so again, I'll know where to find you."

Ida nudged the door. "Dimitri, you should go."

"Wait, Raidan, you can't leave now."

The jittery feeling intensified. Raidan didn't know if he'd be able to control himself if he had another outburst.

Ida got Dimitri's attention by waving a hand in front of his face. "You need to go."

Dimitri squinted at her but backed off. He gave Raidan a last sad look before turning away. "I'll be here."

Ida closed the door. She took a deep breath and released it. "I'll pack for Altrow." Raidan stood in the threshold between the bedroom and the hallway with Cassian fast asleep, snuggled up to his chest. Ida stepped past him. She opened the hall closet and retrieved an overnight bag. Raidan would help in a moment, but for now, he needed a minute. He crossed to the sitting room and sat in the armchair, cradling Cass.

They were leaving. Going to Altrow would give him the time he'd need to come up with a plan to rid himself of the magic. He'd even endure Esef's exasperating groans.

Raidan could already imagine what he'd say when they showed up at his door. *I told you marrying a Dairner was trouble, Ida. I warned you. The Dairner name is bad luck. You should have listened . . .* yada, yada, yada. It seemed that after all this time, he was not wrong.

Raidan's eyes settled on Cassian's sweet face and pouting lips. His closed eyes twitched, and Raidan hoped he was dreaming good dreams.

His love for his family was more than he could contain. He'd already nearly gotten himself and Dimitri killed with a magic he couldn't control. He wouldn't be able to live with himself if he ever put Ida and Cass in that kind of danger.

"I'll find a way to get rid of this," he whispered to his sleeping son. "Whatever it takes, I won't let anything happen to you. I promise."

Chapter 12

What has Ilan done now? was the question Kingston Valca asked himself more times than he liked.

A handful of townspeople had gathered in protest: What did Ilan do?

The dam had a leak: What was Ilan up to now?

The cattle down on Mairno's farm were dying: Ilan *must* have had something to do with it.

Kingston sat at the grand oak table, picking at an array of seafood, across from Duran Morocan. He'd been invited to dine with the king of Tsein to discuss a future alliance. Kingston himself was not royalty, though his name could imply it. He was a ruler who took what he wanted. People feared and respected him because of it. Referring to himself as royalty was distasteful, though Duran was right to address him as such. Treating him to the best he had to offer, giving him the best guest room in his lavish palace, making a show of his wealth and splendour by serving him his finest spirits and sparing no expense on the meal—he'd rightly judged Kingston's position of high standing.

Ilan happened to be the topic of interest at their table this evening. And Taaura, Duran's daughter, she would be good for Ilan—or rather, her nobility would. All that was needed was for Ilan to show an interest.

Seeing Ilan take things seriously for once? That would be the day. Kingston's confidence in his son's capabilities was less than hopeful, though he would not let on that he felt that way to Duran. Duran would believe whatever Kingston wanted him to believe about Ilan. And right now, he would say whatever Duran needed to hear to ensure his son's betrothal to the princess of Tsein.

Placing Ilan in Tsein in a position of power would be critical to taking the country one day. And drafting the citizens of Kartha to expand upon his army was going to be useful when that time came. While Tsein was larger in landmass, its population was smaller than Kartha's. If Kingston ruled both, he could increase his recognition in the neighbouring countries and extend his reach farther into the larger nations.

Duran finished his last bite of his salmon and gave a satisfied moan. "Very good." He set down his serviette. "We shall set a date to have them meet as soon as possible."

Kingston picked a piece of crab meat from his teeth. "Yes, yes. Ilan will be pleased. I will speak to—"

He was interrupted when Owen—Kingston's bumbling assistant who had somehow managed to keep his position for a month now—barged into the room to drop a note into his palm. Immediately, Kingston's thoughts turned to Ilan. *What has he done now?*

Kingston glowered at Owen, then opened the note and read it.

The news he'd brought was unusual, and if true, Kingston supposed it might have been worth the interruption. Maybe he'd keep Owen after all. For now.

Owen scurried off, and Kingston rose to his feet.

"I must go. I'll be in touch." He made sure to make it a statement, a matter of fact. He didn't need to ask permission. He was Kingston Valca.

"Is everything all right, Mr. Valca?" Duran asked, as if it were any of his business.

"Yes, thank you for the meal and hospitality. We'll speak again soon." He excused himself and found Owen waiting for him at the door. Duran's attendants escorted them out. Kingston and Owen walked together down the wide, arched hallway toward the foyer. In the foyer, the high ceiling was graced with an exquisite chandelier. A staircase sat at both ends of the room. The stairs joined at the top, creating a balcony that overlooked the entryway.

Outside, Kingston's handful of guards who'd accompanied him to the dinner slouched by the carriage. They perked up as he exited.

What had they been doing while he was inside? Sleeping?

The sun hovered low on the western horizon. Kingston squinted in its shine, waiting as his men pulled the coach around the U-shaped road. It stopped in front of him, and the driver hopped down from his seat and opened the door for Kingston.

The sluggishness of his men would have to be addressed later. He couldn't very well be seen by King Duran Morocan as a ruler with his subjects in disarray.

Owen stood at attention before him. "What's the order, Your Greatness?"

Kingston didn't like the sound of sir. It sounded too knightly or military. He was no knight, and although he had been a great military general once, he'd outgrown that position and, with it, the title. Owen didn't hesitate when he called him Your Greatness; it was the reason he still had his job.

"Send someone ahead to prepare my ship for our immediate return to Kartha."

Owen departed, and Kingston stepped into the coach and lowered himself onto the upholstered seat. Red curtains covered the walls and windows, allowing him his privacy. The driver closed the door and took his place. They set off toward the port.

Kingston took out the note and scanned it again. The *urgent news*—as it read—described a purple mist seen in the south of Kartha. It spoke of a song that could be heard from every corner of the country.

A song? Songs were not urgent news. There was music all the time, but with Ilan left to his own devices, it could be anything.

And a purple mist? What could that have been? Whatever it was, Ilan was likely behind it.

This was what happened when he trusted his son to take responsibility. He had one job. How hard was it to collect a few boys to join their ranks to finally do something to prove himself capable? But as usual, Ilan couldn't even handle that.

The journey home would take some time. The port was an hour's ride from the palace, and then the ship would take them across the channel through the night. Kingston loathed being at sea. The smell, the constant misting in the face, the forever feeling of wearing damp clothing—how anyone could enjoy such a lifestyle was beyond him.

Ilan was not going to get off easy for this. Kingston's mind wandered to all the possible punishments he could lay on his son that would teach him to let his obsessions go. All that talk about the Elderace and magic, as if having any kind *magical* powers were more desirable than the power he had at his fingertips. He wished Ilan would open his eyes.

Something had to be done. Once he was back on Karthan soil, he would figure out what. And Ilan . . . maybe he'd finally see reason.

Kingston thought about where he might find Ilan upon his return. By now, he should be nearing Ferenth to collect for the conscription. At least, he hoped that was what he was doing. So long as he wasn't back in that dreaded cursed land, where there was nothing but dead plants and rubble. Yet Ilan spent more time there than he should.

Kingston pulled parchment and a quill from a small compartment in the coach. He started on a letter. There was no one better to call on than the mercenary Scourge. From finding people who didn't want to be found to assassinations and torture, Scourge did it all so long as he was paid well. And Kingston did pay well.

He scribed the letter requesting Scourge's services. It didn't contain specifics. With mysterious songs and purple mists in the south, he was going to need someone on the ground to personally report to him on these matters. And whatever he found, Scourge would follow his orders.

Kingston finished writing and stuffed the quill back in the compartment and pocketed the note. As soon as they arrived back in Kartha, he would send the note with one of his men to deliver the message personally. He didn't trust those pesky vohrsit birds to do the job. If the delivery went wrong, he'd have an actual person to blame.

In his absence from Kartha, Kingston had no doubt Ilan was up to something. He just needed to find out what.

He peered out the window. Couldn't they go any faster!

Chapter 13

The village farthest south of Kartha was pitiful. Ilan entered Veryl through the gates on his horse, Perry beside him, and with the remaining half of the army marching behind. Those on horseback dispersed around the perimeter of the village. Ilan paraded into the sad excuse for a village square.

Rickety shops lined either side of a single road. A wagon with rotting and broken spokes sat in an open green space behind Hastien's Butchery, as it was called. Ilan scrunched his nose at it. Was that supposed to be some kind of significant representation of this place?

Ilan took in the scenery and glimpsed each of the shops. There was a blacksmith's forge, the Veryl Council building, and a grocer's. A woodworking shop, bakery, and the butcher's all lined the opposite side. It was hard to believe people could actually live in a place like this.

Where was the pub? What did these people do for fun around here?

At the end of the road, Ilan turned. The gates were still easily visible. His army poured in and spread throughout the village. Would they all fit? Aside from four hundred soldiers he'd sent on to Hywreath, Ilan had sent another hundred conscripted men back to Valmain with those from Vray and the no-name villages they'd passed through.

Ilan looked around. Did anyone live here? There was not a person in sight apart from his own men.

Perry drew his horse up beside him. "You want an audience?" he asked.

Ilan knew he'd yank the villagers from their homes and drag them to the square if asked. He shook his head. "Not yet. I'll go to Litlen, then address the people when I return." The song pulled at him. The people could wait.

He looked toward the mountains in the west, then turned to Perry. "Make yourselves comfortable. You're in charge while I'm gone."

No sooner had he spoken the words than a man approached them from a cluster of homes. His broad frame matched Perry's, but his face lacked the hardness. This man's dark eyes were kind.

Ilan imagined the villagers huddled inside their homes, protecting their boys. They needn't worry. Not yet anyway.

"You must be Ilan Valca," the man said once he was near enough. "I'm Dimitri. I represent the people of Veryl. We're honoured to welcome you to our village."

Ilan scoffed. He'd seen no sign of honour.

Dimitri went on. "If we'd have known you were coming so soon, we would have prepared for your arrival. We weren't expecting you for at least another week."

Ilan looked at Dimitri with distaste. "Tell me," he said. "What did you make of the song?"

At his question, Dimitri's jaw went taut. Ilan smiled. He'd triggered a reaction.

"They say the music of Kartha has magic in it," Ilan continued. "What someone feels or sees is unique to each individual. So what did you take from the song?"

Dimitri's mouth twitched. "I don't see how that has any relevance to your purpose here."

"Indulge me."

"Nothing. I felt nothing." His tone was resolute.

Interesting. Every one of Ilan's men had claimed they felt light in some way or another. Some felt only a little moved. Others had experienced a strong pull, where, like himself, they thought they might get carried away. For Dimitri to say he felt nothing was strange indeed. Unless this was his way of dismissing Ilan. Either way, Ilan would not stand for such behaviour, but he'd deal with it later. It was already midday, and he wanted to get to Litlen and back before the daylight was gone.

"This is Perry," Ilan said, gesturing to the muscular man at his side. "My captain. He'll be in charge for the time being. My men will remain here until I find what I'm looking for."

"You're leaving so soon?" Dimitri asked. Ilan noted the raised pitch in his tone. He'd bet the man would be happy to see him go.

"I will return. I'm on a quest, you see. That song means something, and I intend to find out what."

"Why come here? We're just a small farming community."

"Veryl's location is . . . convenient. Believe me, I wish it weren't so." Ilan's gaze shifted to the buildings. He wrinkled his nose, then looked at Perry. "You have your order."

Perry acknowledged him with a nod. The men were in capable hands. Now. To see about that song.

Ilan rode past his men, around the waist-high fence that surrounded the perimeter of the village and out the gate, where he entered the Hayat Forest. It was a cloudy day, and the canopy of leaves above darkened the forest within. Apart from his men, who had spread into the forest to fit into the village, there was no one. Soon he left them behind. The farther he trekked toward the mountains, the denser the forest became until it opened completely to a wall of rock—the start of the Teiry Mountain range.

The single passage through the rock was too narrow for his horse. Ilan dismounted and left her there. He didn't think she'd wander far, but if she did, it was likely she'd go back toward the village. If not, he could always get another.

He walked into the passage, staring up at the sky above the tall mountainsides. Already he sensed something was different from his last excursion there. Something had changed in these mountains.

There was a new smell. A fresh smell. And the closer he came to Litlen, the stronger he sensed the newness.

He picked up his pace. His walk became a steady jog as he all but ran toward Litlen and the mysteries it held.

Chapter 14

THE AFTERNOON SUN WAS HOT. CLOUDS DRIFTED ACROSS THE SKY. Laila leaned her head back and breathed deeply, savouring each sensation. Living underground could make you forget the sun's warmth and the sweet fresh air. Her only distraction was Royl, who wouldn't stop turning his head about, watching their backs.

"Would you relax for just a minute, Royl, and enjoy this moment?"

They stood at the Abberbrat, the tree that marked the centre of Litlen. The last time Laila had come here, there were no wispy branches or leaves. The trunk had looked like ash. She used to fear going near it in case it burst into dust at the lightest touch. But now its bark shone deep brown and the leaves had their usual silver glint. Its branches hung similar to those of a willow tree, and its strong, silky leaves were almost as thin as strands of hair. At night, the leaves emitted a dim glow. The mahtuhvv fruit glowed through them, giving the appearance of embers.

It used to be said that the mahtuhvv could cure anything. Laila didn't know if that were true, but now that it was once again growing, she'd test that theory if the opportunity arose.

Just the other day when she'd come through the city, every plant was blackened like char. Everything that once had life and colour—everything that had thrived—had died. Being here now, she didn't want to do anything but embrace the sun's warmth and admire the beauty unfolding around her. She closed her eyes and smiled as a breeze touched her face.

"Standing here isn't going to tell us where the song came from," Royl said.

She opened her eyes. "Maybe not, but look around. Isn't this amazing?"

During every one of Laila's adventures outside, prior to the song, Litlen's cobblestone streets had been grey and lifeless. Not anymore.

Moss covered rubble littered the streets, and grass grew through the cracks of the broken stone. All around, the silence that had engulfed them for so long was replaced with the sounds of rustling leaves and birdsong; the smell of death and fire, replaced with floral fragrances and fresh soil.

"Come on, let's take a walk," Royl suggested.

Laila had no objections.

They walked in silence through the deserted streets of Litlen, with Laila dazed at the beautiful plants growing before their eyes.

Neither of them knew what they were looking for or where to begin, but Laila didn't care. They were outside, and Litlen was beautiful.

"Laila, look." Royl pointed to a cluster of plants. "Some are coming alive, while others aren't."

Laila followed her brother's gaze. In the midst of the newly grown leaves, some remained dead. And some of the trees still looked the dull grey they had been for a century, with no signs of growth.

"Maybe they're just growing slower than the others," she said. "What does it matter? Litlen is back! We don't have to live in the mines anymore. We can have a home again, Royl." The thought made her squeal with delight.

"Keep your voice down. We don't know if anyone's out here. And don't get too ahead of yourself. The elders will have to decide whether it's safe to come back out and start again. There are too many unknowns at this point."

"Always so negative."

"I'm not negative. Just realistic."

Laila was only half paying attention to Royl. Walking past the pink asterocis flowers, she was amazed to see them spring up from their withered state. The tall stem of one rose to its full height, nearly to her waist. Everywhere they went, her senses were inundated. She had to pause just to remember to breathe.

"What does it feel like to you?" she asked Royl, switching topics.

He looked at her. "I don't know."

That wasn't true. Even without her magic, she still had the ability to tell truth from lies. It was a unique gift that never went away, even after the curse, just like Royl's keen senses, which were part of what made him such a great warrior.

"The truth, Royl," she said. "You know what I'm talking about."

Straight-faced, he held her gaze before answering, "Magic. That's what you want me to say, right?"

"You wouldn't have said it if you didn't think so too."

"It didn't work, though. You tried it back in the mines and nothing happened."

She shrugged.

Amidst the regrowth of their city, the ruins remained as they were: debris and rubble heaps from the buildings that once stood in these streets. Certain parts of Litlen were more ravaged than others. On a few occasions, Laila had visited their old home since they'd fled. It had not been hit so bad. The house still stood.

Along the broken cobbled road where they walked now, the houses that once stood strong and unmovable had crumbled into thousands of broken pieces. It would take some time to rebuild the city and make it liveable again.

Whatever was going on in Litlen affected them all. It was her people's responsibility to take it seriously and learn what was causing the growth. The return of their magic could change everything. It could be just what her people needed to leave the mines with confidence, believing they could make a future for themselves under the sun.

Royl slowed his pace. He put a hand out in front of Laila.

She tilted her head. "What is—"

"Shh. I hear something."

Laila listened. Was it another song? Perhaps some wildlife had already returned to Litlen since the land was now habitable.

Royl took her hand and pulled her alongside him toward the Chronicle Monument, staying low. Laila didn't share his keen senses, but she copied his posture and went without question.

The Chronicle Monument was a replicated statue of the six stone chairs of the sacred room in the delegates' cave. The Pool of Sovereignty was depicted at the centre of the chairs that faced one another. The monument stood at the edge of the Forest of Litlen, on the outskirts of the city. Here, the trees were still sparsely separated, but the farther away from Litlen, the closer together they grew.

Royl led her behind the monument, crouching and remaining still as he listened. Laila trusted his senses and did the same.

The chairs and pool were covered in overgrowth. Flowers and creeping vines that were once probably meant to enhance the beauty of the place clung to the stone. The monument looked forgotten. In the forest ahead, hues of green and blue shades mingled in the leaves and grass as they brightened and bloomed before her eyes.

"What is it?" Laila whispered.

"Someone is close. A stranger."

"How do you know it's not one of the scouts?"

Royl gave her a look as if to say that was a silly question.

"What?" Laila protested. "You don't know! Just like they don't know we're Elderace. We could be anyone from anywhere. How are they to know we're from an ancient race living in a secret mine a few miles away?"

Royl shushed her again. She huffed a breath from her nose and peered out behind the monument chair she and Royl hid behind. She saw what Royl was seeing—a blond man traipsed about on the road in his Valca Order uniform.

Laila gasped and Royl shot her a look. He put a finger to his lips.

Though far enough away he wouldn't hear them, the stranger appeared to be as in awe over the state of Litlen as she was. His head swivelled every which way as he circled in place between quaint houses that remained standing. Among them was the one she used to call home.

The man was the first outsider Laila had come across in all her hundred years living in the mines. She'd known that Order soldiers came to the area from time to time but had never encountered them herself.

Whatever this man was doing, his timing was poor. Royl would certainly bring this to the attention of the elders, and they'd see it as an excuse to stay in the mines.

That couldn't happen. She had to convince them to take their place in their city once more.

When she peeked out again, the man's form was diminishing in the distance. Royl's shoulders dropped, and he rested his arm over his crouched leg.

"That was too close," he said. "It's time we go home to the mines. I need to warn the elders The Order is back in these parts." He locked eyes on her. "And Laila, you can't come out as long as there are soldiers around. You put everyone at risk when you leave."

Laila slumped. She leaned against the monument chair. Now was not the time nor place to argue about this. Neither agreeing nor disagreeing to his request, she glared at him.

"We should go," Royl said. "If one man's already made his way through, who's to say there won't be more?"

Chapter 15

THE FIRST PLACE ILAN THOUGHT TO INVESTIGATE WAS THE CITY, where he'd wandered through the rubble and abandoned territory in awe. The restoration happening before his eyes had made his jaw drop. Whatever the significance of the song, it wasn't the only strange occurrence in Litlen. Never had Ilan witnessed such a magical sight.

To give himself time to check out the delegates' cave before dark, he'd had to force himself to get a move on.

The Elderace prisoner in his father's charge had shared with him the secrets of the six delegates—the Six, as he had called them. They used to be Guardians of the Weldafire Stone, and the cave was where they'd gathered for their meetings. Ilan had scoured every inch of that cave four years ago, hoping to find the stone. He'd left no rock unturned but had come away empty-handed.

At the Hayat Peak, Ilan peered down into the basin where the entrance to the cave was—or used to be. The shallow basin was filled with water; the once hollow space, now an actual lake.

Ilan descended the short distance to the shore. The surface reflected sky, and all Ilan could see were clouds and the white peaks of the tall mountains. He bent down and touched the water. It was cold.

Straightening, he put his hands to his hips as he examined his surroundings to be sure he'd come to the right spot. He was certain this was the place where the cave entrance had been. His confidence waned. So much for getting any answers here. All this gave him was more questions. He grunted his frustration. Was it too much to hope that he'd find even a hint of the answers he sought?

The song held a power of its own. Ilan felt it. But now that he'd set his mind back on the Weldafire Stone, the eagerness of his original quest overcame him.

Ripples broke the surface of the lake and a vine slithered over it, worming its way, toward him. Automatically, he stepped back, away from the water's edge. Anything slithering gave him the creeps, especially a thing that looked more like a plant than an animal. Thick as a small tree trunk, it moved like a snake but resembled a vine.

Smaller tendrils from the vine moved alongside it as one. Ilan retreated all the way to the top of the mountain. The vines spilled onto the ground and curled and wriggled where his feet had been only moments ago. That had to be the same creature the prisoner had spoken of that guarded the Pool of Sovereignty inside the cave. Seeing it quickened Ilan's pulse. Fear and excitement—for him, those two emotions went hand in hand. He loved nothing more than the thrill of something new.

At least for now, he did have one answer. He had come to the right place.

*

Back at the sad little village where his army waited, Ilan looked for Perry. There weren't too many places to look, so it likely wouldn't be difficult to find him. His horse had run off, and it had been a long walk through the forest. It was after sun-down by the time the gates of Veryl came into view.

The familiar sounds of his men's boisterous laughter filled his ears. A woman's voice screamed from afar. It seemed his men had found those villagers after all.

Soldiers had pitched tents in the grass around the shops and now huddled around a smattering of fires. Horses were tied to the perimeter fence, bordering the forest and farmland. It was too dark to tell if his own horse was among them. He'd check in the morning.

He arrived at the lonely street with shops, few lamps lighting either side. The smell of ale filled the air. It hadn't taken long for his men to make themselves comfortable. Ilan couldn't care less what they got up to while he was going about his business. Exploring Litlen set him on the right track. That lake at the cave was new and he'd find out what it meant one way or another.

Behind the old wagon, Ilan found Perry in the middle of a scrap. Not unusual for Perry. He took a swing at a man who hung limp between two other soldiers. Ilan recognized the beaten man, bruised and bloodied as he was. What had he said his name was again—Dimitri? That was it.

Six boys clung to each other while watching the fight. Three of them averted their gazes. One boy cried while two goggled. A handful of soldiers supervised.

Perry took another swing. It didn't take much to rile him, but Ilan was sure he had good reason for his actions.

"You about done?" Ilan asked his man.

Perry slicked his hair back and straightened his tunic. Dimitri raised his head. He spat blood and licked his lip.

Feisty. This spectacle was too intriguing to let alone. "I must have missed some excitement," Ilan said.

"This one thinks this village doesn't have enough men to spare for the conscription," Perry said. "So I found these fine boys here to prove him wrong." He indicated the young boys. "I told him these'll do perfect, and that I'm sure you'd have no trouble finding more. Our hero didn't like that."

At Ilan's nod, the soldiers released Dimitri.

Ilan examined the boys. Three of them had some muscle and would make decent additions to the army, if Ilan cared about such things. One boy had too much fat, and the last two didn't have enough.

"We're a village of mostly farmers, and every one of us plays an important role here," Dimitri said, straightening himself. His blackened right eye swelled. "Taking our men will leave us with nothing. I can offer you extra resources in lieu of our people. Belds. We can gather enough to pay—"

"You think you can buy your way out of this?" Ilan asked. He smirked. "My father wants soldiers. Not money. He has enough of that, or did you forget who he is? If Kingston Valca wants ten percent of the men from each city, town, and village, ten percent is what he'll get." This was a waste of time. Ilan didn't actually care about expanding his father's army, but now he felt the need to prove a point.

He stepped over to Dimitri to get in his face. Opening his mouth to speak, he froze. Something glowed white in the inner part of Dimitri's coat. "What is that?" Ilan asked, pointing.

Dimitri glanced down. Quickly, he tried to cover up the object by folding his coat over it, but Ilan pushed his hand away. Dimitri threw an elbow up and smacked Ilan in the face. The two men who'd restrained him in the squabble with Perry grabbed his arms again, preventing him from taking another swing at Ilan.

Ilan rubbed his chin with one hand, and with the other, he reached into Dimitri's coat and seized the glowing object. It was a white flower with blue in the centre. He knew this flower. The prisoner had described a flower just like this one.

"Where is its pair?" Ilan asked Dimitri.

Dimitri's jaw tightened, but he didn't speak.

"This is bethrail," Ilan said after a moment, disregarding Dimitri's defiance. "Where did you get this? These are incredibly hard to come by. But even more rare than the flowers themselves are the people who know their purpose. Where is the other? Who has it?"

Dimitri held his head high.

In these kinds of circumstances, Ilan usually passed the stubborn ones along to Perry until they finally gave in. But the flower. The song. Litlen.

It couldn't all be coincidence. And somehow Dimitri, this villager, this . . . *nobody* had something to do with it. But what? Ilan had to know. He couldn't risk Perry taking things too far and rendering Dimitri unable to speak. No, he needed answers.

He stepped away from Dimitri and twirled the flower by its stubby stem between his fingers, then turned to Perry.

"Get me a horse and a handful of men. We'll return to Valmain. You'll remain here and look after the village while Dimitri is away. I'm taking him to see an old friend of mine."

Dimitri went rigid. He wrenched himself away from Ilan's men. "I'm not going anywhere with you. This is my village. My people need me."

Perry approached Dimitri and stood nose to nose to him. "You seem to forget who you're dealing with," he said. "So, allow me to remind you. There are many ways to hurt you without ever having to lay a hand on you. You care for this village? Got a family? Kids? A wife? I'd be thinking of them right now because this little village and the people you care about are *his*." He pointed to Ilan. "So, unless you want to see it burned to the ground along with everyone who lives here, you'd better shut up and be a good boy. Do as you're told."

Ilan loved it when Perry threatened people; it gave him chills. It seemed the threat did Dimitri some good. The man's posture loosened, and he hung his head. He needed the reminder of who was in charge. An entire army who answered to Ilan were just waiting for an excuse to fight.

Ilan provoked him further. "There's no need to worry about your little village while you're gone. Perry will take good care of it," he said. "This'll give him plenty of time to pick out the best men for my father's army."

Just as he'd hoped, Dimitri reacted, lashing out against the soldiers. Perry stepped in and took care of it by finishing what he had started before Ilan had showed up. It took longer than Ilan would have expected, but finally Dimitri's body sagged when another blow cut across the side of his face. Ilan signalled for Perry to stop before he killed the man. He would have to be sure to bring a strong guard to keep Dimitri in line for the journey back to Valmain.

Now Ilan only hoped that the prisoner in Kingston's dungeon wasn't bitter about his prolonged lack of communication. Would he still be willing to help?

Ilan banished his doubts. Beiron would help. He had to. Ilan just had to make it worth his while. And that, he could do.

Chapter 16

As far as boundaries went, the delegates' cave was the farthest east Laila had ever been. It was over an hour's hike from the edge of the city of Litlen and into the Teiry Mountains. The Hayat Forest lay on the other side of the pass through the mountains, but Laila had never been that far. It made the most sense to use the Teiry Mountains and the Bludesel Mountains as her boundaries, as each of the ranges bordered Litlen—the Teiry Mountains to the east and the Bludesel Mountains to the north, beyond the Forest of Litlen. To the west were the hills that concealed the mines, and to the south, the cliffs.

In the past, after Laila had gotten over her guilt at frequently leaving the mines to explore, she had journeyed to the delegates' cave a few times. Thanks to a particular book she'd found, she was one of the few people alive who knew its location. As far as she knew, only the elders were the remaining few who had such information.

Laila didn't know what to expect in coming here today, but looking down into the basin where the entrance of the cave was meant to be, she exclaimed aloud at the sight of the lake. She reached into her bag and pulled out the book she carried always. Years ago, she'd scavenged it from a half-destroyed home—Beiron's home. It had taken her some time to dig through the mess of strewn-about furniture and broken glass to get to the bookcase. The books were exactly what she'd imagined: strange and unique, filled with facts about plants and Karthan history, Elderace legends.

When she was younger, before living in the mines, she would pass by Beiron's house to get to her home. She'd often wondered what strange things she might find inside. People used to talk about Beiron *thei Pridoor*, as he was called. They would speak of his experiments, saying he committed atrocities in the name of discovery and learning. A person like that had to have a lab, right? The rumours about him intrigued Laila. She'd assumed he'd died in the war and seized her chance to rummage through his home. There was no lab. Her most interesting find was Beiron's books, most of which were about the plants of Kartha. Others told of natural remedies for sicknesses and a few touched on the countries of Ecstein. The book she'd brought with her today was the only one she hadn't turned over to the elders.

It was because of this book that she knew the location of the cave. It was how she knew the Pool of Sovereignty was meant to have a healing power and the ability to boost magic. Laila didn't understand what that meant. She flipped through the pages to the place where she'd read about the pool, though she already knew the content by heart. *The Pool of Sovereignty offers healing magic to anyone who drinks of its waters*, it read. But nothing explained the song or the lake.

The delegates were responsible for all things pertaining to the Pool of Sovereignty and the Weldafire Stone. There was no question that the Six knew of the pool's magic, but did the elders know? Had anyone apart from herself ever tried to restore their magic by drinking from them?

In hopes of getting her magic back, she'd drunk from the pool right after learning of its power. Nothing had come of it then, but she'd never asked if the elders had tried. It was just another secret she wasn't meant to know. To bring it up would risk revealing her source of information.

Laila gazed at the still water. She supposed she wouldn't be drinking from the pool today, which was what she'd come here to do, not with this lake in her way. According to her book, Azure Lake shared similar attributes with the Pool of Sovereignty, though its waters were not as potent. Laila turned to leave. She would head there next. Before she had taken three steps, ripples in the water caught her eye. She blinked and focused on them.

A thick vine slithered across the lake's surface. Laila gasped and moved away from the shore.

She was familiar with this creature. The Anguivina guarded the Pool of Sovereignty. Magic had lain dormant for so long that anything extraordinary like this was new and exciting and frightening all at once.

The Anguivina reached the shore and crept along the ground, slinking closer and closer to where she stood atop the Hayat Point. To move farther away meant to start on the decline down, back in the direction she had come.

Her heart raced. From what she'd read about the Anguivina, she didn't want to be caught in its clutches.

The Six who had been tasked with the guardianship of the Weldafire Stone had controlled the Anguivina. It acted according to their bidding. But they'd been gone for almost a century. What had awoken the creature? Or had it ever truly been dormant?

Not wanting to stick around much longer, she thrust the book into her bag and descended the slope, back toward Litlen and Azure Lake.

The day grew warmer as the sun rose high in the sky. It was easy for Laila to get caught up in the beauty all around as she made her way to Azure Lake. Everything about this place seemed so right. She didn't understand how her people could still be afraid.

She looked from side to side, wary of more strangers. Out of the pass, she headed south into the woodland. The place was devoid of anyone. Even before the war, it was not unusual for these woods to be deserted.

The smell of soil and pine filled her nostrils. Sounds of insects and frogs indicated a nearby water source. Laila's stomach turned. She'd gotten sick after drinking from the Pool of Sovereignty the last time;

it took her days to recover. If things didn't go well now, on her second attempt, she had to prepare herself for that possibility.

But with the feeling of restored magic in the air, Laila suspected that drinking from the lake would be different this time. Assuming the book was accurate, anyway. If so, it would be of great use. Given that she'd claimed the book from Beiron's home, she originally thought Beiron the author, but the initials engraved in the bottom right corner in the leather were T. C. She couldn't think who that might be. The text inside was neat and precise; the details, definitive. It contained records about various plants.

If not for the book, she'd never have known that churase affected a part of the mind that controls speech. Or that hypnot, when ingested, caused temporary paralysis. Laila could only guess how anyone came to make those discoveries. She learned about the effects of particular plant combinations, about blood magic, and about dangerous concoctions that frightened her.

Many of the methods were too cruel for her to imagine experimenting with herself. The only people she thought would be privy to such information were the delegates, but she couldn't imagine any of them exploring such concepts. From the stories she'd heard about Beiron, it was not so hard to believe he'd been the writer.

She'd made it to the lake. After a slight pause, she took cautious steps toward the shore. The evergreens surrounding the area made for good cover, as did the rocky crags that made up the foothills of the Teiry Mountains. As she neared the lake, the evergreens dwindled, exposing her. She needed more eyes to see. Watching for strangers in the vicinity and keeping an eye on the water at the same time was making her dizzy.

As she came closer to the shore, she focused only on the water. Maybe it was silly, but what if the Anguivina could inhabit other bodies of water as well as the lake in the mountains at the Hayat Point?

Canteen in hand, she crouched down over the water and stretched her arm to fill it, all while keeping her eyes on the icy blue surface. On the other side of the lake, tall pine trees rustled in the light wind. As soon as her canteen was full, she backed away and didn't stop until she was under the shelter of the trees.

Her hands shook as she brought the canteen to her lips.

Even though so much had changed already, something told her things were about to change even more. Perhaps this would be the turning point for her people, the moment that would finally end their hidden existence. Perhaps her people could reclaim their magic and thrive in Litlen once again.

Here was to hoping, she thought as she drank.

Chapter 17

IT WAS GOOD TO BE HOME. ILAN AND HIS GUARD OF TWO DOZEN MEN rode through the gates and into the inner grounds of Valmain with Dimitri in tow. Two towers sat at opposite ends of the high stone walls that encompassed the city. The massive stone structure resembling a castle in the middle of the grounds was the keep where Ilan and his family resided. The integrity of the structure was as strong as the day his great-grandfather had it built, as were the perimeter walls and the towers surrounding it.

They'd left the little village before sunrise that morning and arrived at Valmain well into the late evening hours of the following evening. Dimitri had been quiet along the way. He was in restraints, and Miles, Ilan's strongest guard, kept a close watch on him. The bethrail in Dimitri's possession was Ilan's only clue to figuring out the cause of the changes in Litlen. Could this mean there were other Elderace people out there who'd survived and given Dimitri the flower? Or, perhaps, was Dimitri himself Elderace? Ilan would know soon enough.

There were certain plants that were just not known to the general population, and bethrail was one of them. Thanks to Beiron, Ilan knew about a host of rare plants. Just like he understood the Eldrace language and knew about the Weldafire Stone. Having his own tutor in all things Elderace came in useful.

Apart from Beiron, Ilan had only ever heard of one Elderace man rumoured to have survived the war. Once, he had hired a private investigator to look for the man called Adrik. He got nowhere with that search. The last time he'd heard any news about Adrik was more than two decades ago.

Ilan dismounted at the Keep and strode through the entrance with Miles and Nielsen hauling Dimitri along. Miles, who wore a ring through his nose like a bull, grasped Dimitri's arm in a tight grip. Ilan led the way to the far left corner of the Keep, where a door divided the halls from a stone spiral stairway in the tower.

They descended the stairs. At the bottom was an unlit stone passageway. Nielsen, the guard whose ears stuck out too far from his head, held a torch high. They reached the end of the passageway, where the only way to go was right. A lantern rested on a stool, and two torches on one wall cast flickering orange light around the jailer's room.

Two guards sat at a table with playing cards dealt between them and a pile of belds in the middle of the table. They were the same two guards Ilan had dealt with when he used to sneak down here to see Beiron. He'd been sure to address them by their names and keep their pockets heavy with extra belds each time. For their silence.

Ilan entered the room first, followed by Nielsen, Miles, and Dimitri, who struggled against Miles's hold on him. A useless effort—there was nowhere for him to go.

Nero, one of the jailers, stood when he saw them enter. His knee knocked the table as he got up, making the belds jingle. Cain, the second jailer, snarled at his partner. The thin hairs on his head had receded back further since the last time Ilan had seen him.

Cain put his hands on his hips as he rose. "What's this then? Ilan Valca's decided to drop in to see his old friend? What's it been? Five years? Six?"

"Four," Ilan said. He looked sideways at Dimitri, who flared his nostrils.

Nero rubbed his knee. The burn scars on his face and neck were distracting to look at. "What makes you think he's even still alive?" he asked.

Ilan chuckled softly. "Haven't you guarded him long enough to know he's not the kind of man to up and die? He's still here." He took a pouch of belds from his pocket and laid them on the table beside the ones being used for their game. "Same as our previous arrangement . . . for your silence."

Cain cast a glance at Dimitri's cuffed hands. "What about him?"

Ilan looked at Dimitri. He had yet to try anything, but Ilan was not unprepared. "For now, expect him to be here long term." He added another sack of belds from his pocket to the table.

By way of acknowledgement, Cain handed Ilan a ring with two keys attached. One for each of the two cells in the next room.

From the jailer's room, they crossed to the side door leading into the adjoining room. Ilan went first. Miles kept Dimitri in step behind Ilan, and Nielsen took the rear.

Ilan opened the heavy door and descended three stairs further down, into the dark and cold dungeon. The single torch on the wall ahead provided the only light in the room. It was between the two cells facing each other, just out of reach of either cell. Nielsen carried their torch, bringing new light into the hollow space. The three of them made their way down the narrow hall and faced the cell on the left.

Ilan squinted, trying to see Beiron in the dark.

"I thought you might be stopping by," Beiron said. His gruff, husky voice echoed from the black corner of his cell. "It's been a while."

"I, um . . . I got busy," Ilan said. "My father. You know."

"Who's your friend?" Beiron asked.

Ilan had to give Dimitri credit for not giving in to panic yet, but the strain in his face was evident. It was only a matter of time. "Dimitri. A villager from . . ." Ilan waved a hand. "I can't remember its name. Some village near the Teiry Mountains."

"Veryl," Dimitri cut in. "It's called Veryl." He took a step toward Ilan like he might try to head-butt him. Nielsen and Miles grabbed him and pulled him away.

"What did you bring me here for?" Dimitri shouted in Ilan's face. "I don't know anything about a song. You've brought me here for nothing."

Ilan waited until his guards had a firm hold on him. Dimitri settled down, but the muscles in his arms twitched.

"You can go," Ilan said to him. "As soon as you tell me how you came across a bethrail flower and where its pair is."

Beiron stepped out of the shadows and into the light. His dark eyes were unnatural and menacing as he stared at Dimitri. A long scar traced along the left side of his face, stretching from the corner of his brow to the top of his ear.

Dimitri startled at the sight of Beiron. Beiron did have that effect on people.

When Ilan had first met him fifteen years ago, he'd looked deathly pale and thin. He'd had long scraggly hair and a wiry beard. But since then, Beiron had cleaned himself up. Little by little, with each of Ilan's visits, he'd perked up and looked more human than wounded animal. Ilan saw to it that he was well fed. It was the most he could offer at the time. His father didn't know he'd spent his days and nights in this dungeon, learning about the Elderace. In exchange for simple pleasures—things like strawberries and grapes—Beiron had offered to educate him. Beiron never asked for anything too difficult. Oftentimes, he'd requested a bunch of leaves from outside. Ilan thought it odd, but all Beiron did with them was smell them. He'd keep them until they'd withered and lost their fresh scent, then ask for more in exchange for a new lesson.

"You look familiar," Beiron said to Dimitri. "Have we met?"

"No," Dimitri said.

"Huh. I must be confusing you with someone else. Come closer."

Ilan didn't expect Dimitri to go willingly. He signalled his guards to bring Dimitri closer to the cell for Beiron to get a better look at him.

Miles shoved Dimitri against the bars. Beiron reached out and touched a hand to Dimitri's chest. Dimitri winced, and his breath stuttered. When he slackened, Beiron pulled his hand away and took a step back. The corner of his lip turned upward slightly.

"What did you do?" Ilan asked.

Beiron stared at Dimitri. "That is interesting."

"What is? What just happened?" Ilan had never seen Beiron like this before. So . . . pleased? Excited, even?

Beiron turned to Ilan. "I take it you heard the song and have come looking for answers. That's why you're here, isn't it?"

"What is interesting?" Ilan asked. Beiron's acting like he knew something Ilan did not was infuriating. Ilan breathed audibly from his nose. "What did you just do?"

Dimitri looked pale and weary from Beiron's touch.

"It was a test," Beiron said. "Did you find what you were looking for since we last spoke?"

Ilan scowled. "Don't you think I would have brought it to you if I had?"

"You stopped coming to see me. I assumed you'd found it and stashed it away in your little collection you spoke so much about."

"What good would that have done me if I couldn't do anything with it? The deal was that you'd teach me magic if I brought you the stone."

Ilan heard Dimitri's intake of breath. He turned to him.

"Something wrong?"

Dimitri stared hard at Ilan. He narrowed his eyes. "I need to be with my people. I can't help you with whatever it is you're looking for."

Before Ilan could argue, Beiron interjected. "That's not true though, is it?"

Ilan looked at Beiron. "You think he knows something?" His tone raised a little too high.

Beiron tilted his chin up. "It is possible."

Ilan cleared his throat. "And you, um . . . you have something that can make him talk?" He had always wanted to see a demonstration of magic, but Beiron claimed it couldn't be done without the Weldafire Stone. The look in his eye, however, made Ilan think twice.

"I can do better than make him talk," Beiron said. "You still have your collection of plants?"

"Of course." Ilan had goosebumps just thinking about what Beiron might suggest.

"Good," Beiron said. "I could use some of them."

Unable to hide his delight, Ilan grinned. "Tell me what you need."

Chapter 18

Tomb-like. That was the word Laila used to describe the mines.

She took quiet steps through the mine's passageways on her way to the assembly chamber. Rounding a corner, she almost bumped into a woman whose back was to Laila. Over a thousand people crammed in the large space, barely fitting within. The chandelier made from tree branches hung in the middle, candles burning on it as always in this dark place. At the front of the room beside the elders, two large goblets blazed with fire, enhancing the dim light of the chandelier.

Standing beside Vix at the front were two other elders—Maire and Zulu. Of the eight from the time before, only four remained. Vix, the oldest of them all, faced the people as he led the meeting.

Laila groaned. This was going to be a while.

Vix was a wise old soul, kind and sweet, but slow—slow in speech, slow in responding, slow to get angry. That last one had been a saving grace for Laila on more than one occasion.

"What we know is that Litlen is changing," Vix was saying. "Yes, it is exciting and frightening. But we must remember that the Valca Order is still a threat. Landon may be gone, but his children and grandchildren have kept up the hunt. Only the other day a Valca soldier was spotted in Litlen."

Nothing about this meeting was news to Laila. She scanned the faces in the crowd for her brother's and found him near a second opening into the chamber near the front. She had to get to him without drawing attention to herself.

Magic coursed through her veins, and her awareness of the power it held was energizing. She was whole again. What she had discovered could begin a new era for her people. This couldn't wait.

She squeezed through the crowd, pushing past shoulders. People parted for her. She took her time as she went, so as not to disrupt Vix's dragged-out speech about the safety of the people and the importance of staying unseen.

Yes, yes, they'd heard it all before.

Beside Royl was the elder Darrin. Laila crept beside Royl, close enough that he'd hear her whisper. With his acute senses, he'd hear.

"Royl," she said, barely audible, keeping her gaze forward.

From the slight turn of his head, she knew he had heard her. He straightened his neck and kept his eyes on Vix.

"Royl," she said again, just a touch louder. This time, she looked at him.

Darrin glanced her way. He was blind in one eye, and the pupil and iris in that eye were clouded in an eerie white.

Laila bowed her head and averted her gaze. Darrin turned back to Vix. Royl hadn't reacted to her second call.

"Royl, I need you." Her whisper came out strained. He had no idea how big this was.

Royl didn't respond. Darrin shifted his seeing eye toward Laila while keeping his head forward. He pinched his lips.

"Royl," Laila said again.

This time, he turned to face her. "Not now, Laila. It's not a good time."

Vix had stopped his speech to look their way, drawing the attention of others. Angry eyes fell on her. Those nearest stared.

Suddenly, the room seemed very warm. Laila forced a smile at the many pairs of eyes on her.

"Is something wrong, Royl?" Vix asked.

Royl glowered at Laila. "Nothing that can't wait. Apologies for the interruption; Vix, please carry on." He turned his face from Laila and didn't see how much his dismissal upset her.

Vix, in his way, was slow to start speaking again. Laila took that as an opportunity. She had hoped to share with Royl first, but she couldn't keep her secret any longer.

"No, actually," she said loud enough to demand attention. "It can't wait. This is too important."

She caught Royl's glare, and Darrin's, who managed to curve his eyebrows so far down that Laila thought they might get stuck that way.

"Laila," Royl whispered. "We can talk about this later."

"Everyone needs to hear this." Laila looked past Royl toward Vix. "If I may, Vix, I have something to share."

Vix gestured for her to carry on.

"A long time ago, I read that Azure Lake was like the Pool of Sovereignty and that its waters have the power to heal. It's just . . . not as powerful. I read that not only does the water have the power to heal, but that it can also enhance magic." Her voice went up on the last word as if it were a question. It was strange to be explaining this to the elders—shouldn't they know these things?

"I drank from the water many years ago after reading that," she said.

"Azure Lake, Laila!" Royl interjected. "That's well outside the boundary—"

"Royl, please let me finish."

A muscle in his cheek twitched, and he shut his mouth. He'd have words for her later.

Perhaps she should have felt bad for embarrassing him in front of the elders, but she was right about this. She wasn't going to let him shut her down, apprenticing elder or not.

"Nothing happened then," she went on. "Not that I expected it to." She did, but the fib was harmless. "I think it was because of the curse. But when Litlen came back to life, I thought I might try it again and see if things would be different. And so I went back, and . . . well . . ."

She didn't know how to say it. Showing them would be better. Joining her hands together, she cupped them as if she were holding a small ball. She imagined she was going to make the ball a thing to be seen and not just imagined.

Concentrating on producing something where there was nothing, she slowly pulled her hands apart as if to expand the size of her ball.

"*Vint*," she whispered, speaking her trigger—the word for *life* in Eldrace. Between her parted hands, there was light. The small blue ball of light she'd made was bright enough to illuminate the entire room. She smiled at her success. Having only done it a few times, it would likely take some getting used to.

It was incredible to have magic move through her, starting from her thoughts and travelling into her being, as if she could feel every pulse of blood swimming through her veins. This was a part of who she was, and having it move through her again, she felt whole. Magic was a part of each of them. They'd been missing it for so long.

She glanced up, expecting gasps of amazement and excited reactions from her viewers. Instead, the room went quiet. Her previous excitement dwindled, and she grew aware once more of all the pairs of eyes on her.

Royl, Darrin, and everyone in her vicinity gawked at the ball of light. It was as if they'd never seen magic in their lives, even though each one of them had once had this kind of power themselves.

Royl looked from the light to Laila. His expression turned to one of concern. She'd gone too far, she knew, but for this, it was worth it.

A small murmur broke out and increased in volume. So many people were trying to speak to her at once. Laila backed up into more people. Their words were all a jumble around her: *Azure Lake, magic,*

Litlen, broken curse. She couldn't make sense of the questions. If they were questions at all.

Finally, Vix raised his arms to silence the group. It took a few minutes to settle everyone down, but as soon as the room was quiet, he said, "This is a good time to break."

Some people grumbled. Someone in the back asked what for. Others turned eagerly to talk to their neighbour.

Laila's show of magic seemed to have finally stirred excitement. She spotted her mother, Freya, in the crowd. Their eyes met, and Laila detected the same worried look in her that Royl liked to give her. Often. Someone turned to her mother and said something to her. Freya gave Laila a slight nod. That meant they would talk later.

By saying break, Vix was referring to the elders' huddle, which consisted of the four elders plus Royl. The elders began making their way to the private room adjoining the assembly chamber. Vix motioned to Royl, then turned to Laila.

"Come."

Chapter 19

Laila's skin prickled on her arms. Her surprise at the invitation was intermingled with a thrill of excitement, but also a bit of worry. Feeling like a child being accepted into the conversations of grown-ups, she followed Royl and the elders.

The private room had been carved out of the far wall of the assembly chamber after they had lived in the mines for a decade. Its size was made with only the four elders and Royl in mind. With the five armchairs in a circle, mimicking the layout of the stone chairs in the delegates' cave, Laila felt like an extra. No one sat once they were gathered inside, an indication that this wasn't to be a long meeting. The chatter from the assembly room decreased significantly when the door closed.

Royl wasted no time. He turned to Laila. "I can't believe you went so far as Azure Lake. What if something happened to you? No one would have heard if you called for help or—"

"That will do, Royl," Vix interrupted. "Laila, tell me, where did you read about Azure Lake and its connection to the Pool of Sovereignty?"

Laila's face flushed hot. She'd hoped they wouldn't ask about that.

The pressure to speak was intense with the elders' expectant eyes on her. She closed her mouth and tried to control her racing heart by drawing in one long breath. There was no point evading the topic.

She bowed her head and replied, speaking to the floor, "In a book I took from a house before everything was burned."

"Do you still have it?" Vix asked. He didn't sound angry or upset. But that was the thing about Vix—he always seemed like he was contemplating life, as if his mind was far off from the rest of them.

Laila didn't want to give up the book. It was difficult to explain, but it felt like it was part of her—or like she was part of it. If the elders had it, would they be able to sense her in it?

It didn't make any sense to think that way, but the idea frightened her. Yet, she had just been accepted into an inner gathering of elders. Lying would break their trust.

She sensed their eyes still upon her. If she refused to give it up, would she get in trouble? It had to be important to them. After all, they'd disregarded her display of magic only to ask about the book. She nodded, hesitant.

"May we see it?" Vix asked.

She nodded again and resisted wiping sweat from her brow. She reached into her bag and pulled out the book she'd carried with her for so many years. The pages were discoloured, and its leather cover was a dull grey, weathered and cracked. Laila thought it might have been black at one time. The initials were hard to read.

Maire, a small woman with silver eyes, gasped and put a hand to her mouth. The others frowned at the book. Except for Royl. He kept his eyes on Laila. For once, she couldn't tell what he was thinking. His face held disappointment, but he looked like he was masking other emotions as well.

"We cannot trust anything that comes out of that." Zulu, the large black man with accentuated brow and cheek bones, pointed a finger at the book.

Darrin nodded. "I agree," he said. "We don't know if it's safe to try anything from it."

Vix extended a hand. "May I, Laila?"

Laila handed him the book, then wiped sweaty hands on her skirt. She'd hid it all this time. In one way, giving up Beiron's book lifted a weight from her shoulders, but she was reluctant too. The book had some power, some hold over her she couldn't name.

Vix's bushy grey eyebrows furrowed as he turned the pages, taking a short glance at each before turning another. The others leaned in around him.

"Thank you, Laila," Vix said. "This gives us much to think about."

"Did you know?" Laila asked. The secret was out and the book was theirs now. She had to know. "About Azure Lake and its power?" She expected Royl to reprimand her for being so forthright, but he was unusually quiet.

Vix closed the book and tucked it under his arm. "You're aware, I suppose, that when the Chronicle Storm changed our world as we knew it, our elders of the time split into factions, each preserving knowledge concerning their division. Information pertaining to the Weldafire Stone and the Pool of Sovereignty was the responsibility of the delegates. It seems Azure Lake was known to them . . . or at least, Beiron must have known, as this is his book, is it not?

Hair raised on the back of Laila's neck. How could he know that?

Vix continued. "I believe I speak for all of us here when I say we had no knowledge of Azure Lake's connection to the pool. We shall look further into it. If all goes well, perhaps we can bring some magic back into our lives."

Royl straightened. "Vix, if I may? Laila has gone outside on many occasions and is clearly venturing well beyond the boundaries. Those boundaries are in place for a reason. On top of that, she's kept this dangerous book a secret."

"Dangerous?" Laila's mouth fell open. "What are you—"

Royl held up a hand. "There should be a consequence for such disregard for the rules—rules that are there for *everyone's* safety."

Darrin folded his arms and nodded.

"And what do you suggest that be, Royl?" Vix asked.

Darrin piped up. "Locked in confinement for a month, I say."

Laila wished everyone would stop talking. Her anger at Darrin was overridden by her hurt at Royl's call for punishment. Was his position really more important to him than their relationship?

"I suggest she be monitored and prevented from leaving the mines until further notice." Royl looked at Laila. "You've been lucky, but sooner or later, your luck will run out."

Laila wanted to cry but forced herself to hold back her emotion. Royl's suggestion was out of line. He knew how much she hated this place.

"Given the promise of hope of this new discovery," Vix said slowly, "I believe we could offer some leniency here."

A tear slipped past Laila's defences.

"But you are not wrong, Royl. We have those rules in place for a reason, and no one is above them, including you, Laila. We will give the sentries instructions to prohibit you"—he nodded at Laila—"or anyone to go out unless they are meant to, until we have determined if it safe to do so. Are we all in agreement?"

Maire and Zulu nodded. Darrin gave a small nod and snarled at Laila.

Royl met Laila's eyes, but only for a moment. "Yes."

More tears streamed down Laila's cheeks. She hated looking weak in front of the elders.

Vix concluded their meeting. "Darrin, see that the scouts make it a priority to bring back some containers of water from Azure Lake. Zulu, please speak to the sentries about the increased restrictions. Maire, if you would address the community and let them know what we've decided to do. Please tell them no one will be permitted to go outside for the time being."

Each of the elders acknowledged their orders.

"As for me," Vix said, holding up the book, "I've got some reading to do. Royl, once we have the water here and it has been deemed safe, I trust you'll assist with distributing it."

"Of course," Royl replied.

The four of them broke from their huddle and departed from the room.

Royl stayed back with Laila. It was quiet—except for the sniffle Laila couldn't hold back.

"Laila," Royl said. The sadness in his voice better have been guilt at what he'd done. "You know why I had to."

Anger rose in her. "You didn't have to! It's not going to stop me; I've already told you. I can't stay here in this . . . in this . . ." She didn't have an appropriate word to describe everything she felt about the mines. She opted for a different thought instead. "I can't believe you did that."

The silence between them was uncomfortable. Laila wanted to go, but she didn't want to be seen like this in front of everyone while Maire wrapped up the meeting in the assembly chamber.

"*Tsarioc*," Royl said gently.

"Don't! I'm not anymore, am I? You've just clipped my wings."

"You'll always be a little bird, Laila. And sometimes, little birds get hurt." He paused. "I love you and I don't want to see that."

"Stop treating me like a child. You say you don't want to see me hurt, yet you're the one doing the hurting."

"It's for your protection."

Laila shook her head. She was too upset to keep arguing. This would have been a good time to walk off her anger in the fresh air.

She collected herself. That was just what she'd do. It was like she said. This wasn't going to stop her. There were other ways to get out. Rules or not, she was not going to be kept from flying free.

Chapter 20

A KNOCK SOUNDED AT THE DOOR TO THE STUDY. KINGSTON CALLED out without looking up from the pile of parchment on his desk.

"Enter."

Owen peered inside, first glancing around everywhere, checking for flying objects, probably. More than once, Kingston had chucked a book at him when things weren't going his way.

Since Kingston's return to Kartha, his situation was not out of control as he'd suspected it might be. He felt no need to throw things just yet. Perhaps he'd come back early from Tsein for nothing.

"Your Greatness," Owen said. "Ilan has been spotted entering the Valca grounds with a guard of men and a prisoner."

Kingston waved his hand, dismissing Owen. Owen bowed his head as he left the room, closing the door behind him.

The large wooden desk before Kingston was covered with rolls of parchment and letters. The topmost letter was from Duran Morocan, who had requested Kingston's presence in Tsein two months ago. Now they'd dined together, Kingston could devise the next steps in his plan. Getting a foot in the door was only the first stage in taking Tsein. There was still so much to do.

Kingston looked to the right, where the bookcase took up the entire wall. Too bad there was nothing in there about how to make time move forward. Taking Tsein couldn't happen soon enough.

He sighed. For too long, he'd done everything on his own. It was wearing on him. He needed Ilan to take his future seriously, show he was capable of ruling, giving Kingston the confidence to leave him to it and not have to correct his mistakes along the way. Kingston hadn't thought Ilan would be around upon his return, but he was glad. He could tell him the good news sooner.

He stood and stepped away from his desk, making his way to the door and out of the study. If Ilan had a prisoner, he'd likely be at the jail. Kingston would look there first.

The narrow halls of the Keep were busy with servants. In Kingston's unexpected early return, they scurried about to light lamps and start a fire in his room. The weather was growing colder each day. The Keep was solid and fortified, but it lacked the warmth that Duran's palace held. Ilan didn't realize just how comfortably he'd be living in Tsein.

Kingston stopped on his heel when Ilan exited the library and nearly walked into him.

"Father," Ilan said. "You're back."

"As are you, I see."

A servant hurried past them down the hallway, avoiding eye contact.

"Aren't you meant to be somewhere right now?" Kingston asked.

"I was just . . . I was doing that. The conscription. Perry's on it. You'll get your men."

"*Your* men," Kingston corrected. "Ilan, this army is for you. You should be with Perry. The people need to see you. They need to know that you are to be feared and that they answer to you. What are you doing here?"

Ilan fiddled with the shoulder strap of his satchel. "I'm just . . . um . . . I met someone in—"

"Put a stop to it," Kingston said. The last thing he needed was Ilan finding his soulmate at a time like this. "I'm making the arrangements, and you're to marry Duran's daughter, Taaura. You'll bring us one step closer to taking Tsein."

"Father, I've already told you, I don't want to leave Kartha. I'm happy enough to take over and rule here."

"It's not a matter of what you want. This is your duty and responsibility as a Valca. You'll do as you're told."

Ilan's face became sombre. "Yes, Father."

"What's this I hear about a prisoner you've brought in?"

The sombre look disappeared, and his eyes widened. Ilan should know by now that Kingston knew everything that went on around here.

"He's just a villager who tried to defy me," Ilan said.

"Hmm." Kingston put a hand to his chin. It was good to see that Ilan was stepping up and doing something about it. "You'll have to make an example of him. Nobody tries to defy a Valca and gets away with it."

"Of course, Father. I'll see it done."

"Right. Good. Where are you off to now?"

"I'm going to send word to Perry that I'll be rejoining him soon."

"Very well. Send one of my men. Don't use a vohrsit carrier. You can never trust a beast to do a man's work. Once you're finished and back from gathering the men for your army, we'll deal with that prisoner of yours together."

Over the last few years Ilan's mannerisms had lost a certain . . . enthusiasm. Kingston had noticed it most when Ilan stopped arguing with the orders he'd been given. With an air of defeat, Ilan would agree and do as he'd been told, and that was that. It was not necessarily a problem. But it was clear his heart was not in it. Kingston wished he could make him care.

"Ilan," Kingston said before his son could go on his way. "You're not . . . keeping anything from me, are you?"

Ilan's eyes searched Kingston's face. It was so hard to tell these days what Ilan was thinking. Was he hurt by the question? Or guilty and hiding something? "No, Father," Ilan said. He walked away, adjusting his satchel on his shoulder as he went.

It didn't look like Ilan was involved in the song or purple mist after all. But Kingston needed to investigate the matter. He'd sent the letter to Scourge and expected to hear back in the next day or two. One could never be too careful when it came to ruling a country. The Great Battle at Reen had taught him never to underestimate the forces of a few angry villagers. Thankfully, they were still too few to match the forces of the Valca Order. But he had to be careful not to let his guard down regardless.

His shoulders remained tense. Ilan claimed he was not involved in anything, but Kingston didn't buy it. Some things in life were too good to be true.

*

Metal clanged on metal as the dungeon door shut behind Ilan. Now that he had returned, he was joined again by Nielsen and Miles, who'd stayed with Nero and Cain in the jailer's room to await his orders. In the opposite tower, below the Keep was where he'd hidden his collection of plants. He wished he hadn't taken that shortcut through the library. He might have avoided his father.

Dimitri, still in restraints and now locked in the cell across from Beiron, stood up at their entry. Beiron stepped slowly up to the bars of his cell. Ilan approached and wedged the satchel through the bars, handing it to Beiron. Everything he'd need was in there.

"We need to move quickly," Ilan said.

Beiron peered into the bag. "These things take time."

"We may not have much of it. My father is back and thinks I'm up to something. If he catches us, he'll execute you both and lock me away."

Beiron indicated Dimitri. "I need him in here."

Ilan faced Dimitri.

"You have one last chance," he said. "Tell me what you know."

Even if Dimitri did decide to tell him anything, Ilan planned to proceed. He wanted to see how these plants would affect a person.

Dimitri's lip quivered for an instant. Then his eyes hardened and he jutted his chin.

Just as Ilan had thought—he wasn't going to talk.

He gave the order for the guards to transfer him over. Nielsen unlocked the door to Dimitri's cell and dragged him out. He handed him over to Miles and unlocked Beiron's cell door next. Dimitri struggled against Miles's grasp, but he fought a losing battle. Even if he were to get away, where could he go?

Miles threw Dimitri into Beiron's cell. Dimitri tripped and landed in Beiron's arms.

"I'll need someone to hold him," Beiron said. He shoved Dimitri aside and pointed to Miles. "Sunshine there. I could use his help."

At Ilan's nod, Miles stepped forward. Nielsen closed the door behind him and locked him in the cell together with Dimitri and Beiron.

Chapter 21

Ilan took the keys off Nielsen. "You can go now. Wait in the other room and watch for my father."

Nielsen hesitated.

"What are you waiting for?" Ilan asked. "I'll shout if anything goes wrong."

Whether that made Nielsen feel any better about leaving was irrelevant. He had his orders and would do well not to question them.

Nielsen left, and Ilan stood alone in the hall between the two cells. There in the dungeon with Beiron, whose strength and power was a mystery to them all, and Dimitri, who'd proven persistent in his defiance. Miles stood tense, his hand grasped around Dimitri's upper arm. Between Miles and Beiron, Ilan trusted they wouldn't have any trouble subduing Dimitri.

Whatever Beiron had in mind, it had better work. Ilan stepped closer to the cell and gripped the bars. Beiron opened the satchel and held up the lacrut, a yellow four-leaf plant with no flower.

He tore off a bit of the long root and ate it, then tore off another bit and waved it at Dimitri. "Eat this," he said, "or I shove it down your throat. Take your pick."

Dimitri looked at the plant. He seemed to be weighing his options.

"What's that do?" Ilan asked, unable to restrain himself.

Beiron glanced his way. "The lacrut's magic allows the users to share a thought connection."

Ilan's eyes lit up. "Magic?"

"It was banned by the Elderace long ago," Beiron said. "Many still continued to take advantage of its unique effects, myself included." He winked.

It had not been an easy plant for Ilan to get his hands on. It grew on the lower parts of the cliffs and in the craggy holes of the rock. There, the sea water splashed up against the cliffs, making it particularly dangerous to acquire. It had been worth it, though, to have such a unique and uncommon plant as a part of his collection.

Beiron held the root out toward Dimitri, whose neck muscles strained. Dimitri tugged on his arm, and Miles released it so he could take the root. He ate it, grimacing.

Beiron pulled out the flask from the satchel and drank. He proffered it to Dimitri, then retracted it.

"You spill this and I'll kill you myself. Understand?"

Dimitri studied the flask. Ilan had scooped its water from the Pool of Sovereignty years ago. Good thing too, since now the cave was inaccessible.

Beiron offered Dimitri the flask. "As before—drink it or I make you drink."

Dimitri reached out with both hands that trembled, making the chains on his restraints rattle. He eyed the liquid warily. "What is it?"

"Water," Ilan said. "Nothing more."

"This shouldn't frighten you," Beiron added. "You've drunk from the pool before."

Dimitri fixed his wide gaze on Beiron.

Ilan scrunched his eyebrows together. "How do you know that?"

"Drink," Beiron said. He waited until Dimitri did so, then capped the flask.

"That test I did earlier," Beiron said as he dug through the satchel to retrieve the other three plants. "I have magic deep within me that allows me to distinguish the Elderace from the mayanon. Dimitri is mayanon, yet he has a magic in him that could only come from drinking from the Pool of Sovereignty. My touch would not have affected him otherwise. It only affects the Elderace and those who have drunk from the pool. But I detected something else in him and intend to find out what it is."

Beiron emptied the contents of the satchel. He held up each plant, identifying it before placing it before him on the ground. First was the dangerut, a common purple flower that reminded Ilan of a lilac. It was known to help ease pain. Next, Beiron held up the pink raimai. Its three rounded petals were small compared to the three large leaves the flower rested upon. It could be found in any healer's home. The leaves consisted of an absorbent gel-like substance that worked well as bandaging.

The divinite, a red-speckled, clover-looking plant, had been the most difficult to obtain. Ilan knew from Beiron that it supposedly acted well as a sedative but also had a paralysis effect. It allowed the person under its influence to be fully aware while physically unresponsive.

Beiron laid each of them out, then pulled out the pestle and mortar Ilan had provided. He took apart each plant and added the parts he needed to the mortar. He ground them together with the pestle, adding water from the Pool of Sovereignty.

"Get him on his knees," Beiron told Miles.

Beiron had gone from prisoner to commander. He held himself high as he mixed the concoction in the bowl. For so long he had been Ilan's teacher in all things Elderace. Ilan hardly recognized him as the same man he'd stumbled upon fifteen years ago as a broken and chained prisoner.

Miles kicked Dimitri in the leg, catching him off guard, and shoved him down onto his knees. He swung his fist into Dimitri's ribs. Dimitri doubled over sideways, and Miles held him steady.

Beiron mixed away, adding drops of water between every stir. He commentated while he mixed—like a teacher addressing a student.

"The toxins from the dangerut draw out the chemicals in the divinite that inhibit the mind. In this particular blend, the pink raimai will help stabilize his heart rate. The lacrut, as a two-way plant, could allow him to reach into my thoughts. This mixture will prevent that."

Ilan soaked it all up, knowing this lesson was for his benefit.

Beiron set the bowl down and reached into the satchel for the last plant. The harbury was a grape-sized berry with a hard casing. Picking one berry from the branch of six, Beiron smashed it on the hard floor. The casing broke and he rubbed the bright red fruit under his nose, then handed it to Miles.

"You too," he said. "It will keep you stimulated."

Miles took it and did as Beiron had done, rubbing the berry above his moustache, bumping his fingers against his gold hoop in his nose. Beiron gave it to Ilan next.

"Even from a distance, the smell of this blend can affect the mind. You'd do well to do the same."

Ilan rubbed the berry under his nose. Its scent was strong and sweet.

"Now hold him steady," Beiron told Miles. He picked up the bowl and finished mixing, then approached Dimitri. Sticking his fingers into the mix, Beiron rubbed the pasty substance between his fingers and thumb and applied the paste on Dimitri's nostrils.

Beiron was right, the smell of the mix was strong, even through the scent of the harbury. It was foul, and earthy, like the stink of death and decay. He crinkled his nose and tried to only smell the harbury.

"This is to help you relax," Beiron told Dimitri matter-of-factly. "Breathe deeply." He spread more of the paste across Dimitri's upper lip and on his temples. "Don't hold your breath," he said.

Beiron was in charge now. He had a precision in the way he worked and an intense focus. He set down the mortar and pestle and massaged Dimitri's temples with his fingers. Dimitri started to hyperventilate. "You'll make it worse by doing that," Beiron told him.

Dimitri's body started swaying back and forth.

Each of his breaths grew slower than the last, until finally his head lulled. Miles had to catch him so he didn't fall on his face, but Miles wasn't looking very capable himself. Ilan didn't think he'd be able to hold Dimitri's weight for much longer. His eyes were drooping.

Beiron paused his massaging to help Miles ease Dimitri down onto his back, his head rested on Beiron's lap. Then Beiron shooed Miles away and went back to rubbing Dimitri's temples. He closed his eyes as he worked.

Miles leaned against the far wall and watched, his eyes glassy.

Beiron smirked. "This seems like a good place to begin." His eyes opened, and in them, Ilan could see only white as Beiron became lost in a trance.

Chapter 22

RAIDAN SAT BOLT UPRIGHT, HIS EYES DARTING ALL AROUND AND HIS heart pounding hard. Ida stood over the make-shift bed of blankets on the floor, with Cassian crying in her arms. He searched for the thundering crash that had woken him. He had a vague awareness that the ground had just been trembling. Esef's loduloc was lying on its side on the ground. The long hollow log instrument reverberated its low sound. It must have fallen from its stand.

"What happened?" he asked Ida.

She watched him, unblinking, while bouncing Cassian close to her chest. There was restraint in her voice when she answered. "You were screaming in your sleep."

"I must have been dreaming." Raidan knew full well he'd been having a nightmare. A vivid image of the slithering vine and Adrik came to mind. He shuddered.

A new face haunted his dreams—a face with a pair of unnatural black eyes. He had a deep sense of Dimitri's presence in the dream as well. Rarely apart from his twin for longer than a few days and never on bad terms, Raidan couldn't shake the feeling that something was not right.

He ran his hands through his hair. Rain pattered against the door, which led onto a balcony outside on the second floor of the home. Cassian's cries grew louder.

Ida tore her gaze from Raidan to hush Cassian before he could wake her cousin, Esef. He slept at the other end of the house and on the first floor. It was a lonely home, with only him living in it. He'd responded to their arrival just as Raidan had guessed. But after briefly giving Raidan a hard time, he'd hugged Ida, happy as ever to see his cousin and to meet Cassian. He'd proceeded to pinch his tiny toes and welcome them in.

Ida rubbed Cassian's back while rocking him. Despite her efforts, it seemed Esef had woken. The sound of his racing up the stairs was like the roar of thunder behind the closed bedroom door. He burst in, out of breath and in his nightclothes, looking bug-eyed between Ida and Raidan.

"Is everyone all right? I heard a noise. I—" His eyes caught on his fallen instrument and he leapt over to it. "My loduloc," he said with a quiver in his voice. He crouched down and scoured it from top to bottom.

Raidan's legs were tangled in the jumble of blankets on the floor that made up their bed. He freed them and got to his feet, holding his breath in hopes that nothing had broken. The wooden prongs carved from the top of the hollow log were all intact. The log itself didn't seem to be cracked. Esef's shoulders relaxed, and Raidan released his breath.

Esef rested the loduloc firmly against the wall. His eyes fell on Ida and Cass as Cassian's crying turned to a sad whimper.

Esef scratched the top of his head with a finger. "I don't know what's been going on lately," he said. "We never get earthquakes around these parts. Ever. And that's not even the strangest thing. Only a few nights ago, there was this enchanting song. I would have loved to have known the woman who was singing. Her voice was so . . . smooth, so . . . familiar. Like a warm greeting from an old friend."

"That's a nice way to describe it," Ida said. "We heard it in Veryl too."

"And then there was the purple haze," Esef went on. "Even in the night, people could see a mist hovering low over the south. That, the earthquakes, the song. And now some claim Litlen is reviving. I'm not sure what to make of all this."

Ida held Raidan's gaze with a straight face. Litlen's revival was something they hadn't heard before. Cassian quieted, and she cradled him in her arms.

"Is your loduloc okay, Esef?" she asked.

"It'll take a lot more than an earthquake to break it." He looked at his instrument and stared at it for a full minute, then shook his head, coming out of his reverie. "I'll put it right in the morning. Wouldn't want it to fall again." His eyelids drooped. "I'm going back to bed." He waved his hand and left them, already half asleep as he closed the door.

When he was gone, Ida—Raidan's Ida, who rarely ever asked anything from him—came close and put her hand on his arm. His shoulders relaxed at her touch.

She caressed his prickly cheek. "This can't keep happening, Raidan. I know you don't like it, but you need to learn to control this. If it's true that Litlen is revived, that might just be the place to go. Isn't it where magic was supposed to have come from?"

Raidan's chest sank as he released a heavy sigh. "So people say. I don't want to control it, though. I want to get rid of it."

Ida removed her hand from his face and adjusted Cassian, getting ready to set him down.

"Well," she said. "Litlen is the most likely place where we're going to figure out how to do either." She put Cassian on the bed of blankets, then lay down beside him, extending her arm for Raidan to join her.

With the prospect of going to Litlen—a place of magic of all things—and his nightmare still rattling around in his brain, Raidan didn't think he'd be getting any more sleep tonight. He wrapped his arms around Ida. She faced Cassian, who slept peacefully. Raidan's lips brushed against the top of Ida's ear, and he breathed in the honey-sweet scent of her hair.

It would be better to leave this well enough alone, but he was not willing to take the chance of something happening to Ida or Cass because he couldn't control this power in him. A trip to Litlen might be worth it if it meant he could get rid of this magic—assuming there was anything to be found in the cursed land at all.

Chapter 23

On the cold dungeon floor, Ilan sat with his legs up and his arms tight around them to keep warm. He was between the two cells and may as well have been alone in the dungeon. Miles was passed out, leaning against the far wall in the cell. Dimitri lay supine inside, his head resting in Beiron's lap. Beiron remained in a sort of trance with his hands pressed onto Dimitri's temples. His pure white eyes were such a stark contrast to their usual darkness, Ilan averted his gaze.

Ilan had asked once about his unnatural eyes. In response, Beiron had stopped the lesson and refused to teach him anything more that day. That wasn't the only time that had happened. Beiron didn't like personal questions. Ilan had given up trying to learn more about him so long as it meant he could learn more about the Elderace. This particular lesson was beginning to drag on. It had been more exciting at the beginning.

He sat up straight and arched his back. It was the middle of the night, though down there you wouldn't know it. There was no telling when his father would suspect he had not left Valmain. With the number of spies Kingston had all over the country, Ilan was surprised he hadn't already come storming down into the dungeon.

Beiron's breathing sped up from its steady rhythmic pattern. Ilan scrambled to his feet, keeping his eyes on him. Beiron blinked, and when he opened his eyes, they were back to their normal, unnatural dark. He looked at Ilan and grinned. Grinning was good.

"What did you see?" Ilan asked.

"Everything."

"What does he know?"

"A lot more than you think."

Goosebumps spread up Ilan's arm. He pressed his face against the bars. "Tell me."

"I want something in return," Beiron said.

"Yes, yes, of course. What do you want?" Now that Litlen was full of life, finding plants wouldn't be as challenging as it had been while it was cursed.

Beiron moved Dimitri's head off his lap, resting it gently on the floor. He stood up and stretched, then walked over to the bars until he stood face-to-face with Ilan. "You bailed on our last deal and left me here without so much as a goodbye."

Ilan's ears felt warm. "I'll take up the search again and bring you the stone."

"So that I can sit in here and rot to my death? No, I want something more this time."

This new confidence in Beiron was unsettling. Ilan gripped the bars tight and stared into Beiron's hollow eyes. This was the first real progress he'd made in understanding the song and the changes in Litlen—the first time a lesson was more than just a lesson. He'd spent years wanting more, and finally, he was closer than ever to becoming a part of the world of Elderace and magic.

"Anything," Ilan said. "Name it."

Beiron's lip twitched. "I want my freedom. And I want some men from your army to assist me in retrieving the Weldafire Stone."

Ilan's grasp on the bars slipped. He wiped his sweaty hands on his trousers. Wide-eyed, he gawked at Beiron. He didn't ask for much, did he?

If Ilan released him, Kingston would have his head, but refusing Beiron might end his only chance to pursue this further.

"How can I trust that what you say is the truth?" Ilan asked. "That you're not making up something to trick me?"

In mock disappointment, Beiron asked, "You don't believe I would tell you the truth?"

"You don't get a name like *pridoor* by being a trustworthy kind of person," Ilan remarked. He had no idea how Beiron got the name, but once a traitor, always a traitor.

Beiron's eyes twinkled as he gave a crooked smile. "No, I don't suppose you do. When Dimitri wakes up, ask him about his brother. His reaction will be all the confirmation you need."

"His brother? What about his brother?"

"Our deal?" Beiron persisted.

Ilan looked into his eyes. To turn him down now would mean giving it all up—his research, studying, learning, all for nothing.

He shook off a chill. "If you tell me everything and show me how to get magic of my own, then I'll grant you your freedom."

"I can't give you magic. No one can do that. Or don't you remember anything I taught you?"

Ilan lowered his head. He remembered it all. The Chronicle Storm—the event that changed the Elderace people—was the reason the Elderace had magic and the mayanon did not. It occurred to Ilan that releasing Beiron would mean relinquishing his teacher. He still had so much he wanted to know. "Then bring me with you, and you'll have your freedom and my men at your disposal," Ilan said.

Beiron rested his head against the bars, facing Ilan. He grinned, showing straight teeth. "All right, Valca. We'll shake in an agreement sealed with magic." He held his hand out through the bars.

Ilan reached to shake Beiron's hand, then jerked his hand back. "Wait, what does that mean?" he asked. As exciting as it was to make a magical deal, he didn't know the rules.

"It means that if I don't tell the truth, I die. And if you don't release me after I've told you the truth, you die. A deal sealed in magic makes honest men out of the deal-makers, or dead ones."

Ilan nodded. His nod became more vigorous the more he thought about the bargain. "I'll agree to that," he said. "But you have to tell me everything."

"My life is on the line, and I don't plan on dying today," Beiron said matter-of-factly.

"So what?" Ilan asked, ready to make this deal. "We just shake and that's it?"

"You have a knife?"

Ilan removed his dagger from his belt. Beiron's hand was still poking through the bars. He motioned for the dagger.

Dimitri rolled onto his side, his face turned away from them. He moaned. Miles's face twitched in his sleep. Giving Beiron his dagger seemed like a bad idea. Beiron was locked in a cell with one of his own men and Dimitri, the man who supposedly held the answers Ilan sought.

Beiron followed Ilan's eyes and twisted his head back to look at Dimitri. He faced Ilan again, his confidence clear in his slanted grin.

"I wouldn't worry about him. I need him. The brother too." He nodded at Ilan's dagger again. "To make a deal in magic, we have to use blood." He opened his hand. "You do it if you don't believe me. Make a cut in my palm. Do the same to yours, and then we shake."

Ilan had no reason to think Beiron was lying. Making this deal gave him his freedom. Why wouldn't he tell the truth?

He handed Beiron the dagger. Beiron took it and sliced a cut into his palm, just as he'd said. Ilan took back his dagger and winced when he did the same to his own hand. They shook hands and a shock jolted through Ilan's system. He let go and studied his hand. The cut he had just made was healing over with a black line tracing over it. It didn't hurt, nor did it bleed.

"That line is a reminder of our deal and what the consequence will be for not following through," Beiron said.

Ilan stared at it, breathing hard. He wouldn't forget anytime soon.

The deal made, Beiron stepped back from the bars. "You might want to sit," he said. "There's quite a lot to tell."

Ilan couldn't sit now. With so much at stake, he hoped this was worth it. Beiron sat down next to Dimitri's head. He leaned back, supporting himself with his hands, and told Ilan everything.

Chapter 24

There was too much chatter in the streets, too many disturbing rumours going around. Kingston hated the gossip of the common folk. Nothing was ever true until he'd heard it directly from his sources. But he kept hearing about a song, a song, a stupid song!

Back in his study, he was doing the math, seeing how many men he would need to overthrow the Morocan kingdom once Ilan took his position there. It would, of course, take some time for him to gain their trust and win over their militants. Or buy their allegiance. That could work too. Ilan just had to get his head out of the clouds and stop wasting so much time on . . . whatever it was he was doing. Fooling around with women, going to the taverns with the soldiers like some commoner—that was all going to have to stop.

Kingston hardly slept at night anymore. The hour was late, but there was too much to do and not enough time. It was no secret that he spent most of his nights in the study. The desk, though it was massive, looked small in the grand room. Facing the room with his back to the outer wall, which was more window than wall, he sat poring over his plans. Rarely were the curtains ever opened. The tall, ceiling-high bookcase made up the far wall to his right, and the door was directly in front of him. Owen opened it without knocking. He was getting too comfortable in his position. Fortunately for Owen, he'd proved himself more reliable in getting things done than Kingston's own son.

"I thought you might be up," Owen said. "I'm sure you've been hearing, but I wanted to inform you that the rumours are true. Litlen is indeed thriving. The reports from your spies have come back saying it's like magic."

Magic? He had to say magic.

Kingston grabbed the gold paper-weight off his desk and threw it across the room at Owen. He missed. Owen cowered and hid behind the door. Kingston stood and looked for something else to throw. When he found nothing, he clenched his fists.

"There's more," Owen said, his voice quivering. He shrank back further behind the door and peered in. "Ilan has left his army in a village in the south," he said. "They're camped out there and awaiting orders."

The only things heavy enough to throw and cause any damage were the books in the bookcase that was too far from him at the moment. Kingston ground his teeth. If he heard one more bit of bad news, he was going to scream, or storm across the room just so he could throw the books. Hitting Owen with one would give him a bit of satisfaction.

Owen stood by the door, his body twitching like he wanted to flee.

"Anything else?" Kingston asked.

"No, Your Greatness."

"Go! Get out!"

In a hurry, Owen went, closing the door behind him.

The song, the mist, Litlen . . . now magic? This was getting out of control. He hated when things got out of control. And what was his army doing in some no-name village in the south? This was too much.

He'd be giving Ilan more credit than he deserved if he really thought he'd had something to do with the mysterious happenings in Kartha. Though it was highly likely that Ilan was forcing his way into whatever those things were, especially as it pertained to the Elderace lands.

Ilan was hiding something. Meeting him in the hall earlier hadn't put Kingston's mind at ease. He needed to stop Ilan from chasing after anymore of this nonsense before it was too late.

Kingston massaged his forehead where an ache throbbed. It crossed his mind to have Ilan placed under house arrest until he could get control of the situation. Fewer distractions for him. Fewer opportunities to throw him off course at this time leading up to his marriage and eventual betrayal of the king of Tsein. Kingston couldn't afford to let his son fall back into his old rantings about magic. It had taken a long time to get him back on track the last time.

Kingston despised the Elderace, not because of the long-standing enmity between his family and their kind, but because of Ilan's obsessive behaviour and fascination with them.

If this did have to do with the Elderace people, Kingston knew just who to see for some answers. He hadn't felt like he had any control in this country since his return from Tsein, and it grated on him. Beiron would tell him what was going on. If he thought he'd be granted his freedom, he'd tell Kingston everything.

Here he was, unaware of the happenings in his country. What kind of ruler was he? This never would have happened in his younger days. It was just a reminder of the sad truth that his mind was not what it used to be. The sooner Ilan stepped into his role, the better.

Kingston scooped his hand across the surface of his desk and flung everything on top of it across the room. He bared his teeth and seethed. He couldn't make any moves without first knowing what he was dealing with.

He left the study and slammed the door behind him as he went on his way to pay Beiron a visit. At the very least, he'd have a target to throw something at.

Chapter 25

The events Beiron recounted to Ilan were far beyond what he'd expected. Partway through the telling, Ilan had sat to listen to the rest. Now stiff from sitting on the stone floor, he ignored his aching muscles and adjusted his position.

Everything Beiron told him was incredible. All of it. What luck he had, finding the man who'd been responsible for stirring up the changes in Kartha. And Adrik was at the heart of it all. Ilan could have slapped himself for having given up his search for him.

"So Adrik is . . . ?"

"In the cave," Beiron replied.

In the cave that had collapsed. Most definitely dead, then. "And the stone?"

"In the cave. I can still retrieve it. It's inconvenient, but not impossible."

Miles's eyes burst open, and he gasped. He was up in less than a second, staggering on his feet. He looked down at Dimitri on the ground. Dimitri's face twitched. Beiron, sitting right by his head, swept the hair from his closed eyes.

Dimitri's eyes tore open, looking straight up at Beiron. His hands still restrained, he sprung upright and scrambled away, only to back himself against Miles's legs. Miles bent down and hauled him up by both arms.

"Good, you're up," Ilan said. He stood and rested his hands on his hips. "Now you can tell me where Raidan is."

Dimitri's head swivelled as he took in his surroundings. His mouth gaped open.

"Where is he?" Ilan asked. "We have some things to talk about."

"We don't need him to tell us," Beiron said. "I know a way to find him."

"What do you want with him?" Dimitri asked. His voice sounded phlegmy. He cleared his throat and yanked an arm free from Miles, then swiped his elbow across his nose. The concoction Beiron used on him had crusted onto his face and came off on his elbow. In rushed motions, he wiped off the rest.

Beiron got to his feet. "He's going to break the magic barrier he created."

Ilan looked to Beiron. "Magic barrier? You never said anything about that. You told me you'd tell me everything."

"I have told you everything," Beiron said. "Everything Dimitri saw. The barrier is a conclusion I came to from what I learned."

Ilan's stomach fluttered. Magic was becoming more than a myth—this was happening. It was all so exciting.

Dimitri stepped toward Beiron and pointed a finger in his face. "I'm not helping you," he said, taking another step and pulling his shoulder free from Miles's grasp. He swung both arms, landing a fist at Beiron, hitting him in the jaw. Beiron stumbled.

Miles shoved Dimitri, who jerked forward, lost his balance, and fell, landing on his hands and knees. Ilan called out for Nielsen to return with the keys.

Beiron kicked his foot into Dimitri's gut. Dimitri curled his elbows into his torso while he gasped and coughed. Miles bent over and grabbed Dimitri's arm, hauling him up. Beiron massaged his jaw. He licked his bleeding lip and chuckled. "Is that all you got? I would have expected more from you."

Nielsen entered the dungeon with the keys. At Ilan's indication, he unlocked Beiron's cell door.

"Secure Dimitri," Ilan told Nielsen. "Then prepare horses for us and gather a guard of a dozen men who are loyal to me."

Nielsen and Miles worked together to restrain Dimitri; then Nielsen left to do as he was told.

Dimitri stared at the open cell door. His upper arm where Miles gripped him was colourless.

"So how do we find the brother?" Ilan asked Beiron.

"I'm going to need some eshuair. The pollen in the flower will reveal Dimitri's connection to Raidan in a visible way. Dimitri will lead us right to him."

Dimitri tried to rip his arms from Miles's hold. "Raidan wants nothing to do with any of this!" Obviously, he still believed he had a say. Miles used both hands to restrain him. Beiron placed his hand on Dimitri's chest. Dimitri cried out. His knees bent and crumpled beneath him. Using his free hand to support Dimitri's weight, Beiron leaned in close. "You've awakened things you know nothing about. For that, I thank you. But you're not done yet. I still need you."

The longer he held his hand to Dimitri's chest, the weaker Dimitri became. Beiron pushed him and Miles caught his weight. Beiron raised an eyebrow at Ilan, motioning his head to the open cell door.

Ilan held his hand out toward the door. "Your freedom, as promised."

Beiron's shoulders lifted. He stepped out into the hallway between the cells. His body relaxed and his lips quirked as he met Ilan's eye. "Lead the way."

Ilan clapped his hands and rubbed them together. His face stretched in a wide grin. Gesturing to Miles to bring Dimitri along, he went for the exit. No doubt, Kingston was in for a shocking surprise when he discovered Beiron was no longer his prisoner. He was not going to be pleased.

Ilan opened the door to the jailers' room, breathing in the smell of stale damp air and smoke. The time had come for his learning to extend beyond these dungeon walls.

Chapter 26

Kingston's shout echoed in the jailers' room of the dungeon beneath the Keep. The jailers—idiots—let Ilan free Beiron! Who did Ilan think he was? The guards even stuck around after to guard the empty dungeon. They weren't too bright, these two.

Out of breath from screaming, Kingston's chest heaved, his rage at an all-time high. He flung the table and the belds flew all over the room. The table smashed into the wall and broke in two.

"Where did they go?" Kingston demanded from the cowering guards.

One of them, the burnt one, spoke up. "I overheard Ilan say something about finding someone called Raidan. S-supposedly he's the other prisoner's brother."

Other prisoner? Kingston had to think who that might be. Then he remembered Ilan was seen bringing a prisoner into Valmain—the one Ilan claimed had defied him, the one they were to make an example of together. How gullible he had been?

Kingston looked for something else to throw. Everything in there had already been upheaved in his initial fury. He screamed some more.

Pointing his finger at the two guards, he shouted, "Don't go far! Those prisoners will be returned here immediately. And then . . . then we're going to have an execution. And Ilan—my deceitful, obsessive, unreliable son—is going to watch."

This time, Kingston's accusatory thoughts of Ilan's involvement were justified. With the idea of magic being restored and the talk of Elderace songs, he'd never get Ilan to focus and take his place as ruler in Tsein. If this went on for much longer, he'd never give up his stupid quest and take his rightful place as Valca Order ruler. And without a Valca to rule, there could be no Valca Order.

Scourge was meant to arrive soon. His rates were outrageous, but if he was anything like the rumours boasted, he'd be worth every bit. And Kingston now had his first orders for the mercenary: bring back the prisoner Beiron and the brothers Ilan had taken an interest in, and get Ilan back to Valmain. Immediately.

It was time to put a stop to this. Ilan was going to have to learn the hard way that this quest of his was over.

Chapter 27

Sweat trickled down Laila's brow. The warmth was unusual for the season; it didn't seem right. Yet despite the heat, she felt the need to draw her cloak tight over her shoulders.

Standing before the house, she couldn't shake the feeling that she should not go inside, but the draw was too compelling. She took one step, then another, following the inaudible calling that lured her in.

Upon entering, it felt impossibly cold for such a hot day. The sunlight was blocked by wood slats nailed horizontally across the window, leaving the house in an eerie kind of darkness. Laila remembered the state of this house when she'd last come. Something was different now, but she didn't know what. It was as if her thoughts were blocked.

She ventured into the sitting room. Everything was neatly in place. The sofa facing the fireplace, the side table positioned in the centre of the room—not at all how it had been when she was last here. She shuddered. It was too perfect.

She walked past the polished kitchen and through the hallway where the bedrooms were. The house was bigger than the one she'd grown up in. A familiar desire flickered inside her to explore, to discover the house's secrets.

To her left, a black hole in the wall caught her attention. The wall opened to a narrow staircase descending into darkness. Her feet moved toward it without her mind willing them to go. They pulled her deeper into the house, deeper into the darkness, where the dark was not just a thing of sight but of feeling. Darkness embraced her as she descended stairs that seemed as if they might never end. Down into the heart of the house. The heart of the city.

No—the heart and soul. The lit-len, where it felt powerful—where *she* felt powerful.

A dim orange glow offered enough light to keep her from tripping, though Laila couldn't see its source. At the bottom of the stairs, she reached the place of calling: the stand where a book rested, closed. Not just a book, *the book*. How did that get here?

It called to her and she heeded its calling. All she could hear as she took slow steps toward it was her steady breathing. She stood over the stand with the closed book atop. The leather was in perfect condition, the shade a luring matte black. Laila squinted at it. That wasn't how she'd last seen it.

She felt as though the book wanted her to touch it, to take it. She knew she shouldn't, but at the same time, what was the harm? It wasn't like it could hurt anyone. It was just a book.

She reached out, drew her hands back to herself, then reached out again and picked up the book. It smelled of old leather and mildew, exactly as she remembered. Odd, considering its new look. She held it with both hands, where it felt right.

She sensed a presence and the hairs on her arm rose. She willed her eyes to leave the book and look up. No one was there. She twisted her torso to see around her. Behind her, in the darkness, black eyes peered at her. It was *him*. His dark hair neatly groomed, his scarred, stubbly face, and his soulless eyes . . .

Laila dropped the book. It hit the ground with a soft thud.

She must be seeing things. She slammed her eyes shut, and when she opened them, she was sitting up in her bed, panting as though she had just been sprinting rather than sleeping.

That dream. It felt so real, the details so vivid. She'd never actually seen Beiron before, but his image was clear in her mind. Somehow, she knew it was him; she knew without a doubt it was his eyes that gazed back at her.

Freya stirred in the bed across from hers. Her voice broke through Laila's thoughts. "You want to talk about it?"

Laila cleared her throat. "Not really." Seeing Beiron in her dreams was not something she wanted to discuss. "Sorry to have woken you."

"You didn't."

Laila squinted in the dark to try and see her mother across the narrow space between their beds. She considered using her magic to light the room, but she didn't want to disturb her mother's sleep further. "You okay, Mama?" Laila asked.

"Mhm. I've just got a lot on my mind."

"You too, huh?"

Freya chuckled. The wooden frame of the bed groaned under her mother's weight as she shifted. Laila sat upright and leaned against the wall. A bright blue light filled the small space. Freya sat similarly to Laila, with her back against the wall. Her eyes sparkled. Above her hand, the blue light hovered, and her thumb rubbed her silver locket. For as long as Laila could remember, her mother's trigger to ignite her magic was the piece of jewellery that hung around her neck. It seemed using her magic was as natural as breathing for her. Now that everyone had drunk some of the water retrieved from Azure Lake, they were adapting to having their magic back.

Freya let the locket go, and it rested on her chest between her clavicles. She moved her hand upward in a gentle motion. The lightball moved slowly with the motion of her hand. It halted just above her head and illuminated the whole of the room. Freya had such intense eyes, like Royl's. The two had the same brown hair, dark eyelashes, and dark circles around the green in their eyes. Laila's own eyes were green, but hers were brighter to match her fair eyelashes.

She and Freya said nothing to each other for a few moments. Laila spent so much time exploring outside the mines that she didn't get many quiet moments like these with her mother.

"Mum, can I ask you something?" Laila said.

"You know you can ask me anything."

"Do you like it here? In the mines?"

Freya let out a soft laugh. "Does anyone like it here?"

Her reply surprised Laila. "But you . . . you seem so happy here."

"I'm happy you and Royl are safe and together. Coming here was not a difficult choice to make when I knew what it meant to stay in Litlen."

"Royl likes it here."

"He doesn't. Your brother knows what is safe, and he'll do what he thinks is right to keep you out of trouble. He's looking out for you, Laila. He's protective because he loves you."

Laila said nothing as she stared at her clasped hands resting over her knees.

"You don't think I know what you get up to?" Freya asked.

Laila pulled her blanket over her shoulders.

Freya smiled. "I'm your mother. It's my job to know my children. And I know you could never be held back from adventuring and exploring the world around you. Royl knows it too. He just doesn't understand it."

"And you do?"

Freya chuckled. "More than you know."

Laila didn't consider her mother adventurous in any way. And having never met her father, she couldn't say what he was like. Royl had known him. Sometimes that used to make Laila jealous, but then, she'd always had Royl. Even when he was trying to clip her wings, she loved him.

"He needs to leave me be," Laila said. "Telling the elders about me isn't going to make me stop. I told him that." If her mother truly understood Laila's need to be outside the mines, maybe she could speak to Royl on her behalf.

Freya slid out of bed and took the short few steps over to Laila's. Laila moved over to give her room, and they sat together. Freya brushed a lock of Laila's red curls away from her face. "Don't be mad at him, Laila. He's under a lot of pressure. The responsibility of a future elder is not an easy burden."

"Then maybe he should have stuck with being a warrior, like he first intended."

Freya tilted her head down. It was she who'd convinced Royl to flee to the mines instead of joining the fight during the warriors' most desperate time of need. Even as a trainee, Royl had been one of the best warriors in Litlen. He'd woken Laila up, all those years ago, and told her to pack a few things quickly. While she packed, she remembered having to listen to Freya and Royl argue in the other room. Weeks had gone by before Royl spoke to their mother again after that night.

If it were her, Laila would have fought. Truthfully though, she was glad Royl had stayed. Besides him being her brother, it was nice knowing someone as skilled as him was here to train up a new generation of warriors and look after them all. But his skills didn't stop at being a great warrior. The elders had seen his potential to lead and recruited him in the early years living in the mines. The role of an elder suited him well. Too well.

"Be grateful he's with us." Freya said.

Laila rested her head back. "I am, Mother."

Freya squeezed Laila's shoulders in a sideways hug and kissed the side of her head.

"He loves you. Don't stay mad at him." She took her arm off Laila, scooted out of the bed, and crossed back to her own. "I'm going to try and get some sleep while it's still night."

"How do you know it's still night? It's always dark down here."

Freya lay down and pulled her blankets over herself. "My body knows. You should try and sleep too."

With the image of Beiron planted in her mind, Laila was too afraid to go back to sleep. What if she saw him again?

She shook her head. "I think I'll take a walk and clear my head."
Freya was turned so that she was facing Laila. "Outside or in?"
"What do you think?"
Her mother's eyes stayed fixed on her. "Just remember, don't let your curiosity—"
"—lead me astray," Laila finished for her. "Yes, Mother. I know. I won't."
Freya's tired smile was one of patience. She extended her hand out from under the blanket and closed her fist, snuffing out her blue light. "Stay safe, *deihara*."

Laila let her shoulders relax and smiled at the term of endearment. She left the dark room and stepped into the dimly lit hallway. To conserve oil, a few torches on each of the walls were extinguished in the nights and re-lit in the mornings.

Laila meandered down the hall toward the barricaded exit. She admired her mother's drawings, which were spaced apart about ten feet from one to the next. There were a few drawings of the Abberbrat shown in varying colours and times of day. Night was Laila's favourite, when the tree looked like it glowed and could be seen from afar. The Chronicle Monument was depicted in one drawing, the Forest of Litlen in another. Then came the Teiry Mountains, and the cliffs off the western coast of Kartha on the other side of these hills. There was one drawing of the hills of Litlen, and though it was pretty, Laila associated it with this place and didn't like it for that reason.

She couldn't stop thinking about her dream. Had she missed something the last time she'd visited Beiron's house? There hadn't been stairs then. She'd found his book on a shelf in a bedroom, not in a cellar.

Since Royl had made her life more difficult, the main entrance was out of the question. The barricaded passage was her next best option out of the mines. Other exits went deeper underground and farther west. Long ago, it'd been decided that the alternate passages throughout the mines should remain accessible in case the people needed to evacuate. Two exits had already been collapsed and destroyed before the elders agreed to enhance the supports of the others. It was Laila who'd raised the argument of emergency situations and the need for alternate exits. With two exits gone, she'd already felt trapped, like she'd never see the light of day again. How could the others not feel the same?

The barricaded passage led to tunnels that spread out under Litlen City. Too many people had gotten lost trying to find their way around down there, so that section had been deemed off-limits. The people had no reason to go that way anyway when all their resources were within the mines in the hills. The stream that ran through the hills provided their drinking water, while the hot springs deeper down allowed them to bathe. Gatherers brought food to the kitchen, and the waste crew saw to their work in maintaining sanitation.

Laila made it to the barricaded passage. It wasn't much of a barricade. Three planks of wood had been nailed horizontally across a dark opening that led into the long and winding tunnels beneath Litlen. She ducked between the bottom and middle planks with ease. Too many times, she'd gotten lost while learning her way around the tunnels. But a hundred years was a long time to familiarize herself with every turn and bend, every exit and entrance. Now she knew the places that were too low to walk through, too narrow, or too hazardous. Going this way was no trouble for her, just inconvenient.

She rounded the first bend and lit her blue light. Soon, she'd be back outside again, where she didn't have to look over her shoulder—outside where she truly felt free.

If her people stopped worrying so much, maybe she wouldn't have to sneak around to take a simple walk. If only they could see what they were missing.

Chapter 28

The pounding in Raidán's head was almost too much to bear. Having to listen to Cassian's sobbing without being able to soothe him was harder. But this magic in him . . . Cassian hadn't settled down with him once in their long journey from Altrow. They had to be getting close to Litlen now. He walked a little ahead of Ida, trying to hide his frustration. Anytime he tried to hold Cass, his son cried. Hunger was not the issue. They'd stopped frequently to feed him.

Ida strode up beside him with Cassian finally settled in the sling around her body, sleeping peacefully. "It's not you, Raidan," she said. "It's like I said back at home: he can sense your unease."

Raidan kept his gaze ahead. He knew she was not to blame for any of this; none of this was her fault. He was the one foolish enough to go to Adrik in the first place.

He stopped and Ida halted at his side. It was dark out, and they had been walking through a forest for some time now. The rumours that Litlen was alive were accurate enough. The colours in the trees' leaves were vibrant and bright. Torches or lanterns were not necessary, as the forest had a glow to it. The combination of colours—purple hues with blues and greens in the grass—was incomparable in beauty.

The trees ahead opened to a clearing. Surely they would get to the edge of the forest soon. The trees spread fewer and farther between.

It wasn't just the trees and grass that had a soft glow to them. Almost every plant did, as did small insects that floated by. Some areas throughout the wood were not lit up like the others. Black or grey patches poked their way between the bright places. Raidan couldn't make sense of them, but neither did he understand the sudden revival of an entire region.

"Cassian recognizes you're anxious, and it's making him anxious," Ida said. "Yes, Raidan, you were wronged, but would you let yourself relax? Look around you. I don't know how you can see all this and say it's evil."

It was all internal: the ever-present tingling throughout his body, the constant ache in his head, the lack of his usual energy. Everything felt wrong. Without sounding like a child complaining, he couldn't make her understand. She had no idea. Even as they stood talking, a strong sense of unease rose in his belly. There was an urgency in it. He had a sense of Dimitri. His stomach fluttered.

Whatever their connection as twins, Raidan didn't understand it. Why did he keep seeing glimpses of Dimitri in his mind? More than glimpses, actually. He listened and could hear—or, rather, sense. As much as he hated leaning into the magic, the urge was so powerful, he couldn't ignore it.

"All I'm saying is—"

"Shh." Raidan cut Ida off.

She scowled at him, but then her eyes softened. She looked from side to side. "What is it?"

Something nagged at his mind. A warning. Raidan turned in the direction he felt it was coming from. The intensity of its pull could not be ignored.

Dimitri was close. And he was worried for him. Raidan didn't know how he knew this, but he was certain. He looked back over the territory he and Ida had covered, through the trees and colourful underbrush. In the distance, he thought he could make out shadows moving through the night. He squinted. Those were definitely people on horseback. His pulse throbbed in his ringing ears. Dimitri's warning was loud and clear. There was no words or visions, just a thought: danger was coming.

He turned to Ida, aware that his fright was alarming her. "Run." He looked toward the riders. They were getting closer.

"What about—"

"I'll distract them. Just get Cass out of here."

She paused and glanced down at Cassian. Her gaze darted toward the approaching danger, then fixed on Raidan. Her face set, she nodded. "Be careful."

She turned and ran toward the clearing. She held Cassian close to her body, minimizing the jostle. Raidan jogged behind her. He veered to the side, leading anyone coming toward them away from his wife and son.

Buildings were visible in the distance, past the open plain. Light glowed from within the city ahead. Even from this distance, Raidan could tell the source of the light was bright. He glanced over his shoulder to locate his pursuers. Outrunning riders on horseback was not possible, and the trees here were too sparse to take cover. He stopped jogging. He had to buy Ida some time to get away.

The riders were close enough now for Raidan to make out tan armour with a bright red "VO" engraved into the leather. Raidan took wide steps toward them, waving his arms. A little over a dozen riders slowed as they came to where he stood.

Among them, Dimitri sat atop a horse, shared with a Valca soldier. His hands were cuffed in front of him, and his eyes were swollen like he'd been beaten recently.

Raidan looked at the faces of the others. They formed a circle around him. He backed up and tried to avoid being fully surrounded. It was not possible, he knew, but the more time Ida had to get away, the safer she and Cass would be.

The blond Valca soldier motioned to one of the riders. "Go after the woman."

"NO!" Raidan shouted and reacted without thinking. He jumped in front of the horse.

The ground trembled, unbalancing him, and the riders held tight to their reins to steady their horses. Shaken, Raidan stumbled and fell back. The rider who had been ordered to go after Ida and Cass yanked on the reins of his horse, and the horse reared. Raidan rolled out of the way before its hooves could come crashing down on him.

The rider took off after Ida. A second rider joined him. Before Raidan could follow, the others closed in around him. Raidan got to his feet as one of the riders jumped off his horse and strode over to him. Apart from Dimitri, he was the only one not wearing Valca attire. Raidan recognized him. He was the same man he'd seen briefly when he thought he'd been dreaming—the man with the dark eyes.

Surrounded now, Raidan had nowhere to go. He held out an arm. "Don't come any closer!" he shouted. He may not have had control of this magic, but he would do whatever it took to protect Ida and Cassian.

"Raidan," Dimitri said. "I'm so sorry; I didn't mean for any of this to happen."

The soldier he shared a horse with put a knife to his throat. "Save your reunion for later."

The man with the dark eyes kept a steady gaze on Raidan as he moved slowly toward him. His cool expression revealed no fear. Either he was not afraid of what Raidan might do, or he didn't believe Raidan could stop him at all.

Blondie, who'd given the order to go after Ida, dismounted. The way he carried himself made him appear large. With his chest puffed out and his nose stuck up in the air, he had the air of a man who had everything and could get anything he wanted. This was Ilan Valca. What had Dimitri gotten himself mixed up in?

Dark-eyes took another step toward Raidan.

"Stay back," Raidan said, keeping his hand extended.

Dark-eyes put his hands up in a show of surrender. "We just want to talk."

"Leave me and my family alone," Raidan said, addressing them all. "I don't want to have to hurt anyone."

"We don't want to hurt you either," Ilan said. "But we will if we have to. You're coming with us."

Raidan glanced at each of the riders. His chance of escape was slim. Using magic might work, but he had no control. It wouldn't take them long to figure that out.

"Come where?" he asked, stalling.

"The delegates' cave," the dark-eyed man answered. "You have unfinished business to attend to."

Raidan looked at Dimitri. What had he told them?

He didn't know how much they knew, or if playing dumb would do him any good. Their presence here and their reference to the cave meant they knew something. It didn't matter. He was not going back. "There's nothing left there," Raidan said.

"Then it will be a quick stop." Ilan leaned back and crossed one arm over the other, maintaining his hold on his reigns.

"What unfinished business?"

"You'll have to wait and see," Ilan said.

Distracted, Raidan wasn't prepared when the dark-eyed man lunged at him. He put his hand to Raidan's chest, and the air felt like it was being sucked from his lungs. Raidan gasped. He grabbed the man's hand and tried to wrench it away, but he was growing weak. His legs wobbled and gave way. The man supported Raidan's weight while keeping his hand pressed to Raidan's chest.

From the corner of his eye, Raidan saw Dimitri's face contort as he clutched at his own chest. The dark-eyed man looked at him, then smirked at Raidan. "Twins, huh? So much I have yet to learn," he said. "I look forward to it." He removed his hand from Raidan's chest. Raidan collapsed on the ground, panting as if he'd just exerted all his energy in a sprint.

"I'm Beiron," Dark-eyes said. "You and I will be seeing a lot more of each other over the next little while."

Whatever he'd done, Raidan still couldn't stand. He looked out toward the edge of the forest to the clearing, praying Ida got away. He let his head drop and slumped his body. Beiron lifted Raidan by the front of his tunic and steadied him. Legs shaking, Raidan planted his feet.

"Tie him up," Beiron told the others. "He'll ride with me." He rested his hand on Raidan's shoulder and leaned in to whisper in his ear. "My knowledge of Elderace power gives me a great advantage over you. Best keep that in mind, Dairner."

Chapter 29

PAYING A VISIT TO THE HOME OF BEIRON *THEI PRIDOOR* IN THE NIGHT was probably not the wisest thing to do. Really, any time was not a good time to go there. But something about that dream made Laila wonder. She couldn't shake her curiosity.

Signs of dawn were visible as the sky lightened and birds chirped. Apart from them, the city was quiet. Not the barren and hollow quiet of before—this was a peaceful kind of quiet.

A woman's scream cut through the silence, breaking the peace and startling Laila. The voice didn't sound far. Without a second thought, Laila deviated from her course. She moved toward the sound, breaking into a run when another scream pierced the air.

In between each stone house in the block were gaps big enough to fit through. Laila ran between two houses. The woman's voice sounded like it was coming from the Forest of Litlen, or thereabouts. Her desperate screams were now accompanied by the sound of a baby wailing.

Laila's heart jolted, and she picked up her pace. The spray of dew from the fresh morning grass wet her ankles. From one block to the next, she darted down the most direct path.

The screaming turned to begging. "No, please!" the woman cried. "Please don't take him; he's just a baby!" Her voice cut out abruptly, and the baby's wailing grew louder.

Closer now, Laila slowed as she made it to the last house. Behind it was a field. She stopped between the houses, not daring to leave her cover. Just beyond the house, a short distance ahead and to the left was the Chronicle Monument. Behind that was the Forest of Litlen. If she stepped out into the clearing, she could be seen by whoever was out there. She chewed her thumbnail while debating what to do.

No more sounds came from the woman. The baby choked as he cried.

"Can't you shut that thing up," a man's voice said. Laila snuck along the outer wall of one of the houses, keeping within the shadows. She reached the corner of the house and peered out.

Two men—soldiers by the look of their uniforms—stood over an unconscious woman. One of them held the baby and attempted to soothe the screaming child. The other held the reins of their two horses. He glanced from side to side and behind them. "Come on, let's just take the kid," he told his partner.

"What about the woman?"

"Leave her. Unless you want to get stuck babysitting her until the master is done with her?"

The one holding the baby scrunched his face. He shook his head.

Laila kept her back right up against the house. She gripped whatever stones she could so she wouldn't do anything stupid, like run out there and reveal herself to those soldiers. Who knew what they'd do if she tried to take the baby from them?

She dropped her head back and winced when it hit the stone wall of the house. Rubbing the sore spot, she argued with herself that she could, of course, use magic. But if she did, she'd be putting her people at risk by exposing that the Elderace still lived. And in every scenario she imagined, there was no refraining from using her magic.

Exhaling a heavy breath, she peeked out again.

The men walked with the crying baby and their horses in tow, leaving the woman behind as they made their way into the forest.

Again, Laila contemplated going after them to take the baby. She had to do *something*.

And so she would. But what?

Royl's voice nagged at her thoughts, scolding her, telling her not to do something reckless. Even when he wasn't there in person, she couldn't get him out of her head.

The men were in the forest now, out of sight. The quiet settled again. Laila shook her head at herself for what she was about to do. She stepped out of the shelter the houses offered. The open plain was before her.

First things first, she needed to check on the woman. She ran to her and crouched over her limp form. The woman's chest rose and fell in a steady rhythm. She was breathing. That was a good start.

Her blond curls spread loosely around her head, and the tall grass rose over her supine body. Laila checked her head for any wounds. A bruise was beginning to show on her temple, but there wasn't any blood.

Laila looked back toward the forest. She'd missed her chance at getting the baby. Going after them now would be too dangerous. Who knew how many more of those soldiers were out there?

On high alert, she glanced around, all the while hoping the woman would wake up soon. They were going to have to take cover before anyone saw them. As long as they remained in the open, they were in danger.

*

They were ready to go. Raidan sat uncomfortably atop Beiron's monstrous horse with Beiron seated behind. Hands tied, Raidan found it difficult to balance. Even more uncomfortable was the fact that Beiron was as close as he was.

On the eastern horizon, the sun had just risen. Streaks of light shone between the tree trunks. To the south, beyond the clearing and off in the distance stood a smattering of buildings. Houses, perhaps, but having never been to Litlen before, Raidan didn't know. He could only hope Ida had made it there and taken shelter.

Ilan led the group away from Litlen. Raidan cast a glance at Dimitri. Angry as he was with his brother, he couldn't help but check that he was all right—well, as all right as either of them could be for their situation.

Raidan knew Dimitri could sense his gaze, but his brother kept his eyes ahead.

People used to ask if, because they were twins, they could communicate telepathically. But no one could do that. At least, not that Raidan knew. He and Dimitri were aware of each other in ways others weren't. From Dimitri's posture to the way he avoided meeting Raidan's eye to the quicker-than-usual rise and fall of his chest, Raidan knew his twin was planning something. But what, Raidan could only guess.

The sounds of leaves crunching underfoot and the rustling branches above them were interrupted by a baby's cry.

Cassian!

Ilan raised a fist to halt the group.

Raidan tensed and turned his head. The two soldiers who'd ridden after Ida were returning. One carried Cassian, wrapped in his grey wool blanket Ida had made for him before he was born. Raidan's throat tightened. Where was Ida?

A sharp point dug into Raidan's back, and he straightened. Beiron leaned forward as he pressed his knife through Raidan's cloak. The words he spoke were for him alone: "Don't try anything stupid."

Raidan ignored the sharp pain in his back. "That's my son," he said to Ilan. "Give him to me."

Ilan rode over to the soldier carrying Cass. He crinkled his nose at the thrashing swaddle of blankets. "Where's the woman?" he asked, then pointed at Cassian. "What am I supposed to do with that?"

"I'll take him," Raidan said over Cassian's cries. "Please."

Ilan cocked his head at him. "Do you think I'm a fool?"

Raidan looked at Dimitri, who'd been uncharacteristically quiet. The soldier with the ring through his nose had returned his knife to Dimitri's throat. Dimitri was kept on a short leash by the knife held to his neck. His biceps bulged. Finally, he looked at Raidan. There was a fierce determination there, a pre-warning, letting him know to be ready for what was coming. Whatever he was going to do, Raidan didn't want Cassian caught in the middle of it.

"I can calm him down," Raidan said to Ilan. "Please. Just let me take him."

Whether or not he thought Cassian would settle with him was beside the point. None of Ilan's men could be trusted with his son. The soldier holding Cassian was trying to rock him, but Cassian was too distraught. At this rate, he'd end up crying himself to sleep.

Might he get off the horse and make it to his son without getting himself killed? Or the life drained out of him again by Beiron and his little tricks? He felt a rising power in himself and knew that more of that ground shaking could come back at any moment. He didn't know how to make it happen, though. He couldn't rely on power he couldn't control.

In his mind, he thought it through. He'd have to push his weight back onto Beiron to swing his leg over the horse's neck so that he could dismount. The knife would pose a problem, but he'd brace himself for the pain. Once on the ground, he could rush the soldier and take Cassian. But then what?

There was no time to figure out the details. He had enough of a plan to start.

Chapter 30

Psyching himself up to make his move, Raidan flinched when Beiron went rigid and poked the knife deeper into his back. There was not much Raidan could do to put any more distance between himself and Beiron. He bit his cheek and leaned forward as much as he could to alleviate some of the sting. Beiron's other hand tightened on the reins. Had he somehow guessed what Raidan was about to do?

But Beiron didn't try to stop him. He narrowed his eyes and looked around like he was searching for something.

"What is it?" Ilan asked.

As quickly as Beiron had tensed, he relaxed the knife at Raidan's back and loosened his grip on the reins. Raidan twisted his torso around to better see Beiron, who glanced at him before turning to Ilan. Something had changed in him; Raidan just didn't know what.

Beiron focused on the soldier carrying Cass. "What you're doing is not working." If he was annoyed at the nonstop crying, he didn't sound it. "Try holding him another way. He's a baby, not some wild animal that can't be tamed."

The soldier moved Cassian from his cradled arms to rest him against his chest.

Beiron looked at Ilan. "The cabin we passed in the forest, bring the baby there, leave some of your men to look after him. Was the Abberbrat intact when you last saw it?"

Ilan gave a slow nod. "Yes."

"Good. Have one of your men bring some of its fruit to the cabin. It's good for the baby and will suffice for feeding him. Women who've struggled to feed their babies have been using it for centuries."

"He needs his mother," Raidan said. "Where is my wife? Where is Ida?" The question was directed at Ilan and the two soldiers.

Cassian's crying faded. His stuttering exhausted breaths made Raidan want to cry.

"You have other things to concern yourself with," Ilan said. He turned to the two soldiers. "I assume you've returned without her because . . . ?"

One of them filled in the blank. "She was not in any state to walk or ride." The two men hardly raised their chins enough to meet Ilan's eye.

Ilan clicked his tongue. "Is she going to be a problem that *I* need to worry about?"

"No, sir," one of them said. Raidan thought he detected a tone of uncertainty.

"You don't sound sure of that." Apparently, Ilan hadn't it missed it either.

"She won't be a problem," the other guard replied. Cassian had settled down in his arms and was nearly asleep. Raidan longed to be the one holding him, comforting him, telling him everything was going to be all right even if it might not be.

Ilan's forehead wrinkled. He nodded. "Right." He pointed to the two soldiers who'd returned with Cass. "You two, take the baby to the cabin. You—" He pointed to another of his men.

"What do you want?" Raidan demanded. His heart was nearly bursting from his chest. "Why are you doing this?"

Ilan glowered at Raidan, then resumed his order to his soldier. "Get the fruit from the tree in the centre of Litlen and bring it to them for the baby. Wait there, and we'll rendezvous at the cabin after Beiron and I finish at the cave."

The mention of going back to that place made Raidan's stomach twist in knots all over again, but more pressing was his son's safety. He clenched his jaw and went back to planning his escape. He caught Dimitri's eye, which still had a spark of determination. The knife at his throat remained a hindering factor.

Ilan's soldiers turned and went on their way with Cassian, deeper into the woods.

Dimitri would act when he could. This was Raidan's last chance to act on his plan. No more hesitation. He pushed himself back into Beiron and the knife. Beiron was ready for him. He pressed the knife into Raidan's lower back before Raidan could stretch his leg over the horse's neck. The knife dug further in than it had before. Raidan jumped at the sharp pain and cried out. Then came the ground shakes.

Beiron wrapped his arm around Raidan's shoulder. He placed his hand to Raidan's chest, draining his strength. The quaking stopped, and Raidan squeezed his eyes shut to make the pain more bearable. Dimitri moaned, and Raidan knew he somehow felt Beiron's touch too.

"You want to protect your son?" Beiron said. "Then do what I tell you." He released his hand from Raidan's chest, not taking as much of his strength as before but enough for Raidan to lose his momentum.

Dimitri yelled and threw his head back, hitting the soldier in the head, hard. It seemed the quake had caused the soldier to lower his knife to steady his horse. Dimitri fought for control of the reins and whipped his elbow behind him, twisting his whole upper body. He knocked the side of the soldier's head and got control of the horse, then pulled on the reins. The horse reared and Ilan's man fell off.

Beiron returned his hand to Raidan's chest, sapping more of his strength. Within seconds, Dimitri let go of the reins and fell to the ground, landing on his backside. He clutched his chest.

The horse calmed. Ilan dismounted his own horse to intervene while his other men or Beiron's—Raidan didn't know exactly who was in charge—positioned themselves so that Dimitri wouldn't be able to run. Their horses inched closer together, creating a tight circle around him, Ilan, and the bloody-nosed soldier. Dimitri rolled onto his side and gasped.

Beiron took his hand away from Raidan's chest, and Raidan's whole body slumped forward over the horse's neck. On the ground, Dimitri coughed.

Ilan helped his man up. The septum soldier stood tall and wiped blood from his face. The gold hoop that had been between his nostrils was gone. He brushed off his clothes, then grasped his hand around Dimitri's throat, lifting him to his feet. Dimitri choked, and when the soldier didn't let up, Ilan smacked him on his shoulder. "We don't want him dead, Miles. Just compliant."

The soldier—Miles—released Dimitri. He wiped under his nose again and looked around on the ground, presumably for his nose ring.

Raidan caught a last glimpse of the soldiers who had Cassian as they moved farther away. His eyes burned. He'd find a way to save Cassian. The cabin Beiron had mentioned was not one Raidan knew, but he would find it. He had to. He'd find it and save his son.

And Ida. His heart ached for her. He had to believe she was all right.

Ilan switched Dimitri's bonds so his hands were behind him. Two of his men hefted Dimitri back onto the horse. Beiron hung back while Ilan and the soldiers began to depart.

"What are you doing?" Ilan asked.

"I'll meet you at the entrance to the pass," Beiron said. "There's something I need to get."

"What is it? We'll all go."

"No. I won't be long."

Ilan scoffed and jerked his head toward Raidan. "What about him?"

"He's with me. We'll—"

Ilan spoke before Beiron could finish. "What do you have to get?"

Beiron's breath was hot on Raidan's neck as he sighed. "Just meet me at the entrance to the pass. We'll be there shortly."

"Why are you taking him?" Ilan pointed to Raidan again.

"Because I don't think you can handle him."

Raidan wasn't sure if he preferred to go with Beiron or Ilan and his company, staying close to Dimitri. Ilan seemed the lesser of two evils. Beiron had shown that he was powerful and he commanded obedience from Ilan's men. And Raidan didn't like that Beiron could disable him so easily. It almost made Raidan wish he knew how to wield the magic within him so that he could use it against Beiron. Almost. At the very least, he wished he could control it enough to protect Ida and Cass.

"Be quick about it then," Ilan said. Even Ilan Valca obeyed Beiron.

Raidan hoped Beiron would head in the direction of the cabin, toward Cassian, but they went the opposite way. His breath became shallow. He twisted his body to look back, as if he could still see the soldiers with his son. They were long gone already, but he squinted anyway. Beiron nudged Raidan to face forward.

Ilan and his group branched off in another direction.

"Dimitri," Raidan said before they parted ways. His voice caught. He couldn't breathe. He looked to his brother for help, searching for the right words, but he didn't know what to say.

This was it. Cassian was gone. Ida was gone.

"It'll be all right, Raidan," Dimitri told him. "We'll get them back."

Get them back. Words Raidan clung to. Yes, he had to. If something happened to them, he'd never forgive himself.

Chapter 31

Scouts would be out. If they overheard the commotion as Laila had, they could be close and would spot her crouched over the unconscious woman in the open. Laila glanced over one shoulder and then the other.

"Wake up," she said as loud as she dared and gave the woman a gentle shake. She bit her lip and checked around again.

The woman's eyelids fluttered open. She blinked in the morning light and sat up, taking a moment to get her bearings. Her hand flung to the empty sling wrapped around her body, and she gasped.

"Cassian!" She looked at Laila. "My son!" Standing up too fast, she wobbled on her feet. "Where is he?"

Laila put her hand out as if to offer support. The woman was slight, but Laila herself was small and mightn't be able to support her weight if she fell.

The woman put her hands to her head. She turned in a circle, then stared into the forest. "They took him," she said. "No, no! They took him away!" She walked toward the forest, looking like she might fall.

Laila offered a hand to steady her. "You don't look too good. You took a hit to the head."

"I have to find my son—and my husband. They're in trouble." The woman hugged herself. Tears rolled down her face.

"You're in no condition to help them," Laila said. "Why don't you take a minute and tell me what happened. Maybe I can help. What's your name?"

The woman took notice of Laila as if only seeing her now. There wasn't much to see: just a red-headed girl in a dirty, tattered dress, who to her, probably appeared younger than her.

"My name is Ida. And who are you?"

"I'm Laila."

Ida put a hand to the bruise on her head and cringed.

"You're hurt," Laila said. "I know a place nearby where you can rest. There might be something there that can help with the pain."

Ida's shoulders slumped. She turned her face to the forest. "Did you see my son?"

"I . . ." Laila hesitated. "I heard you scream and I ran here as fast as I could. By the time I got here, you were out of it and . . . well, I did see two men take a baby into the forest. I'm not sure what I could have done."

It was a poor excuse. She knew she could have used her magic and gotten Ida's son away from those men, but she was already going to be in trouble just for being out here. Royl would have her head if he found out she went out of her way to help a mayanon and risk exposing their people. Going after those soldiers—attempting to take them on with her magic—would have been like waving a red flag in their faces, saying, *Here we are, come and get us!*

"Which way did they go?" Ida asked.

Laila pointed. "That way. I didn't know if there were more."

"There were," Ida said. "We came looking for answers, and they came out of nowhere. My husband . . ." She walked in the direction Laila had indicated but didn't get very far before collapsing onto her knees in the tall grass. She dropped her head into her hands and sobbed.

Laila caught up to her and did another check around. Royl's keen senses could have served her now. He'd know if other soldiers were coming.

She stood in the clearing, mostly exposed. The Chronicle Monument didn't provide much cover, but it hid them from anyone within the forest who might look their way. The houses were behind them, back toward Litlen. To the east were the Teiry Mountains and the Hushno Rekam—the Quiet River. The Forest of Litlen took up the whole north border of Litlen and ended at the mountains.

"Ida," Laila said. She spoke in a gentle tone, trying to be sensitive. "I'm not supposed to be out here, and since there are more of the soldiers, could we go somewhere to take cover? The place I know isn't far. We can find something for your head, and I can help you make a plan to get your son back."

Ida let her hands fall into her lap. She didn't bother to wipe her tears.

Laila crouched down to her level. "I want to help you. But you can't help your son like this. Please. Let's get out of the open."

"Why do you want to help me?" Ida asked, staring at her hands in the tall grass.

The question took Laila aback. She couldn't say why exactly. Someone was in distress and needing help, and it was within her power to do something about it. At the very least, she could offer shelter and a place for Ida to collect herself. "I don't get too many opportunities to help people," Laila said. "You say you came here looking for answers. I want answers too. Maybe by helping you, we can learn more about what's happening here."

Ida's body tilted forward, and she looked to be having a hard time keeping her eyes open. She gave a single nod and made a weak attempt to get up. Laila pulled her to her feet.

"Where is this place you have in mind?" Ida asked.

The mines were not an option. The days of getting out of there would be over for good if she brought a mayanon back to their place of hiding. Her old home was as safe a place as any. "There's an old house in the area that I've been to a few times," Laila said, half lying. "There's a bit to eat there as well as a few supplies."

It wasn't much, but it would have to do.

Chapter 32

Laila had returned to her old home many times since living in the mines, though she'd visited more often in the early days. Her old bedroom felt safer than the suffocating dark dwelling beneath the hills west of Litlen.

Coming here with a stranger seemed wrong. Laila led Ida into the house. It was located on a rounded street. Two more avenues adjoined it, and down one of them was Beiron's house at the end of a dead-end road. His home was visible from the back of her own house. Other similar-looking stone houses lined the streets, all built close together.

Laila entered the sitting room and stood awkwardly in its middle. A layer of dust drifted in the stale air. Ida coughed, and Laila waved a hand to get it out of their faces. She hadn't been here in over a year. Everything was as she'd left it. There were no more lingering scents from her childhood. The house smelled of dust and rotting leather. All the furniture was upright and neat. Plaster on the walls peeled at the bottom and corners of the rooms. The closed curtains blocked the daylight, giving the room a dull red glow.

When The Order destroyed Litlen, everything had been turned upside down and rummaged through. Furniture had been thrown about. Anything that could smash or break had been broken. Shutters had hung ajar from the windows. Similar to how she'd found Beiron's home years ago. Laila had cleaned up what she could and transformed it into something inhabitable.

Ida looked around, her eyes glazed.

"Have a seat wherever," Laila said. "I'll see if I can find something for your head."

"Who lives here?" Ida asked. She took tentative steps into the middle of the sitting room, watching her feet so as not to step on broken pieces of stone or clay.

"No one." Laila looked around at the room. It was sad, but it was the truth. "No one lives in any of these houses anymore."

"Why come here? Why this house?"

Laila took a moment to consider her answer. Telling Ida that this was her family's home a hundred years ago might not be the best idea.

"It's got supplies," she said. "I've been through most of these houses. There's not much else left of this city. If you wait here, I'll go find something for your head." She left the sitting room before Ida could ask any other questions.

The best place to look for medical supplies was in her mother's old room, where she'd kept a collection of herbs for healing. Freya was a bit of an unofficial healer. She'd always had an interest in the plants of Kartha and their medicinal uses. Laila accredited her mother for her own interest in those things.

In her mother's cabinet was a wooden crate full of jars of various plants. Laila studied each jar's contents. Back when they'd lived in the house, Laila only knew what a few of these plants were. Now she had a whole plethora of knowledge thanks to that book.

At the bottom of the crate were dried flowers wrapped in cloth. Laila unfolded the linen around the first plant. The motus was easy to tell apart from the others because of its sharp-pointed seven petals sticking out on top of its tuft-like flower head. It grew in varying colours, but Freya had a yellow motus. The fragrance of the yellow induced a state of joy. Each colour of the motus could change one's emotional state of mind. Blue brought about sadness; red, anger. The fragrance of the green could spur on nausea, and the purple made you forgetful.

Next, Laila took out a pink raimai flower. She set it down and reached for the next one. She unwrapped a mertivez, an upside-down flower with the leaf at the end of the stem and the flower at the base near the roots.

Caln, a highly poisonous plant that everyone knew, was in the crate. Her mother must have known of its medicinal uses when used in combination with other plants—something Laila knew because of Beiron's book but never considered how her mother had learned it. Most of these plants were known to the majority of her people, but a few were ones Laila thought only she knew about.

Marple was next. This one was green, but the marple could also be blue. It was a bulb-like vegetable that helped focus the mind, according to the book.

In one of the jars at the corner of the crate was a drooping sorrosee. Laila smiled at that one. It wasn't there for any purpose except as a keepsake. Laila had brought it home one day for Royl, thinking she'd picked him a pretty yellow wildflower. When she brought it in to show him, her mother caught her first. She'd informed Laila that the flower was not a wildflower at all but, in fact, a drooping sorrosee, a flower that could cause an irritating rash when touched. Laila ended up itching for nearly a week. And to think she was going to give it to Royl. She'd been more careful with the plants she'd picked after that. Her mother must have kept this for the memory.

The only plant in the crate that might help Ida was the pink raimai or the caln and regtal. The pollen from the regtal would counter the poison of the caln and would allow Ida to stay alert and focused. On the other hand, if she ate the petals of the pink raimai, it would alleviate her pain and probably knock her out for a while. Laila's hand hovered over the pink raimai. She bit her lip, then decided to take all three. She put the rest away and tucked the crate back in the cabinet.

Before leaving her mother's room, she stopped to look out the little window facing out the back. The one where Beiron's house was visible. Seeing it reminded her about her whole reason for having gone out earlier that morning.

Her vision blurred, and suddenly, she was standing in Beiron's house, in his sitting room—not in her home, viewing his from the window in her mother's room. She froze as Beiron turned to face her direction. His posture tensed, and his eyes peered around the room, squinting, searching. Laila didn't recognize the man beside Beiron in the entryway, but he didn't look like a willing companion with his hands restrained.

From the corner of her eye, Laila noticed that everything here was exactly how she'd remembered it, except maybe with a few more cracks in the walls and dust balls and cobwebs. The sofa was turned over, and the tea table by the window had been thrown across the room and smashed to pieces. Stones from the fireplace littered the floor.

She took it all in. The mouldy smell, the chill in the air, the morning sunlight trying to seep through the boarded windows, and the warmth from its ray stretching across her shoulder. Rather than comfort her, the sun's touch her made her uneasy. It was strange that she could feel its warmth. Surreal. Wrong.

The man who appeared to be Beiron's prisoner glanced around the room. "What are we doing here? What exactly—"

"Quiet." Beiron's gaze fell on Laila, but it was as if he looked right through her. Could he see her?

Laila stood perfectly still and held her breath. Her racing heart beat loud in her ears. Beiron was staring right at her. He created a light with his magic, never taking his eyes from the place where she stood. A blue glow filled the room. The prisoner's eyes grew, and he stepped away.

Laila stared into Beiron's dark eyes, trying to determine if he could see her. How was she here? Was this happening in real time?

Beiron's prisoner shuffled his feet. "Where did your men take—"

"Sh." Beiron interrupted. "Quiet." His voice dropped in pitch as he spoke again. "You've stolen something from me."

"What are you—"

"Not you." Beiron's patient tone wavered as he scowled at his prisoner. "The thing you've taken—" His eyes flicked around the room. "I'm going to be needing it back."

Laila's breathing quickened. Afraid he might see her if she moved, she stood still as a statue. Was he speaking to her? Should she say something?

"I can sense you," Beiron said.

That answered her question as to whether he could see her.

"And your fear," he went on. He took three steps closer to where she stood and tilted his head as though listening for her. She covered her mouth and nose to make herself silent.

"I'll find you," Beiron whispered.

Her whole body was shaking. *Wake up!* she told herself. *Wake up!* This had to be a dream, it couldn't be real.

WAKE UP!

She squeezed her eyes shut tight and then opened them and was back in her mother's old room, looking out the window at Beiron's house. She let out her breath, panting. Was Beiron over there right now?

Heart pounding, she wiped sweat from her neck. Beiron's whisper echoed in her thoughts. What did he mean, he'd find her? How had he sensed she was there? She shook the thoughts away. If Beiron was back, she had to tell Royl.

Before the war, there had been a warrant out for Beiron's arrest. When Landon Valca and his army invaded, and the curse took their magic, all else was forgotten while everyone either fled or fought.

If Beiron was back and looking for—what? His book? Is that what he thought she'd stolen? She thought about its contents. From what she remembered—which was all of it since she'd studied it nearly every day for decades—there was nothing of great significance that might cause him to come looking for it. Unless it held sentimental value to him.

She watched for any movement at his house. It was too far to see inside from here. There was something about this whole thing—all of it. Ever since the song and Litlen's revival, there'd been so many strange occurrences. The Valca soldier in Litlen. Ida, chased down by Valca soldiers and separated from her baby. Beiron and his prisoner. What was going on? What did it all mean? She had to know.

If Beiron was involved, Royl would be sure to investigate further. He'd know what to do. Laila knew very little about Beiron, except that he was a wanted man and a traitor to her people. Supposedly, he had shared Elderace secrets with Landon Valca. Why he would do that, Laila hadn't a clue.

A whimpering cry from the sitting room pulled Laila from her thoughts. *Ida!* She'd almost forgotten why she was here in the first place. She made her way back to the sitting room, where Ida sat on the floor, leaning against the sofa and hugging her knees while she cried. She looked so broken.

"Ida?" Laila said. "What were those men after you for?" She'd asked so forcefully that she thought Ida might not answer. Softening her tone, she tried again. "I'm trying to understand why Valca soldiers are in Litlen and what made them go after you."

Ida dried her eyes. "I don't know," she whispered. "I think it might have to do with my husband, Raidan. He's . . ." She paused. Her lip trembled.

"He's what, Ida? What's he got to do with the Valca Order?"

"Nothing. That's just it. I don't understand. Just over a week ago, he met with his brother and didn't come home until morning. After that, everything was different. We were coming here to try to find someone who might be able to help him."

"Help him how? No one's lived here for years."

"We heard Litlen had come alive, that it was like magic. They say that Litlen is where magic began in Kartha, and we thought that . . . maybe, if someone was here, they could help him."

"Help him how?"

"He's got magic!" Ida said. "He can't control it. He loses control and the ground shakes. He's terrified of it and wants to get rid of it."

Laila said nothing. A mayanon had magic? But how? She rubbed her clammy hands on her skirt. The silence between them grew, and Ida sniffled.

"How?" Laila asked at last. "Only the Elderace are supposed to be able to have magic."

Ida shook her head. "I'm not sure. He told me Adrik did this to him. I don't know if you've heard of him, but Raidan—"

"Adrik?" Laila interrupted. She knew that name. Wasn't he the son of Norick? One of the Six? New questions formed in her mind. "Was there a stone involved?" Laila asked.

Ida nodded. "Yes, I think he said something about a stone. How did you know?"

Laila's hands shook. Was she excited? Scared? If someone had been bound to the Weldafire Stone, that could have caused Litlen's revival. It made the most sense. Though how someone had been bound in blood without the delegates was a mystery. The ceremony required all six, and Laila was certain none of the delegates had survived the war.

In any case, it sounded like Ida's husband might be the Guardian of the Weldafire Stone. That meant that he was responsible for protecting it and with it, Kartha. The stone and Kartha were connected. Whatever happened to the stone would affect the land.

Knowing that someone was potentially bound to it, the elders would have to do something to help Ida. Laila could take a good guess as to what the Valca Order wanted with her son now. Leverage to use against the Guardian of the Weldafire Stone and total control over all of Kartha. Not that The Order didn't already have that. Laila's mind worked to fit the pieces together. If The Order already had total control, what did they want the stone for?

She really had to find Royl now. Whatever was going on, it was time her people got involved. No more hiding and waiting to see what happened next. Now they needed to act.

She would have to convince them. With Ida, she had a better chance.

Chapter 33

Raidan guessed the house was Beiron's, or had been at one point. It didn't look like anyone lived there now, nor had they for a very long time.

The furniture was thrown across the room. The window was boarded. The fireplace, crumbling to pieces. Beiron hadn't wasted any time when they'd entered the house. He'd gone straight to the far room at the end of the hallway and disappeared for a minute before returning. His face was a little redder, and the crease in his forehead deepened. The man was not well. He'd been talking to someone, but there was no one there.

Beiron stood motionless, his eyes squinting at the empty space he spoke to. Then he blinked and seemed to remember Raidan. "Time to go."

They stepped out of the house. Raidan tried to orient himself and remember which way Cassian had been taken.

Beiron lifted him onto the horse to continue on their way to the mountains, back to Ilan, Dimitri, and the others. Raidan scanned the direction where he thought Cassian was. If he knew the location of that cabin, he'd have gone already to rescue his son. But without that knowledge, he'd end up wandering for hours and Beiron or Ilan would get there first. Raidan didn't know what they might do to Cassian. He had no idea if they'd go so far as to hurt a baby.

He kept his eyes out for Ida. He took not seeing her as a good sign, if only because he had to believe her safe.

Creeping vines grew up along the sides and fronts of the houses they passed. Gardens overflowed with plants, flowers, and lush grass. Flowers blossomed in every direction, in front of every home. Their floral fragrances reached Raidan. It truly was an awesome sight. It was hard to believe no one lived here.

Prompting conversation with the man who'd taken his son went against his nature, but it was a long ride to the pass, and he had questions. He knew nothing about Beiron or what he wanted. It might be worth learning a thing or two about the man who was currently his only shot at getting Cassian back.

Raidan turned his head to catch Beiron's eye. "Was that your house?"

"It is my house," Beiron said. He spoke casually, as if he were not the man who'd threatened his family. "It's been a long time since I've been back there. Obviously."

"Who were you talking to in there?"

"I'll find out soon enough," Beiron said.

He'd been talking to no one, and not even *he* knew who it was? If this was some form of Elderace magic, Raidan didn't care to know more.

Thinking of Elderace magic sparked a new thought. "I thought all the Elderace were wiped out in the war a hundred years ago," he said. "But you're Elderace, are you not?"

"I am. I don't know what's become of my people. Clearly, Adrik survived, unlike his father. I'm sure others did as well."

"You knew Adrik?"

"A long time ago."

"Then I guess you won't like hearing that he's dead," Raidan said. It had been his only comforting thought of late.

"Adrik was no friend of mine. And I'm not convinced he's gone."

He was no friend of Raidan's either, though he didn't know if that made him feel any better. It didn't matter. Adrik was gone, even if Beiron didn't think so.

"He is," Raidan assured him.

Beiron chuckled. "You know nothing of magic and curses."

Well, that much they agreed on. To veer away from the topic of Adrik and magic, Raidan asked, "What were you looking for? Back in the house?"

"Something I hid years ago. It's not there anymore."

Raidan considered the state of the house. "Is that really so hard to believe?"

"Yes!" Beiron snapped. "I took measures to ensure it could not be taken or removed from its place, so yes, it is."

Whatever measures he was talking about, his casual tone turned harsh, and Raidan backed off.

They passed the last house and rode down a dirt road, straight toward the Teiry Mountains. Judging from their distance to the foothills, it would take them at least an hour to get to the entrance to the pass. The space north, to the left, was all open field. The trees farther out were the beginning of the forest where Ilan and Beiron had picked up Raidan. Somewhere in there was Cassian.

To the right, the trees in the woods were mostly evergreens. The road broke off into three directions: one went straight to the mountains; another went left; and the other, right. They continued straight.

Raidan's tailbone ached from the long ride. He squirmed, trying to adjust his position with his hands tied.

The looming mountains ahead grew bigger. In the distance, riders were visible on their horses. Ilan and the others must have already gotten there and were waiting.

"What do you think you'll find at the cave anyway?" Raidan asked. "I'm sure Dimitri's told you what happened. There's nothing left of it."

"Patience, *Sudneil*. All will be revealed soon enough."

"*Sudneil?*" Raidan asked.

Beiron didn't reply.

Raidan cast a backward glance at him. Beiron was smirking. Trying to ignore the growing fear in his gut, Raidan faced forward. The first time he'd gone to the cave, he'd had the choice to turn back. Why hadn't he just followed his instincts and left well enough alone when he'd had the chance? Then none of this would be happening.

Raidan squirmed some more in the saddle. Beiron gave his back a little shove and Raidan winced. His wound was still sore from Beiron's knife-point earlier.

"Are these cuffs really necessary," he asked.

Beiron's smile was audible as he breathed, making a mirthful sound. "No," he said, but didn't bother to take them off.

The pass was close. Raidan picked out Ilan's blond hair ahead. If Beiron wasn't going to divulge why they were going to the cave, maybe he could learn something of equal value. "Why are you working for Ilan Valca?" Raidan asked.

"Ilan Valca is a joke. He's nothing more than a child whose only wish is to do magic."

"A child with an army."

"There you go. You've just answered your own question."

Raidan thought about it. From the way Ilan acted around Beiron, it wasn't so hard to believe that Beiron was only using Ilan. But what did Beiron want?

"You share that with anyone," Beiron warned, "and I'll make sure you never see your son again.

There went all of Raidan's thoughts on pitting the two against each other. "Why go after my wife and son in the first place?" Raidan asked. "You've made me your enemy by threatening my family."

"That wasn't my idea. Ilan made the call. But I'll admit, it's an effective move."

Raidan said nothing. Arguing wouldn't change the fact that Ida was missing and Cassian was lost.

Closer now, Dimitri's broad shoulders were clear to see. He was still mounted on the horse with the septum soldier. The sun was high at nearly midday. It was hot, shining down on them.

"How can I be sure my son is safe with those men?" Raidan asked. "And that you'll return him to me when this is over—whatever this is."

"You do everything I say," Beiron replied, "and your son will be unharmed and returned to you."

"Who's to say you won't kill me after I do whatever it is you want me to do?"

"Guess you'll just have to trust me. Besides, where we're going is no place for a baby."

Beiron was not the kind of man who inspired trust. It was true that the cave was the last place he'd want to bring Cassian, but at least, he'd be with his father and not in the care of Valca soldiers.

They arrived at the pass and joined the others. Ilan's lips pressed together, and he glowered at Beiron. "Where have you been? We've been waiting for you for almost an hour."

The others dismounted and Dimitri was helped down.

"We're here now, aren't we?" Beiron said, dismounting and yanking Raidan down from the horse. He took the key for the restraints and uncuffed Raidan.

"Why are you taking those off?" Ilan asked. "What if he tries something?"

Beiron winked at Raidan. "He knows what's at stake."

Raidan didn't want to know what Beiron had planned for him at the cave. He swallowed past the hard lump in his throat. He'd thought Adrik was bad, but Beiron's threats against his family were much worse.

Yes, Raidan knew what was at stake. And he was running out of time to come up with a way out of this.

Chapter 34

Only the gardens and houses across the street could be seen from Laila's front window. Laila gazed across the empty space between. She let the curtain fall and turned to face Ida, who sat on the sofa, her head in her hands.

"We should find my brother, Royl," Laila suggested. There was no easing into the topic naturally. After seeing Beiron only a block away, she felt the urge to hurry.

"I need to find my son." Ida stood. "I need to go back into the forest."

"The forest covers a lot of ground. Those men will be long gone, and we don't even know where they're going. Come with me to get my brother. He's skilled in combat." Laila looked Ida up and down. "I suppose you can't take on more than two armed soldiers on your own?"

"Maybe not," Ida said. "But if we could spot them, we can go back for help. There's still a chance they've not gone far."

"Ida, there's nothing in the forest. It's trees and more trees. They're not going to stick around there for long. My brother can track them. I'm telling you, he's the best at what he does! We'll only waste time if we go back."

The longer they argued, the sooner Beiron would be gone from his house and Laila would lose track of him. She needed to get to Royl before Beiron could go far.

Ida hung her head and covered her face with her hands as she began to cry again.

"Ida," Laila said. "I cannot imagine what you're going through right now, but—"

"No. You can't." Ida cut her off. "You have no idea!"

Laila gave her a moment. She waited until Ida had calmed down enough to listen. She had to make a call and get a move on, even if it meant parting ways.

"I want to help you, Ida. I do. But if going back into the forest is what you want to do, then I can't go with you."

Ida's heavy eyelids betrayed her exhaustion. Laila didn't know why it was so important to her that Ida go with her. She'd only slow her down. She let go the idea of having Ida join her and shifted her feet, ready to go. "I hope you find your son," she said. "And I hope we meet again." She went for the door.

"Wait!" Ida said.

Laila froze and looked back.

"How long will it take to get to your brother?" Ida asked.

"It's a bit beyond the other side of the city. We could make it there in twenty minutes if we run."

"And your brother . . . you're sure he'll help me?"

"I believe he will." So long as he wasn't too busy killing Laila for what she was about to do. Revealing her people to an outsider, showing Ida right to the doorstep.

If not Royl, someone would seek punishment for her actions, but she'd worry about that later. If the implications of this situation were as big as she thought, it was worth chancing it.

"All right," Ida said. "Let's make this quick then."

*

It was becoming clear to Laila that soon she would have to divulge information about her identity if she was going to keep Ida's trust and lead her into the mines. It wouldn't be right to leave her alone outside. Plus, she might need Royl to hear Ida's story for himself.

They were nearly at Spry Lagoon, the hidden entrance to one of the tunnels. It was boggy and wet there, but at least, they wouldn't be detected by whomever stood sentry at the main entrance to the mines.

Ida slowed to a stop and looked at her feet, wet from the saturated ground. She clutched her side, panting. "Where are we going?"

Laila stopped beside her. She knew this was coming. Out of breath, she turned to face Ida and bit her bottom lip. *Here goes nothing.*

Her stomach was in a flutter and her words came out fast and as one. "I live with my people in the mines that are beneath the hills. There's an entrance just ahead." Laila put a hand out before Ida could interrupt. "There's more. . . ." She made a fist, opened her hand, and said, "*Vint.*"

Her sphere of blue light appeared. It hovered above her palm and glowed the colours of the sea. Ida gasped and took a step back. She gawked at Laila.

"You have magic," she said, stating the obvious. "Are you Elderace?"

Laila nodded. "No one is supposed to know about us. I'm probably going to get in huge trouble for revealing myself, but the Weldafire Stone is everything to my people. It represents life and healing, and it's a sacred piece of our history. If your husband is bound to it, then my people will do whatever they can to protect him, you, and your family. My brother will know what to do to help you find your husband and son."

Ida stared at Laila's blue light. "What else can you do?"

Laila's feet were sinking into the soggy earth. She closed her fist around her light, extinguishing it, then stepped out of the sinking spot. "Like all Elderace, I have the ability to manipulate the elements," Laila said. "Each of us usually has more control of one area over another. My strongest element is earth. My brother favours wind. Some people, like me and my brother, have a kind of inward magic, beyond what's visible. I can distinguish truth from lies. Royl has keen senses and an incredible awareness of his surroundings."

Her mother could sense when Laila was upset, though she wasn't entirely sure that was a magical gift. That might just be her mother's way. "It's different for everyone," Laila added.

Ida lifted her feet, making a suction sound as she pulled free from the earth. Laila moved to keep from sinking again.

"It might be best if you hide in my room until I've spoken to Royl. My people are wary of outsiders. The sooner I can convince my brother to help you, the less time we sit around discussing if you're a threat."

"A threat?" Ida said. "Why would they think that?"

Laila shook her head. "I know you're not a threat. And once I can get Royl's help, he'll make it known to the others. He trusts my judgement. But until then, it's better if you stay unseen."

"Why don't I wait out here?"

"You could do that, but we have scouts that go out and check around these parts. You could be spotted, and they'd be suspicious of why you're here. But by all means, wait here. I just can't guarantee you won't be taken for a trespasser."

Laila walked toward the hill that rose directly in front of them. Just ahead, tucked away in the slanted angle of the hill was a dark tunnel, almost like a human-sized burrow inside the mound of earth. The height and width of the space would be a bit of a squeeze for most men and some women, but for Laila, it was a comfortable size. Ida would have no trouble either.

Ida remained where Laila had left her, shifting her feet in the sloppy mud. When Laila was nearly at the burrow-like entrance, Ida ran to catch up, then stopped when she saw the hole. "You want us to go in there?"

Out of habit, Laila glanced in all directions but saw no one. She looked at Ida. "This is the way in." Lifting her feet in the mud, she shambled into the tunnel and waited for Ida, lighting her blue light in the meantime.

Ida followed, her steps slow and cautious. Her eyes fell on Laila's light again. "You can make that appear on demand?"

Laila led the way through the tunnels. "I can. Everyone has their own trigger. Mine is a word. I just speak or think the word for life in the Eldrace tongue, and it makes my magic strong."

Having never spoken to an outsider before, it felt strange to explain such a simple concept. Everyone knew about triggers. She went on. "Some people have other words as their trigger. Some have an item of significance they keep on them always. Others have to perform an action."

Ida was quiet, listening.

"In the entire first year of our education," Laila said, "we have to learn and master our own trigger. Oftentimes, we inherit similar triggers from our parents."

"My husband," Ida said, "he can't control his magic. Do you think it's because he hasn't learned his trigger?"

Laila shrugged. "It could be."

Truthfully, the power of the Weldafire Stone was something Laila knew little about. She knew what it represented, but as for the mechanics of its power, the Guardian had to figure that out for himself.

Light appeared from the torches in the halls ahead. Laila put out her light and Ida gasped. The sudden darkness was startling.

"It's all right," Laila assured her. "I just don't want us to be seen. Ahead, the tunnels merge into the mines."

They crept along the tunnel until they arrived at the barricaded opening. Ida stared at the drawing of the Chronicle Monument across from them. Laila ducked between the two planks, going from the tunnels into the mine's halls. She looked in both directions. Ida ducked through next.

This particular hall was never busy with people. Laila half expected to find Royl standing there waiting for her. She didn't, but they weren't in the clear yet. She took the right path and led Ida toward her quarters.

"This way." Laila opened the door to the room she shared with her mother, hoping to avoid finding her mother inside. There'd be time to explain her guest later, but not now.

"Stay here," Laila told Ida. "I'll be right back." She raced out of the room before Ida could protest.

Finding Royl would not be difficult. Laila ran directly to the assembly chamber and to the adjoining room meant for private meetings. The door was half open, and just as she thought, her brother was inside with Vix, Darrin, Maire, and Zulu.

With effort, Laila pretended like she wasn't out of breath. She peered into the room.

"Royl," she said, speaking slow to calm her heart rate without being too obvious. "I need to speak with you. Now."

Chapter 35

Her tone suggested urgency. Royl excused himself from the elders. Vix had his usual look of deep reflection. Zulu held a hard gaze on Laila. He might have been irritated at her interruption, but she couldn't tell. He always looked like he was angry. Maire's silver eyes studied Laila. They were kind and soft.

Laila nodded sideways at Royl, and her brother followed her to the far end of the assembly chamber. He turned to her. "Laila, you can't keep interrupti—"

"It's the stone."

Royl cocked his head. "The stone? What are you—"

"The Weldafire Stone. That's what's caused the change. A mayanon was bound to it, and I think that's why Litlen has come back to life. And Beiron is back, and I think he knows something about it, but—"

"Beiron? Why would you think he's back?"

Laila had already decided not to tell him about her visions. Not yet. Not until she understood them better. She hadn't figured out how to answer that just yet, and seeing as Royl appeared tense, it didn't seem like a good time for him to meet Ida.

Wiping her sweaty hands against her skirt, she fidgeted. There was no way to go about this without him finding out she'd gone out again.

"I met a mayanon woman. She told me that Adrik bound the stone to her husband—"

"You met someone!" Royl looked toward the door to the private meeting room and lowered his voice. "Laila, how do you know Beiron is back?"

In a flash of sunlight, she glimpsed mountains around her. She froze. Then she was back underground, standing with Royl.

Royl raised an eyebrow at her.

What she saw didn't make any sense. There were no mountains here. Royl's eyes were round and expectant.

Suddenly, she was standing outside again. Mountains towered high above her: the Teiry Mountains. Among her party was Beiron and his captive from the house, another prisoner who looked like the captive—except his eyes were harder—and a handful of Valca soldiers. Laila recognized the blond one in Valca Order attire as the same man she and Royl had seen wandering in Litlen after the song. This group of people, the mountains, the prisoners who looked like they could be brothers—Laila was pretty sure she knew exactly where they were going. The only one missing was the baby.

"Laila!" Royl waved a hand in her face, drawing her back from her trance. No, not trance, a vision?

There was no time to explain it all now. Beiron was already headed into the mountains. It would take Royl some time to get there. "You have to go to the delegates' cave," Laila said. "I'm sure that's where you'll find Beiron. He's on his way there now."

Except for the two of them, the assembly chamber was empty. Silence settled over them. The torches at the front of the room were out, and only the chandelier offered light while no one was gathered. Royl's forehead wrinkled. He motioned to the door to the private room. "Come with me."

Laila straightened. She'd been prepared to do a lot more convincing. Royl led her to the meeting room, where the four elders sat in their designated seats. They turned their attention to the two of them entering.

"Vix," Royl said. "I'm sorry to interrupt, but I could use a group of warriors to come with me to investigate something. Also, I'd like to request that someone please take Laila to her room and make sure she stays there until I get back."

Laila opened her mouth to protest.

"There have to be consequences, Laila." Royl turned on her before she could speak. "You've not taken this seriously, and I can't do my job if I'm worried about the trouble you're getting into."

Zulu stood, and Laila took a step back. "I'm not staying here, Royl," she said. "I'm going with you."

He shook his head. "No, Laila. Not for this."

Vix's eyes moved from Royl to Laila, then back to Royl. He rubbed his chin. Laila hoped he'd defend her, or that any of them would. But no one doubted that Royl took his role as head warrior seriously and would not have requested extra warriors if he thought it unnecessary.

Vix nodded at last. "Maire, would you gather the warriors and have them wait for Royl in the assembly chamber? And Zulu, see that Miss Madx gets to her room safely."

Laila's heart sank. "Please don't do this, Royl." Her eyes blurred with tears that threatened to loosen any second.

"Maire," Vix prompted. Maire got up slowly and passed Laila at the doorway to carry out her order.

"I'll stay out of your way," Laila pleaded. "What if he's gone before you get there? I can help you find him again."

"Him?" Darrin asked.

"Zulu, if you could, please?" Royl said as he waved a hand for him to take Laila.

"Who is she talking about, Royl?" Darrin asked, rising.

Laila pulled her arm away from Zulu as he extended his hand out to her. She stepped away from his reach. "Beiron's back," she said. "He's here in Litlen, and I can find him. He's with others, Royl, you have no idea what you're walking into. Please, let me help!"

"Enough, Laila! You're staying here until I get back, and I'll speak to you then."

At that, Zulu wrapped his hand around Laila's upper arm and gave her a tug. Laila yanked her arm, but he held fast. She winced when his fingers pinched her skin.

"How do you know he's back?" Darrin asked while she was almost out the door. "And how are you meant to find him?" He turned to Royl. "I hope you're planning on explaining this before you go anywhere."

"I don't know that it's true yet. That's what I intend to find out," Royl said. He glanced her way just before she was taken from the room. His sad eyes were stamped in her mind as she was pulled from his sight.

Zulu kept a tight grip on Laila's arm all the way to her quarters. She couldn't let him go inside and see Ida. Then they'd both be brought before the elders for questioning.

Laila held back her tears. She'd gone and brought Ida here only to get trapped in her room with her. "I'll go myself," Laila said as she ripped her arm from Zulu's hold. He let her go.

She rubbed her sore arm. As she went into her room, she could feel his eyes watching her until the door closed.

Ida was right there, her eyes wide. "Well," she said. "Is he going to help?"

Laila looked at her new friend and frowned. What did it matter now if Royl was going to help? They didn't need him anyway.

"No," Laila said. "And now I've been put under watch and can't leave this room."

"What do you mean?" Ida looked at the door, then back at Laila. "Why don't we go together and speak to him?" She reached for the doorknob. "Maybe if—"

"No, don't go out there right now!" Laila stopped her. "I'll get us out of this. We need a distraction. Something to get Zulu out of the way so we can get out of here."

After this, there was no way she was going to stick around in this place. This was it. As soon as she could get back outside, she was not returning. Not ever.

Chapter 36

WALKING TO THE CAVE A SECOND TIME WITH DIMITRI AND THEIR company, Raidan found himself grateful for the time it took to get there, while wanting to get this over with. His anguish over Ida and Cassian's involvement made him weak with sorrow. He needed to find his wife and come up with a way to save Cassian from those less-than-capable guards who'd taken him to some cabin in the woods. It pained him, knowing they were responsible for his son.

Instinctively, Raidan glanced over his shoulder as he walked, looking back as if he might miraculously see Cassian there. He knew he wouldn't, but he checked anyway.

The pass had been too narrow for any horse to attempt, so they'd left them at the entrance and continued on foot. Trekking the uneven ground and keeping within the narrow walls of the pass, they moved along in a single-file line. Ilan led and a few of his men followed. Dimitri was ahead of Raidan with three Valca soldiers between them, and Beiron was directly behind Raidan with two more soldiers ending the procession. Onward they walked, ducking under overhanging rocks and squeezing through the narrower spaces until, finally, they veered from the path and hiked up the mountain that led to the cave.

Ilan's men got to the top first and waited for the rest to catch up. The clouds drifted across the sky, briefly blocking the low sun.

When Raidan reached the mountaintop, he stood beside Dimitri and gazed out across a lake. That hadn't been here before. Seeing it almost brought him relief. Even if there had been a chance of getting into the cave before, digging their way through the rubble, there was no way to get in now.

But then a voice, like the wind, called his name. *Raaaidddann.*

It hissed. It reminded Raidan of the snake-creature that attacked him the last time he'd been here. He shivered and stepped back. No way did he want to encounter that thing again.

The voice called again. *Release me.*

Raidan knew that voice. But Adrik was dead. How could he be hearing him now? He looked at Dimitri.

"You hear it too?" Dimitri asked.

So it wasn't just his imagination. Raidan squinted at the water. His chest ached from Beiron having used his magic against him earlier, and from contracting every muscle in his body. He'd never thought he'd have to return here or hear Adrik's voice again.

"Love what you've done with the place," Ilan said, his arms spread wide. Raidan had no idea what he was talking about.

Beiron moved right behind Raidan and Dimitri and shoved them both forward. The two of them tripped but balanced their footing on the downward slope. The group started on the decline toward the shore.

"I wouldn't get too close," Ilan warned one of his men who was about to dip his hand in the lake. "There's a creature living in these waters."

Raidan's chest tightened. He hated to think just what that creature was, but he suspected he already knew.

Raidan. Dimitri. Adrik's voice called to them, sounding more urgent than before. Raidan looked at the faces of the others to determine if anyone else heard the echoing voice. No one reacted.

The tall mountains cast shadows over them as the sun dipped lower. A chill ran down Raidan's spine. He had to find a way out of this. Undecided which was worse—his back to the lake or his back to Beiron—he determined that the lake currently posed no threat, whereas Beiron definitely did. He faced Beiron, a solid force standing in his way.

"What are we doing here?" Raidan asked. "What do you want?"

"You're to go down there and break the barrier." Beiron gestured to the lake. "You put it there, and only you can remove it, allowing for anyone to go in or out."

Raidan stared at the reflective water, which appeared dark and ominous in the fading light. Any barrier he'd put in place was not on purpose, though it was there with good reason. What lay beneath, within that mountain at the base of the basin, was a place he never wanted to see again.

Ilan's men were lined in staggered formation. They covered every part of the slope. Apart from swimming across the lake and attempting a climb up the steep mountain face on the other side, there was no way to get past them all without a fight—one that Raidan knew he'd lose.

Raidan spoke to Beiron. He seemed to be the one in charge. "Why should I believe that when this is over, you'll let us go and return my son?"

Beiron held up his hands. "Once we're done here, you have my word that you can have your son back and go on your way."

"Your word means nothing to me."

"Fair enough. But I assure you, I am a man of my word. If you break the barrier and give me the Weldafire Stone and its power, I'll personally see to the safety of your son. We'll make a deal and seal it with magic—"

"No way are we giving the stone to you," Dimitri interjected. His fists were clenched, his legs apart in a fighting stance.

As much as Raidan wanted to be rid of this magic, he agreed with Dimitri. He could sense the capacity of power within him and didn't care to wonder what that might look like in the hands of Beiron. And yet, if this was the way to get Cassian back, he'd be open to an arrangement. Preferably without the use of magic.

He shook his head. "No magic."

Beiron cocked his head and smirked.

Ilan marched over. "What's your problem with magic?"

"No magic," Raidan repeated.

Dimitri turned his eyes to the lake. He smacked Raidan's arm. "Look," he said, pointing at the surface. "There!"

Raidan looked. There, slithering across the surface of the water, was the vine-snake creature. He stepped forward to get away from the shore, but Beiron blocked him.

"Don't!" Raidan shouted. He thrust out his arm to stop Beiron from pushing him any closer to the water. As soon as his hand made contact with Beiron, a surge of power coursed through his arm. Beiron flew backward and landed on his backside, six feet away.

Raidan looked at his hand. It looked the same. It felt normal. Except for the fact that he'd just thrown Beiron back with nothing but his touch. His hand quivered, and he clenched his fist to control its shaking.

Beiron scowled at Raidan. Raidan wanted to check for the vine, but he was afraid to take his eyes off Beiron. Dimitri inched closer to Raidan.

A shriek cut through the air. Raidan and Dimitri both turned their heads.

Ilan screamed, "Get it off! Get it off me!" The vine had wrapped around one of his legs and was tugging him toward the water. Miles and another of Ilan's men scampered to his aid.

Distracted, Raidan didn't see Beiron rise and come at him. He grabbed hold of Raidan by the front of his tunic with two hands. The fabric curled in his fists, and he lifted Raidan off his feet. Dimitri chopped his hand across Beiron's arms, and Beiron removed a hand from Raidan's tunic to swing a well-aimed elbow into the side of

Dimitri's head. Dimitri staggered back, and Beiron shoved Raidan toward the water, maintaining his hold on his shirt.

His nails clawing at Beiron's hands, Raidan tried to pry them off. Beiron held on until they were at the water's edge. "Get in the water and break the barrier," Beiron spat. He propelled him into the lake, and Raidan's feet landed in water up to his ankles.

Ilan shouted again. His screams intensified, and Raidan suspected that the vine was reacting to his struggle, tightening its hold as he fought.

Come, Adrik beckoned Raidan over the noise.

Raidan put his hand out to ward off Beiron, who narrowed his eyes. Beiron's posture went rigid and he gasped, glancing at his arm, where blood seeped through a new tear in the fabric of his sleeve. Raidan didn't understand what had happened, but then the call of a battle cry drew his attention away.

Behind Beiron, a dozen or more people spilled over the peak with weapons drawn.

Chapter 37

One of the attackers descending the summit had a bow; the others, swords. They were not Valca soldiers, but they didn't exactly have a friendly approach.

One of them extended a hand toward Beiron and Raidan. Raidan felt wind whip past his face. It caused Beiron to wobble.

They had magic!

With Beiron distracted, Raidan stumbled out of the water. He swerved left around Beiron, but Beiron grabbed his upper arm and squeezed tight. Raidan winced. Beiron glanced back at the new opponents advancing toward them. He reached his other arm out. "*Bludevint.*"

A blue light shot from his hand like lighting and struck one of the magic fighters. The man he hit clutched his chest and scowled at Beiron, but he kept coming. The light attack barely slowed him.

Beiron tightened his hold on Raidan's arm. "Come with me, and I'll take you to your son."

Raidan's heart jolted. Would he really take him to Cassian? Just like that?

To their right, Dimitri brawled against one of Ilan's soldiers, an opponent that matched his size. The soldier hit him hard in the head, then drew his sword to fend off the armed magic attacker who came at him.

Beiron shot another blue light toward two more coming their way, keeping Raidan's arm locked in his grip all the while. A flash of blue struck Beiron's shoulder. He groaned but held firm.

Ilan had wrangled himself free from the vine and joined in the fight with his men against the magic users. The lake to their backs, no one was watching for the vine when it burst out of the water. It sprang at one of the magic fighters, wrapped itself around his waist, and dragged him toward the lake. He screamed, and his cry was cut off as he hit the water.

An arrow landed beside Beiron's feet. Beiron looked from it to the peak of the mountain, where the shooter stood with his bow still ready. While he reached for another arrow, four of the attackers with magic moved in toward the two of them. Each had a sword in one hand, and the other hand extended, palm out. With cautious steps, they closed in, blocking every direction but the lake.

Beiron turned to Raidan. "They're not going to help you. They'll bring you back for questioning and all the while your son is left with those imbeciles. Do you want your son back, or are you going to keep wasting time?"

There was no time to think. He needed to get to Cassian, and if Beiron was going to take him, he'd go now and ask questions later.

"Take me to him," Raidan said. The blood rushed back into his hand as Beiron released his arm.

Beiron faced the four men coming their way. He threw his arms out and, as if he were lifting something heavy, raised his hands. Four massive boulders rose from the mountain and hovered in mid-air. They were nearly the same size as Raidan. Beiron manoeuvred them as though they were nothing. He thrust his hands forward, launching the boulders at the approaching men.

While those four were either smacked by a boulder or jumping out of the way, Beiron took long strides past them. Raidan followed.

One of the men cried out, his arm crushed under the weight of the boulder. Raidan cringed, feeling the man's pain. He turned his head away and tried to block out his howls. Cassian needed him. He had to get to Cassian.

Beiron lifted another two boulders and thrust them at two more attackers who came running at them from the top. Raidan walked on, right at Beiron's heels, not looking to see if they'd been hit. Their cries verified that they had been.

Between the soldiers and the magic users, everyone was fighting someone. In the growing night, flashes of light illuminated the area. On the slope, two pairs of men fought. Near the shore were another three, including Dimitri, who'd teamed up with one of the magic fighters to oppose Ilan's man. He'd somehow gotten hold of a sword and was wielding it while the magic fighter waved his hands about and raised water from the lake to encircle it around his opponent. At the top of the mountain, the archer aimed his bow at Beiron.

"Watch out!" Raidan called and pointed. While the mountain's shaking was subtle, it caused the archer to lose his footing. Beiron thrust a boulder toward him. The archer tried to leap out of the way, but the boulder crashed into his leg and he fell face forward. Beiron used his magic with ease, like his power was an extension of himself.

While fighters were preoccupied, Beiron and Raidan hiked the incline and made it to the peak. One of the magic wielders came running at them from down by the lake. He moved with a fluid sway, like he was born to fight. He raised his hands, readying them for an attack. Beiron surprised the man by turning and running toward him. He shot a burst of his light magic at him. It hit the man's hand, causing him to drop his sword. That was all Beiron needed to lunge at him and put his hand to the man's chest. As soon as he made contact, the man gasped and his breath caught.

Recognition flashed in Beiron's eyes. He drew his hand away and, instead, grasped the man's tunic at the collar. "Stay out of my way,"

Beiron told him. He threw him back, and the man fell to the ground. Beiron got back on track, leading Raidan to Cassian.

At the top of the mountain, before descending on the other side, Raidan took a last look down at the battle. Dimitri would understand why he had to go now, why this couldn't wait.

The water rippled in the lake. "The vine!" Raidan shouted. The mountain shook at his call.

"Let's go," Beiron said. He grabbed Raidan's wrist and pulled him along before Raidan could see the outcome of his warning. The fighting sounds on the other side of the mountain hushed, replaced with a splash. Raidan tried to pull away from Beiron to go back and look, but Beiron tightened his grip and yanked his arm.

One of the magic fighters followed them. He jumped out in front of Beiron with his sword pointed. Beiron dealt with him immediately. Blue light hit the man's torso and he dropped his sword so he could clutch his chest with both hands. Beiron threw the man's hands aside and put his own to the man's chest, just like he'd done to the other, except this time, he held it there until the man collapsed, gasping for breath. Raidan grimaced. He knew all too well the feeling of that particular assault.

Beiron released the man and tugged Raidan along. As much as Raidan didn't like being pulled around like a child, he waited until they'd cleared the dangers of the battle before ripping his hand from Beiron's clutches. Beiron kept moving. He pointed away from the pass. "You can bet there'll be others waiting in Litlen at the end of the pass. We can avoid them if we go this way."

Avoiding the people who could potentially help him with his magic problem? Raidan looked back. Was he doing the right thing, going with Beiron? Clearly whoever those people were, they were no friends of Beiron's. But it appeared they knew each other.

Darkness surrounded them as the sun was about to set beyond the mountains. If not for the moon, it would have been too dark to see anything at all. Beiron blazed the trail ahead in his confident stride.

Raidan was not oblivious to the fact that Beiron only wanted him along so as not to lose track of him. He still needed him to break the barrier, whatever that entailed.

Thinking of magic, Raidan scoffed. He'd been getting too accustomed to the constant muscle shakes that never went away. For only a second, the jitters had ceased when he'd hit Beiron. There was a moment of peace, and then the jitters were back and he remembered how much they irritated him. At least, he didn't have the headache now.

While getting rid of this magic was a priority, finding Ida and saving Cass took precedence. And Beiron was his way to Cass. He caught up to Beiron, leaving Dimitri behind with the magical attackers, Ilan, and that terrifying vine.

Chapter 38

From the corner of his eye, Ilan saw what Beiron had done. The way he'd just thrown those boulders at those men and stalked off. And Raidan with him!

If not for Raidan's warning, Ilan might not have gotten out of the vine's way in time as it re-emerged from the lake. The plant left a mark on his leg.

Xander, one of his men, had not been so lucky. The vine had wrapped around his waist and dragged him into the water. The second man to get taken down so far. Ilan was just glad it hadn't been him. The unpredictability of the vine's attacks caused everyone to edge away from the water as they fought. They'd come to this place as thirteen in total. Ilan counted only seven remaining.

One of the magic wielders lit a light. It glowed bright and blue. He pushed his hands upward to let it float up above his head. With the space now brightly lit, it was easy to see all that was going on.

Ilan duelled with one of the attackers. Miles cut his blade across his opponent's chest, then came over to help Ilan. Shaw was holding his own against two opponents, one of them being Dimitri. He'd teamed up with one of the attackers against Shaw, but Shaw happened to be an excellent swordsman, one of the best.

A gust of wind from nowhere brushed by and nearly knocked Ilan off his feet. Miles staggered as well. Their assailant took their loss of balance as opportunity to step away from the two of them as they fought two against one. He snapped his fingers and fire appeared in his hand.

Ilan's jaw dropped—and then he understood what was about to happen. He jumped out of the way as the man thrust his arm forward to throw his fire as if he were throwing a ball. But the fire diminished before it left his hand and it sparked to nothing. The man scowled and shook his hand. Ilan didn't think that was meant to happen.

Miles lunged at the man and whacked him on the head with the hilt of his sword. The assailant fell, unconscious.

When the attackers had come down on them from the top of the Hayat Point, their groups had been close to even in number. But these fighters had an advantage with their magic. It was hard to focus when all Ilan wanted to do was learn who they were. But to surrender would be to submit and turn themselves over. And to keep fighting . . .

Ilan had already deduced they had to be Elderace. He didn't know, but he didn't want to become their enemy. He didn't want to fight them.

With the Elderace fighters busy battling his men, no one else came at him and Miles. Ilan looked up to where Beiron and Raidan had gone. They were no longer in sight. Who knew if they'd gotten very far.

The leader of the Elderace attackers—the one whose actions were so casual and easy, as though he weren't in the midst of a fight—stood near the peak, no one opposing him, as Ilan's own men were down in number. He, too, glanced back the way Beiron and Raidan had gone.

Only three of Ilan's men were left fighting near the shore of the lake. The others lay unmoving on the slope of the mountain.

The Elderace leader caught Ilan's eye. Ilan lowered his sword, letting it be known his desire was not to engage in battle. The man didn't seem too eager to come at him and fight. He called out to his men. "Let's go!" He pointed to Dimitri. "You're with us!"

Their people outnumbered Ilan's men only by one. Shaw, who'd been fighting against Dimitri took a swing with his sword and struck Dimitri's. Spinning around, Shaw extended his leg out, kicking the Elderace assailant he'd also been fighting. He came back at Dimitri with a second strike that made Dimitri stagger.

It was a good effort, but the Elderace man swept up a gust of wind with his hands and thrust it at Shaw, pushing him backward and causing him to lose his footing.

Dimitri wouldn't be inclined to stay with Ilan, and there was little chance Ilan or his remaining men would be able to force him to stay. Not when the Elderace had the elements at their disposal.

The Elderace obeyed their leader, and as expected, Dimitri did not protest at going with them. Water swirled up from the lake and danced all around them. Ilan's heart jumped. He looked to the lake, thinking the vine had returned. The water blocked their vision on all sides. When it splattered to the ground and Ilan could see past it, the vine was nowhere to be seen and the last of the Elderace were disappearing, taking with them Dimitri and the only light they had.

Ilan didn't want to stick around for much longer. Not with the vine still looking for victims to claim. "Move out!" he said to whoever was left still standing. He considered going after Dimitri and the Elderace, but with so few of his men remaining, it would not go well for them. He ran up the slope and stood at the top of the Hayat Point. Accepting the fact that he'd lost this fight, Ilan let his shoulders slouch. He had so many questions, and the only ones who could give him answers had just left. But he still had Raidan's son. That would ensure Raidan would be back.

Ilan swore. Beiron knew where the baby was. That must have been where they were going. What was Beiron playing at?

Ilan would have to hurry if he was going to get there in time to catch them. Maybe letting Beiron roam free hadn't been the best idea. Ever since he'd been freed, he'd taken far too many liberties over Ilan and his men. That was going to have to stop, although something told him it was a little late for that.

*

Laila never had much reason to worry for Royl until today. She bit her nails and paced, undecided if she was angry at him for leaving her or afraid for him and what he was getting himself into, running off after the infamous Beiron, who seemed to have an army of Valca soldiers by his side.

She paced in the narrow space between the beds in her room. Ida stood by the door with her ear to the wood, listening for sounds. The ceiling was not very high, and with every passing minute, it felt like it was closing in on them.

More than a few times, Laila had to talk Ida down from marching out to speak to someone about finding her son. Each time was harder than the last. At one point, she'd almost embraced the idea, but then she shut it down. Ida would not be welcomed by her people. Many still despised the mayanon.

Zulu stood watch outside her door. Laila had peeked not long ago to check if he was still there. It was going to be impossible to slip past him unnoticed.

She stopped pacing and pulled her hair, growling her frustration. This was taking too long. She couldn't stand being here.

"I think I hear someone coming," Ida whispered.

Laila darted to the door and opened it. Her room was near an intersection adjoining a main hall. To get from the main-way into the mines and to the assembly chamber, one had to pass this way. Laila stepped outside her room, leaving the door slightly open. Zulu turned to her. He took up the majority of the hall, blocking any way past.

"I want to see my brother," she demanded. "That's him returning now, I can hear him. Let me pass."

"He'll come get you when he's ready," Zulu replied.

"Royl!" Laila shouted down the hall. The enclosed space of the braced walls here swallowed her voice. "Royl!" she called again. Zulu didn't stop her from calling out. He just wouldn't let her around him.

Royl appeared at the end of the hall. He had his men with him, worn out and dishevelled. There were so few. Surely he'd taken more warriors than that.

She took a step toward him, and Zulu matched her step to stop her. Royl and his group stood at the intersecting halls, eight feet away. Laila knew all the warriors with her brother but one. The man was blindfolded, but she did recognize his figure. He was the one she'd seen with Beiron in her vision—if that's what she could call it.

The realization made her cold, and she shivered. A part of her had hoped it had been some strange dream. But she didn't doubt its reality now.

"Not now, Laila," Royl said. He sounded tired. "I'll come and—"

"Dimitri!" Ida exclaimed. She ran out of the room and stopped where Laila stood, blocked by Zulu.

Zulu's big eyebrows raised high as he looked first at Ida, then turned an angry gaze on Laila. "Who is this?" he demanded.

Laila shrunk, startled by his booming voice. Dimitri, the stranger with Royl, removed the blindfold and stepped forward from the group of warriors. "Ida!" He stumbled down the hall a few paces. "You're all right! We saw . . . the soldiers, they—"

"Laila," Royl interjected. "What is going on? Where did she come from?" He faced Ida. "Who are you?" he asked. "How did you get in here?"

Ida ignored his questions. "Dimitri, they have Cass!" she said. She cried and tried to speak at the same time. By the few words Laila understood through her sobs, she knew Ida was trying to explain what had happened, but it was incomprehensible as she cried.

"Who is he to you?" Royl asked Ida, pointing at Dimitri.

Ida hiccupped and calmed down enough to speak. "He's my brother-in-law. Valca soldiers have taken my son. Laila said you could help me." She sniffled.

Royl's looks of disappointment for Laila were becoming too common a thing. But she wasn't thinking of his disappointment just now. Instead, she was thinking how this was going to affect her argument for ever leaving the mines. "Royl, they need our help," she said.

Royl raised his shoulders and stood tall. "Back inside, Laila. You"— he pointed to Ida—"with us."

Ida looked at Laila, unsure. Zulu grabbed her arm and shuffled her past him, then continued to block Laila's way. "Royl, let me come. I can explain everything."

Royl waved a hand, indicating Ida go with him. "Tell me later. It's best if I don't see you right now." To Zulu, he added, "I'll be back soon. Will you be all right here?"

Zulu nodded. Royl gestured for Ida to go. Stefan, who was too tall for the low ceiling in this hall and had to slouch, came to escort Ida away. Ida glanced back at Laila but said nothing as she went with Stefan.

Laila already couldn't stand to be in her room. Now she'd not even have the company to make it more bearable. "Royl," she said as he turned to go. "Don't leave me here. Let me come. I won't leave your side. Please."

Without turning his head, he said, "I'm not ready to deal with you just yet." He left her there and followed the others. Then they were gone.

Zulu faced Laila. "Go on, Laila. He'll come when he's ready."

"He's not putting them in containment, is he? Ida's not a threat to our people. She's someone who's lost her son and needs our help."

"I don't know where Royl is taking them. That's not your concern. Go on. Back inside."

Laila's shoulders slumped as she re-entered her room. She was going to have to get rid of Zulu so she could get out of here. She paced again, trying to think.

Just as she sank onto her bed, the door opened and her mother came in. "Mum!" Laila stood. "I'm glad you're here. I could really use your help."

Freya stood an inch shorter than Laila. "What's going on? Why is Zulu out there?"

"I'll explain later." Laila took her mother's hands in her own. "But right now, I really need you. Will you help me?"

Chapter 39

The mountains were enveloped in darkness. At some point during their trek, the moon hid behind clouds. Raidan didn't think it would emerge. Things had been going so terribly wrong that it seemed appropriate the weather wouldn't cooperate; he almost expected it to start lashing rain. The dark was unsettling.

Beiron walked at a steady pace, and Raidan struggled to keep up. The pass trail had been fairly straight and easy, as frequent use had trodden it down, making it distinguishable as a path. Here, Beiron swerved all over, responding to the angle of the mountain and the depth of the slopes. The peaks rose higher above them the lower they descended toward Litlen. The shadows deepened.

Raidan tripped a few times. His legs were sore, and he was exhausted. Although no one followed, he couldn't help but check over his shoulder every few minutes.

Hearing Adrik's voice at the lake and realizing he was not gone stirred his anxiety. If breaking a barrier in that place would potentially release him, all the more reason not to do it. Raidan had no problem letting the barrier remain, keeping the stone and Adrik right where they were: far away from him and his family, and out of their lives.

Now to get his family back. He hoped Dimitri hadn't been harmed during the fight. He couldn't explain it, but he sensed he was alive, which was more than he knew for sure about Ida's well-being.

At last, they passed the final walls of mountain surrounding them and came to a wooded area, the same one in which Raidan hoped he'd find Cassian. The unusual colours of the branches and grass stood out in the night. It was autumn, but the trees here didn't seem to know that. Rather than the leaves turning their usual browns, reds, and yellows, here, they were brilliant green with hues of blue and purple. And, just as when he and Ida had first set foot in Litlen region, everything had a sort of glow: the grass, the trees, the flowers and bushes, the insects. It really was—and he hated to admit it—magical. But magical in the way that he'd first imagined what magic was meant to be like, before that frightful night with Adrik all those years ago.

Raidan walked faster, knowing they were nearing Cassian. It was much easier to move at a quick pace here than it had been in the mountains. If only he knew where the cabin was, he could leave Beiron behind.

"We should discuss what's going to happen when we get to your son," Beiron said.

"What's going to happen is I'm going to take him far away from here and we're leaving this country like we should have done in the first place."

Beiron chuckled. "It's a nice thought, but that's not how things are going to go down. We've had a minor setback, that's all. As soon as I'm sure we won't encounter Royl and those warriors again, we'll go back and finish what we started."

So Beiron did know the attackers. "Those people?" Raidan said. "They were Elderace, weren't they?"

"You're very observant."

Raidan pressed his lips tight and ignored Beiron's mocking tone. "How?" he asked. "I thought they were all meant to be gone. And now, you all keep popping up everywhere. Why?"

Beiron gave an exasperated sigh. "Landon gave it his best effort, but still my people prevail. It's no surprise. To think that a worthless mayanon could conquer the Elderace—it will take more than your lot to destroy us."

"My lot?" Raidan almost laughed. "Weren't those *your* people back there attacking *you?*"

Beiron scoffed. "My people still have much to learn. They don't grasp what I'm doing yet, but they will."

"And what is it that you're doing?"

"Restoring balance to our country . . . making things the way they should be, the way they always should have been."

Raidan hated to think what Beiron meant by that. "So what do you need me for?" he asked, purposely leaving Dimitri out.

"Are you really so dull?" Beiron asked. "You're to break—"

"The barrier, yes, I got that part. But why?"

"For the Weldafire Stone. It's still in the sacred room, and you're going to give it to me. And its power with it."

The very idea made him go rigid. "Even if I wanted to do that, Dimitri won't. Don't you need both of us?"

"I do," Beiron said. His candour came as a surprise. "And as long as you're with me, he'll come for you."

Raidan laughed softly. "What makes you think that?"

"Your brother likes to be a hero. He'll do anything when it comes to you."

After recent events, Raidan could have denied Beiron's observation. But in truth, Dimitri did have a thing about saving people. If he knew Raidan was in trouble, he'd come for him. And as long as Beiron had Cassian, Raidan would do anything to protect his son. Evidently, Beiron knew how to play this game.

Raidan opened his mouth to speak, but a cry pierced the night. He froze. Though it was distant, there was no question what the sound was. It was a baby. *His* baby.

He stood perfectly still, listening for Cassian's further cries. Then before Beiron could stop him, he ran. He sprinted through the glowing woods and thought he could see the dim glow of firelight ahead. He weaved between tree trunks, running toward it.

Cassian's screams escalated the closer he got. He was hysteric, angry. What were they doing to him?

Raidan ran faster. He lost track of where Beiron was or how close behind he might be. It didn't matter. Cassian needed him. His boy needed his father.

Raidan sprinted over uneven ground. His chest burned the harder he ran, dodging trees and low-hanging branches. He ignored the throbbing in his head.

A handful of men stood outside the door to a cottage. More than Raidan could recall were meant to be here. Stealth was out of the question at this point. There was no time to slow down and plan his way in. He was going to save his son, now.

With Cassian's life in the balance, he was fearless. Invincible. Protecting his son was his duty. His responsibility. His joy. Nothing could stop him.

He ran at the men at full speed and—it must have been pure adrenaline that gave him the strength to knock three of them to the ground and out of his way. The other two didn't make it to him in time before he'd made it to the door and burst into the cottage.

The wall in the small landing divided it from the rest of the house. He stepped out of the landing and gasped at the sight before him. The sitting room was too small for the eight men crowded inside. Three of them, Raidan recognized as Ilan's men. The other five, as well as those outside, Raidan didn't know. They wore no colours to indicate they were Valca soldiers, but they all had different markings on their faces. One man had an extra eye painted on the centre of his forehead. Another had horns painted on either side of his head, which looked like scars protruding from his skin. One of them had made it look like his smile extended all the way back to his earlobes. And then there was the soldier—Ilan's man—holding Cassian, trying to calm him down.

The man had no idea what he was doing. He had Cassian facing away from himself and toward the terrifying-looking men, and he was bouncing him up and down too hard. Cassian's face was scrunched up, and his legs kicked the air.

Ignoring the hideous faces of those around him, Raidan took a giant step across the room. One of the ugly-faced men stepped in front of him. This one had his eyebrows slanted downward at an unnatural curve to make him look perpetually angry. Yet, he smiled a wide, wicked grin.

They all carried weapons, swords mostly. Two of them carried a baton, and one held a club. Someone else had a machete, which was not typically seen or used in Kartha. The one with the angry eyebrows had no weapon that Raidan could see. Directly behind Raidan, the man with the machete closed in on him.

The magic in Raidan stirred. He was beginning to recognize the way it bubbled inside, ready to burst from him at any given moment. There was no telling when that might be. "Move!" Raidan shouted and felt the rumble beneath his feet. If not for Cassian, he might have almost welcomed the quake. But he couldn't risk the cottage coming down on them. "Give him to me," Raidan said, quieter. The ground did not tremble this time.

The man with the angry eyes raised his thin eyebrows, and his lips formed an O. His pupils went all the way to one side and then the other before they landed on Raidan. "Ooohh." He giggled. "Was that because of you? I was told there was magic here. I see it is not at all like what I imagined." His body shivered. "So exciting!"

Cassian hiccupped between every breath as he cried.

The man with the angry eyebrows took a step closer to Raidan. "You must be the father?" he said. "I know that look in your eye." He put a hand out, blocking Raidan. On his hand was a glove with stringy attachments and pieces of metal attached to the tips of each finger.

The man jerked his hand back, looked at it with wide mouthed wonder, and flashed his grin again. "You like?" he said. "I have a kind of magic of my own, you see. I'm not from here. Perhaps you've heard of me, though. They call me Scourge. It's a bit . . . dark, but I like it. Makes me seem so . . ." His gaze rolled downward, across the floor, then came back up to Raidan, and his lip slanted upward. "Dangerous," he said. "What do you think?"

"I think you're in my way." Raidan brushed the man's hand aside and took a single step before a shock surged through his system. Every muscle in his body contracted as he convulsed and fell.

Scourge crouched over Raidan's paralyzed body. He showed his gloved hand to Raidan. "See?" he said, wriggling his fingers. "Magic. Where I'm from in Nuwnot, we've made some very exciting progress in our weaponry. This one mimics the effects of a lightning strike. Have you ever been struck by lightning?" He waited for a response.

Raidan gave none. No words would come. His nerves felt tingly, and his weakened muscles were not working properly.

Scourge shrugged. He stood, then said to his men, "Get him in the wagon." When he turned his eyes back down to look at Raidan, his painted eyebrows made him look fearsome.

"Kingston requests your presence in Valmain," Scourge said. "He's hired me to deliver, and so I shall." The next bit was for his freaks and Ilan's men. "Be sure Ilan gets this message," he said to the soldier holding Cassian, handing him a crumpled note. To his man, he said, "Menace, be a good lad and see that this father gets to the king who's not a king. I have others to round up before I collect my payment."

Cassian was asleep in the arms of Ilan's man. His poor baby had once again cried himself to sleep. Raidan felt as though someone had ripped his heart out and crushed it. The ache in his gut paralyzed him as much as the electric assault had.

Two of Scourge's freaks dragged Raidan to an enclosed wagon, heaved him in, and shut the door, locking him inside. It took every bit of his strength for Raidan to get onto his knees to look through the barred window out the back door of the wagon. He looked for his Cassian, expecting to see him in the arms of the soldier. But Ilan's man never came out of the cabin. And Beiron was nowhere to be seen.

The wagon started moving, and Raidan steadied his balance on his knees to match the movement. As they rode farther from the cottage, Raidan heard Scourge address his men.

"Make sure he gets to his accommodations. I'm not finished here yet." He came into view as he rode on horseback in the opposite direction that Raidan was being taken in.

Raidan shoved his weight into the solid door of the wagon. He sat back and kicked at it with both legs, desperate to get to Cassian before he was too far away. He kept kicking until his legs had no strength left, then rammed his shoulders into the sides of the wooden walls that stretched up and around him on every side. As if it made any difference, he pounded his fists against the door and screamed a pathetic, weak cry. There came the rumble, but that was all. It wasn't even enough of a quake to make anyone stop to look. Why did it work sometimes and not ever when he wanted it to?

Defeated, Raidan leaned his back against the wall and rested his head. He needed to get out of here. It was looking like the only way that was going to happen was if he used magic, however he was supposed to do that.

He took a deep breath. He'd made it work on demand a couple of times, but he didn't know how. Snapping? Clapping? Waving his hands around? He'd seen some of those magic wielders do that back at the lake.

Raidan snapped. He made fists and opened them fast, expecting to see that blue light. He tried clapping and waving his hands like a maniac. He even tried smashing his hand onto the floor of the wagon, but all that did was make his hand hurt.

When nothing worked, he groaned and sat back again. It was difficult not to succumb to his weariness. The motion of the wagon swayed and rocked him. His heavy eyelids stayed closed for a longer length of time every time he blinked. As he thought of Cassian, tears leaked from his eyes.

I'll find you, Cass, he told himself. *I'll come back for you.*

Chapter 40

THE ROOM WAS HOTTER THAN USUAL. OR MAYBE IT WAS LAILA'S IMAGInation. She was back to her pacing, trying to block out the fact that she was still in these stupid mines. She hated the way the walls seemed to inch closer together. The two narrow beds and the desk and chair where her mother did her drawings were the only pieces of furniture in the room. There was not enough space to stretch her legs properly, and walking back and forth the same few steps every thirty seconds was making her crazy.

Although she couldn't change how she'd wound up here, she could do something to get herself out of this little room. At her request, her mother had gone to summon Royl. She needed to speak with him. Until then, she would wait. And pace.

She lowered herself onto the bed. Her body was so restless, her legs jittered. She tried to distract herself by thinking about how she was going to convince Royl to let her leave her room. In her hand was a crinkled-up note that she intended to hand deliver to Ida. Royl was trustworthy, but she couldn't show him what she'd written. If he knew what she had planned, he'd take extra precautions to stop her. There were times when his status with the elders had come in handy, and he'd used it to help get her out of trouble, but he'd never used it against her. Until now.

She stood again to pace, just in time for her mother to return with Royl following behind her. He came fully in the room and closed the door.

"You wanted to see me?" Royl folded his arms across his chest.

"I need you to get a message to Ida for me. Can you do that?"

Royl exhaled and closed his eyes, pinching the bridge of his nose. "What message?"

"Tell her I'm sorry I brought her here, that I thought you would help her—not make her a prisoner here. I really did want to help her find her husband and son."

There was a lull of silence while Royl stared at Laila with his lips pressed together. "Laila," he said at last. "There—"

"You wouldn't even know about Beiron being back if it weren't for me," Laila continued. "And if not for me, we'd still be without magic and without any knowledge of the Weldafire Stone being bound. The least you could do for me is allow me to go and speak to Ida myself. It's not her fault she's here. Please, Royl." It had to be enough. She'd been counting on his usual brotherly compassion.

"About that," he said. "We still need to talk about the fact that you led a mayanon right to us, and about how you came to know where to find Beiron."

"I'll tell you everything, but first, would you please let me out of here? I'm going out of my mind."

Royl looked sideways at Freya. "What do you think of this, Mother?"

Freya dipped her chin at him. Royl must have already told her about Beiron being back in Litlen because she hadn't acted surprised to hear his name. "I think a lot of things." Freya stepped over to Royl and placed a loving hand on his arm. "I hate to see you two like this. I know you're only looking out for Laila, but consider how this will affect your relationship."

Royl backed away from her touch. "Yes, but, Mother . . . it's—"

"I know," she interrupted. "I know, Royl."

The depth of her gaze was meaningful, though Laila had no idea why. Royl and Freya understood each other in ways that Laila didn't get, though, to be fair, the same could be said for herself and their mother.

Their silent communication sparked Laila's interest, and she thought to ask what was not being said, but Royl's eyes were softening and she didn't want to ruin her chances at getting her way. He looked at Laila and sighed. "I'll take you to her and see about getting you in to speak with her."

Laila's heart skipped a beat. She almost yelped in her excitement but refrained.

"But you've been pushing it with the boundaries," Royl added, "and that has to stop. I'm sending someone to guard the access hall into the tunnels. You're to stay in the mines until we figure some things out. Deal?"

Until they figured things out could be too long. Laila nodded but could not verbally agree to such an arrangement, especially if she was going to be of any use to Ida in helping her find her baby.

Royl didn't press for anything more. He led the way out, and Laila hugged her mother before leaving, squeezing her extra tight.

"Be careful, Laila," Freya whispered.

When Laila pulled away from the embrace, Freya's smile didn't meet her eyes. There was that resemblance to Royl and his famous look of concern.

Laila followed Royl into the hall. Royl dismissed Zulu, then ushered Laila through the halls to the private meeting room, where Ida was being kept with her brother-in-law, Dimitri, like prisoners, though she knew Royl would disagree.

Bailey and Stefan stood outside the door like jail-guards. As if the two people inside the room were dangerous. Laila didn't know Dimitri, nor did she know Ida well, but the woman was distraught; she was barely keeping herself together. Besides, Laila was certain that even if they did try to get past Bailey and Stefan, they'd not know how to exit the mines.

Royl indicated to Stefan that Laila could go in. She walked past the two of them, feeling short next to Stefan as he opened the door for her. He was taller than anyone she knew, and she didn't like having to look up so much to meet his gaze. But for the fierce warrior that he was, there was no hardness in his eyes as he let her in. He even gave her a small smile, which Laila returned.

Inside the meeting room, Dimitri sat in a chair, his head in his hands. He stood when she came in. Perched on the floor with her back against the stone wall opposite the door, Ida hugged her knees. Her eyes were glazed over, and she stared at the ground without so much as a glance at Laila. Royl came up behind Laila and stood at the open door, arms crossed.

"What do you want?" Dimitri asked. His tone was harsh, but Laila supposed she couldn't blame him. At least they'd been given the private meeting room with the comfortable chairs, as opposed to the containment room for those who had broken the rules and faced judgement. A place Royl had spared Laila from on more than one occasion.

The private room seemed much less crowded now, rather than the last time she was there with the elders and Royl. The five armchairs were vacant. Outside the circle of chairs, Ida looked lost in her thoughts. Royl waited by the open threshold. She'd have to be careful what she said. She needed to figure out a way to get Ida the note without Royl seeing.

Laila turned to Royl. "Can I have a minute please?"

She understood his reluctance to leave her. His eyes met Dimitri's and narrowed at him, then turned onto her. "I'm not comfortable leaving you in here with him."

Dimitri's fists clenched. Laila could sense the growing tension between the two men. "I'll be fine," she told Royl, then faced Ida's brother-in-law. "It's Dimitri, right?" she asked him rhetorically. "I'm Laila. You're not going to hurt me, are you?"

"Are you going to tell us why you're keeping us here?" Dimitri said. "And who you are and where you came from?"

"You have a bit of explaining to do yourself," Royl said. "Like how you got mixed up with Beiron and what you were doing with him and the Valca Order."

It would be the next day before Laila would get out of here. "Okay," she said before anyone else could speak. "We'll get to all that." She looked between Royl and Dimitri. "Evidently, we all have questions. We're not enemies here. But before everyone has a sit-down for hours on end to exchange stories, can I please just have a minute with Ida?"

The two glared at one another. Finally, Royl backed off. He stepped out of the room. "I'm just here, Laila." He closed the door. That wouldn't stop him from hearing everything, but at least, he wouldn't see her give the note.

Ida seemed unfazed by the arguing men or by Laila's presence. Laila wasn't sure if she'd blinked in all that time. She sat unmoving, staring at the ground. Laila couldn't imagine what she was going through. She wanted so badly to help. She was, after all, a little bit responsible for those soldiers getting away with her son in the first place. It had always only been a matter of time before her people would be exposed. If only she'd have stopped them from taking the baby, they'd not be here now. And now here was Ida, beside herself about all she'd lost.

"Ida," Laila said. She wasn't sure if Ida was okay. She didn't look it. "Ida, I'm so sorry." She pulled out the little piece of parchment on which she'd scrawled her note. At the moment, she didn't think Ida would receive Laila well if she went over to her. She handed her note to Dimitri instead.

He took it. "What's this?"

Laila shook her head and put a finger to her lips. She pointed at Ida, indicating the note was for her. Dimitri nodded.

"I just wanted to say I'm sorry. I really do want to help you, Ida." Laila raised her eyebrows at the note, and Dimitri opened it and scanned it. She hoped he understood her quick, messy script. The note simply read:

I'll make this right. I'll find your son and return him to you.

She'd meant it. As soon as she was clear of watchful eyes, Laila was getting out of here and would find Ida's baby.

"I should be out there looking for Cass," Dimitri said. "It's my fault that any of this happened."

Laila glanced at the door. She imagined Royl pressing his ear to it, listening. The thought made her smile. That'd be something she'd do, not Royl. But she had no doubt he could hear them nonetheless.

"Tell my brother all about it," she told Dimitri, "and maybe he'll get you an entire team to help look."

Now that she'd done what she had come to do, it was time to go. She went to the door, opened it, and Royl was right there, just like he said he'd be. He let her out and closed the door again, then walked with her. His overbearing protectiveness was like a shadow attached to her. If she was going to rescue Ida's baby, she'd have to get rid of Royl's constant hovering, which was growing increasingly more difficult.

Chapter 41

IN THE HILLS OF LITLEN, THE ASSEMBLY ROOM WAS SITUATED IN THE middle. The tall ceiling extended higher than all the other rooms in the tightly enclosed space of the mines—so close to the outside, and yet, mounds of earth between Laila and the sun.

The room was void of people, save for Laila and Royl. The tree branch chandelier was alit with candles, and the big goblet torches were cold where no fire burned.

"Laila." Royl reached out, stopping her before she could leave the cavernous space on her own. He faced her directly and rested his hands on her shoulders. "Remember what I told you."

She gave a small nod and avoided his gaze.

"Where are you off to now?" he asked.

There were ways out other than the barricaded access point leading to the tunnels under Litlen. Adjoining the eating room, the kitchen's chimney and ceiling trapdoor led out for the purpose of ventilation. If Laila could get there before a crowd came, she could leave the mines unseen. But Royl didn't need to know that.

"Anywhere that's not my room," she replied.

He stared at her for a minute until she finally looked at him. She sensed he wanted to say more. He searched her face, and she was afraid he'd somehow acquired a gift of mind reading on top of his already acute senses. She stopped thinking about where she was planning to go just in case he could see into her thoughts.

"You're in my way," she said.

His shoulders dropped slightly, and he returned his hands to his sides. "I'll come find you in a while and see that you're all right."

"You mean to see if I'm still here."

Royl made an exasperated sound. "I'm trusting you to do as you've been told. You've broken the rules, and I've already kept you from a more severe punishment. I understand that you're angry with me, but I'm trying to protect you, Laila."

Well stop trying and stay out of my way, she held back from saying. Punishment for what? Wanting to be free of this place and to live outside? She'd happily go and not come back if it made them feel better about keeping their secret safe. Although, keeping it a secret now was unlikely. Royl had just led an attack on Valca guards and exposed their presence in Litlen to their enemy.

Laila had nothing more to say. She brushed past Royl and left the assembly chamber. He let her go without further remarks. Today, he was not acting like her brother. Today, he was acting like an elder. Laila didn't know what she thought of that. She was proud of him and his role—training up the warriors and protecting the heritage and history of their people. But these past few days, he'd been interfering with her freedom.

Laila longed to breathe fresh air again. She couldn't handle getting stuck in her room a second time. The sooner she left the mines, the better. She would look for Ida's son, starting with Beiron's home.

No. That was a bad idea. The visions of Beiron in her head came back to her, and she shook them off. No, not his home. She'd have to begin somewhere else. But where?

She hardly paid any attention to her surroundings as she made her way round the bends and down each hall. Few people passed by at this early hour.

When she arrived at the eating room, more people were coming and going. Judging by the smell of freshly baked bread, she determined it must be time for breakfast. Some of the residents in the mines had tasks and jobs both day and night, and the time of day didn't matter much to them. But most people, like her mother, had that internal instinct, telling them when the days should begin and end.

Out of the thousand-plus people living there, everyone had been divided into three groups, and each group was allotted certain time slots in the eating room before the next group came. It was just not a big enough space to hold everyone at once.

Nearly to the kitchen now, she still didn't have a plan as to how to bypass the cooks on duty. They rotated shifts per meal, along with the other kitchen helpers. Laila had no idea how many people she'd have to sneak past.

A sudden light shone and blinded her. She squinted and blinked, putting her hands out in front of her to block the low eastern sun from shining in her face.

Sunlight? Inside the mines? Laila closed her eyes tight. It was happening again. How did this keep happening?

She opened her eyes, and there were trees everywhere. This place was familiar. She recognized it as the Forest of Litlen. Beiron was on her left, and a Valca soldier walked to her right, carrying a baby. She gasped and Beiron looked right at her. Taking a step back, she walked into something solid and turned to see what it was.

Her vision dissolved. Now she was back in the mines and completely disoriented. She'd walked into a wall in the eating room. The few people nearest to her saw what she had done and were watching her.

The blond girl who approached was a friendly face. Dynelle was close to Laila's age, and they had been friends since before the war. They lived on opposite ends of the mines, though, and didn't see a lot of each other, probably because Laila spent every moment she could outside the mines and aboveground.

"Laila, are you all right?" Dynelle asked, touching her arm.

"Dynelle? What are you doing here?"

Dynelle raised an eyebrow. "Cooking duty. Don't you know where you are?"

Right. The kitchen. The ventilation and the trapdoor leading out. Laila looked around her, dazed, playing up her confusion a little. Now she had a plan.

"Should I send for your brother?" Dynelle asked.

"No! No, don't do that. That's not necessary." The kitchen was only a few feet ahead. Laila brushed herself off and stood up straight.

Those who had been watching her when she'd backed into the wall resumed their business.

"I'm fine," Laila said. "I just need some air." To play it up further, Laila put her hand to her forehead and closed her eyes.

Dynelle smirked. "Come with me. I know just what you need."

She took Laila's hand and led her into the kitchen. Lihna, the woman on duty with Dynelle, looked up from her kneading. With a nod, Dynelle assured her that Laila was there with her. Lihna turned her focus back to her task, ignoring the two of them.

In the kitchen, the fireplace took up the majority of the far wall. The chimney was equally big. Laila could have stood under the large space and looked up to the sky from beneath. A clay oven sat against the right wall, and Lihna kneaded dough at a nearby table. One wall had a shelf lined with pots and bowls, and ladles and other cooking utensils. Under the shelf, knives of all sizes dangled from hooks. Herbs hung in bundles from the ceiling.

Dynelle showed Laila to the far left corner, where the earth had been built up enough that one could stand and touch a flat hand to the ceiling. Dynelle pushed open a hidden hatch and sunlight filled the room.

Laila shaded her eyes with her elbow. Squinting past her arm at the morning's blue sky, she sucked in a breath of air and savoured it. She couldn't help herself.

"I know," Dynelle said. "Sometimes, I come in here just to do that." She grinned.

"How could you not? It's the worst down here." Laila stepped onto the raised mound to reach her arm through the opening. It was big enough that she'd be able to climb through. She'd just need a boost.

"It's good that we're safe here, though," Dynelle said.

Laila said nothing. She needed Dynelle to help her get through the trapdoor. And she needed to do it without provoking a heated discussion about the risk.

Dynelle stared at the sky. "They're saying the curse broke and Litlen has come to life again. I never saw it in its cursed state. My family got here before it hit." She met Laila's gaze. "What about you?" she asked. "Did you see it?"

"I saw it," Laila said.

The sounds coming from the eating room were growing louder, and Dynelle turned her face that way. Laila needed to distract her from getting back to work.

"It was bad," she said. "There was no colour, no birdsong or leaves rustling in the air, no beautiful fragrances." She breathed in again and could smell the sea air, mixed with the wildflowers growing in the hills. The cattle would be grazing nearby, and the cliffs and sea were near.

"Dynelle," Lihna called from her workstation. "I need you to get back to work. People are coming."

"I'll be right there, Lihna." Dynelle looked at Laila and smiled with sad eyes.

Lihna left the kitchen with the fresh loaf of baked bread in hand. This was Laila's only chance.

She raised a corner of her lip, smiling back at Dynelle. "I'm going to take a walk."

Dynelle's forehead wrinkled and her lips parted. "What do you mean? We're not supposed to go outside."

"I'll be all right. I just need to breathe the fresh air and take it all in." Laila checked the threshold for Lihna. There was still time. "Here."

She lifted her leg and indicated Dynelle give her a boost. "Help me get up there, then close it behind me. I'll walk around the hills and return at the main-way."

Casting a nervous glance toward the eating room, Dynelle shook her head. "Laila, we could get in trouble."

"We won't. I'll get to the entrance and explain everything to whoever's on sentry duty. I won't mention you at all, I promise."

After another glance at the door, Dynelle gave a hesitant nod. She clasped her fingers together and made a step for Laila's foot. "Okay, quick then. Before Lihna comes back."

Laila put her foot on Dynelle's hands. Together, with her bouncing up and Dynelle pushing her hands upward at the same time, Laila reached both arms over the trapdoor's opening and pulled herself up. Once settled above, she peered back in. "Thanks, Dynelle."

"Just come right back, okay? And stay safe out there."

"I owe you one. I'll see you around."

Dynelle closed the trapdoor and Laila relaxed. She was exhausted mentally, physically, and emotionally. She was in no state to rescue a baby from a dangerous, wanted man and a Valca soldier. She needed a plan. And sleep. Her old home was the only place that she could think of where she'd be able to rest and devise a course of action.

She took slow steps out of the hills. Sheep grazed nearby. Any of the workers who tended to the gardens and orchard would be out harvesting fruit and vegetables at this time. The last thing she needed now was to get caught and brought back inside to face Royl.

It was slow going, getting to her old home from this far in the hills, but at least, she was out of the mines. Now if only it could stay that way.

211

Chapter 42

THE COTTAGE WAS EMPTY BY THE TIME ILAN ARRIVED WITH HIS FOUR remaining men. Nielsen and the baby were missing, and his other two soldiers lay dead on the floor, blood pooling around their heads. Judging by the stained floorboards, they'd been dead for some time. The stench of blood and faeces filled the small dwelling. Ilan's stomach turned. He looked away.

The fire in the fireplace was out. Ilan went to it and pinched the ash between his fingers. It was cool. The wagon tracks in the mud outside indicated someone other than Beiron had been here. Whoever they were, they were long gone by now.

The quaint little cottage had only the one room with two couches and a fireplace. The walls were made up of white rocks, and a thin, thatched roof topped it off. One little window let sunlight in through crooked wooden shutters.

Shaw bent down and retrieved something from one of the dead man's hands. It was a piece of parchment tinged with blood. Shaw was not only an excellent swordsman, but he had twisted sense of humour. One that earned him a slap across the head on numerous occasions. He handed the parchment to Ilan.

"Don't think Trent'll be needing this," he said with a snigger, indicating the dead man on the floor. Ilan lowered his eyes. He didn't share

Shaw's humour. He may not have known Trent and Syrus all that well, but they were still his men, there on his account, doing what he'd told them to do.

Ilan took the parchment and read it:

I have someone you're looking for. Come to Valmain.
~Scourge~

Ilan crumbled the note in his hand. Seeing the name, he had no doubt it was intended for him. Ilan had heard of Scourge, the mercenary from Nuwnot known for his freakish looks and unusual methods of torture. There was no question in Ilan's mind how he had come to be involved. Kingston must have hired the man. Ilan guessed that might have been in part due to Ilan's releasing Beiron.

Whomever his father had, Ilan didn't think he'd like what he'd find in Valmain, but all the same, he had to know.

He turned to Miles, Jack, and Tate. "You three, go and check in with Perry in that little village we left him in. See that he's not receiving orders from elsewhere and that things are running smoothly." He nodded at Shaw. "You're with me. We're going back to Valmain. I need to see what my father wants."

Without any questions, Miles, Jack, and Tate left the cottage.

Shaw gestured to the bodies on the floor. "What do you want to do about this?"

Ilan didn't look at them. "When we arrive back in Valmain, I'll send someone to retrieve the bodies from the lake and here and to return them home." He walked outside.

The sun shone bright in the east. It was low, and the light filtered between the leaves of the trees. Ilan looked toward Litlen. There was so much he wanted to know about the Elderace people who'd attacked them. Where did they come from? How did they survive? Were there more of them?

Ilan hoped his father wasn't aware of them. He could imagine how he'd react to knowing the Elderace were still out there—and with them, their *magic*.

Shoulders heavy, Ilan sighed. He checked the time on his pocket watch. It was too early for his father's games. Valmain was the last place he wanted to be right now. He stuffed the watch back in his inner pocket.

"Here we go," he whispered under his breath. Time to see what Kingston wanted.

*

"Survivors!" Kingston shouted at the informant. "How many?"

Clay was only in his early twenties, still practically a child. Kingston had selected the young man as his spy among Ilan's party, thinking Ilan wouldn't suspect the boy.

Kingston sat at the long table in his dining hall. He had been enjoying a lovely breakfast of poached eggs and jam on toasted bread. Clay's return this morning brought the unwelcome news.

"I don't know exactly how many," Clay said. "They came—"

"What do you mean you don't know!" Kingston searched nearby for something to throw. His choices included his plate, the cutlery, and his cup. He picked up the spoon first and clenched it in his fist.

Clay took a small step back.

"Elderace survivors. How is that even possible?" Kingston asked, then waved a hand. "Never mind. I don't care. I want them gone."

"Yes, of course, Mr. Valca." Clay was backing up.

"I'm not finished with you," Kingston said.

Clay froze.

"What news do you have of my son?"

"I, uh . . . I left before the fight was over," Clay stammered. "I wanted to be sure to make it back here and let you know about the Elderace."

Kingston stared at the boy. Then he chucked the spoon at him. It flew across the room and hit him in the ear. Clay yelped and clapped a hand to where he'd been hit. Kingston grabbed the fork next. Clay backed away further.

Kingston rose and stepped toward him. "You didn't think to help my son in battle? Instead, you just left him!" He threw the fork, and Clay dodged it.

"I'm sorry, I didn't think . . ."

"No, you didn't! Get out!" Kingston shouted. Clay scurried out of the dining hall.

As he exited, Owen entered. "Bad time?" he asked.

"What do you want, Owen? This had better be good." He didn't think he could take any more bad news.

"It is, Your Greatness. There's someone to see you. Shall I send him in?"

Kingston waved a hand to accept the guest. Owen went out and returned a moment later with a three-eyed man. Or so it appeared. The man had painted an extra eye on his forehead. The painting of the face was a signature look for Scourge's men. This must be one of them.

"You work for Scourge," Kingston stated.

"Yes, Mr. Valca. A keen observation. I come bearing a gift."

Good news indeed. "Where's Scourge? Why is he not delivering this gift himself?"

"Scourge is fulfilling the rest of his duty." The three-eyed man spoke with a lisp, and Kingston could see why. His tongue was filed at the tips like that of a snake's. Kingston's mouth curled in disgust.

"What I bring you today is only a part of what you've required," Three-eyes went on. "Your prisoner is right where you requested we bring him."

"Very good. I'll check on him in a moment. You'll receive the final payment when the job is complete. And what of my son?"

"He's been made aware of your newest guest. He'll come."

"Did you see him? Did he seem all right to you?"

"I wouldn't know. We didn't see him, but the man in your dungeon might have answers to your questions."

Kingston loosened his grip on the fork in his hand and an indentation remained in his skin. He set the fork on the table. "That'll be all then. You may go."

Three-eyes left, and Owen poked his head back in. "Anything else you need?" So eager the man was.

"In fact, there is. Find an alchemist and have him concoct black powder. My grandfather's cannons will need to be dusted off and made battle-ready. I may be using them soon."

Owen gave a curt nod and exited.

Kingston pushed his plate aside and sat back down. With his elbows on the table, he rested his head in his hands. Dealing with Elderace survivors after so long was not how he had intended to spend his time. He was so close to extending his reach into Tsein. This whole Elderace business messed with everything. He'd have to take care of it quickly and move on before Ilan became too involved. He wouldn't make his grandfather's mistake. Landon had been careless to allow survivors. Kingston would be known for ending the Elderace, and for doing it right.

Chapter 43

A CHILL SETTLED IN THE AIR AFTER THE CELL DOOR CLOSED. VALCA guards locked Raidan in the dungeon and left him there alone. Raidan's breathing came out raspy, and his eyes darted from one corner of his cell to the next. The torch just outside was dim and didn't give off much warmth. Beyond the narrow space between his cell and the one across from him, the room was dark.

The memory of Cassian's screams resonated in his head. He approached the bars and one by one pulled at them, checking their strength. The surge of adrenaline coursing through his veins made him strong, but it was not enough to rip apart the thick round bars. He stopped his tugging. The cell was sturdy. He turned to the stone wall behind him, studying it for any weak points.

Despair threatened to overtake him. His legs threatened to give way, but he wasn't going to stop trying. There had to be a way out. Cass was still out there. He had to get to him. He had to find Ida and know she was okay. The not knowing made his heart ache.

Looking at his hands, he tried to piece together what made the magic work. He snapped; nothing. Did it again. Still nothing.

He groaned. "Why won't you work!" he shouted as he snapped. As he did so, blue light flashed in his face and hovered over his hand.

He gasped, startled. What had made it appear? And how might it aid his escape?

The door to the adjoining room clanged and Raidan's heart leapt. Someone was coming. He dropped his hands and the light followed his right hand down. In a panic, he waved his hand, trying to make the light disappear. Instead, the bright sphere moved from his hand and bobbed through the bars, hovering in the passage between the cells. First, he couldn't summon the magic, and now he couldn't make it go away.

The light glowed blue and filled the space of the dungeon. It illuminated the entirety of the cell across from his and the broad figure coming from the door. Raidan shook his hand and the light wobbled, brightening. He crossed his arms, tucking his hands in.

The man entering looked to be in his late fifties or so and had light hair that matched Ilan's. His eyes were the same green eyes as Ilan's, and as if that weren't enough to verify his identity, the Valca Order emblem of the V overlapping the O, encompassed by large elk horns curled up around the lettering was emblazoned front and centre on his costly garb. This was Kingston Valca, the man feared by all in Kartha.

He looked at the light, then scowled at Raidan. Veins protruded from his neck. "What is that?" he asked, pointing.

Raidan didn't answer. He didn't have an answer.

"Make it stop," Kingston said.

The light seemed to pulse with the rhythm of Raidan's rushed heartbeats.

"You deaf, boy? I said put it out!"

"I—I don't know how."

"*I—I don't know how,*" Kingston mocked. "Figure it out, or I'll have you taken from here and flogged in the square."

Raidan untucked his hand and moved it in a sweeping motion. The light shifted sideways, away from Kingston. That didn't work. Kingston eyed him through narrow slits. He had to get control of the light.

"Go out," he told it. It was the only thing he could think to do in his panicked state, but it worked. The light disappeared. His and Kingston's shadows were cast upon the walls by the torch outside Raidan's cell, the only remaining light in the room.

His victory was snuffed out when Kingston put his face up to the bars. "Do anything like that again and you can be certain I'll make your death painful and slow." He backed up and brushed off his shoulders. "I guess I don't need to ask if you're the one my son has taken an interest in. That little display was answer enough."

At the mention of his son, a boldness rose inside Raidan. "Where is my son?" he asked. "My baby, he was—"

"I don't know anything about your son." Kingston waved a hand. "I just wanted to see who's been distracting Ilan from his work."

Raidan's boldness withered. Kingston had no idea where Cassian was, which meant he was likely still at the cottage with Ilan's men and Beiron. His shoulders drooped. "What do you want?"

"What do I want?" Kingston threw his hands up with a shrug. "Well, how nice of you to ask." He started to pace. "What I want is for my son to get over this foolish obsession of his and to get on with his responsibilities as future ruler. I want him to realize what power really is and to stop chasing after magic and all its silly tricks. Magic is not power; it's trickery, sleight of hand, deception. I want—"

"What does this have to do with me?" Raidan cut him off, weary of being dragged from one danger to the next.

Kingston tightened his lips to a thin line. He tilted his head at Raidan, a warning, Raidan gathered, not to interrupt him again.

"Everything," Kingston said. "If you're what Ilan wants, he'll come for you. When he does, I'll have my son back under control."

"I'm not what Ilan wants," Raidan said.

Kingston puffed out his chest. "Well, I suppose we'll find out."

Raidan had no doubt Ilan would show up if he'd heard he was being held there by his father. "Please, I need to find my son."

"Your son is not my problem. You are. Ilan should already have received the message that you're here. I should think he's on his way as we speak."

"What happens when—if he comes?" Raidan asked.

"I'm going to lock him up to keep him out of my way. He let my prisoner go after he'd been here for an entire century, if you believe it. He's been too caught up in this obsession of his, and I can't have him in my way while I march my army on Litlen. I intend to finish what my grandfather started. I'll kill Beiron and destroy everything magic and Elderace—everything Ilan has fixated his mind on and neglected his other duties for, starting with you."

Sweat beaded on Raidan's forehead. He hoped he misunderstood. "With me?"

"If he's distracted by it, it goes. Unfortunate for you, of course, but I must do what's right for clearing his head of this nonsense. I'm helping him see what's right in front of him: the power he already has at his fingertips."

The room spun, and Raidan's hands shook. Not just his hands, his legs too. His knees wobbled.

Kingston turned to go. He'd made his plan clear. Now he was probably going to prepare an army for war. He just needed to wait for Ilan to get there so he could return, kill Raidan, and begin his liquidation of the Elderace. "I'll be back with Ilan," Kingston said, then added "I'll make it quick."

Referring to his death as quick was not a comfort.

At the door, Kingston turned. "I'll have someone bring you something to eat in the meantime." He opened the heavy door and left.

How thoughtful. He was going to feed him before he executed him.

With Kingston gone, Raidan was left with nothing but his thoughts. His mouth was dry, and he couldn't breathe. He was fully sweating now, and the room around him spun.

Everything that'd happened since he'd made the choice to follow Dimitri to the cave had led to disaster. Tears fell silently down his cheeks. The more he allowed himself to wallow in self-pity, the more hopeless everything seemed. His cries turned to sobs and then became anguish.

He was going to die here. Cass would be without a father; Ida, without her husband . . . if she was even still alive. Raidan lay curled on the ground, head pounding and body aching. Thoughts of Ida and Cassian filled him. He clung to their images.

This couldn't be it. He still had time. Although he felt numb, he forced himself onto his knees. He looked at his hands for a long time. Telling the light to go out had made it go out. If he'd been able to do that, perhaps he could do it again.

Thinking of magic made something harden in the pit of his stomach. He closed his eyes and thought of Ida and Cassian again. They needed him. If he died in this dungeon because he refused to use the tool at his disposal, he'd fail his family.

He opened his eyes. It wasn't as though he was accepting it. He'd only be using it temporarily. But if he was going to use magic to escape, he would need something more powerful than a little light. Something more dangerous. Something like fire.

Closing his eyes, he envisioned what he hoped to achieve. He opened his eyes, snapped his fingers, and spoke. "Fire."

There was a spark, but nothing more. He focused, taking slow, even breaths, and closed his eyes again. When he opened them, he had an odd sense of clarity. Within the darkness of the dungeon, determination rooted itself in his mind. He would get it right. With nothing but time until Ilan arrived, he would get it to work.

And then . . . then he'd be ready.

Chapter 44

She felt like she wasn't alone. In her old room, in her bed, Laila had fallen asleep, but the sense of being watched woke her up. She opened her eyes.

Beside the door, leaning casually against the wall with his arms crossed, was the frightening man from her dreams . . . watching her while she'd slept. He was exactly as she'd seen him in her visions, except he'd combed his hair and shaved.

She propped herself up onto an elbow to sit in a more upright position than the flat, side position she'd fallen asleep in. Afraid to move any more than that, unsure if this was real or another vision, she closed her gaping mouth and tried to slow her breathing to disguise her panic.

Beiron pushed off from the wall and grabbed the chair next to him. He dragged it over to the bed and straddled it. He leaned in close enough to her face that she could smell the scent of pine blended with some sweet fragrance of incense, something floral. He was so close she could taste his scent. She shifted away slightly, but for fear of looking away or being distracted, she didn't shift very far, and she still wasn't liking her position.

She swallowed past the lump in her throat and stared back at him, afraid to breathe.

"I'm going to need my book back," he said. "It doesn't belong to you."

How did he know she'd had it? How did he even find her here? "I don't have it," she told him truthfully.

He took a noisy breath. "Well, that's not good because that means someone else has it and can read it."

She tried to remember if there was any sensitive information from the book that Beiron might not want others to read, but she couldn't think right now.

"Who has it?" he asked.

No way was she going to tell him. "I don't know," she said, not caring if it sounded believable or not or if he knew she was lying.

He stood up, and she scrambled back on the bed. Her knees sank into the thin mattress, and she put her hands protectively in front of herself, ready to push him away if he came any closer. She didn't have a whole lot of places to move, and her new position wasn't much better than the last.

"Bring the book to me here tomorrow or the baby dies," he said. He walked out of her old room.

She waited until he was out of the room before calling out to him. "You would kill a baby?"

His footsteps halted. "If that's what it takes."

She got to her feet and ran out of the bedroom. Maintaining her distance from him, she stood at the end of the hall, facing him at the front door. "You're a monster," she said. Maybe it wasn't so wise to provoke him, but how could he hurt an innocent child?

The corner of his mouth curled up. "I've been called worse." He exited the house.

Laila stood there, breathing hard, unsure what to do.

She couldn't go back to the mines. Not now. Not after she'd just gotten free from that place. If Royl found out, he'd have her guarded again and then she'd never get out. And how was she supposed to get the book from Vix, assuming he even had it? And if he did, was it in his private room, or did he have another hiding place?

But what of Ida's baby? If things went wrong, Beiron would kill him. Whether or not Laila believed he'd do such a thing was irrelevant. If he said he would, she had to believe he wasn't bluffing. She'd told Ida she would help. Getting her baby killed was not helping. But now she had the chance to do *something*.

An idea struck her and she ran outside after Beiron. "Wait!" she called.

He stopped in the middle of the road and turned. It was nearly midday now, and the warmth of the sun had a calming effect on her. She forced a courage into her steps. She was only partially mindful of the fact that scouts could be out anywhere and might spot them. That might not be such a bad thing.

She stopped when she was close enough that she didn't have to raise her voice but far enough to be out of his reach—unlike moments ago, when their noses were nearly touching.

"A trade," she said. "The book for the baby." She hoped he wouldn't reject the idea. Beiron stepped closer to her, closing the gap until they were an arm's length away from each other. Laila planted her feet.

He looked her over—admirably? She wasn't sure. She didn't want to even begin to try and understand the mind of Beiron and unravel his thoughts.

"All right," he said. "Bring the book to the Abberbrat by tonight. Come alone and you've got a deal."

What was it about the book that he wanted badly enough to relinquish the baby? From what Laila understood, Ida's son gave Beiron a hold over the Guardian of the Weldafire Stone. His agreeable manner made her wonder if she should return the book after all. But, of course she was going to. A baby's life was at stake.

She considered what it meant to agree to Beiron's arrangement. She'd have to find the book without getting caught. Then she'd have to sneak away with it and somehow get out of the mines *again*, unseen, to meet with Beiron—alone and on purpose. All the while, he would still walk free after the deal was done and her people wouldn't be able to catch him in a trap. To do as he asked was not going to be simple.

"Give me three days," she said. "You bring the baby to me unharmed and allow me to return him to his mother. Those are my terms."

"You have until tomorrow afternoon."

Laila's mind raced. That could be cutting things too close. But what choice did she have? He could just as easily walk away and hold to his threat to kill the baby. She slowly nodded. "Okay," she said. "Tomorrow afternoon then."

He produced a knife from his pocket and she stepped back. He gave her that crooked smile again. "You've read the book, haven't you? I take it you know how this works?" He cut the knife into his palm.

Laila's breath caught. It was a deal sealed by magic. She'd read about it and understood what making this kind of deal could mean. Beiron's hand showed a thin red line of his blood.

"That kind of magic is forbidden," she said. The instant she'd said it, she wished she could take it back. Of course, he knew it was forbidden, but what did he care?

"Is that a problem for you?" Beiron offered her the knife.

She hesitated. To go forward with this kind of deal and not follow through would cost her, her life. Was she ready to make that kind of commitment? So many things could go wrong.

"Come alone tomorrow afternoon to the Abberbrat," Beiron clarified. "Bring the book. I'll bring the baby—unharmed—and you can go on your way and return him to his family."

Laila didn't see any other way to save Ida's baby. Beiron's eyes looked hollow and . . . deep. She took the knife from him and cut her palm. He reached out to her, and slowly, she extended her arm and shook his hand, agreeing to the arrangement. Her magic surged within her and she felt its power, its strength.

He let go of her and backed away quickly, looking her up and down like she'd given him a shock. She met his gaze and swallowed hard. Beiron snatched his knife back, then turned on his heel and walked away.

"Come alone," he said over his shoulder. "Don't forget that's part of our deal."

Laila looked at the black streak across her palm where she'd cut. Like she needed reminding.

Chapter 45

Laila did not take the main-way back into the mines like she'd told Dynelle she would. At the time she'd said it, she had no intentions of returning at all, at least not without a baby in her arms.

Clouds drifted across the sky, growing heavy. It looked like rain, and here she was, about to retire to the mines and miss this fresh rainfall. The rain in Litlen during the cursed years was dirty and felt just as cursed as the land was. She'd been looking forward to an uncursed rain.

She stood for a long time at the Spry Lagoon entrance, watching the sky and the gathering clouds. Whatever way she returned to the mines, she was taking a risk getting caught sneaking in. Dynelle was likely to be off duty in the kitchen by now, and the next person on shift had probably already taken over. Whoever that may be, Laila couldn't be sure they'd not report her directly to the elders if she went back in through the trapdoor.

She could go to the western cliffs and make her way in from there, but that was dangerous and would take much longer. She only had until tomorrow afternoon. What was she thinking, making a deal with Beiron?

Her muscles tensed, and she held her arms around her stomach. It was like her body knew it was on borrowed time. She just had to get this over with.

Crouching down to clear the opening of the burrow-like tunnel entrance, she shuffled through and stood to her full height inside. She summoned her blue light with her magic and headed toward the halls of the mines. As she walked slowly through the narrow tunnels—sometimes ducking to avoid hitting her head on the ceiling—she thought about whom Royl might have assigned to guard the barricaded access point. It was possible he'd just asked the men who were on sentry duty to swap locations from one access to another. Of the five who rotated shifts, they all knew her to frequently come and go. She always tried to avoid running into Chandler; he was a stickler for the rules. He'd made it his personal goal to stop her and reported her every attempt to leave. Knowing Royl, that was exactly who she'd have to deal with coming back.

She extinguished her light as she rounded the last bend. Ahead were the barricade and the halls adorned with torches and artwork. Creeping along the side of the tunnel wall, Laila arrived at the three horizontal planks nailed across the opening. No one was visibly guarding it. She peered out, looking from left to right. Still no one. She ducked between two of the planks and stood there for a moment, holding her breath, hoping this wasn't a trap.

Something was not right. Where was the guard who was meant to be watching the access point?

With cautious steps, she walked down the hall to the right, heading toward her room. These halls were less busy, so it wasn't surprising to find them vacant. She checked inside her room and found it empty, then made her way toward the assembly chamber. Halfway there, and still no one crossed her path. Where was everyone?

Then she heard Vix. His voice carried from the assembly chamber. Laila slowed her pace as she neared the filled room. What appeared to be the entire community of her people was gathered within. The torches at the front were lit; the two blazing fires illuminated the room. Vix held everyone's attention. Darrin, Zulu, Maire, and Royl stood at the front with him, facing the group. Laila looked around. Three of the sentries were accounted for. Bailey and Chandler were the only two she didn't see. But she supposed someone had to keep an eye on the main-way.

She searched for Dimitri and Ida. The door to the private room was closed, and she didn't see them anywhere. They must still have been inside.

"We have learned a few things of importance," Vix said in his usual drone as he addressed the crowd. "First, that Litlen's revival is connected somehow to the Weldafire Stone."

Faces of those nearest Laila expressed shock and surprise. Whispers swept around the room. It was not unusual for these meetings to be void of interruption. It seemed this meeting was no exception.

"How?" a man from across the room called out, loud enough to be heard. Laila couldn't see who it was. "I thought the delegates were gone?"

Vix bowed his head. "Yes, we are getting to the bottom of it all. We have asked you to gather here so we may discuss what lies ahead for our people."

Apparently, what lay ahead was more conversation about the changes and less doing something about it. Vix droned on. That seemed to be all anyone wanted to do. Talk about what was happening. How were they not grasping the importance of recent events? How were the people not demanding they take a stand and step out into the light already? Everyone was so behind on the things happening around them. Laila didn't have time for this.

Royl caught her eye and straightened. He turned to Zulu beside him and whispered something in his ear, then left his place at the front to come toward her.

She wasn't sure she could hide her secret from him. It was easy enough to fool others, but Royl always knew when she was keeping something from him. She would have to push him away.

Folding her arms to hide her shaking hands, she set her jaw and refused to meet his eye as he came closer. When he made it over to her,

229

he placed a hand on her back and guided her away from the crowd. They stood just outside the assembly chamber, hidden in shadow.

"Where were you?" he said. "I looked everywhere for you, and then when you didn't show up on time for the meeting, I was starting to think you took off again, but no one saw you go."

So, he was checking up on her. While Laila was still angry with him, she had too much on her mind to be concerned about his overbearing protectiveness. For now, and for the sake of getting him off her case, she acted like she normally would have—indignant.

"I was sleeping," she snapped.

"Where? I checked your room."

"Does it matter? I'm here now, aren't I?" She hated the way his eyes went sad at her harsh tone. There was so much going on that she couldn't tell him. Her carefully guarded emotions were seeping through the cracks. Tears welled in her eyes, and she looked away so he wouldn't see.

"Laila." Royl reached for her shoulders. "*Tsarioc.*"

She stepped back and shrugged his hands off. His sudden gentleness wasn't helping her stay strong. Her walls were about to come crashing down. Already her cheeks were wet with what she feared was only the beginning of what was to come if she didn't get a grip. "Leave me alone, Royl." She wiped her face.

He opened his arms for an embrace and she backed away.

"Don't!" she said, putting a warning finger up. "Just leave me alone. I don't want to talk to you right now."

She'd hurt him. She knew she had.

A new batch of tears was near breaking point. She took a deep breath to hold it back. Her resolve set, she shook her head. "I'm going back to my room. I need to be away from you right now."

In truth, it wasn't him she needed to be away from; it was these stupid mines. And every passing minute without Beiron's book brought her that much closer to death. She needed to get a move on. Time was running out.

She walked away from Royl, listening for his footsteps as she went. Would he follow her?

With everyone preoccupied in the meeting, this was her chance to sneak away to search Vix's room. It was also possible the book was in the private meeting room where Dimitri and Ida were being guarded. If that were so, she'd have to find a way to get in there again and search the room without drawing attention to herself.

No footsteps followed in pursuit, and she allowed herself to relax a little. With her goal set, she picked up her pace, made a brief stop in her room to collect her bag, then jogged through the tunnels toward the main-way. Vix's room was straight ahead from there, at the very end of a dead-end hall. Having no good excuse to be down that way, she'd have to hurry before the meeting ended. She didn't want to get caught lingering.

She arrived at the dead-end and entered the last room. It was dark inside.

"*Vint*," she whispered, and her glowing blue light hovered over her hand. Scanning the room, she searched in the obvious places first.

Vix's room was a little bigger than her own, and he didn't share it with anyone. She supposed being the senior elder had its perks. The single bed at the far end was neatly made, and the desk and chair were left tidy. The book, if it was in here, hadn't been left out in the open. She was going to have to do a deeper search. But where to start?

She closed her eyes. Maybe she could sense the book. She opened her eyes—what a strange thought?

She closed them again. It was worth a shot.

The atmosphere around her was still and quiet. She listened, feeling as if she could taste the dust floating in the air. She breathed it in, allowing her senses to open up.

The smell. She could smell its musty leather. But now something else mingled with its scent. It smelled like Beiron. Like pine and sweet incense. Had that always been there?

She opened her eyes and turned her attention to the bed. It felt strange to feel a book's presence.

She approached the bed and lifted the flimsy mattress. Tucked underneath was the book. She recognized the familiar faded black leather, engraved initials, and torn edges. She'd had it for so many years that it felt like it belonged to her.

Picking it up, she stuck it in her bag and patted the blanket on the bed down to hide her presence. She had what she needed, and now it was time to go.

She paused to listen for sounds in the hall. Hearing no one, she left and walked back toward her own room. The closer she got, the louder the noise from the assembly chamber grew. It sounded like the whole crowd of people had erupted into chatter at once. Zulu's low, booming baritone voice carried over everyone else's, quieting them all.

Laila turned left and had just passed her room when Royl called out behind her. "Laila, wait up!"

She turned. He caught up and looked to his left at the door to her room, the one she'd just passed. Ahead were a few other rooms and the access point into the tunnels under Litlen—and her exit.

His eyes narrowed at her bag. No believable lie occurred to her. She was in an impossible situation. There was no time to explain the seriousness of a deal sealed in magic, nor to get into a discussion about dabbling in forbidden blood magic with a wanted traitor.

Instinct took over. Laila turned and ran. The sound of blood rushing in her ears and her fear at being caught blocked out Royl's shouting. He called her name and ran after her.

Tears burned in Laila's eyes as she willed her legs to go faster. She'd gotten a bit of a head start, but was it enough? She was almost at the access point. If she could just get through, she could lose him in the tunnels. No one knew their way around in there like she did.

Royl stopped his pursuit. "Laila, stop! Wait." He sounded like he could have kept going, but he didn't. "I don't want to chase you, Laila!"

At the three planks of wood barricaded across the darkened tunnel, Laila paused and looked back. Royl stayed where he was.

"Please don't go," he said. "Don't leave. I'll send someone with you. Just . . . don't go out there alone. Please."

She couldn't stop now. And there was no time to stand around waiting for an escort—an escort that went against the rules of her deal with Beiron. She let out a sob and shook her head. "I can't, Royl. But I'll be back. I promise. And then everything will be okay."

Royl stood around ten feet away. Even from there, Laila could see in his eyes that he had questions. He was crying now too, and it was that much harder for Laila to leave.

"Then I'm coming with you," he said. He took a step forward, and Laila put a hand out to stop him.

"No! Not this time. You can't."

He looked at her, his lips slightly parted. "What aren't you telling me? Whatever it is, Laila, we can work this out."

Laila pulled herself together. "I'll tell you everything when I return. You just have to trust me."

Royl took another step closer. Laila knew what he was up to. He was trying to distract her so he could get close enough to stop her. That was her cue to go.

Years of slipping through the planks of wood across the passage made it easy to glide through quickly. She did so and Royl threw caution to the wind and ran to close the gap between them. Laila darted farther into the tunnels, creating more distance. The darkness swallowed her, and she didn't dare light the way now.

"Laila, wait!" Royl stood at the access point on the other side of the planks.

"I'm done waiting!" she called back to him. "You don't have to worry about me, Royl. I'll be all right." She hoped.

She ran into the darkness and kept running, past the first bend, still with no light. She couldn't even see her hand in front of her face, but

233

that didn't matter. Each step she took was one made with confidence. This was a place she knew well.

Royl wouldn't try and follow her here. He'd get lost for sure. Though now she had to be wary of anyone waiting for her on the outside. Royl was probably already on his way to send someone out to get her.

With that thought, Laila chose not to turn toward the exit at the Spry Lagoon. She'd gone around enough bends and turned enough corners that she finally felt it was safe to make a light. These tunnels went everywhere under Litlen. In her head, she imagined the web of paths. One would take her out of the tunnels near the south end of the city, through a cave at the waterfall where that section of the River Lin ended. From there, she'd go the remainder of the way aboveground to make the exchange with Beiron. Alone.

She took a shaky breath. What if something went wrong? What if Beiron was using her for some evil scheme? That he agreed to hand over the baby seemed too easy.

Laila knew everything written in his book—every plant, every word, every detail and concoction that had been recorded. If she'd somehow missed something, she wanted to know.

Her mother's words came to mind. *Don't let your curiosity lead you astray.* Freya said it to her often. Laila was beginning to grasp its meaning.

How far was she willing to go all for the sake of knowing?

Chapter 46

THE ABBERBRAT'S THIN WISPY BRANCHES SWUNG PEACEFULLY, THE exact opposite of the way Laila felt as she arrived at the meeting point, in the middle of Litlen city. Beiron had not arrived yet, but that was no surprise. The sun had just set on the same day they'd agreed to meet. Her fears about not making it on time were put to rest, but that didn't ease her other anxieties.

So many things could go wrong with this meeting. She didn't know what to expect from Beiron. But what she did know of him was not good.

Laila stood with her back to the trunk. She leaned against it and folded her arms. Closing her eyes, she tried not to think about the what-ifs.

The branches of the Abberbrat swung soundlessly in the light wind, and the mahtuhvv gave off its illuminating glow in the night, looking like fire-lit embers. By now she expected Royl would have a whole search party out looking for her. If Beiron didn't hurry up, this meeting might not happen at all. Having arrived so early, she'd likely be waiting all night for him.

Her restless mind kept her from being at ease. Her thoughts wandered to the book in her bag and all that it contained. She opened her eyes and decided to take one last look at it before handing it over. Retrieving it from her bag, she opened it to an entry Beiron had marked about the use of blood magic. Someone called Gilia was mentioned, who supposedly was gifted in using that particular kind of magic. It was noted that she could carry her peace into others who were suffering turmoil.

Laila could use magic like that right about now. She read from the place in the book:

Her mind, body, and soul worked unanimously to draw power from her very being, as though she herself were one of the elements.

Put that way, it didn't sound so bad. The way the elders spoke of blood magic, it was like an evil that corrupted the soul.

The sound of a baby's playful cooing startled Laila. She closed the book and looked up. Beiron walked toward her, carrying the baby in one arm. She'd have expected Ida's son to be loud and angry at having been separated from his mother for so long. Yet there he was, smiling at the most dangerous man known to her people.

Beiron stopped directly in front of her, close enough to hand Ida's son over to her, which he looked in no hurry to do. Cassian—as she recalled Ida or Dimitri had called him—seemed quite content with Beiron. His brown eyes were just like Dimitri's. And from the brief glimpse she'd gotten of the father, she recalled that he too had the same chestnut-coloured eyes.

"Thought you said you'd need three days," Beiron said.

Laila looked away from the baby to meet Beiron's eye. "Things went more smoothly than I anticipated."

"You have my book?" He gestured with his eyes at the book in her hands.

Laila gripped it tight, knowing this would be the last time she'd hold it. After a moment, she offered it to him. He was gentle as he took it from her, then skimmed through a few pages.

"Who is T. C.?" Laila asked.

Beiron looked her over like she was some curious object. She didn't know if he'd answer her question. He stuck the book in his waistband at the back of his pants and relaxed his shoulders. "Terrin Cailt. My father."

It was hard to believe that someone with a reputation like Beiron ever had a father or a mother. Prior to seeing him in her dreams, she'd always imagined him as some sort of beast, emerging from the soil in a dark place on a terrible stormy night, foreboding a darker time to come.

"That sounds so normal," she said without realizing she'd spoken it aloud.

He chuckled. "It surprises you?"

Laila looked away. This conversation was getting a little too friendly. She shook her head. "No, I just . . ." She trailed off. They were getting off track.

Cassian held his arms up, trying to reach Beiron's face with his chubby fingers. Beiron tilted his chin away, maintaining eye contact with Laila. He didn't seem ready to hand the baby over to her yet. And as much as she wanted to, she couldn't just take him. The way the deal worked, she had to wait until Beiron said so. Taking him before then would count as a cheat or breaking the rules, thus resulting in her loss. Loss of life, that was.

She shifted on her feet, his gaze making her uncomfortable.

"You have a name, girl? Or do I just call you *voroc*?"

Little thief was not a nickname she wanted. "My name is Laila, and I'm not a thief." She pointed at the book. "The—" Pain erupted in her chest, and she lurched back. Something was wrong.

Ahead of her—behind Beiron—three figures in the night moved about. Laila was only partially aware of Cassian's crying. Manic laughter came from behind Beiron.

Beiron swivelled his head about, taking in the figures, then looked at Laila's chest, which radiated with pain. She followed his gaze. The handle of a dagger protruded from her chest. Her breath stuttered.

Her chest burned and she cried out. She raised her hand to touch the handle and the pain intensified at her touch. A little more to the left, and the blade might have hit her heart.

In the back of her mind, she registered that one of those figures had thrown the dagger. They seemed far away, but Laila couldn't be sure.

She was having a hard time making sense of reality. It hurt to breathe, and her vision blurred.

She couldn't bring herself to remove the dagger. She wobbled and fell to her knees. Warm liquid oozed from where the dagger had buried itself into her. She was going to die here.

Fearing she might drive the dagger further into her chest if she fell forward, she made a conscious decision to fall backward. She let herself go and anticipated the impact of her body hitting the ground.

The impact never came. Beiron caught her fall and placed her down gently. *Why would he do that?*

"Don't die on me, Laila," Beiron said. "We're not done yet." He disappeared from her sight.

Everything hurt, and her focus was fading fast. She closed her eyes to make the world stop spinning. From somewhere beyond the sound of the baby's screams—which felt like they were right in her ear—she could hear grunting. Like people were wrestling. Then came a disgusting gurgling. The choking sound that followed was unmistakable as someone dying. Something thudded to the ground—a body, Laila assumed from her haze. And she was next.

It felt like an eternity, lying there in agony. The noises around her were muffled, and all she could hear now was the blood pumping through her ears, slowing down with every weakened beat of her heart.

Her mind gravitated to Royl. She'd left in such a hurry and hadn't properly said goodbye. Now it was too late. She would never see him again. Tears burned on her skin as they slid down her face and fell into her ear.

The last thing she heard, right before her world went dark, was a man letting out a painful howl. And then she heard nothing.

Chapter 47

HER EARS WERE RINGING. LAILA SQUEEZED HER ALREADY CLOSED EYES tight to try and tune out the sound. She was lying down, and through her eyelids, she could tell it was going to be bright if she were to open her eyes. The ringing changed to more of a buzzing. She breathed in the earthy scent of grass.

Grass? Turning her head to the side, she opened her eyes and used her arm to shield them from the sun. Tall grass tickled her face. She sat upright and winced.

Her hand went to her chest, where the sharp pain brought back the memory of what had happened. A quick glance down at herself verified there was no dagger there, but the shirt she wore was not her own and was much too big for her.

Cassian sat in the grass next to her, his blanket tossed aside. The boy's face and fingers were covered with the purple-green colour of the mahtuhvv, the fruit of the Abberbrat. Cassian had the mahtuhvv in one hand and was sucking on the soft, round fruit while using his other hand to pull blades of grass from the ground. He snatched a handful of some and waved it up and down.

Beiron sat in the grass on the other side of Cassian. Facing the lake before them, he had his knees drawn up, his elbows resting upon them, and was reading from his book. She felt like she'd interrupted a picnic.

Laila took in the rest of her surroundings: the dark evergreens encircling the lake; the flow of water coming down from the mountain run-off and into the lake. She knew this place.

"Why are we at Azure Lake?" she asked. Her voice was hoarse, and she cleared her throat. "How did we get here?"

At her words, Cassian stopped waving his hand with the grass in it. She met his chestnut gaze and kept her eyes on his until he was done looking at her. He went back to sucking the mahtuhvv and waving the grass in his hands.

"If I didn't bring you here, you'd be dead," Beiron said, eyes on the book. "It would have been better if I were able to access the Pool of Sovereignty. Then there'd have been no mark left at all."

Laila peered back down at her aching chest. Curiosity got the better of her, and she pulled the collar of the loose garment away from her neck to examine the injury. Underneath the navy shirt, the bodice of her dress was torn where the dagger had pierced her. The fabric had been cut further for the wound to be treated, and there was dried blood everywhere. How was she not dead?

The wound was sore and healed over, looking at least a day or two old already. She clutched the collar of the shirt and tucked it in close to her neck, holding her arm across her chest. How had she survived?

"Why did you save me?" she asked.

Beiron's head barely moved, but his eyes found hers. Then he shifted his attention to the book. "Our deal was incomplete. If you died before my part was through, where would that have left me?"

Cassian made playful sounds, experimenting with his voice as he waved another handful of grass. All the while, he clutched the mahtuhvv and made a sticky mess up his sleeve. He went to take a bite from the fruit, but he ate from the wrong hand and dribbled grass out through puckered lips.

"What happened to the people who did this?" Laila asked. "Who were they? Why did they try to kill me?"

"They were there for me. Madmen Kingston Valca hired. I took care of them."

So, Beiron wasn't working with the Valca Order? "What does that mean?" she asked. "Will they be back?"

Beiron shook his head. He turned his face toward her. In the daylight, she could see beneath the darkness in his eyes, a speck of light blue. "You were in the Madx home," he stated. He spoke to her as if they were old friends, catching up after a long time away.

The fact that he knew her family name made her uneasy. He'd never struck her as a neighbourly sort of person. "I was," she said. "How did you know I'd be there?"

"You're Freya's daughter," he said, as if that were an answer—or perhaps a question. Laila gave a slight nod.

Beiron put the book down beside him and looked out at the lake. "You've got quite the search party out looking for you," he said. "Your brother's doing, I presume?"

Laila glanced around them as if Royl might be there somewhere, hiding among the trees. He was not, but she was wary now. Had Beiron tricked her, bringing her there to ambush the warriors who sought to arrest him? "What do you know about my brother?" she asked.

Again, he disregarded her question. "Did you tell him about our arrangement?"

Laila adjusted the way she was sitting, preparing to stand up at a moment's notice. She didn't know where this was going, but she wanted to be ready to get away from Beiron if she felt the need. "I didn't tell anyone," she said.

"Good. Because that wasn't part of our deal." His gaze swept from her to Cassian. "And what about your father?"

"What about him?" Laila stood. Cassian took notice of her. He rubbed his eyes and yawned. She hoped he'd be all right during the journey back to the mines. Caring for babies was something she knew little about, but one thing she did know was that when it came to comforting them, mothers did it best. Somehow Beiron had managed to keep him happy. Laila almost thought to ask him how he did it. Any pointers for her long walk ahead would be beneficial. "We're wasting time. I only want the baby."

"You stole my book and read it," Beiron said. "You've gained some insight into who I am. I think it's only fair if I know something about you."

Laila shook her head. The book provided little insight into Beiron's character. The only item within that didn't pertain to the uses of plants and other concoctions—useful for far darker things than curing mild ailments—was the mention of Gilia, the woman with gifts in the use of blood magic. Only the one small section on a single page told of her amazing ability.

Whatever sensitive information the book contained about Beiron, Laila didn't know, but she didn't like being accused of thievery, yet again. "I didn't steal it," she said. "You were gone. I took a lot of things before The Order could destroy them. If anything, I saved your book from destruction. You have it back now anyway, so what does it matter who I am?" She looked at the sky. "Our time to finish the deal is nearly up. After this, you'll never see me again."

Beiron smiled. "Oh, I doubt that." He looked at Cassian, then checked the position of the sun. "We have time. Answer the question."

Cassian whinged and rubbed his eyes again. He needed Ida. Laila let her tense shoulders relax a little. It wasn't as if the information he was asking for was any secret. "He died," she told Beiron. "My father. Before I was born."

Beiron stared across the lake.

She'd expected more questions, but there were none. Beiron got to his feet and picked up Cassian. He brought him over to Laila and handed him to her. "You're free to return him to his mother," he said. "As promised."

Laila gathered the boy into her arms and took three steps away, unsure if Beiron would try something now that he'd relinquished the baby.

Beiron smiled his crooked smile. The gentleness in his eyes made her even more wary of him. "If I was going to hurt you, Laila, I would have done it when you were sleeping, before we ever made a deal."

She didn't know what to make of him. He was acting different from how she'd perceived him prior to their meeting.

Her hand tingled, and she glanced at it. The black mark in her palm where she'd made the cut to seal their deal had disappeared. The deal was done. At last. She let out a breath.

Cassian was light in her arms. He whimpered, and again, he rubbed his eyes and yawned. Laila adjusted him so he was propped up over her shoulder. She cringed when he kicked her chest and squirmed against her body. It took repositioning him so that he was lying back with his head cradled in her arms to make him stop kicking.

Beiron held Cassian's knitted blanket out, offering it to Laila. "Wrap him in this," he said. His behaviour was so unusual for his reputation, Laila didn't know if he was being sincere. She hesitated, then took it.

The material was soft and warm from the sun's rays. It was a beautiful blanket. She wrapped Cassian in it. He clutched a corner of it in his tiny hand and curled his body in toward her, already beginning to drift off to sleep.

Laila let out a breath of relief and smiled at him. His lips pouted, and his thin hair splayed across his forehead.

Beiron handed Laila a fresh mahtuhvv from his pocket. "You might need this too."

Again, Laila hesitated, then freed one of her hands and took the fruit. She had nowhere to put it, so she rested it on the baby's curled-up body.

"When you find Dimitri," Beiron said, "tell him I'll be seeing him." His tone indicated a threat—a jarring transition from his gentleness toward her.

"What do you want with him?" she asked. It was a weak question, and she knew it. It was obvious what Beiron was after. She didn't know much about the brothers, but she did know that their involvement

243

with the Elderace was stemmed from their connection to the Weldafire Stone. But what did Dimitri have to do with it? Wasn't it Ida's husband who was supposedly bound to the stone?

Beiron thrust his hands into his pockets. "You aren't naive, Laila. I think you already know the answer to that."

She wasted no time playing dumb. "I don't see how the stone is of any use to you. Your own book says you need delegates' blood to bind it. Or—unbind it, if that were even possible . . ." Was that possible?

"Let me worry about that," Beiron said. "Go. Your brother must be worried about you by now."

The reminder of the search party out looking for her didn't comfort her. To bring Ida her child, she would have to face punishment for her disobedience. . . . She wished she didn't have to go back at all. But the longer she stood around, the less time she had before Cassian would wake. And he'd been away from his mother for long enough.

She started walking away, then stopped and faced Beiron again. "Who's Gilia?" If this were to be the last time she saw him, she wanted to know about the mysterious woman from his book.

"What?" Beiron pulled his hands from his pockets. His posture stiffened.

"Gilia. Who is she?"

The gentleness in his face was gone, replaced with a cold, distant look. "She was my sister."

"Was?"

"She died. Long before the war."

He had a mother and father, and now a sister. Was it possible he had experienced love in his life?

"Were you close?"

Beiron looked at the ground, then narrowed his dark eyes at Laila for a minute before responding. "Yes," he said, then pressed his lips together.

His change in demeanour said enough. Laila wasn't about to push her luck and ask more.

Should she offer some word of comfort? Probably not. It wasn't her business, and she felt no sorrow for a man who had threatened to kill a baby. She turned and walked away without saying anything at all. The deal was done, and that was that.

Chapter 48

There was something to be said for the attention Ilan received upon his return to the streets of Valmain. As he held his head high and rode through the grounds, his onlookers regarded him with a mixture of awe and fear. Whatever this business of his father's was, he sought to get it over with.

At the Keep, he dismounted and was met by his father's assistant. Owen's ridiculous hair was slicked back. A few weeks ago, Ilan had spotted yellow in his otherwise brown hair. His attempts at matching Kingston's blond hair—though he'd tried to hide it—did not go unnoticed.

Inside the entryway, hallways branched out in three directions. A stairway led to the upper rooms. The long narrow hall to the left led to the dining hall and his father's study. Ilan stepped past Owen to go to his father. Owen was quick to jump in his way.

"Your father's not in his study," he said. "But he is expecting you."

Ilan wanted to smack the smug look off the man's face. "Yes, I gathered that, Owen. Where is he?"

"I'll inform him you're here. There's something he wants to show you." With a smirk, Owen left. The man seemed to think that because Kingston was his direct superior, he was not Ilan's inferior. He'd have to be reminded of his place. Not that Owen would last in his position.

None of them ever did. It was a matter of time before Kingston moved on to the next assistant. Kingston would likely have done the same thing with Ilan if he wasn't his only son. When things didn't go his way, he tended to eliminate the problem rather than deal with it directly.

Assistants could be disposed of. Ilan could not—something his father was well aware of. Ilan saw how his lack of control over his son drove him mad.

Nothing could stop Ilan from pursuing his passion. This desire to know more and immerse himself in the world of magic was rooted too deep in him. He'd come too far to be stopped now.

*

Kingston flung the sheet aside, revealing the first cannon. He had to see them for himself. Dust filled the air, visible in the rays of sunlight shining through the cracks of the wooden building. All three of the beastly weapons were stored in the large old shed, where things were brought to be forgotten.

Why had these been put aside—never to be gazed upon for all time? They were magnificent and powerful, devastating and glorious.

The anticipation of rolling these beauties out made Kingston's stomach flutter. Their use may be unnecessary in ridding the country of any remaining Elderace, but they sent a clear message: his power was not to be challenged.

The door creaked on its hinge, drawing Kingston's attention. Owen peered around the door, eyes searching through the mess of broken and rusting things.

"What do you want?" Kingston demanded. "I'm busy."

"It's Ilan. He's here."

Kingston stroked the cannon's cast iron surface and grinned. Everything was going according to plan.

"Excellent." His eyes met Owen's and his grin widened. "It's time for an execution."

The clang of the dungeon door made Raidan jump to his feet. He stood with his back against the wall, away from the cell door.

The bulky form of Kingston entered from the other room. Two guards flanked him, followed by Ilan and the two guards from the next room over. Ilan stepped out of his father's shadow and came into Raidan's view.

Ilan was here, which meant Kingston could carry out the next step of his plan. Raidan's heart raced. He wasn't ready. Despair threatened to pull him down again, but he wouldn't let it take him.

Raidan didn't recognize the two guards who'd first entered with Kingston. All six men that entered wore the tan leather Valca Order armour, complete with a sword and knife at the waist. Kingston's personal guards unlocked Raidan's cell and joined him inside. One was almost too fat to fit through the threshold. The other's malicious smile revealed a gap where a tooth was missing. Were these to be the last faces he would see before leaving this world? As they came closer, Raidan backed up until he had no more room.

Ilan stepped forward and was stopped by the balding jailer. "Father, what is this? What's going on?" He glanced from Raidan to Kingston.

The two guards grabbed Raidan's arms. They dragged him away from the wall, fighting to make him go along as he struggled.

Kingston straightened his posture and stuck his nose out. "It's time for me to put an end to your obsessions," he said. "This man is guilty of possessing and using magic."

Ilan shoved the balding guard off him. The other jumped in to assist, restraining him from getting any closer to Raidan.

The guard with the missing tooth elbowed Raidan in the ribs. Raidan cried out as pain coursed through him. The rumble that followed did not deter the guards. They pulled him out of the cell and brought him face-to-face with Kingston.

Ilan surveyed the integrity of the walls. It seemed that he had taken notice of the tremor caused by Raidan's voice. Was he concerned that he might bring the whole dungeon down on them?

In the hall between the cells, the guards yanked Raidan's hands behind his back and secured them in iron cuffs. The few links of chain between his hands allowed him little give. Raidan's mouth was dry. He swallowed air and felt faint. Thinking it through was one thing, but pulling off an escape in this moment seemed impossible.

In the narrow space, Kingston drew his sword from his sheath. "This man will die by my sword, marking the beginning of the end," he said. "I will go from here and rid our land of all trace of the Elderace kind—something my grandfather should have finished properly in his time, but I must now see through to completion."

"Father, don't!" Ilan protested. The jailer's hands grasped him tighter. Ilan's face contorted in his effort to push past them. He looked to Raidan. "Use your magic!"

Raidan tugged on the cuffs. What good were his hands when they were behind his back?

Kingston raised his eyebrows at Raidan. "Ha! That little light display?" he exclaimed. "That won't save you from what's coming."

"Probably not," Raidan said. He mustered the courage to say more. "But this might." He snapped his fingers and shouted, "Fire!" sounding ridiculous to his own ears. But it worked. The heat of a flame hovered above his hand.

The fat guard jumped back, and the gap-toothed guard whistled. "Whoa! Neat trick," he said.

Raidan had hoped for more. Although the fire burned brighter than the few sparks he'd produced earlier, he needed his shouting to create a reaction powerful enough to break the chains. He pulled his hands, trying to snap the links. Panic swelled in him. He couldn't catch his breath.

Kingston grinned and tutted. "I told you not to try anything like that again. You see, this is exactly why we're here. You people just don't get it. No one opposes me." He nodded at his guards.

The fat guard snuffed out Raidan's fire with a pat to the hand. He kicked Raidan in the back of the leg and Raidan fell onto his knees. The two guards held him down by his shoulders.

Kingston looked at Ilan. "It's over. This ends now." He turned back to Raidan with determination in his eyes.

Raidan couldn't tear his gaze from the sword. His whole body shook. His mind raced to think of something new to try, but his time to act was running out.

"Raidan!" Ilan said. He tried to shove past the jailers again. "Raidan, this doesn't have to be the end!" His voice rose. "I've seen what you can do! You don't have to die here. Think of your son!"

Raidan snapped his gaze to Ilan. "I am thinking of my son!"

The room shook, and Kingston and the guards glanced around. Ilan tilted his head, giving Raidan the slightest nod.

Raidan scowled at Ilan. "I'm only here because of *you*!" He spat that last word. "My family is missing because of *you*!"

The rumble around them grew.

"Where did you take them?" Raidan demanded. "Where are my wife and—"

"Enough!" Kingston shouted. He eyed the ceiling as dust fell. "It's over! No more Elderace, no more magic."

He drew his sword back, ready to drive it through Raidan's heart.

Chapter 49

THE BUILD-UP OF TENSION IN RAIDAN INTENSIFIED. IT WAS TOO MUCH to hold back. Needing release, he screamed and pulled his hands outward. The room shook. The cuff's chain broke, freeing his hands.

The force that emanated from his body threw Kingston back, along with Ilan and all four guards. Kingston's sword clattered to the ground.

Raidan's screaming stopped, and the shaking ceased. The dust that fell from the ceiling settled. Still on his knees in the narrow hall, Raidan breathed hard. The pure energy that surged through his veins was exhilarating. If not for the imminent threat of dying, he might have almost enjoyed the feeling of power within.

Two of the guards were sprawled against the bars of either cell. Kingston had landed on his back in front of Raidan, unconscious. The jailers and Ilan lay in the darkened space near the door.

Raidan wasted no time. He stood, lunged for Kingston's sword, and dove straight for Ilan. That burst of magic may have been an accident, but he'd use it. He grabbed Ilan by the collar of his tunic and raised him to his feet, pushing him against the closed door. The back of Ilan's head banged against it. Raidan pushed his weight against Ilan's. He held the edge of the blade against his opponent's throat.

"Where is my son?" he screamed.

Ilan did not struggle. He remained perfectly still and eyed the long, sharp edge of the blade. He looked over Raidan's shoulder at the dungeon and the damage he'd done.

Raidan had little time. The others would get up any second, angrier than ever at his outburst. "Tell me where you took him!"

Ilan shook his head. The movement was small so as not to cut himself on the sword. "I'll take you to him."

"No. Tell me. Where. Is he?" Raidan pressed the blade into Ilan's skin. "Tell me where he is!" he screamed. More rumbling. Raidan ignored it. The whole place could come down and he didn't care.

The cuffs were still locked around both of his wrists, and the few links of chain dangled down as he gripped the sword with white knuckles. It felt awkward in his hand, but he'd reached the point of desperation.

Ilan winced. "I'm not telling you. You need me. I know where he is and can take you to him."

Enraged, Raidan pulled him away from the door just so he could throw him back against it. "I'll kill you!" he screamed in his face again, then breathed heavily, attempting to regain control of himself.

Ilan glanced again over Raidan's shoulder. He raised his eyebrows. "Better make up your mind. We don't have a lot of time."

Raidan didn't look away. He didn't know what to do, and having to rush wasn't helping.

"I can take you to him," Ilan said. "Or you can stand around and wait until my father and his guards wake up to finish this. He will kill you. And then what good will you be to your son?"

Raidan seethed through clenched teeth. He didn't have much choice. Ilan was his last shot at finding Cass. He released Ilan, pushing him against the door again out of spite.

Behind him, the jailer with the burn scars on his face got to his feet. He straightened and looked from Ilan to Raidan.

Ilan drew his sword. "We need to go."

Raidan shoved Ilan out of his way so he could open the door. The jailer with the burnt face was coming closer, and the other was getting to his knees. Kingston grunted as he propped himself up on all fours. His arms faltered under his weight. He looked at them as Raidan opened the heavy door. "Stop them!" he shouted.

The door opened, and Raidan went first into the jailer's room. He held the door open for Ilan. The burnt jailer seized Ilan's arm and swung a fist at him, but Ilan spun and elbowed the man's face. The man wobbled, and Ilan landed a second blow to his chin, rendering him unconscious. Raidan held his breath and cringed as the man dropped.

Ilan crossed through the open doorway into the jailer's room. He grabbed Raidan's arm and pulled him backward so he could go first. Raidan opened his mouth to argue, but Ilan cut him off.

"We're under the Keep," he said. The door slammed. Ilan didn't flinch. "The guards up there won't think twice about me going from here. You, on the other hand . . ."

Raidan got the point. The door swung open and the bald guard entered the jailer's room. Raidan tripped over the small two-man table. He banged his thigh and stumbled, dropping Kingston's sword. Ilan pushed Raidan out of his way and raised his sword to block the man's assault. He swung a strike of his own, stepped into it, and removed a hand from the hilt of his sword to weave his arm between the jailer's. He extended his leg behind the guard's heel and tripped him. The jailer toppled backward, and his sword fell.

Ilan's actions were smooth and graceful. While the man was on the ground, Ilan used the hilt of his sword and hit him in the head, knocking him out. Raidan gawked. Ilan smacked his arm. "Let's go."

Raidan bent over the jailer's unconscious body. He patted down his sides, feeling for the keys to the cuffs that dug into his flesh.

Ilan pulled Raidan by the arm. "The others will be on us any second."

"I need the keys." Raidan raised his hand to show his cuffed wrist.

Ilan looked at the bald guard's supine body. He released a harsh breath while glancing at the closed door, then reached for the man's right pocket and retrieved a small key ring. He tugged Raidan, bringing him to his feet and led him into the dark passage toward the stairway.

Raidan ran to keep up, tripping over his own feet. "Give them to me."

"We don't have time."

Raidan dropped his hand, letting it go for now. He followed Ilan through the passageway, then up the stone spiral staircase. They exited the stairway. Ilan pushed Raidan in front of himself. He clasped Raidan's wrist.

"What are you doing?" Raidan threw his hands up.

"Go along with me," Ilan said. "You're my prisoner. No one will suspect anything."

A servant appeared in the corridor. Seeing Ilan, she averted her gaze as she strode past. Raidan relented, allowing Ilan to guide him out of the Keep.

The Valcas and their red: the carpet and the draping along the walls on either side of the Keep were all bold red, topped off with the orange-red glow of the fire-light from the hanging lamps. They made their way down one corridor into the next. As they exited the Keep from the foyer, a skinny man with brown, slicked-back hair stopped in front of them. The midday sun beat down from a cloudless sky, and Raidan squinted in the light.

"Ilan!" the man said. "What are you doing here?" He took notice of Raidan. "And with *him*? You're supposed to be—"

Ilan punched him in the face. The man fell to the ground and rubbed his chin. Ilan looked at Raidan with a wide grin. "I've wanted to do that for a long time," he said, then indicated they keep going.

Raidan didn't hesitate to go with him. For now.

The Keep was situated on the northern end of Valmain. The grounds were vast and spacious on a hilly green. Raidan jogged after Ilan down the slant of the hill toward the stable.

Ilan may not be Kingston, but he was still a Valca and had the backing of his own men. That in itself could present an obstacle, but for the moment, Raidan chose to go along. Did Ilan truly intend to take him to Cassian? Either way, they were far from being out of danger from Kingston and his men. It wouldn't be long before they emerged from the dungeon to spread the word about Raidan's escape and Ilan's treachery, if they hadn't already done so.

Raidan ran faster.

Chapter 50

"She's here!"

Laila approached the mines. She carried Cassian, his curious eyes taking in the new people.

It had been a long walk back. He'd woken, and she'd given him the mahtuhvv. He ate it while she walked, and after some squirming and fussing, she gave him his blanket and he'd calmed down again. He chatted his baby gibberish while she carried him.

Exhaustion wore down on her. Her injured chest ached, her feet were sore, and her shoulders were stiff from holding Cassian the whole way. Chandler's call was almost a welcome sound. Finally, she'd be able to rest. And she could wash up and change her clothes.

She descended the hill, where the entrance was ahead. Stefan came running toward Chandler from within.

"Find Royl and tell him we've got her," Chandler said.

Stefan's eyes fell on the baby. "Royl's not back yet from his search."

"Then go tell the elders!" Chandler barked. He'd taken it upon himself to command orders. Stefan was technically his superior and didn't have to put up with that, but he was too gentle to tell Chandler to back off. He turned and ran back the way he'd come.

Chandler blocked Laila's way, his arms folded across his chest. His wide stance took up the majority of the opening. "You're in a lot of trouble." He indicated the baby with a slight nod. "What's this?"

Laila rolled her eyes. "What's it look like?"

"I mean where did he come from?"

Laila was tired, hungry, and sore, and just wanted to get Cassian to Ida. He was staring with his big brown eyes at Chandler. "It doesn't matter," she said. "He's safe and can be returned to his mother."

Chandler rubbed his chin. "The mayanon woman?"

Laila didn't like the way he'd said it, like Ida was far beneath him. "Yes."

"They don't belong here."

"Neither do we," Laila countered.

Chandler snarled his lip. He stepped forward and extended an arm behind Laila to guide her inside. Laila didn't need to be shown in, but she entered the mine all the same.

Leaving behind the fresh outside air and the low sun, Laila went along, following Chandler. The cool inner air made her arms cold. Cassian squirmed and she gave him the blanket. He grasped its corner and raised it to his mouth.

Chandler lit his magic light. He gave it an upward push to stay above them and move ahead as they walked through the halls. The torches were lit in their sconces on the walls, adding orange hues to the vibrant blue of Chandler's light.

Bailey approached from ahead. Chandler gripped Laila's arm and stopped in the middle of the hall. "Bailey," Chandler said. "Take this baby to the mayan—"

"No," Laila said. "I have to be the one to do it. It has to be me."

Having made it a part of the arrangement with Beiron that she return Cassian to Ida, she didn't know what would happen if she handed him over to someone else. The black mark on her hand was gone and the deal was officially over, but would she risk her life over an assumption?

Chandler shook his head. "Bailey will do it. I'm taking you straight to containment, where you'll remain until further notice."

Laila's knees faltered. Her own weight seemed heavy. Containment's only purpose was to hold people who'd committed a crime worthy of punishment. She supposed her being taken there had been a long time coming.

Chandler nudged her arm. He nodded at Cassian and gestured to Bailey, who cocked his head and narrowed his eyes at Chandler. Unlike Stefan, it looked like Bailey was going to assert his higher position.

Laila held Cassian close to her chest. "Let me take him, Chandler, and I'll go with you to containment without a fight."

"You're going anyway," Chandler said. "This isn't up for discussion."

Bailey put his hands on his hips and shifted his weight. "You overstep, Chandler."

Laila interjected. "I can make things really difficult for you, Chandler."

Chandler smiled contemptuously. "Likewise, Laila."

"Royl is my brother. He can be upset with me, but I'll always be his blood. You, on the other hand, are not. If you ever want a promotion beyond sentry duty, it's him you'll have to appeal to."

Chandler's upper lip curled, and his hands clenched into fists. She almost thought he might grab hold of her anyway and drag her off to containment, fighting the whole way. His slits for eyes focused on her. In front of the two of them, Bailey stood tall with his hands on his hips, watching Chandler. Laila held Cassian closer, ignoring the ache in her chest from the increased pressure.

Chandler glanced at Bailey, then looked back at Laila. His shoulders dropped. "Why do you have to be like that, Laila?"

Laila relaxed her posture. "Because I don't appreciate being treated like a prisoner in the place I'm meant to feel safe in." Cassian wriggled in her arms, and she rocked him gently. His heavy eyelids closed and opened slowly.

Bailey touched his hand to Laila's elbow. "You're all right then?" he asked.

Laila met his eyes. They were a bright icy blue, and they shone in the odd-coloured blend of light. She nodded. "Thank you, Bailey."

He gave her a kind smile and went past the two of them, bumping shoulders with Chandler. Chandler scowled, then turned his attention back to Laila. He gestured for her to proceed. "You're not leaving my sight until I get you to where you need to be," he said. "I'll take you to the mayanon woman."

"Ida. Her name is Ida."

Chandler raised a brow and waved his fingers for her to go. Laila went. Cassian made a face and squirmed. His sudden wailing alarmed Laila. She tried rocking him as she walked, but he just cried all the harder. She wasn't watching where she was going and almost walked into Chandler, who'd stopped to turn right and lead her down a lesser-used, dead-end hall.

"This way," he said.

Laila gazed down the dim hallway. The torches were spaced farther apart along the earth-mounded, braced walls. "They're in the private meeting room," Laila said over Cassian's cries.

"They've been moved. They're this way now. Let's go."

She followed Chandler down the hall.

It seemed Zulu had gotten guard duty again. He stood at the dead-end of the empty hall, outside a room with a closed door. The noise of Cassian drew Zulu's attention. He goggled, speechless.

They were nearly to the door when Ida burst out of the room, eyes wide. Her gaze landed on Cassian, and she came running, straight past Zulu's wide shoulders. "Cassian!" she shouted. Her eyes were red, like she'd not been sleeping. They practically bulged from her head as they took in her son. Zulu turned from Laila to Cassian to Ida, looking stunned.

Ida ran the few extra feet to Laila. Zulu reacted too slowly to stop her, but he did manage to block Dimitri from getting past him. Ida reached out and relieved Laila of Cassian's flailing and ear-piercing screams. She cried as she held him in the middle of the tunnel-hall, cradling him close to her chest and burying her face in his neck.

Behind Ida's reunion with her son, Dimitri swatted Zulu's arm out of his way and clenched his hand in a fist, ready to swing. Laila saw it coming before Zulu did. Dimitri punched him on the side of his head. Zulu shouted and put a hand to where he'd been hit, while Dimitri pushed past him and ran the short distance to Ida, Cassian, Laila, and Chandler.

Chandler drew the fire from the torch on the wall to himself, where it hovered above his hand. He held it out to ward off Dimitri. Dimitri stopped and peered down at Cassian in Ida's arms, eyes glistening. Cassian's cries faded to soft whimpers. Dimitri tore his gaze away from Cassian to look at Laila. "How?" he whispered.

Zulu had recovered from the hit. He marched over to Dimitri and grabbed his arm.

"Wait!" Dimitri resisted. "I need to know what happened."

Zulu set his jaw. His gaze shifted toward the tiny creature in Ida's arms. Neither he nor Chandler seemed to know what to make of this moment. They'd not seen a baby in a hundred years.

Ida sniffed and wiped her face. If she could have snuggled her son any closer to her body, she probably would have. She turned her eyes toward Laila.

Tears snuck past Laila's defences and rolled down her cheeks. She brushed them away. "It's a long story," Laila said. "And I, uh . . ." She looked at Chandler, then back to Ida and Dimitri. "I have to go."

"Did you see Raidan?" Ida asked.

Laila shook her head. "I'm sorry."

Ida released a sob and nuzzled her face into her son's neck. Her chest shuddered as she took a breath. Then she threw herself at Laila, giving her a start as she wrapped her in an embrace. She held Cassian close with one hand and put the other around Laila's shoulder. Chandler's frown deepened. His fire still hovered over his hand. Laila glowered at him to convey that Ida's quick action was a welcome gesture. Chandler's eyes narrowed.

"Thank you," Ida whispered in Laila's ear. She gave Laila a feeble smile.

Dimitri shrugged Zulu's hand from his arm and stepped over to Laila, wrapping his arms around her as well. Laila tensed, but then she relaxed in his hug and returned the gesture. Zulu bounced on the balls of his feet, looking ready to pounce at any given moment while Chandler held his fire hand out toward Dimitri.

Dimitri squeezed Laila's shoulders, then dropped his hands. Chandler extinguished his fire. "Let's go, Laila." He waved his hand as if she didn't know the way. Laila took slow backward steps, drawing out the minutes before she had to go to containment.

"Laila," Ida said. Laila stopped, grateful for another distraction before her time of solitude. "What you've done," Ida said. "It's . . . I don't know how to repay you." Cassian made little grunting sounds, and his hand patted Ida's face and lips. She took his tiny hand in hers and rubbed her chin over it lovingly, then kissed it.

Laila's lips curved in a weak smile. There wasn't much Ida or Dimitri could do for her. She'd gotten herself into this knowing there would be unavoidable consequences. But Ida's reaction had been worth it. Laila sighed. "Just do me a favour, would you?"

"Anything," Dimitri said.

"Trust my brother. If you tell him what's going on, he will help you find your husband," she said to Ida. Then to Dimitri, "He just needs to know he can trust you too."

Chandler grunted, indicating Laila had stalled long enough. Laila turned her back on Dimitri, Zulu, Ida, and Cassian. She had finished what she'd set out to do, and now she was going to be locked up.

She dragged her feet as she followed Chandler. She had nothing to say to her escort. They walked through the assembly chamber and into the hallway that Laila had only once meandered down out of curiosity. This time, there would be no wandering back to her room.

She breathed the stifling air. It felt thick and heavy. Apart from the containment room, there were no rooms down this unlit hall. It was carved out of the hard rock in the hills here and was short, with only one bend. Around the bend, a single torch was visible beside the door.

Darrin must have got the memo that she was being taken there. He waited by the solid wooden door. It was much thicker than the others in the mines and had a latch and padlock. Darrin had one of the keys; Vix had the other. If there were any more, Laila didn't know. It didn't matter. She'd not be getting out of this so easily. For all the times Royl had kept her from containment, she didn't think his influence would help her now.

Darrin stared at her with that ghostly eye of his as she neared. He removed the padlock and opened the door. She stepped past him wordlessly. The door closed behind her. She flinched at the sound of the latch flipping in place and the click of the lock

The room was similar in size to her own room. Two narrow beds took up either side. A desk and chair sat between them against the wall where a lamp was lit, giving off the only light in the suffocatingly small space. It was one of the oldest rooms in the mines, dating back to the time when the mines were abandoned and left alone for years. Cracks lined the grey stone in the walls.

Laila remained by the door, taking it all in. A picture hung on the wall above the desk. It was one that her mother had drawn of the Abberbrat in beautiful pastel colours. Laila studied it. She imagined herself there, feeling the cool, light morning breeze that rustled the wispy branches, making no sound. She closed her eyes and breathed deeply.

Almost as soon as she'd closed them, she opened them with a sense that once again she was not alone. Like when she awoke and Beiron was there, in her old room with her, she felt that same presence. When she looked around the room, there was nothing. But the feeling didn't go away. Her heart pounded fast. She closed her eyes again and tuned in to her senses.

Was this how Beiron felt when she'd been there with him? He'd been able to sense her presence those times.

She opened her eyes again and looked around the room imagining he was there somewhere in the room, invisible to her.

"You're here, aren't you?" she asked, not expecting a response. She listened for a moment, then said, "Say something." Now she was curious if they could communicate verbally in this way, if he really was there at all.

A handling of the padlock on the other side of the wooden door startled her. Laila nearly jumped out of her skin. Her hand flew to her heart. Beneath her wound, the rising and falling slowed as she calmed herself.

The door opened. Royl burst in and made a beeline for her. His embrace caused her to wince. He stepped back and looked at her with a deep crease in his brow. His hands stayed on either side of her arms. "Are you hurt? Where did you go, Laila?" he asked. "I was out looking for you all night."

His eyebrows drew even closer together at the sight of her clothes—the too-big navy shirt over her dress, covering the dried blood and shredded fabric of her bodice, which thankfully he could not see. "What are you wearing?" Royl said. He frowned at her face and hair. She must have really looked like a wreck. "What happened, Laila?"

With Beiron's presence still lingering, Laila was hesitant to say much. He could be there, listening to everything. Royl wasn't giving her much chance to respond anyway.

"And what's this I hear about you returning with a baby? The mayanon woman's missing son?" He removed his hands from her arms and circled the small room before facing her again with softer eyes. "Please tell me what's going on"

There was so much to say. And yet, with Beiron possibly there in the room, she didn't want to say anything. She had so many questions for Royl, like how Beiron knew their family, and if he really was so bad, why did he save her? He'd said it was because of their deal, but . . . if she recalled correctly before passing out, he'd looked genuinely concerned for her. Or maybe that was just her imagination.

Her muscles ached from the tension and stress. She relaxed her shoulders, and her whole body slouched. "You're not going to like it" was all she said.

"Whatever it is, just tell me. We can figure this out together."

It was hard to look him in the eye. After everything she'd been through, she wanted to tell him all of it. But what if her actions appalled him and he saw to it that she never left the mines again? Perhaps when she was not locked up in containment, she'd share. Then she could ensure her chances at leaving the mines. For good this time.

"I will tell you, Royl. Just . . . I'm not ready yet." She wished that feeling of Beiron's proximity would go away.

"Can I go down to the springs and get washed up?" she asked, gesturing to herself. "If I'm to be in here long, I'd like to at least be clean." As clean as one could get when living underground.

Royl shook his head and sighed. "I'm not supposed to let you out. The elders are convening tonight to discuss the consequences for your recent activity."

Laila's face went hot. She sank onto the nearest bed, slumping her body.

Royl stepped over to the bed and sat beside her. "You're to be brought before them to share your account of where you've been these last few days. How you managed to find that missing baby and your reason for bringing a mayanon into the—"

"Stop!" She stood up abruptly. If Beiron was listening, whether he knew about the mines or not, Laila didn't want Royl to unwittingly reveal their location, not like Beiron wouldn't be able to figure it out from the rock surroundings. "I get it," she said. "Then what? What will happen after that?"

"The elders will decide how to deal with you."

How to deal with me? For what? Wanting her freedom? She rolled her eyes but kept her thoughts to herself. Until she felt that presence go, the less she said, the better.

Royl stood. "I'll see what I can do about allowing you to get cleaned up. What are you wearing anyway? Whose is that?"

This was definitely not something she was ready to talk about. She crossed her hand in front of herself and rubbed her opposite arm. Avoiding looking directly at Royl, she said, "You won't like that either."

She sensed his eyes on her. Finally, she met his stare. He shook his head gently. "Get some rest. Someone will bring you something to eat. I've been invited to sit in on the meeting later. I'm going to hear your story one way or another. I just wish you trusted me enough to tell me on your own."

He went to the door and knocked to be let out. Laila wanted so badly to make things up with him. She hated his disappointment. But she said nothing. He left the room, and she was alone again. Or not alone. She wasn't sure.

She turned her head to try and sense if Beiron was still there. It was quiet for a moment. Then, she could have sworn she heard a faint whisper saying, "Until next time."

And the presence was gone.

Chapter 51

Valmain was behind them now. The ruins of Reen were just ahead, and as Raidan was not accustomed to long durations on horseback, his tailbone was sore after only an hour of riding. The horse had no problem with a stranger on its back. It followed Ilan's horse with hardly any guidance from Raidan.

His wrists were raw where the cuffs rubbed against his skin. He couldn't take it much longer. "Stop up here a minute," he told Ilan, then directed his horse toward the ruins. They would offer shelter from the exposure of the open plain, concealing them from anyone passing on the road. Particularly Kingston's men.

Ilan steered his horse after Raidan's and voiced no argument about taking a break. He craned his neck to gaze up at the towering stone wall before them. "It's quite something, isn't it?"

Small trees poked through the crumbled stone floor within the interior of what used to be a grand structure. Raidan wasn't interested in admiring the scenery. He dismounted and stood next to Ilan, who sat atop his horse. Raidan reached up. "The keys."

Ilan got off his horse. He handed over the ring with three keys attached and pointed out which key to use. He then surveyed the ruins, hands on his hips. His head circled about the open space.

There was no ceiling in the ruin, except for a few areas where the structure hadn't crumbled. Those places offered shelter from the afternoon sun.

While Raidan got to work removing the cuffs, Ilan whistled. "I'd love to have seen this place before it fell."

Raidan shook his head and tried to ignore him. It hadn't fallen. It'd been destroyed by Kingston and his army during the Great Battle at Reen. Raidan tried not to think about that. He fumbled about with the keys. The broken chains dangled from his wrists. He shook the key around in the keyhole but couldn't get it to unlock. The magic he'd used to break free must have damaged the locking mechanism or warped the metal.

"You know," Ilan said, "they say the Fronort Templi was once a place to behold and that even the deities envied its splendour."

Raidan glanced up. The place held no splendour anymore. Now it was simply a reminder of what was lost. It had been the Great Battle at Reen in which his father died. Losing his father so young—Raidan's heart wrenched as he thought about his own son. The sooner he unshackled himself, the sooner he could go to him. He removed the key and jammed it back in, grunting.

Ilan turned to Raidan as he struggled. Stepping over to him, he put his hand out. "Allow me."

Raidan swatted his hand away.

Ilan snatched the key. "Just let me do it." He jiggled the key, doing no differently than Raidan had been doing. "What's it like?" he asked. "To use magic?" His mouth twitched like he wanted to smile, but he suppressed it as he continued to twist the key.

Raidan flinched when Ilan pinched his skin. He pulled his hands away and grabbed the keys back to do it himself.

"I nearly had it," Ilan said.

"We're not talking."

"Right," Ilan said. "Not talking. Got it."

Raidan turned the key and twisted it until finally the lock clicked loose. He removed the cuff and got to work on the other, which proved to be not as difficult as the first one. His wrists were raw and hurt to touch. He rubbed them anyway.

"Let's go," Raidan said. He mounted his stolen horse and wriggled his bottom around to get comfortable. They still had a ways to go before they were close to Litlen, assuming that was their destination.

"Good." Ilan got back on his horse and took the lead. "To Ferenth then. I'm famished."

"No. Take me to my son."

"After we've eaten, I will. Come on, you must be hungry as well. When's the last time you ate?"

Raidan thought about the meagre portion of stale bread Kingston's men had brought him in the dungeon. As if his stomach agreed with Ilan's suggestion, it gurgled. He supposed it would be good to eat something. But he had no money. Not that he needed any when he was in the company of Ilan Valca. That was another thing. He didn't like the idea of being in public with Ilan. Nor did he like that this would take more precious time away from him rescuing Cassian.

"Well?" Ilan said.

Raidan gave a slight nod for Ilan to lead the way. He'd need his strength if he was going to be of any use to Cass.

Ilan rode out of the ruin first, Raidan trailing behind. They cantered for a while, then slowed to a walk. The journey from Reen to Ferenth was another couple of hours, and the hunger pangs Raidan experienced intensified with every passing minute. Ilan's talking wasn't improving his mood.

". . . I mean," Ilan was saying. His horse stayed side by side with Raidan's, and he had been droning on for some time already. Raidan was only half listening.

"I've always wanted to know what kind of things you can do with magical abilities," Ilan said, not leaving any room for response between sentences. "Like, fire. Obviously, you can do something with that, but what? To what extent? And at the lake, someone was manipulating the water, using it as a weapon. That's how their magic works, you know? Through the elements, but I don't understand how they can control the element in use or how they can conjure without having the elements handy. Like you made fire from nothing! How did you do that? And what Beiron did with those rocks—hey! Can you fly? I used to think the Elderace could fly. Beiron said they can't, but I've heard of a man from Reij who supposedly flew on the back of a dragon. A dragon, can you believe that? I don't know whether I believe such things, but clearly anything—"

"Ilan!" Raidan couldn't stand it any longer. "I'm not Elderace. You know that, don't you? I'm not one of them."

Ilan cocked his head at Raidan. His mouth twitched. "I know. But you have magic, and that's supposed to be impossible for a mayanon, so surely if you can have magic, then I—"

"You're no more Elderace than I am."

Ilan's pained look gave Raidan a bit of satisfaction. "I realize that," Ilan said. "But it can't hurt to try." He straightened up on his horse, took a breath, and carried on. "How many do you think are out there? Elderace, I mean."

Raidan kept his gaze on the road ahead. "I don't care. I just want to get my son back." He turned his head toward Ilan. "And thanks to you, now I'll have to find my wife. You'd better hope she's all right."

He didn't know what he would do if she weren't. Would he go so far as to murder a man out of vengeance. He didn't think so. But he supposed no one ever truly knew their moral boundaries until put to the test. He shook the thought from his head. She had to be all right. He'd keep telling himself that, believing it.

Ilan shrugged. "What was I supposed to do? You ran. I made a call."

"You could have left my wife and son out of it. They didn't have to be part of this."

Ilan stuck his chin up. "Well . . . it's done now anyway. You'll see your son soon enough. And I'm sure your wife is fine."

269

Raidan hoped so.

The closer they got to the city, the more people there were around. A tree-line separated the highway from the city outskirts. They passed timber-frame homes, where people went about their business in their gardens or hung clothes on a line. When the people glanced up to see Ilan and Raidan pass, they scurried inside their homes. Mothers huddled their children close.

Raidan shrunk back into himself as they passed. He didn't like the frightened looks in their eyes.

"You see the way the people cower?" Ilan asked. "It's that kind of power that my father is always going on about. The power in a name and reputation, but he just doesn't understand. It's not the same as magic. I mean, you know what it's like, right? Which do you think would be better?"

Raidan disliked the kind of attention he was receiving just being in Ilan's company. He was thinking about how many more people would be in the city, and how there were bound to be more Valca soldiers there. Whether they were loyal to Ilan or Kingston didn't matter. Ilan would have the opportunity to reenforce his power with more men by his side. Could he be trusted to not turn on Raidan and make his own demands? This didn't seem like such a good idea anymore.

They passed more people, each reacting in similar fashion. More homes and shops lined the streets; more people scurried indoors. As Raidan feared, the presence of Valca soldiers was already beginning to show. They passed Valca soldiers standing in groups on the street corners or walking about.

Ilan led Raidan to an inn, where there was a pub serving meals. He dismounted, tied his horse, and encouraged Raidan to do the same. Raidan tried not to catch anyone's eye as he dismounted and joined Ilan.

Two soldiers exited the pub. They saw Ilan, saluted, and parted ways to allow Ilan and Raidan to pass.

Ilan nodded at them. "As you were, men," he said, then smirked at Raidan. He opened the door to the pub and found a table to sit at. A barmaid brought them ale. She leaned across the table, purposely flaunting her cleavage in Ilan's face as she placed the drinks down. She took their orders for food, and her eyes lingered on Ilan. She glanced at Raidan a few times but paid him little attention, which was fine by him. After they ordered, she winked at Ilan and walked off.

Ilan looked at Raidan and grinned crookedly. "Ferenth is a wonderful place."

The pub was full of people. A group of soldiers sat at a table nearby, and Raidan tensed in his seat, keeping his head down until the food was brought over. Ilan had taken the liberty of ordering for both of them the roasted lamb and potato dish. Raidan didn't argue. He would eat just about anything at that point.

When the food came, he wolfed it down while Ilan took his sweet time, licking his fingers and savouring every last bit on his plate. Raidan was aware that Ilan was trying to get a rise out of him, probably hoping to see some more magic. They were wasting time.

He stood. "Let's go. We've stopped for long enough."

Ilan looked up at Raidan. "Relax, your son is fine. Besides, I'm not done with my food yet."

"You're done," Raidan said a little too loudly. He'd caught the attention of the group of soldiers from the table over. All four of them slid their chairs back and moseyed over to Ilan and Raidan. The one with the scruffy beard and bald head placed his hand firmly on Raidan's shoulder. He stood a head taller than Raidan.

The soldier looked to Ilan. "Everything all right here, Mr. Valca?"

Ilan sat back in his chair. He folded his arms and looked at each soldier, then Raidan.

Raidan held his breath.

"I don't know yet. Are we all right, Raidan?"

Sweat dripped down at the back of Raidan's neck. The last thing he needed was to cause a scene. Onlookers watched from their tables and from behind the bar. Raidan got Ilan's point. He was the one in charge, not Raidan.

Raidan nodded. The soldier with the beard kept his hand on his shoulder until Ilan gave the okay.

"I think we'll be all right, soldier," Ilan said. "You've done well." He stood and faced the man. "What's your name?"

"Rory, sir."

"Rory. I need you to do something for me. Go to the village of . . ." He looked to Raidan. "What's the name of that little village you and your brother are from again?"

"My village?" Raidan said. "What for?"

"The name, Raidan."

Raidan rubbed his upper arm. He looked around the pub for some support or help, but none would come. He knew that.

Ilan snapped at him. "Come on, Mr. I'm-in-a-hurry. What's the name of your village."

"Veryl." Raidan felt like he was sentencing his village to some terrible fate just by surrendering its name.

"Right, Veryl." Ilan snapped his fingers again and faced the soldier. "My captain is in Veryl and I need him. Go there, find Perry, and tell him to meet me in Litlen, near the tree. He'll know where that is."

The soldier bowed and left. The other three soldiers followed. Ilan looked at Raidan. They stood at the table in the middle of the pub, the people watching, pretending not to be. Ilan gestured to the door. "Let's go then," Ilan said. He seemed to be in a good mood after having eaten and showing everyone how gracious he could be. He walked with his nose up and his chest puffed out.

"I've no desire to make you my enemy," he told Raidan as they remounted their horses. "All I want is to have magic and learn more about the Elderace and their ways. It's all I've ever wanted. And now I know there are more Elderace out there. That song. It spoke to me. It was like a call, leading me to you and your brother . . . to Litlen and the Elderace. I'm meant to know more."

"The song called you?" Raidan asked as he raised an eyebrow. "What exactly did it say to you?"

"The words were not what moved me. It was in the music itself. Like a cloud—it carried me and—oh, you know. You probably felt something similar."

Just thinking about the song again and that whole night gave Raidan a headache. The food had agreed with him, but now he fought to keep his eyes open. "I didn't hear the song," he said.

"What? How? You'd have to have been living under a rock to not have heard it."

"I suppose nearly getting crushed by one could count."

Ilan sucked his cheek and shrugged. "I suppose." He kept his horse in step with Raidan's as they exited the city limits to get back on the road headed south. "Well, it was an old Elderace legend about healing in the land. The song talks about restoration and reconciliation. If you know your history, you'll know there was always great discord between the mayanon and the Elderace. The legend speaks of one who will heal the land, but it hints at a reconciling of the people too. When I heard it, I saw a place filled with song and magic, all for me to discover."

Ilan looked at Raidan with a sparkle in his eye. "I think I'm meant to be the one to unite the people," he said.

Raidan wrinkled his nose.

"Think about it," Ilan said. "Who better than me, future ruler of Kartha, to bridge the gap between races? You happened to get in the middle of this, which is unfortunate for you, but we can make it right. Once we get your son, you can take me to the place where you gained your magic and show me what to do to get it too. After that, I'll find the surviving Elderace and prove to them that I can lead them and don't want to fight them. And then all will be right in the land."

Raidan had nothing to say. He knew little about the conflict between the races. Apart from Adrik, the Elderace had been gone since before he was born.

Raidan nodded, allowing Ilan to believe what he wanted. Ilan was mistaken to think that Raidan would be going back to that place ever again.

He had a plan of his own: get Cassian, find Ida, then find a way to get rid of the magic.

Chapter 52

The red mountains in the distance gradually became larger. Raidan ignored his aching back and kept a steady pace. Ilan remained at his side as they rode on.

For once, Ilan seemed to have nothing to say. They rode in silence for a long while, and Raidan almost wished for the distraction of conversation, even if that conversation was with Ilan. His mind created horrific scenarios of how he might find Cassian and Ida, and his stomach churned.

Out of the blue, Ilan blurted out, "You know, you're easy to talk to."

His statement tore Raidan from his thoughts. "You think so?"

"Yes, I feel like I can really open up with you, you know?"

"How lucky for me."

"Who would have imagined, you and me travelling together to—"

"We are not together," Raidan said quickly.

"No, no, I only meant that we're riding together, and it's been good, you know?"

Raidan didn't answer. *Good* was the last word he'd use to describe these past weeks.

The rise of the terrain happened so gradually that Raidan hadn't realized how far in the mountains they were. The twisting road rounded bends that Raidan couldn't see beyond. They rode up slight inclines, then down steeper slopes. Eventually, the road levelled off on a straight path between the towering heights of the red desert-like mountains. The sandy stone was like shale, breaking under the horses' hooves.

A high peak momentarily blocked the sun, and Raidan peered up on either side of the trail. If not for the red colour and flaky ground, this part of the trail would have reminded him of the pass through the Teiry Mountains. He closed his eyes, trying to remind himself that this was not the same. He was going to his son; he was on his way to save Cassian. He opened his eyes and took a steadying breath.

Movement from the corner of his eye caused him to look up again. There were people in the mountains, walking along with them from above. How long had they been tracking with them?

More people followed along on the opposite side of the mountains, beside them, keeping up in the tall heights. Raidan slowed his horse, as did Ilan. Was this an ambush? Bandits stopping travellers along the road was not unheard of.

Those who were trekking with them from above made their way down on either side of Ilan and Raidan on the trail. They came from behind and ahead. Raidan came to a full stop and looked back. A group of four men and women, all with dark skin and drawn weapons, stood in a line and blocked the road. In front, another group of five came down and converged with a man standing in the middle of the road.—Raidan didn't know where he'd come from. They all had the same angry slant in their eyebrows. Their weapons were mostly swords. One woman held a crossbow, and someone else wielded two short swords, one in each hand.

One of the men stepped forward, palm out for them to stop. He signalled with his fingers that they dismount. "Get off your horses," he said. His accent was not like anything Raidan had heard in Kartha.

Shoulder's back, Ilan looked at Raidan. "I'll handle this." He eyed the speaker, who'd stepped forward from the others. "It's in your best interest to let us pass," Ilan said. "Stand aside and you will be forgiven for your ignorance."

The leader dipped his chin. He crossed his arms in front of himself, and a broad grin spread across his face. He looked at his people on either side of him, who smiled as well. Then they all laughed. The leader had the loudest laugh of them all. His head swung back while his voice bellowed out. Evidently, Ilan's reputation didn't always get him his way.

Disregarding the man's order would be unwise when they were clearly not deterred by Ilan and his Valca Order attire. And using magic, though it had proven useful in certain circumstances, would end up revealing to these people that Raidan had it—a fact he would rather not make known. The sooner he was rid of it, the better.

"Do what he says," Raidan said to Ilan, then dismounted slowly and put his hands up in a show of surrender.

"I will not," Ilan said. "Who do you think you are?" he asked the group of men and women. "You can't stop people on their way like this."

He was one to talk. The Order did it all the time, collecting random tolls to pass at varying points on the roads with no particular reason, except to produce fear and submission, meanwhile increasing the wealth in their own pockets.

Ilan went on, getting louder as two men approached his horse. "Do you have any idea who I am? I'm—"

"They don't care who you are." Raidan warned him with a sharp look.

Ilan was not quick on the uptake. He spoke loud enough to ensure he was heard by all. "I am Ilan Valca, and you have no right to stop me and my companion on my journey."

The two men reached up and dragged Ilan off his horse. Ilan reached for his sword a little too slowly, and it was confiscated before he could act. He waved his arms about, and the bandits—as that was what Raidan assumed them to be—secured his arms to keep him from flailing.

The speaker stepped over to him and dropped his jaw in a surprised gasp. "Ilan Valca?" he said. "Ooohh, I had no idea we were in such esteemed company." The others chuckled.

Ilan caught the derision, and worry played across his face. Clearly, he was not used to such treatment.

Raidan wasn't jumping to Ilan's defence; he'd had that coming. Raidan only wished he didn't happen to be travelling with him right then. This detour was costing him time.

The leader who mocked Ilan rubbed his finger over the small growth of beard beneath his lower lip and cleared his throat, smirking.

Raidan turned to him. "Please," he said. "I'm not with him. He—"

"Save it, rider," the leader said. Ilan shot Raidan a quick glance, eyebrows furrowed. "You are both coming with us." The leader jerked his head for them to move.

"You don't understand," Raidan said to the group of bandits. "Ilan has my son. I need to—"

"Enough," the man interrupted again. "I will hear no more. Come. This way."

Two bandits approached Raidan from behind and encouraged him to follow their leader. Raidan did a double take, looking at the black dots marking the one man's chin, going in a single line down from his mouth. The other who'd come to urge Raidan to move was the woman with the crossbow. She didn't look like much, but Raidan suspected she could be just as dangerous as any of these men.

They marched farther along the road, horses in tow. The leader led them south along the trail until there was a crevice to the right. A few from the group continued on the road, bringing the horses, while the woman nudged Raidan toward the crevice. He had to duck underneath a shelf and shimmy through. Once on the other side, he stood to his full height. Now off the trail and surrounded by tall red mountains, they headed west, deeper into the mountains.

Ilan was pulled along by either arm by two more of the bandits. He shouted all the way about how they were going to regret this and about the imminent consequences when his father got word of this treatment. Empty threats. Ilan knew as well as Raidan that Kingston had other things to see to just then.

"Where are you taking us?" Raidan asked when they took yet another turn, losing themselves further into the mountains.

"No talking. Kameron will decide what to do with you," the leader said. Kameron came out in three syllables with a slight roll on the r, and Raidan figured that Kam-er-on must be their true leader.

The man leading them to Kameron continued to direct them along a winding pathway that eventually led to a clearing with an array of huts scattered about. Many had cone-shaped thatch roofs, and the buildings themselves looked to be constructed of clay. People were out and about. Most of them were dark skinned, like the group who'd brought them there. Some stood and talked, while others walked from one place to another—there was one large rectangular building, and an octagonal one among the cluster of cone-roofed huts. Other people were sparring, and every one of them stopped what they were doing to watch as the newcomers were brought into their hidden village. A few of those who'd been talking left their place to enter one of the bigger buildings. Those who were sparring went back to their practice.

Raidan couldn't think what this place was. This little village wasn't on any map of Kartha, if it could even be called a village. It was smaller than Veryl, hidden well in this valley of the Bludesel Mountains. Raidan suspected it was meant to be that way.

The low sun cast shadows over them. The men dragging Ilan along separated him from Raidan. As they took him away, Ilan glanced over his shoulder toward Raidan.

If Raidan lost Ilan, he'd lose his shot at finding Cassian forever. He turned to follow Ilan, but his escort with the markings on his chin flung an arm across Raidan's chest, stopping him.

"You are this way," he said, pointing in the opposite direction. His accent was the same as the leader's.

Ilan fought as he was led away from Raidan.

The marked chin man wrapped a meaty hand around Raidan's arm and shoved him along. He brought him to one of the huts and told him to go in. Raidan complied.

Based on their mockery of Ilan, Raidan guessed these people did not care for the Valca Order. That was good for Raidan, as they might

279

be able to help him learn of Cassian's whereabouts from Ilan. The only complication was that he happened to be Ilan's travelling companion.

Inside the hut, there was not much. A single bed, barely big enough for a grown man, was positioned against the far wall. An unlit lantern rested on the bedside table. It was more furnished than the dungeon cell.

"You will stay here," the woman with the crossbow said. "If you try to run, we will not hesitate to kill you, and we are very fast, so you will not get away. Do I make myself clear?"

"Perfectly," Raidan said.

"Good. Tala will bring you food shortly," the woman said before shutting the door and leaving Raidan alone in the hut.

Standing in the growing dark of the windowless space, Raidan slouched. Here he was, once again at the mercy of others. He rubbed his tailbone, which was sore from the long ride. Not knowing how long he'd be waiting for Kameron, he drifted to the bed and sat.

The door opened and he jumped up. A woman entered with a steaming bowl of food. Her eyes were strikingly blue in contrast to her dark skin. She did not close the door. Behind her, a man stood at the threshold, facing in. The woman came to stand before Raidan. She smiled, and her eyes sparkled. "I am Tala." Her accent matched that of the others. Tala held the clay bowl to Raidan. "I have brought you food."

It had been a long time since he and Ilan had eaten in Ferenth. The scent of peanuts combined with the stew's earthy aroma made his mouth water. He accepted the bowl but didn't eat. "I can't stay here. My son needs me."

She looked at him, her eyes gentle. "How old is your son?"

"Only half a year. He's in trouble, please, can you tell whoever's in charge that I need to leave? I have to find him."

"What is his name?" she asked, ignoring his plea.

Raidan took a deep breath. She was not the one he needed to be telling. "Cassian."

"That is a lovely name."

Raidan looked at Tala. Her face held genuine kindness. How could he make her understand how desperate he was to leave?

Tala gave a curt nod and headed for the door. She turned to face him once more. "Eat, you will need your strength. Kameron will speak with you soon." She left the hut, and the guard followed, closing the door as they went.

Raidan's jaw tightened. Kameron needed to hurry up.

The smell of the soup tempted him. He ate straight from the bowl, savouring the peanut flavour. He detected the taste of sweet potatoes too. Already his mood had lightened a bit, and his bad temper was eased. It was wise for them to offer him food. Hostilities were likely to be less on a full stomach.

Raidan chugged back the rest of the pureed stew. He swayed, feeling tired. Really tired. It had been a while since he'd slept and properly allowed his body rest, but this was not a natural exhaustion. The bowl slipped from his hand and clattered on the floor. He hardly noticed.

On wobbly legs, he faced the bed and extended his hand, reaching for it. He fell onto the bed, landing prone. His arm draped over the edge. It was impossible to keep his eyes open any longer. He shut them, drowsiness dragging him down.

What was in that soup? he wondered before sleep claimed him.

Chapter 53

RAIDAN LAY NEXT TO IDA IN THEIR BED. HER FAIR, LOOSE CURLS CAScaded over her rosy cheeks. Full, slightly parted lips curved up in a soft smile. Raidan reached for her face. Her skin was warm, and her cheek leaned into his hand.

This was peace.

Cassian's cry pierced the silence. It was a usual kind of cry, nothing alarming. But then it became a scream, as if he were hurt.

Sitting upright, Raidan turned his head to face Cassian's direction. He thrust back the blanket and left the warm bed and Ida, going from his room. Following the sound, he went through his home, past the sitting room and out the front door. Cassian's cries faded.

Outside his home was not as it should have been. This was not Veryl at all. Raidan had entered a familiar room. One he'd been in only once before at the white cottage in the woods, where Cassian was just within his reach. So close.

From seemingly nowhere, the man called Scourge appeared as well as his freaks. They formed a circle around Raidan. Their hysterical laughter echoed everywhere at once. In a dark corner of the room, near the fireplace and armchair, Beiron stood. He held Cassian in his arms and glared at Raidan. Cassian, no longer crying, grasped his fingers around anything he could reach: Beiron's tunic collar, his hair that nearly touched his shoulders.

Raidan breathed through his clenched teeth. Scourge and his laughing men were a nuisance, standing between him and his son. Stepping forward, Raidan moved like a man on a mission toward Beiron and Cassian. He *was* a man on a mission. His blood boiled. From deep within himself, magic stirred.

Scourge and the three-eyed man stood in his way. As Raidan shouldered through the gap between the two men, he gasped and stumbled backward. His hand went to his abdomen, where warm blood oozed. He looked down at the damage, then turned his eyes up to the assailant who'd stabbed him. Kingston towered over him with a murderous glint in his eye, reflected in his blood-soaked sword.

The quaking in the ground seemed surreal. It was faint, but it didn't seem right. He'd have expected there to be more shaking.

Kingston's shout echoed in the back of Raidan's mind. "This ends now!" The voice rang out. The sound of it warped and changed into a deep male voice, shouting at Raidan.

A hand cupped over his mouth and woke him with a start. A black man was crouched beside the bed, level with Raidan's face. Raidan smacked the man's hand away and sat up, remembering where he was: the thatch-roofed hut in the little village in the Bludesel Mountains.

Though he hadn't been conscious to know for sure, he suspected that the shaking he'd caused in the dream was not only a part of his dream—or nightmare, rather—but had been felt by those in the vicinity. He swiped his wrist across his wet lips.

The door to the hut stood open, letting bright sunlight into the room. It looked like it might be nearly midday. Had he slept the whole night?

Another man stood outside, looking in. The man who'd awoken Raidan frowned at him. He had silvery tips in his short, wiry, otherwise black beard. Despite his wizened appearance, the man's gaze was hard. "You were yelling in your sleep," the man said, voice accented as the others.

"You drugged me." Speaking hurt his throat, probably from yelling in his sleep.

The man smiled. "Tala's special ingredient has a kick to it, no?" He laughed. "Apart from its effectiveness, did it not taste wonderful?"

Raidan chose not to answer. "How long was I out? I need to find my son."

The man dropped the humour. He narrowed his eyes and stared fiercely at Raidan. "I am Kameron. And you, my friend, look like a spy."

"I'm not a spy."

"Exactly what a spy would say."

"Also, exactly what a non-spy would say. Look, I don't have time for this; my son is in trouble."

Kameron raised an eyebrow. "Your son, your son," he said. "How do I know this is the truth? If you are a spy, then you are also a good liar."

Heat radiated in Raidan's cheeks. With his newfound awareness of his voice's power and knowing it would reveal his magic, he kept his voice calm. Though if Kameron were observant, he might have already noticed the magic. "I'm only travelling with Ilan because he's taking me to my son. He knows where he is, and he's my best shot at finding him."

Kameron stood to his full height and his head just about hit the ceiling. He put his hands to his hips. "The Valca claims you are together."

Of course, Ilan would say that. Raidan was his key to the Elderace and magic. "We're not," Raidan said.

Kameron took a long, deep breath and looked at Raidan like he was between children arguing over who started a fight. "I cannot let you leave," he said. "Not until I know if what you say is true. But you may walk about within our camp in the meantime. You may be our guest until I know what to think."

Raidan was finding it difficult not to shout. His patience was wearing dangerously thin. "Are you not hearing me? My son is in danger; I need to get to him."

Kameron moved his hands from his hips to cross them in front of his chest. He squinted at Raidan. "You were travelling with the Valca, and you have now seen this place. I cannot let you go until I know the truth."

"I'm telling you the truth. Please," Raidan begged. "Ask Ilan where he is, ask him about my son."

Kameron stared for a long while at Raidan without saying anything. Then his eyes softened. "I will ask, but it does not change anything. We shall see if you speak the truth."

Raidan tapped his foot. He was tempted to scream and see what damage it would do, and potentially give himself an opportunity to run. But to where?

The magic was so unpredictable, he didn't even know if it would work. Besides, to find Cassian, he needed Ilan. Perhaps, if these people could get Ilan to talk, they'd believe him and he could leave Ilan to save Cassian. He was afraid to hope.

"Come, I will show you around," Kameron said. He directed Raidan outside the hut. The man at the door moved aside. "This is Eli," Kameron said. "He will keep an eye on you while you are here."

Eli raised his chest. Even with his long neck, he didn't quite reach Kameron's height.

"This is where you will sleep," Kameron said, pointing into the hut as they stepped out. The sky was clouding over, but the sun peeped through. The late morning was colder in the mountains than it had been in Valmain. Raidan's arms prickled with goosebumps under his thin, tattered shirt sleeves.

"That is the locameen. It is a place where we gather to eat." Kameron pointed to the large rectangular wooden building about a half a kilometre away. The name of the place was unfamiliar to Raidan, but he understood well enough that it served as a place for dining.

"Over there is where legends are made," Kameron said with a smile as he pointed out a green space. "It is a place where we gather to tell stories and play music. I hope you will join us later. You will find many of us there at any point throughout the day. Often, we will have a game of ternex there. Have you heard of the sport?"

Raidan had, but he'd never played the game. He gave no reply, and Kameron didn't push for one.

"That building is the Acteg." Kameron indicated the octagonal wooden building that was between the green space and the locameen. "If the weather is bad, we gather for music and stories in there."

As they walked farther from Raidan's hut, Eli followed closely, his hands clasped behind his back and his posture stiff.

"That over there is the latrine," Kameron said, pointing out the hut to the left, away from the buildings and other huts. Then he threw his hands up in the air in a grand gesture. "This is our camp. Anywhere beyond these buildings is off-limits to you. If you try to leave, you will be caught. I have my people everywhere. If you run, you will be considered guilty of being a spy, for which the penalty is death. In the meantime, I will decide if you tell the truth or not. Is that understood?" Kameron waited.

Raidan's chances at leaving this place without being caught were slim. He slowly nodded, undecided whether he would try anyway.

"Good," Kameron said. "Eli will take you to meet everyone. I have other items to attend to. Eat something; you look like you are needing it. And you can wash over there. Fresh clothes will be brought for you." He pointed outside the camp to a place in the mountain where water streamed down into a creek. "Eli will take you."

Eli's tight facial muscles twitched. He looked as unhappy about his task of watching Raidan as Raidan was of being guarded. Kameron walked away, leaving the two of them.

"This way," Eli said, indicating to where a group of people were gathered by the locameen. Raidan didn't move.

Eli turned to face him. "Or you can sit inside your hut if you prefer and wait until Kameron decides if you lie."

Using magic was something Raidan didn't want to have to resort to. His growing reliance on it was almost as unsettling as the fact that he was considering using it at all. Though he stood perfectly still, his heart raced. To calm himself, he took a breath through his nose. He released it, then stood straight. "I'd like to clean up a bit before meeting others."

Eli rolled his eyes. "Yes, yes, all right. Come, I will show you where." He took a step toward Raidan and waved a finger in front of his face. "But do not think to try anything. As Kameron has said, it will not go well for you."

Raidan raised his hands in surrender. "I wouldn't dream of it."

Eli led Raidan through the grounds of the camp. As they went, Raidan paid close attention to the layout. If he were to attempt to leave, he'd first have to discover where Ilan was being held. There was a chance Kameron might release Raidan and let him go on his way, but he suspected it would not be so for Ilan. If these people could just learn from Ilan where Cassian was, Raidan wouldn't need him anymore.

Behind the locameen, there were fewer huts scattered about. Eli stopped walking and indicated with a wave of his hand the place where Raidan could bathe. A misty haze hovered over the calm water of a small lake. The mountain water that trickled down into it matched the red, sandy colour of the rock. The serenity of the place did help Raidan relax a bit. He waved his fingers in the warm water, closed his eyes, and allowed the tension in him to release. The water's touch eased his jitters, which were a constant reminder of the magic that weighed him down.

For now, he would familiarize himself with this place and find Ilan. He wasn't going to be staying long, though. All he needed was the opportune moment. He opened his eyes.

It would come. One way or another, he was getting his son back.

Chapter 54

What kind of place was this that these people lived like such savages? And that they thought they could treat him like an animal?

Ilan paced the space of the hut. Back and forth, biting his nails. This primitive structure was not enough to keep him in. He looked around, scouring the walls for any weak spots he could tear through.

Then he stopped his pacing and could have smacked his own head. The door. He'd just go out the door. He was trained in combat. Timing would be everything in his escape.

The door opened as Ilan was looking at it. He braced his stance for a fight. Kameron stood at the open door, alongside a woman, who was nearly as tall as him. The man had introduced himself to Ilan last night when they'd first arrived. He'd not gotten much chance to speak over Ilan's yelling. Now he was back, and Ilan had since calmed down.

Kameron stepped into the hut, crowding the small space. The woman waited outside as Kameron closed the door.

"You can't keep me here," Ilan said. "Do you have any idea who I am?"

Kameron raised his eyebrows. "I have an idea."

"Then you should know not to make an enemy of me. I can have my army here to destroy your little village at the snap of my fingers."

He snapped his fingers to prove his point. "My father is looking for me, and he will—"

"He will not find you here," Kameron said. "No one is going to find you here."

Ilan snarled. "You underestimate my father's forces."

Kameron tucked his thumbs into the waistband of his trousers and shifted his weight to one side. "You and your family are responsible for a great deal of loss and suffering to the citizens of Kartha. It is the wish of my people that you face execution."

Ilan opened his mouth.

Kameron cut him off before he could say his piece. "I have suggested a trial for you."

"What good will a trial do when your minds are already made up? What chance do I have?"

"We are just and fair. You will be heard and dealt with accordingly."

It was impossible to be still. Ilan's fingers fidgeted with the loophole at his belt that was intended for his sword. He'd been stripped of his weapon and he felt bare without it. His muscles twitched as he kept himself from acting on his impulse to attack and run.

Timing. He needed to plan this right.

"When is my trial?" Ilan asked.

"Soon" was all the reply Kameron gave. "Your friend. Who is he?"

"Raidan?" Ilan had almost forgotten about him. "He's with me."

"That is not what I asked."

"He's a loyal servant to the Valca Order. Where is he? I demand to see him immediately."

Kameron tilted his head down and smiled. "You do not make demands here, young Valca. What of Raidan's son? Where is he?"

"What?" Ilan assumed his best confused look. "What son? What are you talking about?"

Kameron's lips pressed together. He glared at Ilan and said nothing.

"I want to see Raidan," Ilan said. "Where is he?" If he could learn where Raidan was, they could escape together.

"You will not see him," Kameron said. He went to the door and opened it. The woman waited for him there. "I will return when we have decided when you will be tried. My people will keep a watch on you. As I have already told your friend, it would be unwise to run." Kameron left the little hut. The lamp on the bedside table flickered firelight when the door closed.

Unwise to run. Ilan blew air from his mouth. It had been unwise for them to have brought him to their village in the first place. He went to the door and listened to the sounds outside. It was difficult to say how many people he would have to contend with when the time came to make his escape. This would take some time to plan. With his father's wrath toward the Elderace and Litlen, time was something he didn't think he had much of. He supposed he would just have to be quick about this whole escaping business. The Elderace needed him. And Raidan was his key to finding them.

Chapter 55

THE STILLNESS IN THE AIR WAS UNNERVING. IF IT HADN'T BEEN FOR Beiron's voice still echoing in her mind, Laila might not be so anxious. She sat on the bed with a quill and parchment. The ink bottle rested on the table beside the bed. She'd gotten right to work, writing her recollections from Beiron's book—Beiron's father's book. Knowing now that the book first belonged to his father, Laila thought she knew exactly where the entries changed from father to son. The handwriting was slightly different, but her guess was based mostly on the fact that the first couple of pages were about the Abberbrat and the River Lin. The Forest of Litlen was mentioned as well as some other unique attributes of other landmarks of Litlen. The input didn't fit the pattern of the rest of the book's entries, which slowly took a darker turn. Nevertheless, Laila wrote it all down.

She was clean and back in containment, having been brought a meal and granted her request to bathe. Getting dressed had not been easy with her chest wound causing her discomfort every time she raised her arms or bent down. Covering the wound had been a challenge too. All her dresses were too low cut to cover the purple bruising and red scabbing above her breasts. She'd ended up crisscrossing a scarf over her shoulders and tying it around her waist. It looked strange, but it covered her injury and she'd not have to explain herself.

All the while as she'd washed and dressed, she'd rushed, paranoid that Beiron would return. It was one thing for her to have been able to see him, but that he could see her too made her uneasy. She looked over her shoulder and listened intently. At this point, she'd lost count of how many times she'd done this. She couldn't keep going this way.

The end of the feather quill tickled her cheek as she lost focus on her writing. While copying from memory the information in Beiron's book, she was overwhelmed by the amount of knowledge that was packed into it. Plants she'd almost forgotten about came to the forefront of her mind as she racked her brain. Maybe there was one she could use to help Ida find her husband. A specific plant came to mind and she wrote it down.

The meeting with the elders would be soon. She hadn't decided what she was going to tell them yet. Would she share the truth? All of it?

The thought of pleading with them to banish her had crossed her mind. Nothing would make her happier than being told she could not return to the mines. Maybe then, others could see her make a life for herself in the city, in her old home, and they would venture out to do the same.

The sound of the key turning in the lock pulled her from her thoughts. She rose and put the parchment on the table. In a quick attempt to cover it, she threw her shawl over it, which she'd brought from her room after she'd cleaned herself up. The ink bottle tipped over, and she bent to pick it up as Vix entered the room. The door closed behind him, and she didn't have time to fix the covering over what she'd been working on.

"Vix, I—what are you doing here?" Laila asked, standing up straight.

"I wanted to speak to you before our meeting later."

Laila suspected Vix's eyesight was not great as he squinted often. He came closer, and it seemed easier on his eyes to do so.

"I have a particular item missing from my quarters," Vix said, "and wanted to ask if you knew something about it."

Laila hung her head. "Yes. I took the book. I'm sorry, Vix. I just . . . I needed it." Her face went hot.

"That is all right," Vix said. "But I should like it back. It is not something I wish for anyone to have in their possession."

"Why? I don't understand. I've had it for years and read the whole thing numerous times. What difference does it make now for me to give it up?"

"I understand, Laila. All the same, I should like it returned to me."

Telling Vix she'd given it back to Beiron was guaranteed to keep her locked up forever. "Vix, most of what's in the book is remedies and plants and their uses. I would never try any of the ones that I thought were too dangerous."

Vix bowed his head slowly. "It is not the contents that concern me, Laila." He looked at her. "It is the means by which Beiron came to learn all that is in the book. Beiron has no moral boundary and does what he deems necessary. Even if it is not right."

But he'd saved her life.

Laila shifted away from Vix and the back of her knees touched the bed. She'd been told Beiron was evil and inhumane. But what she saw of him was not so. "Is he really so bad? What if people are wrong about him? Or what if he's changed?"

Vix raised a hand, silencing her. "He is not a good man, Laila. Beiron is dangerous, and if you should ever come across him, run away. He will not hesitate to kill anyone who stands in his way."

It wasn't adding up. Vix had to be wrong about him. She shook her head, and he stepped closer to her. He took her hands in his.

"Sit, please," he said. When she looked into his eyes, his gentle face had become downcast and his eyes filled with tears.

Laila did as he said, and Vix sat down beside her. He held her hands as a father might to console his child.

"There is something I must tell you. It is something I have not shared with anyone before, mostly because I was too ashamed to speak of it. And because it seemed of no use to tell anyone before now. But you need to hear this. Please do not be quick to judge me."

Laila held her breath. Whatever Vix was about to tell her, she wasn't sure she wanted to hear. That wasn't true. She did want to hear it. She leaned in closer, her eyes big and expectant.

"When Landon Valca invaded Litlen," Vix began, "Beiron sought out the delegates. We elders had been informed that Landon had become privy to knowledge of the Weldafire Stone, and it was believed that Beiron was responsible for informing him of our most sacred piece of our magic."

"Why would he do that?" Laila couldn't help herself. The question escaped her lips before she could catch it.

"I do not know. There were rumours about a mayanon who would become bound to the stone. Beiron, son of Terrin Cailt, one of the Six, and nephew to another, Sullivan, believed it was his right to possess the stone and its power. The warriors were given the order to arrest Beiron when he was suspected to have murdered one of the delegates. But with the war having begun, the warriors were preoccupied in the battle. The elders and I were leaving a meeting, and I happened upon Beiron on my way out. He was not in a good way and had a look in him—a darkness. His eyes were changed. Once bright and blue, turned dark. Whatever he was up to, I knew it was not good. He went on his way and I followed him."

Tears streamed down Vix's cheeks. He spoke even slower than usual as he appeared to be struggling to make himself say more. "I followed him in the dark to the mountains, where he came across Anahita, another of the Six. I watched from the shadows as he stabbed her." He paused. "And I did nothing." Vix released Laila's hands and put his own to his face. He wept into them.

Laila stared. Vix was always so strong and sombre. This vulnerability scared her. She looked at the door, wondering if someone would check on them soon. There was no one. She swallowed past a hard lump and rubbed his back consolingly as he took a deep breath and went on with his story.

"I was too afraid to go to her then. If Beiron killed me too, what good would I have been to Ana?" Vix's chest hitched as he breathed in shakily. "Beiron spoke to Ana as she bled out. I was too far to hear what was said, but I was not too far to see him fill his hands with her blood and drink it."

Laila's heart pounded hard. Could Vix have been mistaken? She doubted it. Had she really made a deal with such a man?

"When he was gone," Vix said. "I went to Ana, and she died in my arms. Beiron had left her to die, and there was nothing I could do." Vix sniffed. He said nothing more as he wiped his eyes with his sleeve. Then he looked at Laila, and his grey eyes reflected the firelight of the candle. "You ask if Beiron really is all that we say he is. The answer is yes, Laila. He is that and so much worse."

What Vix had told her was a lot to process. Laila's mouth hung open, and she closed it. Seeing what he'd seen . . . having someone die in his arms and choosing not to tell anyone about it—why had he not told anyone? Surely if Beiron was so dangerous, someone should have been told.

"Would you not have warned the others?" she asked. "The other elders or the delegates? Were you not worried that Beiron would have done the same to them?"

"I was terrified, Laila. That was the same night our magic left us. I don't know what caused the quake, but when I felt it, I knew I'd lost my power. Beiron was not seen or heard from again, and it did not seem to make much difference whether I told anyone or not."

"But why would he do that?" she asked. "He drank her blood?" She couldn't imagine it. Or perhaps to imagine it scared her too much and she just chose not to believe it. All the more reason not to tell anyone about her shared connection with Beiron.

"I do not wish to delve into the mind of someone so evil," Vix said. "And nor should you dig any further into the matter. It is enough that you have read his book. I would remind you to keep your head about you." He pointed to the parchment Laila had set aside. The one she didn't hide so well. "I see you are making notes that look quite like his own." He stood up from the bed and wiped the last traces of tears from his face. "Now, if you'll tell me where I can find the book, I'll be on my way."

Laila couldn't meet his gaze. She kept her eyes to the ground and remained seated on the bed. "I . . . I can't tell you, Vix."

She was certain she'd be the one to finally cause him to lose his calm demeanour. Any moment now, she expected him to raise his voice—something he never did—or tell her she could never leave this place. She bit her bottom lip. Vix was quiet. More than a minute passed.

"I understand I haven't earned your trust," Laila said, finally meeting his gaze. "But please, trust that I have my reasons." It was as if the room was closing in on her. Her brow was wet with sweat, and she wiped it with her wrist.

Vix nodded—slowly, as always, which only made her stomach churn more.

"Very well," he said. He went to the door and knocked. "I will see you later tonight when you will explain your actions to the elders." When the door was opened, he left and she was locked in once again.

Every bit of hope she had of leaving these mines dwindled away. She was doing this to herself.

Leaving her writings alone for the time being, she lay back on the bed and stared at the ceiling. Why couldn't she make something up to appease Royl and the elders and finally be free of this place? Her need to tell the truth nagged at her. She couldn't entertain the thought of lying to her brother. She'd been keeping so much from him lately, and it hurt her heart. As she lay on the bed, unable to relax, she considered all that Vix had told her. His account of the night he followed Beiron was disturbing.

How was she supposed to explain to them all that she had made a deal with Beiron? Or how the two of them even met in the first place?

Laila groaned. She was never getting out of here.

Chapter 56

Laila had lost all track of time in containment. As Zulu escorted her to the private room for the meeting with the elders, she had no idea whether it was day or night. The only indicator of time she had were by the meals that had been brought to her, but she couldn't remember when the last one came. Her legs shook as she walked behind Zulu's tall, broad frame toward where the elders waited.

Zulu opened the door and waved her in.

In the room were the five armchairs. They were not arranged in their usual circle but instead were lined in two rows. Royl sat to the left in the second row. Vix was in the first row, facing directly in front of the chair that had been brought in for Laila. It was a small room to begin with, and the six people crowded in with the six chairs made it seem much smaller.

Laila took a seat and, only as an afterthought, considered that she should have waited until she'd been asked to sit.

The sweat on the back of her neck made her skin itch. She resisted the urge to move her hand to wipe it away. All eyes were on her as she leaned back in the chair and folded her hands in her lap. She met each elder's gaze, Royl's the longest. Typically, she was skilled at reading his thoughts from his expression, but lately, it had been difficult to conclude what he was thinking. Perhaps it was because she'd been keeping things from him.

Vix began the meeting. "Laila. You have been brought before us because you have broken the rules we have in place for your protection and for the protection of everyone here. This is not the first time you've done this, but you have taken it a step further and invited a mayanon into our sanctuary."

Refusing to shrink back under the watchful eyes of the elders, Laila raised her chin and set her jaw. She would not apologize for doing what was right.

Royl leaned forward and rested his elbows over his knees. He linked his fingers together. Whenever she glanced his way, he averted his eyes.

Vix continued, "Countless times you have left the mines to wander in territory that has been deemed unsafe. In the beginning, you had done a good thing by salvaging books to preserve our history, but that was long ago. You are not a designated collector, nor do you tend to the crops or livestock, nor are you a sentry. There is no reason for you to be outside, away from your place here in the mines. However—"

"And you've not brought anything of use back in years," Darrin cut in. "The least you could have done is brought back some supplies in all the times you've gone."

Nothing of use? Laila didn't see anyone complaining about the fact that they had their magic back. She bit her tongue, not allowing herself to be provoked into an argument.

"However," Vix resumed, disregarding Darrin's comment, "we will take into consideration all that you have done. Thanks to you, we have our magic."

Laila caught Darrin's good eye and suppressed a smirk. Now was not the time to be arrogant.

"And a baby has been safely reunited with his mother," said Vix. "We are now aware that Beiron is present in Litlen once more, and you have brought useful information regarding the Weldafire Stone. It seems that after your friend Ida had her baby restored to her, Dimitri was more than happy to share his involvement. It is an interesting tale to be sure, but right now we should like to hear your story, Laila."

Their expectant eyes fell on her, and she cleared her constricted throat. She hadn't considered all that she would share, but she understood that they'd need to hear something of her adventures beyond the mines. "I met Ida and learned of her husband's correlation with the stone," Laila said, speaking with more confidence than she felt. "I was there when her son was taken from her. I didn't act to help her at that time, and I felt responsible for her and her son. So, when an opportunity presented itself to retrieve her son, I took it."

"What opportunity?" Darrin asked.

Royl had been quiet this whole time. He probably thought that by keeping his head down, he wouldn't be among those condemning her to a miserable fate in confinement—never to see the sun again.

"An opportunity that got the baby back to his mother safely," Laila said simply. "I weighed the risks and made my choices, knowing there would be consequences. I take responsibility for my actions, but I'm not sorry." A strong desire to be done with this conversation came over her. Why were they talking about this when there were more important things to discuss?

"Surely you all know we can't keep living like this," she stated. "In fear of something happening to us if we move forward. I cannot be the only one who thinks this."

Royl finally looked up at her. His grimace did not make her back off. She sat on the edge of her seat.

"It made sense to flee during the war," she said. "When we lost our magic, the battle was already lost. Coming here was a way to survive, and we have. But we're not truly living!"

"Laila." Royl implored with his eyes that she stop talking—that wasn't going to deter her.

"We have our magic back," Laila said. "We have trained warriors. Litlen is mostly restored and alive again, and the Weldafire Stone, within reach. Why are we not planning to find the Guardian? That should be our priority, especially since we're now aware that Beiron is at large, and I presume you all know what his goal is."

The room became still. She'd done it now. This was it. Any moment they were going to lock her away and throw away the key for such insubordination. Even Royl couldn't prevent what was coming her way.

Maire's small voice spoke into the silence. "I agree with Laila.

Laila almost laughed out loud, her nerves were so on edge. It occurred to her that she'd never actually heard Maire speak. Laila always associated her with the four elders without ever paying her much attention. Her voice was different than what she would have imagined from the small silver-eyed woman.

Darrin's wide eyes turned to Maire. "The Guardian? A priority? He's a mayanon. Already we have two here who know more than they should. Perhaps we should let Beiron find the Guardian. At least then the stone would be in the hands of an Elderace, as it should be."

"We are at a pivotal time for our race," Maire said. "Finding the Guardian and ensuring his safety should be our concern, as Laila has said. If Beiron gains possession of the Weldafire Stone, not one of us will be immune from his tyranny. He will be as much a threat to us all as the Valca empire has been, except his power is greater."

"He will have the interest of the Elderace in mind," Darrin argued.

"Beiron acts from self-interest," said Vix. "And he is not the kind of man who should have such power."

"But we do not have a way to find the Guardian," Zulu cut in.

"I might have a way," Laila said. Her latest entry in her version of Beiron's book provided a solution. Eshuair was not the easiest to access, as it grew among the poisonous xhinelet bush, but it could work and was worth a try. She couldn't believe it didn't come to her sooner, it being her mother's favourite flower. Dimitri's blood ties to his brother would lead them right to Raidan. If only she could convince the elders to use Beiron's tricks for their own purposes.

"It will require Dimitri's help," she said, "and I want to accompany the group that goes out to look for him." Maybe she was pushing her luck, but it seemed she now had an ally. To further aid them granting her request, she added, "And when we find Raidan, I'll explain everything. I promise."

Darrin's lips curled back. He pointed a finger at her once more and opened his mouth, likely to reprimand her. Thankfully, Vix did not allow him to say anything.

"Perhaps," he said in a loud voice, then quieted down to say the rest. For all his slowness, he was quick to command the room. "We should consider what Laila has in mind and grant her permission to join the search. She has proved herself capable of handling herself outside the mines. Dimitri clearly trusts her, and will therefore make it easier to gain the trust of the brother. What do you say, Royl?" Vix twisted his torso in his chair.

Royl's eyes widened. He looked from one person to the next. "What do I think? Well . . ." He looked at Laila. His shoulders relaxed, and his eyes softened. "I think that when Laila gets something in her head, she'll make a way to go after it regardless of what anyone says. So, I suppose it's best to allow her to go along. But if she goes, I should like to be a part of the search team also."

"Very well." Vix nodded.

Darrin stood abruptly. "So what? We're going to absolve her of her disobedience and reward her by letting her roam freely again?"

"She'll be with me," Royl said, finally coming to her defence. Even if she had to be supervised, this option by far beat staying locked up in containment.

Vix remained calm as he filled his lungs before speaking. "Is anyone else opposed to this plan?"

Again, all eyes turned to Laila. Darrin remained on his feet, his jaw twitching and his eyes narrowing in on her. No one spoke.

Vix clapped his hands together. "Good. It's settled. Now, Laila, please let us hear what you have in mind."

Chapter 57

THE CLOUDS THAT THREATENED TO COVER THE SKY EARLIER THAT DAY had disappeared. Eli led Raidan to the locameen to meet others. It was nearly time for dinner, and the place was bustling with people.

Round tables were spread out around the room. The inhabitants of the village came and went, and the chairs scraped along the floor as people made room for others to sit. Along the length of the far wall was a bar table filled with hot dishes of various foods. The room had the aroma of blended spices and herbs.

Eli walked toward the bar table, and Raidan stayed close behind. In a new place, it was difficult not to look around and take it all in, but to do so without catching anyone's eyes was impossible. Some of the people in the room ignored him completely. Others glared at him. The man and woman who leaned in toward one another to whisper in each other's ears while shifting their glances at him were not too subtle. One man stared at Raidan, looked him up and down, then hissed at him through his teeth. It wasn't exactly like Raidan blended in here.

Eli handed Raidan a plate and the two moved along the bar counter together, spooning food on their plates as they went. The foods before him were bright in colour: chicken in an orange sauce; vegetables of varying greens and purple; a red stew of some kind, which reminded Raidan of the stew that knocked him out the night before. He avoided that dish. Even the rice was yellow. Eli filled his plate while Raidan selected a few bits distractedly. They sat at one of the few empty round tables.

A boyish-looking young man approached their table with a plateful of food and a broad smile. His hair was woven into short dreadlocks that jutted out from his head.

"Eli, my friend," the man said. "I see you are the guardian of the rider." He laughed and set his plate down. Eli stood up, and the two of them slapped hands. Eli took his seat again, and the friend joined them.

The word "guardian" triggered memories of Adrik. Raidan pushed them from his mind. He had enough problems as it was without the added problem that Adrik lived.

"Eh, you," the man said to Raidan. "You the spy then?"

"Just Raidan will do."

"Well, *just Raidan*, I am Andrei. You already know my brother Eli." His grin was mischievous. "He is not really my brother, but he is the closest thing to it, so do not go making an enemy of him because you will have me to answer to, ya hear?"

It was a playful jest, but Raidan knew he meant it. He felt the same way about his own brother.

Andrei wriggled his bottom and started into his food. "So what is your story, Rider?" he asked. "What is the Valca's plan?"

Eli dug into his food while Raidan picked up his fork and poked at what looked like a bit of pineapple saturated in a brown glaze. He had no appetite.

"What happened there?" Andrei asked, pointing to Raidan's bruised wrists from the restraints. Instinctively, Raidan touched a hand to his wrist. He said nothing. It wasn't as though they'd believe him if he told them.

"You do not speak, Rider? Are you mute?" Andrei said.

"And you don't stop speaking," Raidan said.

Rather than Andrei being discouraged by Raidan's remark, his lips spread wide in a smile. His eyes were slits on his face. "You are right

303

about that," Andrei said, slapping Raidan on the back playfully. He looked at Eli. "You have your work cut out for you here, Eli my friend. This one is very serious." He leaned in close to Raidan again. "You should lighten up, ya?"

Raidan set his fork on the table. He glanced behind him at the door. Already Andrei spoke loud enough to draw attention their way. Raidan would only make it worse if he got up to leave. He picked up his fork again and stabbed a piece of sweet pepper. It was more to distract himself than anything. He raised the fork to take a bite and stopped short, remembering Tala's stew. Eli had eaten half his food, and Andrei was already a few bites in. They both seemed perfectly fine. Still, Raidan hesitated.

"Ah, I see you have had Tala's specialty," Andrei said. "You do not need to worry, though. This is not anything like it."

Raidan took the bite, not because he trusted what Andrei said, but because he'd witnessed others in the room eat it without consequences. Though by Andrei's smirk, Raidan was certain that he thought it was his reassuring words that did the trick.

After swallowing two mouthfuls, Raidan looked around, sensing that people were not as interested in him as they'd been. "What is this place?" he asked.

Andrei and Eli shared uncertain expressions, and Raidan wasn't sure they were going to tell him.

"It is a rebellion," a woman said from behind as she approached. When she spoke, everyone in the locameen turned their attention to her.

"*We* are a rebellion. Is that a problem?" She stopped at their table and crossed her arms. She was tall for a woman and had high cheekbones that complimented her features. Her hair was braided close to her scalp and spilled down her back where it was tied in a ponytail. Like the men and most of the women Raidan had seen in the camp thus far, she wore trousers and a fitted shirt.

"Rider, this is Keshlyn." Andrei was right on top of the introductions. "And she is a wicked woman who will beat you if she likes you. That is how you know her feelings." Andrei found this extremely funny and burst into laughter, joined by Eli, though Raidan suspected only because Andrei's laugh was so contagious.

Keshlyn's lips pouted, and she shook her head. "Andrei, go do some work. You have too much fun for a warrior."

Raidan had to agree. He'd never have believed Andrei was a warrior by his playful mannerisms.

"Well, Rider, is it a problem?" Keshlyn repeated.

"It's Raidan, actually, and no. On the contrary, I think it's something this country needs." He almost laughed out loud at the irony of hearing himself say those words. Where was Dimitri at a time like this?

"You do not disapprove then, that we plan and perform defiant acts on the Valca Order?" Keshlyn asked.

"I know how it looks, me riding with Ilan, but it isn't what you think."

Keshlyn shrugged. "Kameron will say if it is what it looks like," she said. "In ten minutes, we meet," she told them all. "And I hope you will come too," she added for Raidan. Without further explanation, she walked off. The people who'd turned their attention to her resumed eating their dinner.

"Come where?" Raidan asked.

"Music night," Andrei said. "There will be singing and dancing. It is wild! So much fun, Rider. You will love it."

Fun was not what he needed. He needed his family. There was no time for this when Cassian and Ida were still out there, missing.

"It is required; you must come," Andrei said when Raidan didn't answer.

Eli scowled at his friend. Raidan got the sense that Eli didn't want him there. But what else was he going to do? Sit in his hut and drive himself crazy in his own head while waiting for Kameron? Besides,

Ilan was somewhere in the camp. Seeing more of the place might help him determine where they were keeping him. He nodded.

"Good, it is settled." Andrei stood, his chair scraping the floor as he pushed it out from the table. Eli stood too, and Raidan took that as his cue that they were leaving.

They went back outside and walked toward the green space, where some of the camp's inhabitants carried out couches and chairs from the octagonal building. A band prepared their instruments on the grass, facing the couches and chairs.

This camp was a rebellion against the Valca Order. What might Dimitri think of all this?

"What made you start a rebellion?" Raidan asked as they walked at a slow pace toward the green.

Andrei swept his arm across to indicate the people before them preparing for the music night. "For a long time," he said, "we were isolated from the rest of Kartha. Many years ago, Kameron and Keshlyn started this camp as a refuge. It was only after the Great Battle at Reen that we knew we had to do something to help bring a change in our country. We were unaware that the people had taken up arms against The Ord—"

Eli smacked Andrei's arm, making him stop.

"The Great Battle at Reen?" Raidan asked. "That was years ago. You don't look any older than I am, and I was only six when that happened. How could you have been a part of that?"

Eli's lips were a thin line as he gave Andrei a disapproving glare. "It is not your business. None of it is."

Were these people Elderace? Raidan stopped walking and stared at the ground. Eli stopped too and stood poised to grab Raidan if he tried anything. "What is it?" he asked. "What is wrong with you?"

"How many are there of you?" Raidan asked. "Is it just your camp?"

"Ah, Rider, you are accused of being a spy, remember?" Andrei said with a pat on Raidan's back. "We cannot tell you that."

The green space filled with people. Chairs became occupied as people came from all around the camp to take a seat. The band warmed up their instruments, playing a light beat with a steady rhythm.

The sun glowed red, hovering at the tip of a peak, soon to dip out of sight. Eli put his hands to his hips. "Why are you standing there like that?"

To bring up the Elderace was to begin a conversation that Raidan did not want to have. If this group of people were Elderace, could they be the ones to help him get rid of this magic in him? But saying anything about his power and the Weldafire Stone would raise too many questions. Before all else, he needed to find Cassian and Ida. He would save the subject of the Elderace until then.

Chapter 58

Raidan walked toward the courtyard filled with people. Eli and Andrei hopped in step with him, and Raidan could sense them looking at him. They found Keshlyn on one of the couches and went to her. She scooted aside so Raidan could sit. Eli took a chair beside the couch, and Andrei went off and mingled with others. Kameron was still nowhere to be seen.

With no warning or introduction, the band struck a well-timed chord that led them into their first song. The musicians bounced in rhythm while playing their upbeat melody. Three people played different-sized drums. Two had djembes, and one had congas wrapped around his neck and he bounced and played along. Everyone who had joined to hear the music cheered and swayed. Even Raidan found it difficult to keep his feet from tapping out the beat as he sat leaning over his knees.

He relaxed and folded his arms in front of his chest. Then immediately, he sat forward again, not letting himself get too comfortable.

Kameron appeared in the growing crowd as more people trickled over. He sat down next to Raidan. "What do you think?" Kameron asked.

Raidan cocked his head at Kameron. What did he think of what? "Just wait, it gets better." Kameron pointed to the band.

"Have you found anything out from Ilan?" Raidan had to lean over to Kameron and raise his voice to be heard over the music.

Kameron ignored the question. "The music," he said, "do you like it?"

Raidan huffed out a breath. He spoke through clenched teeth. "It's nice."

"Are you listening, though? Truly listening?"

"I don't have time for this—"

Kameron put a calming hand on Raidan's knee before Raidan got too worked up. The reminder was needed, and he wondered if Kameron knew something of Raidan's power.

"Be still, Raidan," Kameron said. Raidan didn't recall giving his name to Kameron, but Keshlyn or Andrei may have shared that bit of information with him. Or Ilan. "Listen," he said.

Raidan tuned his ears in to listen. "It's like nothing I've ever heard," he said truthfully.

"Yes." Kameron sat back and folded his hands behind his head. "Benji has unique sound." He pointed out the man playing a stringed instrument over a hollow piece of wood. The instrument had a low rumble that Raidan could feel pulsing through his body just as he could feel the vibration of the sound on the ground. It was steady and quick. Between that and the three drummers playing, it was hard not to jump up and move his feet. Raidan refrained.

There were two other strange-looking instruments fashioned similarly to the low rumbling stringed instrument that resembled a lute. In the back, beside one of the men playing the djembe was a woman playing a marimba. Raidan recognized these instruments from books he'd read when he was younger. They were predominately played in the country of Ectarin. He'd never heard their sound before now. The harmony of the instruments and the atmosphere in the courtyard was compelling.

Raidan pulled his attention away from the music. "Did you learn anything from Ilan about my son?" he asked again.

Kameron shook his head. "He says many things, but he has not said anything about your son."

Raidan's headache was settling between his brows. He closed his eyes tight and pinched the place where it ached. How could these people believe Ilan and not him? They had to know what kind of man Ilan Valca was. Why was it so hard for them to see he was lying?

The band continued to play through their arrangement of music. After the first few songs that had everyone on their feet jumping and sweating, the next tune mellowed out. Many people remained standing and swayed to the song, while others sat back and fanned themselves ineffectively.

As darkness grew around them, two villagers went around the field lighting the lamps that lined the edge of the green. They danced while they moved from one lamp to the next.

Keshlyn stepped up to the front and sang. Her voice carried a haunting tune, and her song revolved around a couple who had a deep bond with each other, but their friendship and their love could not be. The girl had come from a family of rulers from which she had run away. The boy's own family was once an enemy of the girl's family, unbeknownst to him. The families forbade them from seeing each other again. In defiance, the young couple embarked on an adventure that deepened their bond and brought about reconciliation between the families.

Keshlyn's strong voice didn't waver. Her smooth tones were fierce, yet she somehow made Raidan believe his feet could lift off the ground. Closing his eyes, he listened:

> *In the eve,*
> *at the dawn,*
> *when you go from here to there,*
> *I'll be by your side,*
> *I'll be by your side.*

When all those who come against us,
try to break this bond of ours,
I'll be by your side,
I'll be by your side.

Keshlyn stopped singing, and the music carried out the tune until the band flawlessly switched to the next song.

"Do you know what your problem is?" Kameron tore Raidan's mind from the music. They weren't the only ones to converse at this point. Others talked amongst each other, speaking over the loud music.

"There's only one?" Raidan kidded. Somehow his mood felt a little lighter.

"You have so much anger. You need to let it go. You must allow yourself to let go of the weight you carry."

Easier said than done.

Kameron leaned in closer. His dark eyes reflected the firelight from the lamps, and he rubbed the silver hairs on his chin. "Do this: Let everything go from your mind. Listen to the music, let it carry you. Let it take your weight and lift you. Can you do that?"

Raidan wasn't sure he could let his worries escape his mind. His fear for Cassian was at the forefront of his thoughts. If he allowed himself to stop thinking about him, what if something terrible happened? "I can't," he said.

"Try. You cannot make your problems disappear. I know you are worried for your son, but right now, in this moment, what can you do about it?"

"What can I do? If you let me go, I can go to him."

"So, you know where he is then?"

Raidan shook his head. He understood what Kameron was saying, but it still didn't make sense. "If you believe me, then why won't you just let me go so I can find him?"

Kameron's eyes had turned soft, his compassion genuine. "My point, Raidan, is that you would leave and go where exactly? You claim

Ilan is the only one who knows where your son is, yet you wish so desperately to go and get him right this moment. Where will you go? Even if I free you, the young Valca is going nowhere."

He waited for Raidan to reply, but Raidan had no response. "I may believe what you say, but then I ask myself: Why is the Valca adamant that you are with him and what brought you to him in the first place? Where is it you intend to go from here?"

All Raidan knew was that as long as he stayed, he was no closer to finding Cass.

Kameron went on. "In the same way you do not trust me to tell your story, I cannot trust you to not go from here and expose what we are doing. You understand?"

Raidan did. He didn't like it, but he understood.

"Now," Kameron said. "Right here, close your eyes. Put everything from your mind. All things, good and bad, and just listen."

Raidan took a moment before deciding to go along with it. He wanted to show Kameron he was willing to earn their trust. He sat back and attempted to clear his head.

After less than a minute, Kameron said, "You are not clearing your mind. I can see that you are still thinking."

Raidan shot him an annoyed look. Following Kameron's instructions was not easy. He closed his eyes again and cleared his mind. Really cleared it. The music continued to play its slow tune, and Raidan let it draw him in. It carried him, and his body completely relaxed. He allowed the song to lift him far away and into a place of peace and understanding, of certainty and direction.

He was in tune with his body and could hear himself breathe over the music. He put his hand to his chest and felt its steady rise and fall. Deeper within himself was the power. It was there, and it was in him. It *was* him. He just didn't know how to access it. As he was pulled deeper still into his mind and body, he knew he would not ever be able to control this power as long as he let his anger block him. His anger at Adrik. Dimitri. Himself. It was like a wall, solid and firm, blocking his mind from drawing from the pool of energy and power in him. He knew, truly knew and understood, that unless he could dismantle that barricade, he'd never be able to help those he loved. The question then was, how did he break the barricade?

He opened his eyes. He knew the answer. He didn't like it, but he knew it.

"What did you feel?" Kameron asked after Raidan opened his eyes.

In a word: "Hope," Raidan said.

Kameron's face nearly disappeared in his smile. He clapped a hand onto Raidan's shoulder. "There is hope for you yet."

Chapter 59

Raidan awoke late the next morning after having the best night's sleep in a long time. It was a cooler morning, and he'd been given extra layers of clothing to stay warm in the night. After dressing, he stepped outside, where Eli greeted him. Someone had remained posted outside the door all through the night, but judging by Eli's fresh appearance, it had not been him.

Though he himself felt refreshed and rested, his heart ached for his family. The music last night had taken some of the burden, but another day had gone by where he didn't know Cassian and Ida's whereabouts.

"Where is Kameron?" Raidan asked Eli, hoping to be able to get out of there today.

People shouted and cheered from the courtyard. All the chairs and couches had been removed from the field and were lined along the sidelines, where spectators watched a game of ternex.

"Kameron is busy," Eli said. "Come, Andrei has a place for us at the game, and I am not supposed to leave you alone."

They went from his hut and passed more along the way. Near the locameen, Raidan got a whiff of fresh bread and bacon. His stomach grumbled.

As if Eli heard it, he said, "You missed breakfast. They have already cleaned up. Lunch will be soon."

Raidan breathed in, letting the scent of food be enough for the time being. He and Eli found Andrei sitting alone on the sidelines, fidgeting with a wooden toy boat. At least, that was what it looked like it was meant to be, though it was hard to be sure in its jumbled form.

"What are you doing with that?" Eli asked, taking a seat beside his friend. Raidan sat on Andrei's other side, observing Andrei's attempts to put the thing together.

"It is a gift for Jayde," Andrei said. He turned to Raidan. "She is my cousin."

"Why does Jayde want a child's toy?" Eli asked.

Andrei grinned and pride swelled in his chest. "She is with child."

Eli's jaw dropped. "It is not possible. How could that be?"

"Well, Eli, if I must explain it to you, then we have a problem."

"That is not what I meant and you know it. Does Manny know?"

Andrei went back to his fumbling with the pieces of the boat. "Of course, he knows. Do you not think she would tell the father before anyone else?"

A crowd of people across the field yelled at the players and encouraged their teams. The sport was played by three teams, competing to put a ball through each other's goal posts. Raidan hadn't been paying attention and didn't know who was winning. The teams were distinguished by coloured scarves wrapped around each player's head or waist. One team wore white, another black, and the third red. The field was scattered with players from each colour.

Andrei was getting nowhere with what he was doing. Raidan reached for the toy. "Here, I'll fix it." He'd made many toys like it in his craft. This one shouldn't be too difficult to figure out.

"You know how to fix this, Rider?" Andrei asked.

"Just give it here."

Andrei handed it to Raidan. The toy was made up of a few parts that joined together to make it a whole ship, complete with a wooden sail and turning wheel.

Raidan tinkered with it for a minute. He turned one of the two base pieces upside down. "This piece is meant to go like this," he said, then twisted it all the way around so that the two pieces fit together, making the shape of a boat. "With that done, the bow simply gets attached here." He put the pointed bow in place. Then all that remained was the mast and sail. He connected them for Eli and Andrei to see, then added the final touch with the turning wheel. When he was done, he gazed at the toy in his hand.

Life had been so much simpler when these were the only kinds of things he had to fret over. His worries about Rees's deadline seemed so minor in comparison to his troubles of late. With him and Dimitri gone, Veryl was left without their fearless leader. He wouldn't be surprised if Dimitri had convinced those Elderace to join him in his quest to conquer The Order. It would be so like him to spark a fire in the hearts of those who cared to listen. Who more than the Elderace had reason to hate The Order?

"He fixed it!" Andrei exclaimed, his face full of amazement. "A true magician, you are!" He plucked the boat from Raidan and turned it over in his hands.

There was nothing magical about it.

"That is nothing," Eli said. "You want to see real magic?" He took out a link, the Elderace currency. There weren't too many of those around anymore. The link was a small colourful coin with a hole in the middle. The hole served as the inner part of the yellow sun imprinted on the metal and was surrounded by a blue wave-like circle that looked like water splashing around the sun. The outer edges were an earthy colour that faded to black.

Eli put his hands out, palms up with the link in his left hand. "You see this link? I will transfer it from this hand to the other." He made a fist over the coin in his left hand, then closed his right. He banged them together and opened his left hand first to show that the link was gone. He extended his right hand, and there sat the link, as if transferred there by magic. Raidan couldn't keep a small smile from his lips. Eli smirked and bowed.

Andrei waved a hand. "Phfft, it is not like you are Adrik," Andrei said. At the mention of Adrik's name, Raidan ground his teeth.

A cheer erupted from the players on the field and those watching the game. Someone had scored a goal, but Eli took no notice. He shook his head sadly. "No, no one can do magic like Adrik. Not anymore. But still, he taught me this trick, and it is pretty amazing, do you not think?" he asked, looking at Raidan. His smile dropped and his eyes widened. "You know Adrik?"

Raidan's shoulders tensed. Had he been so obvious? He glanced between Eli and Andrei. "You could say that."

The two men leaned forward in their seats, their eagerness like that of children.

Raidan crossed his arms. "Let's just say he's not all that amazing."

Both the friends' faces dropped. "Not that amazing?" Eli almost fell off his seat. "How can you say that? When I was just little, Adrik came to me after my father's death and showed me magic. He taught me how to do that trick with the link and made me forget about my grief, even if it was only for a moment. I will carry that memory with me forever and am grateful for what Adrik helped me to realize then."

"And what was that?" Raidan asked.

"That even in my sorrow, I could still have joy. I will never forget my father and I will never stop feeling that loss, but I have been able to move on with my life, and I have had great pleasure in showing others what Adrik showed me. Now I can help others experience that same joy and show them it is okay to smile again."

Eli's experience sounded a lot like Raidan's, except that it was the loss of his mother that had him out mourning alone that night. Would his own experience have mirrored Eli's if Raidan hadn't been the heir to the guardian of a magical stone?

It didn't matter. Hearing Eli's story didn't change how he felt about Adrik. Thankfully, before he could say anything more, Keshlyn walked past and Andrei dropped their conversation to call out to her as she went.

"Eh, Kesh, you gonna come and watch me play the next game? You are good luck, you know!" He howled and slapped his knee. Whatever was so funny, Raidan didn't know. Eli raised his eyebrow at his friend and shook his head.

Before Keshlyn could leave his sight, Raidan stood and followed after her. Eli had let his guard down, and he jumped up when Raidan was already halfway to her.

"Where are you going?" he asked, running to catch up.

"I want to speak to Kameron."

Keshlyn was nearly past the last of the buildings, going further into the mountains. Raidan called out to get her attention.

"You are not allowed past this point," Eli said, leaping in front of Raidan before they could pass his boundary.

"I need to see Kameron." Raidan called out for Keshlyn again. She heard him that time and turned around.

Eli tugged Raidan's arm, trying to turn him around. "He is busy. Let us go back to the game." The game they weren't even watching.

Raidan called out a third time, and this time, Keshlyn turned and walked toward them.

"What do you want?" Keshlyn said when she was right in front of them. Eli pointed a thumb at Raidan and accompanied it with an eye roll.

The huts were fewer and farther between where they were standing. Raidan couldn't determine where Keshlyn had been heading to before she'd turned around. "Where's Kameron?" Raidan said. "I need to speak with him."

Keshlyn raised her eyebrows and jutted her chin up. Raidan turned around at her indication. Kameron was coming their way from the locameen, holding a mug that steamed at the top. Even from where Raidan stood, he could smell the coffee. He closed the distance to him.

"What can I do to make you trust me?" he asked before letting Kameron give a greeting. "I can't just stay here, wasting time. Let me prove I'm telling the truth."

Kameron took a sip from his coffee as he stepped past Raidan. He smacked his lips. "I have a meeting to attend that I am already late for. Prove to me after." He carried on his way with Keshlyn.

Raidan went after them and Eli jumped in step. "Allow me to join you."

When Kameron stopped walking, everyone else did too. The corner of his mouth scrunched up.

"The way I see it," Raidan said, "I'm either true to my word and you have nothing to worry about in having me attend. Or I'm not who I say I am, in which case it won't matter what I hear or see because, well . . . you understand my meaning."

With a bit of amusement in his eye, Kameron raised a brow at Keshlyn.

"Don't look at me," she said. "I am not the one to decide. The others will not like it."

Kameron sipped again from his drink. "No. Likely not." He took a contemplative breath. "All right, you may come," he told Raidan. "But do not forget what I have told you. If it turns out you are a spy and you attend this meeting, there will be no leaving this place for you. Ever. You will die here."

Raidan swallowed and nodded. What did he have to hide? Apart from the fact that he had power from a magical stone coursing through his blood.

Kameron dismissed Eli from his duty of supervising Raidan. He gestured for Raidan to come with him and Keshlyn, and they went away from the camp, outside the invisible line that served as Raidan's boundary.

While he hoped to gain Kameron's trust, Raidan also wanted to glean information regarding who these people were and whether they could help him with his problem.

Provided they first established that he was not a spy.

Chapter 60

The doorway into the mountain was unexpected. Raidan ducked inside a dark passageway after Kameron. It brought on memories from the cave with Dimitri and Adrik. He kept his head down while suppressing those thoughts. To get through this and earn trust, he needed to stay calm.

The short passageway ended in a wide-open space. From outside, Raidan would not have guessed this place existed within the mountain. It had been hollowed out into something of a grand hall. The walls, like the rest of the stone, were red. To the far right of the space were two couches and a small table between them. The three people who'd been sitting on the couches rose to their feet when Kameron approached with Keshlyn at his side and Raidan following. The only woman among them pointed her finger at Raidan. Her toned biceps were flexed, and her facial muscles were strained tight.

"You brought the spy?" she asked.

The other two men stared at Raidan, jaws hanging open.

Kameron held his mug in one hand and raised the other. "Yes, yes, Raidan has come. Perhaps he may contribute to our meeting. Who knows? Please sit. We are already delayed this morning."

Kameron sat first and took a sip from his drink. Keshlyn indicated Raidan sit somewhere. By the comfortable corner they were congregated in, he got the impression that meetings here were not generally so tense. The silence was awkward as they each claimed a seat. Raidan guessed he was the reason for their discomfort. He lowered himself onto the two-seater couch beside Kameron. Keshlyn remained standing and leaned against the wall, while the other three sat across from Raidan and Kameron.

When they were settled, Kameron bent forward over his knees. "Right then, Raidan, this is Jazz, Indra, and Yuri." He indicated the three attendees. Jazz was the man who had led the group that brought Raidan and Ilan to the camp from the road. The one with the little growth of beard, just under his lower lip.

Kameron moved on. "Let us begin. Our captive prince has not given any insights into the happenings in the north. Jazz, have you any news for us on the matter?"

Jazz flared his nostrils at Raidan before giving his report to Kameron. "Kingston Valca is preparing to march on Litlen. He has been busy readying his weapons."

"His weapons?" Keshlyn asked.

Jazz gave a nod. "Cannons. Three of them. The same as we have seen before."

Kameron downed the rest of his drink and placed his mug on the floor by his feet. "Do we know his motives for an attack on Litlen?"

"It is not clear," Jazz said. "We have all felt the change, and some of us have seen with our own eyes that there is once again life and beauty there. Perhaps he intends to destroy it as his grandfather did with those very same weapons."

"Perhaps," Kameron said. "But look further into it, would you?"

Raidan sat up straight on the couch and opened his mouth to speak. He closed his mouth abruptly, stopping himself. Would telling them of Kingston's plans make him look guilty of being a spy? Surely it would help Kameron trust him more.

Everyone was looking at him, waiting for him to speak. Raidan decided to take the risk. "There are Elderace who live."

"What?" Yuri asked. "Who? How do you know this?"

Kameron's eyes were intense on Raidan, but he didn't seem surprised by this information.

"I don't know who," Raidan said. "I only met two, but there were more. They . . . they were using magic."

"So, it is true," Keshlyn said. "The curse is gone?"

Indra, the woman who looked like she could snap Raidan's neck with only one of her arms, pointed again at Raidan. "Does Kingston know? Is that why he is preparing his army?"

"Yes," Raidan said. "Well . . . maybe. I don't know. There is one man—"

"You are one of them. Why should we believe you?" Jazz snapped to his feet and thrust his finger at Raidan.

Raidan's face went hot. "If I were one of them, why would I tell you anything?"

Kameron cleared his throat, getting everyone's attention. "Sit down, Jazz. Raidan, who is the man you were about to speak of?"

"His name is Beiron. He was with my son last. I was right there, and then—"

"Beiron!" Indra interrupted. "He was meant to be gone—"

Keshlyn cut her off. "I thought Ilan had your son," she said to Raidan.

"He does. I mean, he did. They were working together."

"The Valcas and Beiron working together," Yuri said. His top lip curled back, revealing his two front teeth.

"What were you doing with Beiron?" Kameron asked.

Raidan shut his mouth. His story was sounding more complex than intended, and he'd given more questions than answers. He leaned back and raised his hands to his head, sighing. "He was with Ilan. Look, I'm not with him. He took my son, and I don't know if my wife is safe. I need to find them. Please." His throat closed up, and he couldn't speak. Tears flowed down his cheeks, and he leaned forward while rubbing the bridge of his nose, where another headache was developing.

"Why would Ilan take your son in the first place?" Keshlyn asked.

That was the question Raidan hoped to not be asked. It did not escape his attention that they knew who Beiron was, or were at least familiar with his name. He wiped his face with his sleeve. "Are you Elderace?" he asked, rather than answer the question.

Kameron locked eyes once more with Raidan. He studied him as if he were a puzzle to be figured out. "We are," he said. "And we are not. But that is not why we are here." He addressed his people. "If it is true that Beiron is lurking about, it would be wise to increase our security around the camp. Yuri, put your guard on watch for Beiron. Jazz, gather a few people to go out in search of him. Indra, secure the perimeter."

Yuri, Jazz, and Indra acknowledged their orders with a nod and took Kameron's tone as a dismissal. Jazz spat at Raidan's feet as he passed with the other two to exit the grand inner mountain. Only Raidan, Kameron, and Keshlyn remained. Keshlyn took a seat on the now vacant couch across from Raidan and Kameron.

"First you are with Ilan and he has your son," Keshlyn said to Raidan. "Then Ilan and Beiron are working together and Beiron has your son. Working together for what? And what does it have to do with you? Where do you fit into all of this?"

For as much as Raidan wanted to earn their trust, he couldn't bring himself to respond fully. If they knew about the stone and his connection to it all . . . there was no telling when he'd be allowed to leave. All that wretched rock did was cause him pain and trouble.

"I'm not with either of them," he told the two of them. "I just want my family back. Please can you help me?"

Kameron placed a hand on Raidan's knee. "We will help you, Raidan. We will speak again with Ilan and see what he can tell us about the whereabouts of your son. But if Beiron had your boy last, then I would venture to say Ilan does not know where he is, as you say he does. Beiron does not answer to anyone."

Chapter 61

THE CLANKING OF SWORDS AND GRUNTING OF SOLDIERS FILLED THE Valca training grounds. Kingston walked at a brisk pace through the field of men as they sparred with one another. He found Mason, his army captain, and made a beeline for him. The men he passed stopped what they were doing and scurried out of his way. One person didn't move fast enough, so Kingston shoved him, causing the man to stumble into a handful of soldiers.

Mason stood with his arms folded over his chest. His earlobes hung low where large gauges were pierced through. They flopped about whenever he turned his head to watch or correct the men as they trained. He turned his head to Kingston and dropped his arms to his sides, standing at attention.

"Where are my cannons?" Kingston asked. "They were supposed to be ready by now!"

The men stopped their sparring to watch the spectacle.

"They're nearly ready, Mr. Valca," Mason said. The cords of his neck were strained. "In the meantime, the men have been training, and they're—"

"I don't care about that. Has anyone found my son? Where is Ilan?"

"He's not been found yet. I sent a group out to look and they've returned this morning with no news."

"Then send them out again. And when he's found, have him brought to the dungeons and locked up until this whole business is done. I can't have him getting in my way at a time like this."

"Of course, sir. I'll get right on it."

Kingston cringed. "Don't call me sir."

Owen's voice shouted from across the field of soldiers. "Your Greatness!"

Kingston smirked. His timing was impeccable.

Owen ran to him. "Your Greatness." When he was in front of Kingston, he panted and spoke between breaths. "They're ready." He put his hands over his knees and panted some more, then stood up straight. "The cannons. They're ready."

Kingston let his smirk grow into a smile. "Good. Mason, tell the men to be ready to set out this evening. It's time I show the people of Kartha just how powerful I am."

*

After the meeting, Raidan had returned to Eli. The game had ended and lunch was being served. Raidan hardly paid any attention to his food as he ate. Kameron and Keshlyn had disappeared.

After lunch, Eli showed Raidan along to a hut that was a little bigger than the one he'd been staying in. There was a shelf on one wall with a weighing scale on top of it. Jars full of what looked like dried herbs, oils, and plants lined the inside of the shelf. A bed took up some of the space in the single room. Beside the bed rested a table, with a bowl and tweezers atop, as well as a heap of linen cloth. A chair was tucked under the table, and on the other side of the bed was a stool. Raidan deduced that this hut served as a place of treatment for the sick or injured.

"Sit anywhere," Eli said. "I have work to do."

Raidan chose the stool, and Eli pulled the chair out from the table and sat. He unravelled the linen cloth and wound the pieces into individual rolls.

Raidan was lost in his own mind, his worries and fears weighing down on him. He thought about what Kameron had said about Beiron not working with anyone. He hated to agree, but it seemed a realistic presumption, especially considering Beiron himself had told him how he felt about Ilan. As much as it pained Raidan to think it, it was probable that Ilan did not know where Cassian was.

A part of him had always known Ilan might not have been telling him the truth, but he'd needed hope to cling to. If Ilan was lying, then all this time had been wasted. Cassian could be anywhere.

Eli watched Raidan as he continued to wind the cloth into rolls. "How do you know Adrik?"

Their conversation from earlier must have still been on his mind. Raidan didn't have the energy to debate whether Adrik was all Eli thought he was cracked up to be. "The same way you do."

"Why do you not like him?"

"I have my reasons." Raidan changed the subject before Eli could inquire further. "Are you Elderace?" he asked, hoping for more of an answer than Kameron had given.

Eli closed his mouth and turned his eyes down, focusing on his hands. "It is not for me to tell you."

"Kameron said you are and you are not. What does that mean?"

"It means we are neither. Elderace, mayanon, they are labels that begin quarrels. As long as we are seen as one or the other, we are creating separation. So, it is as Kameron has said: We are. And we are not. That is enough talking." Eli tossed a handful of the cloth to Raidan. "Help me with these."

While Raidan assumed the task of winding the cloth, Eli stood and picked through the jars on the shelves. He removed some of the contents from the ones with herbs and put them into individual pouches. He placed the filled pouches gently in a bag with straps to carry it by.

"You're a healer?" Raidan said.

"I am. You know the remedies?" Eli waved a small jar in his hand.

"I know of a few." Raidan recognized the green and orange oil in the jar Eli held up. The cenjer seed oil was easily distinguishable by its colours, which swirled together but did not mix. The consistency and warmth of the oil was said to be good for cauterizing minor flesh wounds. At least, that was what Aunt Nell used it for.

"My aunt is a healer," Raidan said, thinking of her. His mother's sister was the one who'd taken him and Dimitri in after their mother had died.

"It is good work," Eli said. "I must keep some things ready to have on hand quickly. I have heard that soldiers are now marching from Valmain."

Eli looked at Raidan as if he might confirm it. Confirmation would come soon enough through Kameron. Raidan gave no response. He finished rolling the cloth, then helped Eli separate the herbs and put them into pouches for easy transportation. They worked until it was dark, then trickled into the locameen for a late supper before Eli walked Raidan back to his hut and said good night.

Raidan hoped his third night in the camp would be his last. Weary from the day and his worries, he lay down, and for once, sleep came easy.

*

Raidan woke to a sound. In his grogginess, he couldn't determine its source. He didn't think he'd slept for long, but his heavy muscles told him he'd woken from a deep sleep.

The sound was there again, coming from outside the closed door to his hut. There was a muffled groan and some scuffling. Raidan eased out of bed and stood. He shook his head, trying to make himself more alert and banish the tiredness. The noises stopped and the door flung open.

Moonlight filled the room through the open door where Ilan stood. His shoulders rose and fell with his heavy breaths. Outside the door, the man who'd been standing guard lay unconscious.

Raidan rubbed his eyes. "Ilan? What have you done?"

"Let's go, we're getting out of here," Ilan said.

Raidan studied the man's body on the ground. "What did you do?"

Ilan followed Raidan's gaze. "He'll live." He reached for Raidan.

Raidan stepped back. "We can't leave here."

"We can, and we have to go now. Don't you want to see your son?"

"You know I do. But if we go, they're going to kill us."

"They're going to kill me anyway. Makes no difference if I stay or go, and I'd rather take my chances out there than wait to see what happens to me here."

A decent point. Ilan's options weren't great. Raidan's, on the other hand, were turning out to be not so terrible now that Kameron had offered to help him. What Kameron had said about Beiron came to mind. Raidan's chances at finding his family were better with Kameron's help than Ilan's.

"I'm not leaving with you," Raidan said. He planted his feet.

Ilan stepped forward, looking like he was about to engage in a fight with Raidan, then stopped when Raidan matched his step, accepting the challenge.

"You going to fight me, Ilan? Is that what you're going to do? You planning on making me go with you?" His eyes having adjusted to the dim light filling the room, Raidan could see Ilan's eyes locked onto his, like he'd contemplated the idea. Then Ilan dropped his gaze and backed off. Ilan may have been better trained in battle, but with none of his men to back him, Raidan had the advantage here. His magic, though unwanted and unpredictable, was there all the same and Ilan had seen him use it. But calling upon it now would be sure to draw attention.

Ilan groaned, then glanced around as though someone might have heard him. He turned to leave, but before he could go, Raidan grabbed his arm. Ilan twisted his head back. His eyes were big and round, probably hoping he'd changed his mind and would go with him after all.

"Do you know where my son is?" Raidan asked. He had to be sure.

Ilan tugged his arm out of Raidan's grasp. "Come with me and I'll take you to him."

"You don't know where he is, do you?" Raidan said, though now he was fairly certain.

Ilan hesitated.

"Do you?" Raidan said again, raising his voice.

Ilan's gaze darted around, checking behind him. His face looked pinched. "Quiet, or you'll get us both killed. Your son is with one of my men. I know where they've gone."

"One of your men? You left three responsible for Cassian. Why is there now only one? And what about Beiron? How do you know he hasn't taken my son and left your men for dead?"

"He wouldn't. He wouldn't betray me like that." Ilan's voice faltered.

"Then you don't know that man as well as you think."

Ilan glanced around again. The man on the ground was still out. It wouldn't be long before someone noticed him. Or the fact that Ilan was gone from wherever he'd been held.

"I'm not leaving," Raidan said again.

"But your son, I can get you to him."

"Tell me where he is and I won't raise the alarm that you're escaping."

"You won't do that," Ilan said.

Raidan considered it. "You'll be caught and forced to tell Kameron where my son is," he said. "Kameron has already offered to help me. So tell me, where is Cassian?" He raised his voice just enough to make Ilan shrink back, putting his hands out, urging Raidan to keep his voice down.

"Shh," he whispered. "I don't know where he is. But I can help you find him. As soon as we're out of here, I'll have my men by my side."

Raidan's shoulders slumped. His whole world came crashing down. It was just as Kameron had said. His bottom lip trembled and he bit down on it.

"Raidan, come—"

"Go," Raidan said.

Ilan gawked at him. "Come. Or I'll go back to Valmain and tell my father you're here. If you come with me now, he won't know any differently."

"If you tell your father where to find me, you'll lose the one person who can get you close to the Elderace without them trying to kill you. Your father will just kill me and everyone else here too."

"These people threatened to kill me first."

"You're not your father, Ilan. And if he doesn't already know about the Elderace who live, he will soon enough. I know you care about them. You know he'll try to finish them off, just like he said he would. If anyone can stop him from starting another war, it's you."

Voices sounded from outside. Ilan turned his head in their direction. Shouting echoed at the other end of the camp.

From the open door, the sky was becoming lighter. The sun would be up soon and Ilan would lose the cover of night. Raidan could sound the alarm now or never. He stood frozen in place.

But he already knew he wasn't going to do it. Ilan was right. Raidan couldn't figure out why, but he'd already decided in his heart that he was not going to try and stop Ilan. He sighed. "You might be the only chance the Elderace have. You say you don't want to be an enemy. Prove it. Put a stop to your father's plans."

Ilan searched Raidan's face. The voices grew louder and were joined by more. The unconscious man on the ground outside stirred. "Come with me, Raidan."

Raidan shook his head. He had to give Ilan credit for his persistence. "Go," he said. "Before they get here."

Ilan held his gaze a second longer, then ran out of the hut, hopping over the prone man. He left the door open, and Raidan stood there, his mouth hanging open at the realization of what he'd just done.

A moment later, Kameron appeared in the open doorway with a frightening mien in his eye. By his face, Raidan sensed that any trust he'd earned these past days had vanished.

Chapter 62

"What has happened here?" Kameron's strong voice made Raidan take a step backward and stare at the ground, his decision to let Ilan leave weighing on him. Kameron would never help him now. What had he done?

Not only would Kameron never agree to help him, but he would never free Raidan now. He could have stopped Ilan and he would have gained Kameron's full trust, but instead, he had let him go. Why had he done that?

Torn between anger and sadness, he couldn't decide if he wanted to scream or cry, so he did neither. He just stood, expressionless and speechless.

The man who'd been taken out by Ilan sat up. In the darkness and at the angle he'd fallen, Raidan hadn't seen who it was, but now as the man sat up, rubbing his head, Raidan recognized Andrei's short dreads.

Keshlyn appeared beside Kameron. "He is not within the grounds."

Kameron's narrow gaze turned to Raidan, but his short words were not for him. "Take a team to search the mountains. Find him." He stared at Raidan. "Ilan was here?"

Raidan nodded. His heart raced.

"Explain yourself," Kameron said in almost a whisper.

Raidan's throat constricted. He couldn't, not because he didn't want to, but because he was still trying to figure it out himself.

Kameron stepped into the room, closer to Raidan. He'd never seemed so menacing before, but now he towered over Raidan. "You did not leave with him," Kameron said. "Why? You claim he has your son and you do not take the chance to escape with him?"

Raidan was frozen in place. No words would come. All he could do was stand there feeling foolish.

"Well?" Kameron prompted.

Raidan finally spoke. "He didn't have my son. He didn't know where he was." How could he have been so stupid? He should have known.

"And still you did not stop him? You could have stopped him, yes?"

Raidan nodded.

"Then why did you not? You say you are not his man, and yet you do not stop him. Do you realize what this means for us? Tell me why you did not!"

Raidan didn't know why. He swallowed, though his mouth was dry.

But then a reason occurred to him. He owed Ilan a debt. Deep down, Raidan knew that was why he'd let him go. Even after all that Ilan had done, he'd saved Raidan, and Raidan felt like he owed him for it. But to tell Kameron that would not be enough. "I thought he could put a stop to Kingston's plans," he said.

Kameron breathed in through his nose. "That was not a decision for you to make," he said. "You will stay here and are not permitted to leave this hut."

Kameron stepped outside and closed the door on his way out. Raidan heard him instruct someone to stand watch. Then the voices dispersed and faded.

Raidan didn't know what had come over him. It took effort to drag his feet toward the bed and sit. He knew the risk he'd taken in letting Ilan walk out of there. Yet, as Kameron had said, he'd let him go anyway. Now how was he ever going to find Cassian?

The tears were back and, with them, the headache. He stretched out his legs on the bed as the aching between his brows intensified.

Vaguely, he wondered what his chances of survival would be if he'd tried to run away. Maybe he should have gone with Ilan after all.

Chapter 63

Ilan panted, out of breath. He'd run for a long time, putting as much distance as he could between him and that camp before the sun rose. Many of Kameron's people were scattered in the vicinity, guarding the perimeter, but on his own, he was able to slip past on light feet.

To be safe, he'd avoided all regular paths. He'd crept slowly in a few places where, if he missed his footing, he'd have had a long fall down the mountain. Now the sun was just over the peaks to the east. He was far enough away from the camp and heading south toward Litlen, where hopefully Perry would be waiting, so long as that soldier from Ferenth had delivered his message.

Ilan made his way down the slopes of the red mountains and back to the road, where he continued on his way, always checking over his shoulder. He watched the peaks and higher slopes as well.

Voices spoke, and horse's hooves clopped at a steady pace from ahead. They were close and would be within view in minutes. Ilan whipped his head back and forth, looking for a good place to duck and hide. There was no foliage or trees to take cover behind, but boulders and rocks lined the side of the road. They would hide him well enough. Ilan skidded over the shale rock and ran to take cover.

The voices became louder, and Ilan recognized one of them. He snuck a peek out from behind the rock. Dimitri sat atop a horse, walking along the trail headed toward the camp Ilan had just fled from. On horseback beside him was a red-headed woman. Next to her was the Elderace man from the lake who'd attacked Ilan and his men. Two more men rode alongside them.

There wasn't much chance they would see Ilan as a friend if he revealed himself now. And Dimitri certainly wouldn't help plead his case. Ilan cursed under his breath. He hadn't just escaped one place to become someone else's prisoner. To make friendly contact, he'd need Raidan by his side.

Dimitri and his party were almost past Ilan's hiding place. Ilan didn't dare look now. He stayed out of sight as they went along, but then the hoofbeats halted.

Ilan sank his back into the rock, keeping still. He held his breath. There was no way they could have seen or heard him. Why had they stopped?

"What is it, Royl?" a female voice asked.

"Someone's here."

How could they know? More voices spoke. Voices with that thick, all-too-familiar accent of the people from that camp. It was some dialect from the country of Ectarin. When Ilan had first heard it, he couldn't put his finger on its origin, but then he recalled a visitor from Ectarin. The accents matched.

"You," one of the members of the camp said. "You come with us."

"We're only passing through," Dimitri said.

"No," the man from the village said. "You will come with us. Kameron will want to meet you." Apparently, Kameron didn't get out much to meet people himself.

Ilan turned his eyes upward to be sure no one had spotted him from up high. He saw no one, but experience had taught him never to let his guard down.

The man from the camp was not requesting they go with him, just as he and Raidan had not been asked.

"Who is Kameron?" It was the voice that had responded to the girl moments ago. Royl.

"You will see. This one here looks like the other."

"Raidan!" Dimitri exclaimed. "You know where he is? Take us to him." At that, the horses' hooves began clopping along again as the groups joined and carried on along the trail toward the camp.

When they were gone and Ilan could no longer hear them, he made himself wait several minutes before checking that the coast was clear.

That had been too close. Ilan knew what he needed to do. He ran down the road toward Litlen, to where he'd asked Perry to meet him.

If Raidan was too afraid to run away, Ilan would take his decision out of the equation. Although Ilan himself was not going back to that place anytime soon, Perry could help with that. Raidan was stubborn. And clearly Kameron had gotten into his head, making him believe that he was his friend and could help him.

Ilan would help, though. He would rescue Raidan. Even if he didn't know he needed rescuing.

Chapter 64

The door to the hut opened and Kameron stepped inside. His presence filled the room and made Raidan feel small, like a child about to be reprimanded.

"Come with me," Kameron said.

Raidan stood. "Where are we going?"

"I cannot think of any reason you would allow the Valca to escape, except that you are his man, and all this time, you have been lying to me. I do not take kindly to being deceived."

"I didn't lie," Raidan argued. "I'm telling you the truth. My son is missing and Ilan took him."

"Then why did he take him, Raidan? What are you not telling me?"

Raidan feared he'd regret saying anything about Adrik and what he'd done to him. He wavered in his decision to keep silent.

Ilan wanted to use him, Kingston wanted to kill him, Beiron wanted to force him back to the cave, and Dimitri wanted him to raise an army against the Valca Order. What would Kameron want from him if he knew? All Raidan wanted was to find Cassian and Ida.

"Where will you take me?" Raidan asked, debating his options.

"I have told you the penalty for being a spy. You have lied to me and had me believe you were sincere—"

"I am sincere. Kameron, you have to believe me."

"Do I? Give me a reason."

Raidan opened his mouth but closed it as a familiar sensation swept over him. The same as he'd felt when he and Ida were taken in the forest, when Dimitri had somehow warned him of their approach. But this time was different—the emotion was not fear but hope.

"Do your people do regular checks around the surrounding areas of the camp?" Raidan asked.

Kameron quirked his head. "Of course. What does that have to do with this conversation?"

"Please I know it's a lot to ask, but can you have your people go out and look around to see if anyone is near?"

"And why would I do that? You wish to trick me now? Does Ilan lie in wait with more men?"

"No, it's not that. Please. I just . . . I can't explain it."

"The surroundings are monitored. If my people see anything amiss, they will report it to me or Keshlyn. Now, let us go."

Raidan breathed hard and fought the urge to scream. Dimitri was near, he knew it. Raidan just had to stay alive long enough for his twin to get there before he was sentenced to death.

"Do not make this harder on yourself," Kameron said.

Without a clear plan in mind, Raidan took one step, then another. He walked with Kameron past the huts and the locameen and octagonal common building. The courtyard was devoid of people. Raidan presumed the majority were out looking for Ilan.

His feet carried him on behind Kameron while his thoughts swirled. He needed to buy himself time. Sweat beaded on his brow.

"What do you want me to tell you?" he asked as they walked. "What am I supposed to say?"

Kameron paused and turned to face Raidan. They were at the edge of the imaginary boundary line, headed in the direction of the hall within the mountain.

"Tell me the truth about who you are." Kameron stood close. He poked Raidan's chest with his finger. "I have given you plenty of opportunities to tell me. Why did the whole camp shake at your shouting when you awoke the first morning."

Raidan froze. He knew the shaking was not only in his nightmare. Kameron had obviously made the connection. Raidan's gaze fell, and he stared at the ground.

With a heavy sigh, Kameron dropped his hand back to his side. "Come. It is time for us to know who you are, whether you want to tell or not." He began walking again. Raidan didn't follow. He kept his eyes down.

"Adrik came to me." He looked at Kameron. "When I was young." He assumed that Kameron knew who Adrik was, seeing as Eli and Andrei did.

Kameron stopped walking again. "As he has done with many children," he said. "When he left here, he found his purpose in helping others to hope. This is something I already knew."

"But I was not like the others." Raidan closed his eyes and swallowed. He took a calming breath and opened his eyes again. "My brother and I are the descendants of someone called Sermarc."

Kameron's eyes flashed recognition. "Marc? I did not know he had any children."

"Neither did Adrik, apparently." That Kameron knew Sermarc's name revealed that he too must have been around for a long time.

"So you are the Guardian?" Kameron said. He reached out his hand once more and placed it on Raidan's shoulder. "And what does Ilan Valca want with the Guardian of the Weldafire Stone?"

"He . . . he—" There again was that sense that Dimitri was nearby. Very nearby. "Dimitri." Raidan spoke out loud.

Kameron squinted at him.

Keshlyn ran toward them from the heart of the camp. "Kameron, you should come," she said. She waited.

"We are not done with this conversation," Kameron said to Raidan, then nodded for him to follow. "Come, we will see what has happened."

Welcoming the interruption, Raidan followed Kameron back into the camp.

As they approached the courtyard, a crowd of faces came into view, most of them unfamiliar. But Dimitri, three men, and one woman were surrounded by Jazz and a handful of inhabitants from the camp. Of those with Dimitri, Raidan recognized the Elderace man from the lake. Raidan picked up his pace.

"Raidan!" Dimitri jumped and went to meet him. Jazz took a wide step in front of him, blocking his path.

"Let me pass." Dimitri shoved him. Jazz drew a dagger and held it out, keeping Dimitri back. "He's my brother," Dimitri said. He leaned his head so he could see past Jazz. "Raidan!" he called. "Ida and Cass, they're all right. They're safe." He rushed the words out like he'd been waiting to tell him the news.

Raidan's knees buckled. Kameron stopped his fall and steadied him as they continued together to Dimitri. Had he heard that right?

Tears streamed down Raidan's cheeks as he closed the remainder of the distance to Dimitri. "How?" he asked, then didn't wait for the answer. "Where? What . . .?" He was having trouble articulating the multitude of thoughts that flooded his head. "Ida . . . was she hurt? And Cass, how was he? How did you—" Tears blurred his vision. He choked back a sob.

"They're both fine," Dimitri said. A few tears slipped down his own face. "Ida's worried about you. Cassian seems to have forgotten the whole ordeal now that he's back with his mother. We came to get you."

Kameron interrupted the reunion. "Raidan and I have unfinished business to discuss." He spoke loudly, taking command of the conversation. "Until our business is sorted, he will go nowhere." He gestured for Jazz to go on his way. He and his crew of six left and Kameron turned to Dimitri. "You must be the brother. And who are these with you?"

The Elderace man ambled forward. "I'm Royl. This is my sister, Laila." He directed Kameron's attention to the red-headed woman at his side, then to his other men. "This is Stefan and Bailey. We've come quite a way to find Raidan."

"Right," Kameron said. "And I should like to know what led you here, but first—" He looked at Dimitri. "Are you a Guardian as well?"

Laila's eyes widened. She stepped forward from Royl's side. "How could you know about—"

Kameron put up a hand to quiet her. Laila closed her mouth and remained silent while Kameron awaited an answer.

"No," Dimitri said. He looked at Raidan and rubbed the back of his neck. "We, um . . . the binding ceremony was incomplete."

Kameron's head turned sideways so he could make eye contact with Raidan. Raidan couldn't read his stony expression. Did he know it was Raidan's fault that the ceremony was incomplete? Did it matter?

"But are you both meant to be bound?" Kameron asked.

"Yes," Dimitri answered.

"So, the curse is not completely broken?"

Royl cleared his throat. "It's not. Only some of Litlen has been restored. How do you know about the stone?" Stefan and Bailey stood together but remained close to Royl, poised for defence while hostilities were still high.

"I make it my business to know." Kameron stood his full height. "The mystery of the lifted curse has only recently been solved. It explains why our lovely Keshlyn here had a song on her heart all those nights ago." He gestured to Keshlyn.

"That was you?" Laila said. Her face lit up in a smile. "We heard your song."

"Everyone did," Dimitri said. "Well . . . mostly everyone." He met Raidan's eye.

The smile Kameron gave Keshlyn was warm and genuine. "Then everyone knows what a beautiful voice she has." He held her gaze a moment longer, then turned to Royl. "And how do you know of the stone?"

While they stood around in the courtyard people returned from various directions of the mountains, heading back to their huts or into the octagonal building. It was already well into the afternoon. Where had the morning gone?

Raidan couldn't keep still. Dimitri was here, and Ida and Cassian were all right. An immense weight lifted off his shoulders just knowing they were safe, but he needed to see them for himself. If only Kameron would release him.

"What business do you have with Raidan?" Royl asked, instead of answering Kameron's question.

"Business that is between us," Kameron replied.

Raidan supposed there was still a punishment for letting Ilan escape. He clenched his jaw. Would a death sentence be on the table even now, after his story had been validated?

"Forgive me," Kameron said. "Where are my manners? You all must be hungry. Let us move our discussion into the locameen, where we may eat and talk." He directed his new guests' attention to the building. With Keshlyn at his side, he put a hand on Raidan's back and nudged him forward toward the locameen. The others went along with them, examining their surroundings. Dimitri was close behind Raidan. Raidan could sense his eyes on him.

At the door to the locameen, Kameron stopped Raidan. "Not you. Not yet." He stood out of the way to allow others inside. "If you would follow Keshlyn, she will keep you company for a few moments while we have a word in private."

Dimitri set his stance. Had he been two inches taller, he'd have been nose to nose with Kameron. "I'm not going anywhere without him."

"Your loyalty to your brother is admirable, but rest assured, he will not be harmed. I only wish to speak to him."

Raidan knew this was coming. He nodded for Dimitri to go on without him.

"You do anything to hurt him and I'll kill you," Dimitri said.

Leave it to him to say such things without considering his position. Still, Raidan was grateful for his brother's defence.

Kameron didn't blink an eye. He bowed his head. "I will bear that in mind."

Dimitri joined the others, walking stiffly until he disappeared inside.

Raidan remained behind with Kameron, who stroked his beard and looked to be determining what to do with him—a question Raidan, too, wondered with dread.

Chapter 65

KAMERON GOT RIGHT TO IT.

"You put my people in great danger when you let Ilan leave this place. I do not blame you for his escape, but you could have done something, and yet, you did nothing." He paused, then indicated Raidan go with him away from the door to the locameen so they could speak without interruption. He stopped on the grassy patch between the two bigger buildings of the camp. People glanced their way but were not privy to their conversation.

Kameron went on. "If you truly have the power of the Weldafire Stone and it is yours to protect, then you should not do nothing. It is your responsibility to keep it out of the wrong hands. Do you have it?"

Raidan's defences were rising. Kameron was beginning to sound like Adrik. The reminder of him seemed to summon the haunting echo of his voice in his head, calling for him to break the barrier. "No," Raidan answered. He thought to say a lot more than that—to tell Kameron exactly what he thought about the stone and this so-called responsibility. Thinking better of it, he kept silent.

"Is it safe?" Kameron asked.

"I suppose it is." Under a mountain in an inaccessible cave was probably as safe as it was going to be.

"But you do not know?"

"No."

"And Adrik? Did he not explain to you your role? The importance of it? Where is he now?"

Raidan gave a slight shake of his head.

"Is he dead?" Kameron asked.

Raidan's head was starting to ache at his temples from keeping his jaw so tense. "I don't think so."

"What does that mean?"

With both hands, Raidan massaged the sides of his head while relaxing his facial muscles. "No," he said. "He's not dead."

"And you know this?"

"Yes. He's alive. Just . . . trapped."

"Trapped?"

"I don't know what you want from me," Raidan said abruptly and a little too loud. A few passersby glanced their way. He lowered his voice. "What does it matter? He got what he deserved."

Kameron stared at Raidan, who averted his eyes and reached his arm across his chest to rub his opposite shoulder. Why did Kameron's reproach make him so uncomfortable?

"When you heard the music, you said you felt hope. What does that mean?"

Music night had been only two nights ago, but it seemed like much longer. Raidan had almost forgotten about the lightness he'd felt while listening. The hope was not something he thought he could explain. It was simply a knowledge of how he could remove the barricade in him that was stopping him from controlling his power.

The power. Not his. He'd get rid of it soon enough. Though now he was beginning to think Kameron wouldn't help him make it go away.

Raidan shook his head. Somehow, he knew in his heart that the thing to eliminate the blockage in him was to break the barricade trapping Adrik. But all of Raidan's hate, all of his fear and anger originated with that one man.

"I can't," he said, without telling Kameron what it was that he didn't think he could do. He wasn't ready to let that anger go. Adrik could stay right where he was.

"Tell me," Kameron said. "Saying it out loud will be good for you."

In the music, when Raidan felt that hope, it carried his burdens. It carried the heavy weight of his anger . . . his inability to forgive Adrik for what he'd done. For the first time in weeks, he'd wanted to smile, maybe even laugh if the reality of his situation wasn't so present in his thoughts. But now to think about going down that road, freeing Adrik . . . Raidan shook his head.

"Raidan," Kameron said, his dark eyes narrowing.

Under his steady gaze, Raidan relented. "I felt like I knew what I was supposed to do. Like I had a direction. But Kameron, I can't. That's not for me. I need to see my family and take them somewhere safe and away from here."

"What is it you think you cannot do?"

Raidan shrugged. "What does it matter? I'm not doing it."

The disappointment in Kameron's expression bothered Raidan. "Then it will be like an itch you cannot scratch," Kameron said. "Now that you have been enlightened, turning a blind eye will not be so easy. You are the Guardian of the Weldafire Stone, Raidan. It is a great honour."

"Then let someone else have it."

"There is no one. The delegates are gone. It is your blood and the blood of your ancestor who is bound to it. He was chosen for a reason."

"Beiron may know a way." Beiron had been intent on getting the stone. Perhaps he'd be one to ask.

Kameron placed a gentle hand on Raidan's shoulder. "Beiron will be the end of Kartha if he gets his hands on the Weldafire Stone. The best thing for you to do is to finish the ceremony with your brother. Break whatever remains of the curse over Litlen and seek out Adrik to give you the knowledge of the stone. And sooner rather than later."

He raised his other hand and placed it on Raidan's other shoulder. "I knew Beiron. If he is looking for you, you can be sure he will find you. He always finds what he wants. The longer you put off what you are meant to do, the more danger you place upon yourself, your family, and all of Kartha. As it stands, as long as you do not understand the stone and its power, you are an easy target. And when Beiron finds you, he will have his way if you are not equipped to defend yourself. There will be no safety for you or your family. Neither will it be safe for any of us if he succeeds at taking the stone's power."

Raidan's eyes burned as he held back tears. To accept the stone as a part of himself was like a life sentence, being left with a power he didn't understand or want. He stepped back, out of Kameron's reach. "I can't go back there. I won't." Raidan didn't think he could bring himself to face Adrik again, to go to the lake in the mountains. "I need to be with my family."

Kameron bowed his head. He sighed. "I know nothing of your journey ahead. Only you know what you must do and can decide for yourself whether you will do what is right. Tonight, we will have music night. You will stay, and I encourage you to think about this further. In the morning, we will speak again."

He stopped Raidan's protest with a hand raised, palm out. "I will not argue with you about this. We've yet to join your brother and the others, and I have another meeting to attend to shortly after. We are waiting to hear word on Kingston's army. Now that Ilan is free and knows where we are, we must consider what action to take."

His statement was like knives in Raidan's heart. The sharp reminder hurt, but it was the truth. He hung his head. Nothing he could say would change Kameron's mind after he'd let Ilan go.

"You may not see it as your concern that Kingston marches, but you should," Kameron said. "the Valca Order has been a tyrannical force against the people of Kartha for years. You and your brother, as the Guardians of the Weldafire Stone, could be a monumental help in the fight that is inevitably coming."

He asked a lot. Raidan dropped his shoulders. The topic of a revolution hadn't been evaded. Behind Kameron, red mountains stretched in every direction. Raidan stared off into the distance, longing to be anywhere but here.

Kameron patted Raidan's back. "Come. Let us join your brother. We will speak more on this in the morning."

With a weary nod, Raidan accompanied him to the locameen. He entered the building, dragging his feet. His hopes of being released had been squashed. He was stuck here for another night, missing Ida and Cass so much that his gut twisted in knots over it.

Kameron followed him inside. Dimitri stood at their arrival. He walked over to Raidan and embraced him. The action nearly broke Raidan and he had to suppress more tears.

"Raidan . . ." Dimitri wiped his eyes.

Andrei had joined their group as well as Eli. They had brought over a second table and joined them close so they could all sit together. It was nearly dinnertime, and the food was being prepared in the kitchen area behind the counter. The scent of cinnamon filled the air, mingled with cooked poultry and the woodsy fragrance of clove. Dimitri offered the seat next to him. On his other side was Andrei, who'd taken it upon himself to introduce himself and Eli, and to give Keshlyn a proper introduction in his own words, laughing at his own jokes as he often did. Laila was the only one to offer a polite chuckle.

Raidan took a seat, and Kameron sat beside him.

"Now I have established who you are"—Kameron gestured to Raidan, then slanted his head at Dimitri—"and am aware of your situation"—he turned to Royl, Laila, Stefan, and Bailey—"the question remains as to who you are."

"They're Elderace," Raidan answered. "They're the people I saw before, using magic."

Royl sat back in the most casual of ways. He pinched his lips, scowling at Raidan.

"Is this true?" Kameron asked Royl.

"Yes," Royl answered, turning his face to Kameron. "Something we're not accustomed to sharing, for obvious reasons." He shifted his eyes at Raidan and gave him a brief glare.

"I understand," Kameron said.

Laila cut in. "Are you Elderace?" she asked.

"Why do you ask?" Kameron said. "Apart from you lot, the Elderace are no more."

Laila shared a look with her brother. She turned back to Kameron. "Because . . . well, locameen is an Eldrace word."

Kameron moved his head slowly across the two tables, meeting everyone's eyes. The room fell silent, each person awaiting the answer. It seemed like whether they could trust each other hung in the balance of his reply.

"Will it change anything if I am?" Kameron asked. His gaze settled on Raidan. Then he leaned forward, rested his elbows on the table, and folded his hands together. "We decided long ago not to associate with the Elderace."

"Why is that?" Stefan asked. He was the taller of the two other men who'd arrived with Dimitri's group.

Kameron leaned back, changing his position again. He rested his elbows on the armrests and clasped his hands together in his lap. "There was always great discord between the mayanon and the Elderace. It was heartbreaking to see the way everyone treated each other as if they were not the same. So, many of us left our homes to make a new one elsewhere. We became a refuge, a place for those who had no place to call home. We gave people somewhere to come where they might belong.

"Through the first years, we grew. And then when the curse touched Litlen, we dwindled. Many from our camp fought in Landon's war. Most lost their lives. Few returned, bringing others with them as they fled the cursed city. When those from our camp whose years do not extend as far as our own passed on, we were all that remained. Some of our members who did not have Elderace blood running through their veins were able to bear children still. A handful stayed and raised their children here, but most left to find a place where their children could learn trades or develop skills we could not offer here."

"What is 'here'?" Royl asked.

"Here is where we defy The Order with small acts of rebellion." Kameron waited for a reaction.

Dimitri's eyes lit up.

"We are the *valients*," Kameron said. "The warriors of the valley. We send out raids to steal from Kingston's stock supply. The supplies he steals from the people."

"We rescue those suffering at the hands of the Valca Order," Keshlyn added.

"And we gather intel on The Order and any new developments that will affect our country and the people of Kartha." Andrei smiled as he shared this information freely now.

"We are Elefthan. We are freedom." Kameron said.

"Was that rehearsed?" Dimitri asked.

Kameron's deep voice resonated in his laughter, and Keshlyn blushed. She chuckled. "We do not get many visitors," she said.

Laila's eyes wandered, taking in the room. "Why couldn't we have fled here all those years ago instead?"

"Are there more camps like this one?" Raidan asked. Maybe this time, they'd not be so secretive about their work, now that he was not a spy.

Slowly, people made their way into the locameen for dinner. Kameron sat at the edge of his seat. "We are the only ones. Until yesterday, we did not know there were Elderace survivors apart from those who reside here, including those who have lived here and gone elsewhere." He stood up. "I have someplace to be. Eat. Visit. Music night will start after dinner. You are welcome to take part." His quick glance at Raidan was subtle, but Raidan caught it. He cocked his head and gave a little wave, then left. Off to discuss Kingston and his army. And Ilan. And what came next.

Chapter 66

THE MUSIC HAD ALREADY BEGUN BY THE TIME LAILA SHOWED UP IN the courtyard. She had taken some time to freshen up at the nearby creek, using the excuse to check on her wound before joining the others. She had greatly underestimated the powerful waters of Azure Lake, as there was hardly a mark remaining after only a few days since her injury.

A band played music in front of the crowd. Royl sat in the back row. Stefan and Bailey sat next to him, staying close by. Dimitri and Raidan were on his other side, joined by Andrei and Eli. The lot of them took up almost the entire back row of seats.

Eli caught Laila's eye and motioned to the unoccupied seat beside him. She walked over with a little extra spring in her step. Sure, there was the coming war and Beiron was on the prowl, but Laila pushed them from her mind to be able to enjoy one evening of fun. They were out in the open and right now; that was all that mattered.

Although it had been a long time since Litlen held such festive events, if she thought hard enough, she could recall the music from her home. Litlen's music had made your hips sway and your feet move, but this music was different. It was faster. Deeper. More like feeling than sound. The powerful bass that vibrated through her chest kept a steady rhythm that made it impossible to be still. The marimba's hollow woodsy sound filled the beating heart with melody. But the djembes were what really stole the show. The drummers showed off their skill in intense duelling between each other until they joined their sound as one, completing the shape of the song. The music was vibrant and full of colour. Laila couldn't help but rise from her place so she could move about freely.

The man playing the low-rumbling bass instrument handed off his instrument to another. He came over and introduced himself to Laila, shouting over the loud music. "I am Benji," he said. "You dance?"

A little embarrassed at being put on the spot and thrilled to have been asked, Laila joined Benji at a clear spot. They danced along with others on the grass, under the starry sky. She worked up a sweat with all the jumping around and twirling, but she didn't care. She couldn't recall a time when she'd had this much fun.

She stole a glance back at their chairs, where Raidan remained seated, his face serious. Dimitri was among a crowd, excitedly waving his arms as he spoke to people with a smile on his face. Royl appeared to have gotten dragged along to dance as well. On the grass, he shuffled his feet around in swift movements. Even when he danced, he had that casual sway that she knew so well. Laila laughed at him and joined him in a dance after Benji had gone back to his instrument. She danced until she was completely out of breath.

There were more empty seats than full now as the music had everyone crowded together and on their feet. Laila took a seat in an empty chair so she could catch her breath. Her timing was not terrible—the music shifted to a slower tempo, and the swaying bodies adapted their movements to the sound. She sat back in the chair to listen and enjoy. Slowly, every thought melted away as she was drawn into the music.

The people in the camp called themselves Elefthan. Freedom. It was a fitting name. Laila had never felt so free.

The music continued to pull her deeper into her spirit and her core. At the surface of her mind, colours swirled about—hues of purples, blues, pinks, beiges. Her shoulders relaxed. Thoughts mingled with feeling and colour. She had a sense of knowing, an inner knowing that one day her knowledge would expand and grow. There was no limit to what she could learn or the places she could go. The world was hers to explore, and all she had to do was spread her wings. Then she'd be truly free as a bird. She let herself get taken deeper into herself as she swayed back and forth, listening to the music and embracing utter peace.

The peace vanished when a pain started in her stomach. She left the place in her mind where the music was carrying her to. The pain grew subtly, and she took a sudden, sharp intake of breath as it reached her chest.

Drawn back to reality—back to the camp—she looked around. Those around her continued to sway to the music, oblivious to her shock. She grimaced and leaned forward, holding her arms close to her chest. Whatever that was, she didn't think it was supposed to happen. Royl glanced her way. When he saw her face, he walked over to her.

"You all right, Laila?" he asked. He had to lean close to be heard. Laila didn't think it was possible for Royl to look at her without that tinge of concern that lingered behind his eyes.

She didn't know if she was all right, but he didn't need another thing to worry about. She smiled and stood up, tilting her head back. "Don't look at me like that," she said. "I'm perfectly fine. Just warm. I haven't moved like that in . . . I don't think I've ever moved like that." She gave a light laugh.

Royl didn't share her amusement. His eyebrows furrowed. "You sure you're okay?"

Laila straightened. For his sake, she took a minute to seriously consider how she felt by sucking in a deep breath. The pain she'd felt a moment ago in her stomach and chest was gone, along with any residual effects. She smiled. "I'm fine. Nothing a walk through the fresh air won't fix."

Royl frowned and looked around their dark surroundings.

"Royl," Laila said. "We're among friends here."

This didn't seem to appease him as he locked onto her gaze. She sighed. "I'll stay close. Please don't hover."

Finally, he relented with a resigned nod. She grasped his hand in hers and squeezed, then turned to walk away, all the while sensing his eyes on her as he watched her go.

She left the lamplit courtyard and walked to where she might be out of the light to get a better view of the stars. The sound of running water lured her to the creek where she'd washed earlier. It was just a narrow stream that passed through the mountains. The shadows of the mountains all around offered a feeling of protectiveness. From this spot, Laila could see the whole camp. The lamps spread around the perimeter of the courtyard revealed all those who were within the light. She could make out the shapes of the huts, the octagonal recreation building, and the locameen.

How could this place have been here this whole time and they'd not known? She'd always known there had to be others who'd fled elsewhere in the time of Landon's war. She would so rather have been here instead of living underground in mines like trolls.

The sound of the water soothed away any thoughts of the mines. Laila crouched down and touched her fingertips to the cool stream of the creek. Music carried from the courtyard, and she closed her eyes to listen, hoping to sense that peace she'd felt earlier.

A voice spoke in the darkness. "Ah, now it makes sense."

Laila gasped. The voice was accompanied by a presence.

Beiron's presence.

Chapter 67

Laila stood and did a full circle, checking her surroundings and expecting to see Beiron. She did not, but there was no doubt that he was there, though not physically.

She closed her eyes tight and whispered under her breath. "Go away," she said. "Leave!"

Silence followed for a full minute. She opened her eyes and perked her head up a little, thinking it'd worked. But then Beiron spoke again.

"Well, that was entertaining." He chuckled.

Whatever it was that made them able to meet like this was worrisome. Should she find Royl? She didn't want to be alone with Beiron ever again. But she also didn't want to let on that Raidan and Dimitri were here. If she went back to the group, Beiron would see and know.

"I was wondering what I felt, but now I see," Beiron said. "So they survived after all this time too then, did they? Is Kameron still running things here?"

Laila held back her gasp. *He* knew this place was here? She wished she could make him go. "Get out of my head," she said.

"You were in mine first."

"That was an accident. It won't happen again."

"By all means, I don't mind. In fact, I rather enjoy your company," Beiron said.

She couldn't say the feeling was mutual. Not being able to see Beiron or know where he stood, Laila turned her head from side to side as if he'd magically appear.

Beiron let out an annoyed sound. "I need you to do something for me," he said. "Say: *veralnin tushov*."

Laila understood and fervently shook her head. "No."

"It's not as if I'm actually there, Laila. I'm miles away, I promise. The only thing it will do is allow you to see me."

"I don't want to see you. I want you to leave."

"Just say it. You're making me dizzy with the way you keep turning your head around looking for a face to my voice."

"If it bothers you, leave."

"Please," Beiron said. The softness in his voice surprised her.

Laila looked out toward the camp. The music played and people danced. No one was anywhere near, but still she worried. "Will anyone else be able to see you?"

"No. Just you."

Everything within her told her not to, but she could not ignore her own curiosity. There was so much she didn't understand about this kind of magic, so much she could learn. If she revealed him there, would she be able to hurt him? To physically touch him and somehow use that to help Royl and the warriors capture him?

Again she glanced at the camp. The lamps lit up the courtyard enough for her to see the throng of people gathered, but not enough to make out details. She had no idea if Royl was still among them.

She breathed in deeply. When she released her breath, it came out as a sigh. She gave in and said the Eldrace phrase for Beiron to reveal himself, then jumped when he suddenly appeared beside her. The instant she looked at him, she wished she hadn't said the words. He really was quite frightening, especially in the light available to her by the nearly full moon. The place where colour should have been in his eyes was dark, almost black. According to Vix's story, Beiron's eyes used to be bright and blue. What had happened to make them so dark? The scar on his face didn't help his appearance, and his beard was bristlier than the last time she saw him.

"How did you know that would work?" Laila asked as she took a step away from him.

"I didn't. It's called an experiment. You could learn a lesson or two from doing them. You'd learn you have so much more power than you could ever know, and yet, you're not being taught to your full potential. All it takes is a little bit of experimenting, and you'll see what I mean." There was fire in his eyes. "What were they teaching you back home anyway? How to make light-balls and play games? There's so much more to know, but all you know are secrets. The elders don't want to teach you any more than a few tricks and defence skills because they're too afraid of what you could really do."

Laila tilted her chin up. "I'll bear that in mind."

The music played on in the distance. Water trickled from the mountain into the creek, the sound filling the silence. A light throb returned to Laila's chest, reminding her why she was here and not enjoying herself with the others. She rubbed the place where it ached.

"Is it normal to get outbursts of pain from this?" she asked Beiron. He was, after all, the one who'd saved her. "Everything was fine, and then I was struck with a sudden stabbing pain here." She indicated the place of the wound.

Beiron squinted. Then his face lit up in understanding. "Oh, that?" he exclaimed. "No, that was me. I had to make you stop doing whatever it was you were doing."

Laila's jaw dropped. "Why?"

"Because it was awful."

"You had no right." Her fists clenched into balls, though she had no idea what she intended to do with them.

"It got your attention anyway, didn't it?" Beiron said, smiling. "I enjoy talking to you."

Laila didn't know how to respond to that. After hearing Vix recollect the night he'd witnessed Beiron kill, Laila had half a mind to walk away and hope he'd leave.

"I know you do too," Beiron went on. "Otherwise, I don't think I'd still be here."

"Why are you still here?" she asked.

"You don't mind. I'll prove it. I know you have things you want to talk to me about, so here's what we'll do: ask me anything—anything at all, and I'll answer your question."

Laila's heartbeat quickened. The invitation was tempting. She'd regret it if she passed up an opportunity to learn something from Beiron, knowing there were few who told her things.

She thought of all the questions she could ask him. She could ask about their connection and their ability to meet this way. She could ask about what happened to him the night Litlen was cursed, or what he thought he could do to get the stone's power.

"I'll take your quiet to mean there are too many things to choose from," Beiron said. "Either that or I misread you and there's nothing you wish to learn from me."

Laila made up her mind. "Why did you"—she paused, then forced herself to say it—"why did you kill the delegate Anahita and drink her blood?"

Beiron was as still as a statue with his eyes locked on Laila. "How could you know about that?" His eyes went distant; then he focused on her again. "It was the old man, wasn't it? Vix. He always did have a knack for sticking his nose in places it didn't belong." Beiron nodded. "Well, I am a man of my word, so I'll tell you. I took Ana's trace of element."

"Trace of element?" Laila blinked. She was aware that each of the delegates had a trace of element representing the elements through which the Weldafire Stone was formed, but she didn't realize it meant they literally carried that element in their blood. "What does that mean?"

Beiron raised a brow as if to say she already knew the answer and to not ask stupid questions. And while her understanding wasn't totally clear, she did suppose she'd already put together what it meant. Rolling her eyes, she asked, "So why not just cut her and leave it at that? Why kill her?"

"I learned that drinking the blood wasn't enough. The element was weak in my blood. By eliminating the original source of the element, it became stronger in me, giving me full access to the trace of element. It had been my plan to bind the Weldafire Stone to myself before it could become bound to someone else. Unfortunately, it'd already been bound to the mayanon, Marc." Beiron growled the name with contempt.

Laila got the impression that he took great issue with the fact that Marc—being a mayanon—took the Elderace title of *Ser*. "Did you kill the others too?" Laila asked. That Beiron might have been the one responsible for the death of all the delegates made her stomach turn. What was she doing even talking to him?

"No, I didn't kill them all," Beiron said. It did little to ease her stomach. He spoke freely about it, as if it were a perfectly normal thing to kill at all.

"Did you . . . ?" Laila hesitated. "Did you take all the delegates' traces of elements?"

Beiron smiled that confident, crooked smile of his. "I see where you're going with this," he said. "And it isn't your concern. What's done is done."

What was done was done, but Laila wasn't done. "Did you kill the ones you took from?"

Beiron took a long full breath. For a moment, she thought he might not answer. But then he relaxed his stance and shook his head. "No," he said. "My uncle and my father were delegates. I'd never kill my own blood."

From afar, Royl called out for Laila. Beiron looked past her shoulder to where Royl's blue light hovered in the night. The music continued to play in the courtyard, strumming out a light tune. The amount of people there had lessened significantly. Royl called out again.

"Protective, isn't he?" Beiron asked.

"Go away," Laila told him in a harsh whisper.

"And miss this? I don't think so."

Laila took a step to go to Royl, then stopped. She had no way to keep Beiron from listening, and there was no way she was going to tell Royl that Beiron was here.

She stood still and kept quiet, hoping Royl wouldn't come her way. But it seemed he knew her well enough to know she'd have been drawn to the water. He walked her way and cast his light upon her. It was bright to her unadjusted eyes and she shaded them with her arm.

"There you are," he said.

Laila was very aware of Beiron standing near and within the light's beam. Royl showed no recognition or surprise at his presence, so she could only assume he did not see him.

"You never came back," Royl said. "Everything all right?"

Laila nodded. "Just enjoying this night. Being outside. You know me."

Royl dipped his chin. "I do. So much so that I also know when you're hiding things from me, *tsarioc*."

This was true. His senses were never off. Her nickname brought a gentle smile to her lips despite herself. She'd missed hearing it in his playful tone. "It's nothing, Royl, really." Beiron's presence was unwelcome and she hated not speaking her mind to Royl. She hugged herself, rubbing her arms. "I'll return shortly. I'm going to stay here a little longer."

"You look cold," Royl said. He removed his cloak and wrapped it around her shoulders. "I wanted to let you know I'm calling it in. I'll be bunking with the Guardians in one of the bigger huts tonight. Will you be all right on your own?"

Laila cringed at the mention of Raidan and Dimitri.

"Is that a no?" Royl asked.

"No. I mean, yes. I'll be fine. Sorry, it's just been a long day."

There was that look again. Royl didn't try to hide his concern. "You sure you're all right?"

"I am, Royl. Thank you for asking. You can go now."

Royl's smile didn't meet his eyes. He hugged her, then stepped back. "Good night, Laila."

"Night."

His light faded as he walked away. He glanced back once, then disappeared amid the huts in the dark.

"So that's where the brothers have gotten to." Beiron broke the silence. "I lost track of Raidan for a while and wondered. Thank you for helping me find him again."

Laila didn't turn to look at him. Her stomach ached from constricting her muscles for so long. She didn't feel well at all. There would be no way to keep Beiron from knowing anything if he kept this up.

She was growing tired of his presence and wanted him to go—really wanted him to go. This was exactly the kind of thing she had been worried about happening. She thought to give his idea of experimentation a try.

"*Farino!*" she declared. She didn't have to look to know that his presence had gone from her.

Good to know. All she had to do was tell him to go.

Chapter 68

A HANDFUL OF PEOPLE APPROACHED FROM THE LOCAMEEN, CARRYING trays with bread, jams, tea, and coffee for everyone. They'd be up all night at this rate.

Raidan shifted to the edge of his seat. Getting into the music tonight was impossible. Thoughts of Ida and Cass overwhelmed him. Kameron wanted him to think about his role as the Guardian, but he didn't even know what that meant.

Dimitri had made friends and was talking with a group of people across the courtyard, as was Royl's man Bailey. Laila had gone off some time ago, and Royl had left to look for her. Stefan was immersed in the music and was sitting forward in his chair with his head in his hands. Andrei sat down next to Raidan. He leaned back in his seat and clasped his hands together behind his head.

Raidan stood up and Andrei looked over. "You going for some food?"

"No, I'm going to bed."

"Ah, Rider, you are no fun."

Maybe that was so. Raidan shrugged a shoulder at Andrei. "Night, then."

At least, Kameron didn't see it as necessary to have Raidan guarded as he had been before. The moon was bright tonight. Raidan glanced at the endless sky as he walked to his newly assigned hut. Royl had requested to bunk with him and Dimitri in order to get to know the Guardians better. In truth, Raidan was glad for Dimitri's company, even after everything that had happened in the cave. So much more had occurred since, and he missed his brother. Royl was an unknown, though. Raidan was already tired of constantly being on edge with every new face and situation that came his way. At this point, he didn't care who Royl was. He just needed to sleep, restful in the knowledge that Ida and Cass were safe.

Raidan entered the hut. Royl was already there and had already claimed one of the two beds. The floor had a makeshift bed made up of blankets and cushions. Raidan opted for the floor. It looked as comfortable as either bed. He lay down on the heap without undressing, landing on his stomach. After moving around until he was comfortable, he lay there thinking of what he might say to Kameron tomorrow to convince him to let him leave. Was Kameron planning on keeping him there until he'd agree to free Adrik? Was that what this was?

Royl spoke, making Raidan gasp. His voice cut into the darkness. "Dimitri told me everything."

Raidan's bed of blankets was closer to the empty bed that Dimitri would be sleeping in tonight. The room itself was big enough to sleep eight or more. Royl was on the other side, which left an open space between them. It seemed like such a big space compared to the last hut Raidan had been restricted to.

"Of course he did" was all Raidan could think to say in response.

"You know, a lot of people would have killed for the honour of becoming the Guardian of the Weldafire Stone."

If Raidan's eyes weren't so heavy with sleep, he'd have rolled them. Again with the honour. "When something is forced upon you, it's a little hard to be grateful, especially when it's something I don't know anything about."

"You mean you didn't receive the knowledge of the stone?"

Raidan's silence was his answer.

Royl shifted around in his bed. When he spoke again, his voice sounded more direct, like he'd turned to face Raidan. "The stone is like the life of Kartha: pure in every way. It must be protected from corruption and evil, so that Kartha can thrive as it has for centuries past. If I'm being completely honest, I don't think the stone was ever meant to be bound to anyone at all. The hearts of men are flawed and self-seeking. It was why six delegates were responsible for it rather than one. They had to be accountable to one another."

Raidan moved onto his back and stared at the ceiling. "If it was never meant to be bound, then why was it? What was so special about Sermarc that he was bound to it in the first place?"

Royl was quiet for a minute. "I don't know anything about Sermarc. I understand you've met Beiron?" He didn't wait for a response. "He and Adrik were the two living heirs of the six delegates. If ever there came a time that the stone would need to be bound to a bloodline, they were the candidates for the guardianship. Why Adrik wasn't chosen, I couldn't say. I didn't know him personally. But I would say that because of Beiron's actions, someone else was selected instead of him.

"At the time when Litlen was cursed, I was training to become a warrior. We had a warrant out to arrest Beiron for murder. One of our delegates, Cole, had been killed. Beiron was the prime suspect. To entrust it to him would have been a mistake. Once bound, the stone becomes locked to that bloodline. After it's bound, only the delegates, together with their blood and the blood of the Guardian, can transfer the power of the Weldafire Stone."

Raidan lifted his head slightly. "It can be transferred to another bloodline?"

"Not anymore. Not without the delegates, and they're all dead."

"All of them?" Raidan asked, his brief hope leaving as quickly as it had come.

Royl exhaled forcefully. "That stone is everything. It is up to the Guardian—or in your case, Guardians—to ensure that it is protected.

Our people look to you and your brother to keep it safe and out of the wrong hands."

Raidan rolled onto his side. That was a heavy load to carry. How was he meant to do that when he couldn't even protect himself and his family? Now he was expected to take responsibility over all of Kartha?

He wanted to end the conversation but didn't know what to say. His mind grew weary of trying to come up with an excuse. Finally, he said, "Well, I hope I can live up to the expectations."

Royl said nothing, and after a few minutes of silence, his breathing had become a slow and steady rhythm.

Raidan lay still for a while, unable to sleep. Tired as he was, he couldn't stop his mind from buzzing. Some time later, Dimitri came in, saying nothing as he collapsed in the empty bed and was snoring almost immediately.

Raidan scowled. Dimitri had wanted this all along. The revolution and the magic. Secret meetings and sabotaging The Order. This was his dream, and Raidan had been dragged into it. But as he lay there thinking, he had to admit that the magic itself was not such a bad thing. He blamed Adrik for instilling fear in him that had never left. But perhaps the magic was not the problem. After all, it had gotten him out of trouble on multiple occasions. Though, of course, he wouldn't have been in any of those situations if it hadn't been for the stone and Adrik. Still, the idea of breaking down the walls in him that stopped him from accessing the extent of this power was alluring.

It was evident that Beiron was no friend to the Elderace, or to anyone for that matter. After speaking with Kameron and now Royl, it was not hard to figure out who *the wrong hands* meant. Raidan sighed and turned onto his back.

Why was he having such a hard time deciding what he should do? It should have been simple. But nothing about this was simple. Not if he was to be stuck with this magic for all time.

He raised his hands in front of his face and examined them in the dark. It had been a while since he'd tried using any magic. Now that his secret was out in the open, he had nothing to hide.

"Fire." He whispered the word and snapped as quietly as he could manage. Above his fingers, a small flame flickered. It was no wonder it did nothing to help him in the dungeon. The flame was suitable only for a candlestick. He stared at the ceiling, his eyes slowly adjusting to the bit of light and able to distinguish more of the shapes in the room.

The door creaked on its hinges. He turned toward the sound. Figures entered the hut, silhouetted by the moonlight outside the open door. Even in the little light, Raidan could see the pale skin of the first man who'd stepped inside.

His heart jolted. These were not Kameron's men.

Chapter 69

THE FLAME ABOVE RAIDAN'S FINGERS FLICKERED LOW AND TOUCHED his skin. He winced and shook his hand to put the fire out. The flame disappeared, and the first of the figures that had entered the hut rushed silently over and whacked Raidan across his jaw, making him see lights. His face stung where he'd been hit. With one hand, he rubbed his chin, and with the other, he swung up and out, hoping to make contact with the shadow above him. He missed and was treated to another clout on the opposite side of his face.

A hand grasped his throat and squeezed, giving him no opportunity to call out. He clawed at the hand as more shadowy figures moved in around him and seized his arms, pinning them above his head. His legs were useless with the weight of someone pressing onto him. Without enough oxygen, his efforts to free himself weakened.

His first attacker grunted as he was thrown off him by a powerful wind that swept over them. He landed next to Raidan's face. The moonlight coming in through the open door revealed a dragon tattoo on his neck. The gust of wind caused whoever was pinning his arms to loosen their grip, giving him an opportunity to move.

"Dimitri!" Raidan shouted as he rolled onto his side and jumped to his feet. He cast a quick glance at the beds. Royl stood, fighting off what looked like three assailants. His arms waved about as he blew gusts of wind across the room while doing a sort of dance with his feet, fighting with precision and poise. Dimitri waved his arms about too, yelling as he rolled onto the floor out of his bed.

Raidan's millisecond distraction cost him. Someone grabbed him from behind, linking their arms around his. The man with the dragon tattoo was on his feet and he faced Raidan. He snarled and angled a punch into Raidan's stomach. Raidan doubled over, gasping, arms restrained. The dragon-tattooed attacker wrapped his thick hand around Raidan's throat again. He squeezed. Raidan's knees buckled, and his attacker took the weight and held him up.

A burst of blue light whipped past and struck the dragon-tattooed attacker. He grunted and loosened his hold on Raidan's throat. Raidan gasped and coughed. His arms were still linked in the second attacker's grasp. The attacker wailed in Raidan's ear and released his arms as Dimitri dove at him, throwing everything he had into his punches. Raidan stumbled away from them. Winded, he fell to his knees while spots danced in his vision.

His head was yanked back by his hair, then whipped forward. He hit the ground face-first, and his skull felt like it split open. The world spun when he raised his head too fast. Looking around, he could only make out moving shapes in the dark.

He pushed himself onto his knees and was steadied by Dimitri's hand on his shoulder. Moving sluggishly, he twisted around to look up at his brother. His mind didn't register the face above him. It wasn't Dimitri at all. A stranger had his hand on Raidan's shoulder while Dimitri was still tackling someone on the floor. This person had a shining tooth that glinted in the sliver of moonlight. He looped his arm around Raidan's neck, wrapping him in a headlock. Raidan tried to scream, but the arm around his throat pressed harder. His voice made no sound. He elbowed behind him, making contact but failing to free himself. His head throbbed where it'd smacked against the floor.

In front of him were fast-moving bodies, jumping about from one side of the room to the other. Royl was distinguishable by his graceful motion. He moved and the wind seemed to follow. It whipped about like a sudden gale.

Raidan's focus blurred. His body slackened in his assailant's arm, but that didn't encourage the man to release him. He kept him in a firm grip, his arm squeezing around his throat.

Royl moved in closer to them. He crouched down and extended an arm, directing it at Raidan as if he were pointing a sword. He narrowed his eyes as if to aim. Raidan slammed his eyes closed but could see the blue light from behind his eyelids as it whipped past his ear and struck down his attacker. The arm around Raidan's neck went limp, and Raidan fell to the ground with the weight of the man on top of him.

Royl stood and bounded over to Raidan. He shoved the shiny-toothed man off and subdued the man by securing his hands behind his back and keeping him down with his knee.

"You good?" Royl asked Raidan, out of breath.

Raidan blinked. He didn't understand the question. His head felt like it was on fire.

"*Lit*," Royl said, and above his hand a blue light hovered. It lit the whole room better than the moonlight had.

Dimitri rushed over to Raidan and attempted to help him up, but Raidan was not yet ready to stand. He managed to push himself onto his knees, then sat back on his heels.

Six unconscious men lay close together on the floor. Raidan stared at them. Funny, he'd thought there were more.

He blinked. Dimitri let his hand fall at his side when Raidan didn't accept his offer for help.

"We won?" Raidan asked, his words slurring a little. His voice came out raspy, and it hurt to talk.

Royl chuckled. "We did. You did good."

"Really?" Raidan didn't think he had.

"No," Royl said. He gave Raidan a tired, genuine smile. His smiled dropped, and his forehead creased. "You don't look too good."

A dark figure filled the doorway. Kameron carried a lamp, but his face became clearer when he stepped into the room filled with Royl's light. His eyes flitted from one body to the next. He glanced first to Royl, then to Dimitri and Raidan. "Who are these people?" he asked.

Dimitri kicked over the man with the dragon tattoo on his neck. "I recognize this one. This is Ilan's man."

Ilan? Raidan rolled his head back to look at the ceiling.

Kameron stepped over the bodies to approach him. He crouched down and examined Raidan's face. "Send for Eli," he said, waving a hand at Royl. "Then find Keshlyn and tell her I need her to send out search parties immediately. Ilan may still be close."

Royl nodded and left the hut, taking his blue light with him as he went. Kameron's lamp seemed so dim in comparison. The crease in his eyebrow deepened as he scrutinized Raidan's face. "Ilan has sent men after you now? You did not tell me what it is he wants with you."

Raidan looked at Ilan's men, each fallen in various positions. Six men for one man—a part of him was flattered Ilan thought so highly of him.

"He thinks I'm his connection to the Elderace. He and his father don't see eye to eye in regards to the Elderace and the war. Kingston is—"

"Kingston is marching now," Kameron interrupted. "He and his army have already left Valmain."

Eli ran into the hut, eyes wide. He took cautious steps over to Raidan, avoiding Ilan's men and opened his bag of remedies. Kameron set his lamp next to Raidan, then stood up and got out of Eli's way. He went to the door and left the hut without another word.

Eli crouched down and examined Raidan's head, then dug in his bag and pulled out one of the bandage wraps they'd wound together.

"I'm fine," Raidan said, tilting his head away from Eli's touch.

"You are bleeding." Eli took a small bottle of clear liquid and spread its contents on a cloth. He reached for Raidan's head. Raidan swiped the cloth from him and held it to his own head. "This will do," he said, motioning for Eli to put the rest away. Eli ignored him and took his chin between his fingers. He tilted Raidan's head back, studying his eyes intently. Raidan didn't have the strength to protest. He let Eli continue with his examination.

A minute later, Kameron returned with Andrei and Benji at his side, each with their own lamps. The two of them paused to take in the sight before entering the hut fully.

"What will you do with them?" Dimitri asked.

Kameron directed Andrei and Benji to start tying Ilan's men's hands behind their backs with rope. "Our camp is not equipped with the proper facilities to hold prisoners," he said. "We will keep them secured in the mountain until we can arrange something more appropriate. They may be of some use against Ilan if we do not detain him."

Eli finished checking Raidan over. He packed away his bag and handed Kameron his lamp. "Someone will need to keep an eye on him for the night."

"He will not be left on his own." Kameron signalled Eli to go. "Thank you," he said, then faced Dimitri and Raidan. "Moving them will take some time. Come. You may stay elsewhere for the remainder of the night."

Dimitri put his hand out again to help Raidan, and this time, Raidan accepted his offer. His head swam as he got to his feet and followed Kameron and Dimitri, massaging his temples.

Kameron showed them to Raidan's old hut, leading them by his lamp. The small space seemed confining after being in the bigger room. Kameron lit the light on the table. He turned to Raidan and held his gaze for an uncomfortable amount of time.

Even in his fuddled mind, Raidan understood what Kameron's look meant: tonight had revealed another reason why he shouldn't *do nothing*.

Dimitri shifted his gaze between the two of them. "What is it?"

Kameron let up his intense stare. "Get some rest. Morning will be upon us soon. We have much to speak about then, but in the meantime, sleep. I will have cushions brought for a second bed," he said, then added to Dimitri, "Keep a close watch on your brother tonight. Call for Eli if you need anything."

As soon as Kameron was gone, Dimitri turned to Raidan. "What was he staring at you like that for?"

"Kameron thinks I should free Adrik."

"What? Really?" Dimitri's voice rose in pitch, and he suppressed a smile, though not very well. The corner of his mouth twitched up ever so slightly.

"And? Are you going to?"

Raidan lowered himself onto the bed. He thought about how Royl fought with such confidence in the hut, using his magic as if it were an extension of himself, just as Beiron had done. Even Dimitri held his own in the fight. Raidan wanted that kind of sureness.

Kameron was right. If he didn't do something to get control of his power, he'd be helpless against anyone who came after him, just like he'd been helpless here tonight.

Beiron was powerful and would have no trouble getting his hands on the stone. A twinge of possessiveness overcame Raidan. Whether or not he accepted responsibility to protect the stone from people like Beiron, he couldn't ignore its importance to the Elderace. If it truly gave life to Kartha, it was worth protecting—not just for the Elderace, but for him and his family and friends too.

He hated that feeling of weakness, the inability to defend himself he'd displayed tonight. Kameron's advice weighed on him, and he saw no way around it. He was going to have to go back to the cave and free Adrik, then do as Kameron had said and bind the stone to Dimitri, breaking whatever remained of the curse over Litlen. That should remove the blockage preventing him from accessing the magic. If that meant accepting it as his, then so be it.

As long as he had a target on his back, his family would not be safe with him. But if Royl's actions here tonight were any indication of the Elderace protection, he was assured that Ida and Cassian were in capable hands.

He met Dimitri's eyes and voiced his decision. "We leave tomorrow."

Chapter 70

THE NEXT MORNING WAS COLD AND WET. RAIDAN STEPPED OUT INTO the rain, headed for the locameen. Royl slept elsewhere after Ilan's men attacked—Raidan didn't know where—and Dimitri was beginning to wake as Raidan left.

His first order of business for the day was to find Kameron. He was sure at this point that Kameron would not stop him from leaving, but all the same, Raidan would go to him first. After deciding to free Adrik, he'd gone straight to sleep. The details of how he was going to do that hadn't come to him yet, but somehow, now that he'd set his mind to it, it didn't seem so frightening.

The locameen had few people inside. No one had been in the grounds outside either. Kameron sat at a table with Keshlyn and Royl.

"Where is everyone?" Raidan asked as he approached.

"In the Acteg," Kameron said with a wave of his hand in the general direction of the octagonal building. "Kingston is on the move as we speak, and Jazz is informing everyone who did not already know. We will be taking up arms to assist the Elderace in this fight against The Order."

Royl gave Kameron an appreciative nod. Kameron invited Raidan to take a seat, and Keshlyn slid over to give him space.

Royl leaned forward and linked his fingers together on the table. "I've sent Bailey and Stefan back to the mines to inform our people about this place. They'll prepare for Kingston's coming. We've been in hiding for so long, trying to avoid this very thing from happening, but it seems Kingston has forced it upon us, and we cannot afford to fail. We're all that's left of our people."

"The mines?" Raidan asked. "Is that where Ida is?"

"Your wife? Yes, she's there. My men will tell her you're here. They'll see that she and your son are looked after."

Raidan bit his bottom lip to hold back his emotions. Royl had no idea how much that meant to him.

"Have you considered what I said?" Kameron asked. Apparently, this conversation was no longer private.

"I know what needs to be done," Raidan said. "Dimitri and I will go today. Provided I'm free to leave."

Kameron's eyes softened in his smile. "I am happy to hear this. It is what is best. I will see that you have what you need for the journey. It is a few hour's ride to the Teiry Mountains from here. Once you are in the pass, you will have to go on foot."

"On foot to where?" Laila asked as she entered the locameen. She joined them at their table and sat next to Royl.

"Raidan and Dimitri have a responsibility to the Weldafire Stone," Kameron said. "They are going to retrieve it and finish the binding ceremony."

Dimitri came in next and obviously had heard the last bit. He grinned like a mischievous child as he took the last available seat at their table. "When we're finished with that, I want to help fight against The Order. Tell me how I can help."

"We need more people," Keshlyn said. "Without more people, we cannot succeed."

Raidan silently agreed. If they didn't add to their number, they'd be just as doomed to fail as they had been during the Great Battle at Reen.

Dimitri sat back in his chair and ran a hand through his hair. He was in his element here. "I have connections," he said. "I've been speaking about this with a representative from Altrow for some time already. Gunther is all in. He's been communicating with others in Ferenth, Vray, and Hywreath. As soon as the word is given, he can have an army at his side to join the fight. There are also some in Veryl who have made it known they will stand with us. When the word is out, there will be others. If you send someone to speak with Gunther, tell him I sent you."

Raidan knew all too well about Dimitri's desire to start a revolution, but he had no idea just what lengths he'd gone to in getting it started.

"Thank you," Royl said. "When the binding ceremony is complete and you have the power of the stone, I hope you will join us. Together, you two could be an extreme asset in winning this war."

A revolution—the very thing Raidan had been trying to avoid. Although, it seemed different now. Kingston was bringing the fight to them. The people were never in any position to start a fight with Kingston Valca that they could hope to win. But now the Elderace were being threatened and they needed help.

Royl and his people had done a good deed for Raidan in protecting his family, and that meant everything to him. There was no question that when the time came, he would help. He just hoped Dimitri's recruiting would pay off. The people of Elefthan were not many, and Raidan had never seen the Elderace population. But if they were living in a mine, he couldn't imagine they were enough to contend with the Valca Army.

"What of Ilan?" Royl asked. "He wasn't captured last night, and he could be anywhere. Will he not try a second attack?"

Ilan himself was no threat to Raidan, but his men were rough last night. And getting thwarted from his path was something he couldn't let happen. To make matters worse, Beiron was still out there somewhere. He posed a greater threat, one that Raidan was not equipped—as Kameron had clearly stated—to defend against. Traversing to the mountains with Beiron searching for him could present a problem.

"Why not send a few men with Raidan and Dimitri," Laila suggested.

Kameron shook his head. "We cannot spare anyone at this time. Already I will be sending some to Altrow and Veryl to inform Dimitri's friend. We cannot afford to lose more when the fight is so near. I can offer horses to speed the journey, but that is all."

"What about the tunnels beneath Litlen?" Royl said. "Could they go through there?"

"And who's going to lead them through?" Laila raised an eyebrow at her brother. "You?"

"Actually," Royl said. "I thought you might."

*

Her? Royl was asking her to lead them through the tunnels?

"Me?" Laila vocalized her disbelief. "You want me to go? What about the elders? Won't they have something to say about that?" Having been reprimanded too many times for this very thing, wouldn't that stir up disagreement?

"Vix was right. You've proved that you're capable of handling yourself. It's about time I trusted you. I'll speak to the elders. I don't think they'll worry too much about it once they hear news of Kingston's coming."

The fact that he trusted her to do this made her heart melt. But his timing—it was because of her that Beiron now knew exactly where Raidan and Dimitri were. If he visited her again and found out they were returning to the cave. . . .

"Royl . . . I—"

"I know you can do this, *tsarioc*. Keep underground and out of sight, and you should be able to get to the delegates' cave unseen."

Tsarioc. Laila glanced at the faces around the table. It was the first time he'd called her that in front of anyone. It told of his faith in her. If only he knew why she was hesitant.

Kameron sat forward in his seat, resting his elbows on the table. Keshlyn sat back in hers. Raidan tapped his heel under the table, and

Dimitri squirmed in his chair like he was ready to jump up and go now. This was her chance to prove herself. To show the elders she could be trusted with important matters. And what was more important than personally guiding the Guardians of the Weldafire Stone to the delegates' cave so they could break what remained of the curse over Litlen? Nothing.

"All right," she said. "As long as you two want me as your guide." She glanced between Raidan and Dimitri. Since returning Cassian to Ida, Dimitri had warmed up to her, but she didn't know Raidan at all.

"I trust you'll lead us where we need to go," Dimitri said.

Raidan looked at Royl. "You're not coming too?"

Royl's eyes smiled, though his mouth barely moved. "No. I lead the warriors. I'm needed in the fight. But you can trust Laila. She's tougher than she looks."

"We won't run into trouble in the tunnels," Laila said reassuringly. "And on the off chance that we do, I'm sure the two of you could handle yourselves well enough."

Royl raised a brow at Raidan and shook his head. "I've seen him fight." He glanced at Laila. "He's kind of useless."

Raidan winced, then the corner of his mouth curled up. "It's true," he said. "Dimitri can fight well, but if Royl says you can get us there unseen, I'll take his word for it."

Laila stood tall, feeling a renewal of energy. Her excitement about his confidence outweighed her worries about Beiron finding her. They would be underground. Beiron would have no way of knowing where she was going. And even if his presence appeared, she now knew how to make him leave. All she had to do was keep him away until the Guardians completed their task, and then they'd be on their way back to Royl and the others.

She gave a single nod. "Right then. When do we leave?"

Chapter 71

Ferenth was a busy place today. Ilan left his room at the inn to walk about and discover the source of excitement.

Perry hadn't returned with Raidan in the night, which was not a good sign. He'd sent six men and hadn't considered they might fail. Raidan was one man! And he explicitly told Perry not to allow him to scream or yell. It was simple: surprise him while he slept, knock him out, and haul him to Ferenth, where Ilan would be waiting. Perhaps Kameron and his people were more organized than Ilan had thought. Though his own escape had been all too easy, perhaps they'd raised their defences after that.

In any case, without Raidan around to get him in with the Elderace, he'd have to find another way to make them see that he was with them, not against them like his father.

Outside the inn, people scurried off the streets. The buildings lined along the strip were all closing, and people were shutting their blinds and shutters. It was not yet afternoon and hardly anyone was outside except for Valca soldiers. They were everywhere.

"The Valca Order demands your cooperation!" one of them shouted in a grisly voice. "Anyone who stands in the way of Kingston Valca will suffer the consequences."

Ilan made his way over to him. More soldiers rushed from building to building, closing doors and clearing the streets.

"What's happening?" Ilan asked the soldier who'd been shouting. He didn't like that he had to ask.

"No one is to be out. Get inside—" He looked at Ilan and his eyes grew. "Ilan! My apologies. I didn't realize . . . I thought you were—"

"Get on with it," Ilan said, waving his hand. "Why is everyone being ordered to go in?"

"Your father's arriving any moment with his army. A command has been given that anyone in his way will be killed where they stand. We've been directed to make way. I thought you would have known."

The streets filled with panicked cries. Citizens rushed inside the nearest buildings, soldiers dragged more out of their way, and others yelled, mostly at people who were moving too slowly, but also at each other to line up and stand at attention.

Ilan looked north, where his father was approaching cannons visibly in tow. Ilan stood frozen for a minute. It was happening. His father hadn't lied about his intentions.

"There he is!" someone behind Ilan said. Ilan turned. The soldier with the red hair was pointing his finger, but not at Kingston and the coming army. He was pointing right at Ilan. Four men flanked him.

"Get him!" the red-haired soldier shouted.

Ilan's stomach dropped. He turned to the grisly-voiced soldier who'd been ordering people about. "Buy me some time," Ilan told him, then moved before he could get a response. It was hard to say whose loyalties lay where.

He ran.

Footsteps followed. Without turning back to see, he sensed more than one soldier was gaining on him. Through the abandoned streets, he knocked over vendor stands, hoping to slow them down. With no one in his way, he built some momentum and sprinted. Skidding around a corner into an alleyway, he slipped onto another street. From there, he turned into another alley and continued down another street.

That should have bought him enough time. He stopped in an alley to catch his breath, bending over and resting his hands on his knees. He had to get out of here. The Elderace needed to be warned.

That was it! That could be his key to proving he meant them well.

Ferenth was swarming with soldiers. Normally, that was good, but not today. Ilan stood up straight and poked his head out from the alley, looking left and right. To see the busy crossroads city so empty of its usual bustle was chilling. Ahead, to the south were the Bludesel Mountains he'd just come from. To the left of there was the Gap. That was his best option for getting to Litlen, so long as he could avoid getting caught by his father's men. The longer he stood around here, the sooner they'd catch up to him.

Ilan took three quick breaths, then ran.

Chapter 72

Laila resisted the urge to check over her shoulder. She'd already done so too many times and was sure to draw attention if she kept it up. With everything she'd learned about Beiron, this connection they shared frightened her more and more.

She, Raidan, and Dimitri had taken up Kameron's offer of horses and had set out from the camp a little over an hour ago. They wasted no time in packing their canteens, dried fruit, and nuts for the journey, plus a little extra that Kameron had cooked up for them to enjoy.

Heading for the nearest entrance into the tunnels, they rode east at a canter for some time, making their way to the place where they would leave the trail. The rain had let up for most of the ride, but every so often, clouds threatened a downpour.

Laila was aware that the perimeter of the camp was guarded by Kameron's people, and she took comfort knowing they were near. But now they'd be leaving that protection, and she couldn't help but feel somewhat vulnerable. She kept ahead of the brothers by a few paces and slowed her horse to tread with caution across the jagged ground as she led them off the trail.

"Are we going to the place where Ida and Cassian are?" Raidan asked.

Laila shook her head. "No. Until Royl has spoken with the elders, it's best we stay away from the mines."

Dimitri caught up to ride beside her. "Did you get in trouble with them?"

She could hardly be surprised he'd figured that out. "Sort of," she said. "No one is supposed to leave the mines except warriors and those who are assigned to aboveground jobs. But I hate living there." Laila left it at that. She didn't want to let her guard down in case Beiron should intrude.

The tunnel access in the Bludesel Mountains was not far now. She stopped for a moment to gain her bearings. Her explorations in these parts had been a long time ago, and she had to remember the way to the entrance. Here was too open. They weren't low enough.

She dismounted and walked her horse farther to where the ground dropped into a shallow valley. Dimitri and Raidan followed suit. In the valley, Laila recognized the stack of stones towered high and leaning like they might fall, yet somehow they remained sturdy and unmoved.

"It's too steep to bring the horses down," she said. "We'll have to go without them from here and hope they find their way home." She removed the bag of supplies from the saddle and walked to the edge of the rock to find the best way to hike down. She'd only ever come from the other way, out of the tunnels.

Raidan scanned the area, looking down. A moment later, he pointed. "There. Think we could climb down from that spot?"

Where he pointed was not a steep climb. The drop into the valley itself wasn't far down even if she did fall.

She nodded, and Raidan went first. Once he was down, Laila turned to climb down backward. She got a firm grasp of a stone jutting out and found another a little ways down. Three more rocks, and she leapt the rest of the way. Dimitri came last.

The open rock faces before them had the appearance of dozens of caves. Most looked just large enough for someone to tuck underneath the ledges and take shelter from bad weather. The towering stack of stones leaned at an angle, pointing the way into the opening which would eventually merge into the tunnels. Laila walked ahead and into the shelter of the open rock face. She spoke her trigger word to ignite her magic light. The blue light sparked and appeared above her hand. Dimitri's eyes widened, and a grin spread across his face.

"This the way?" Raidan asked, pointing ahead.

Laila nodded. "This is where the tunnels begin." She faced the darkness, knowing they were about to plunge into it for a good portion of the day. What was one more day underground in light of the rest of her life?

Hopeful that this would be the last time, she stepped into the long dark twisting tunnel, hidden from the sun and all life.

Chapter 73

THEY WALKED IN SILENCE FOR LONG ENOUGH TO NO LONGER SMELL the fresh air from outside. All that remained was an earthy, damp scent and cold, stagnant air.

There was room enough to spread out a little and walk with straight backs. That would change once they left the Bludesel Mountains and crossed the narrow spaces beneath Litlen.

Raidan broke the silence. "How do you control it?"

Laila turned toward him, unsure of his meaning. He gestured to her light. Oh—of course. Using her magic came so naturally to her. She'd forgotten it was still a new concept to him and Dimitri.

"I suppose with practice I've learned how to control it," she said. "It's much stronger when I actually say my trigger out loud."

"Trigger?" Raidan asked.

"Yes. Mine's *vint*, the Eldrace word for *life*. Saying the word helps me better control my power. Do you know your trigger yet?"

Raidan shook his head. "No, but my voice does seem to affect how it works. Or, when it works, I should say."

"That makes sense. I can control my magic without speaking my trigger, but like I said, it's stronger when I do."

Raidan nodded. "What is Sudneil?"

"Sudneil?" Laila asked. "It means vessel. Is that your trigger word?"

"No, no, I don't think so. It's what Beiron called me."

Beiron had called Raidan vessel? Laila could only guess as to why. She glanced around again, tuning in to her senses to be sure they were alone. "Come on," she said, picking up her pace. "We've got a long ways to go."

*

Raidan looked at Dimitri, who just shrugged at Laila as she walked off ahead of them. Dimitri followed, and Raidan went last, in single-file. The wide space around narrowed, and Laila barely stayed within sight as she rounded one corner after another. The ceiling dropped in a few places, and they crouched down to duck under it. Then it abruptly rose, and they were able to stand again. But where the ceiling extended higher, the walls gradually drew in. As the space closed in around them, Raidan slowed his pace.

No one seemed to notice him falling behind. When they reached a place where the walls were so close on either side of them they had to walk sideways, Raidan stopped. Standing between the narrow walls, he became aware of his fast breathing.

What was he doing? There were other ways to get to the cave that were better than this. Why did they have to come this way?

Laila had gone too far ahead, and he was left in complete darkness. He closed his eyes and there was no difference from when they were open. Laila's comment about triggers came to mind, and he opened his eyes to see nothing. His hot breath bounced off the wall in front of him. Disoriented without the use of his sight, he put his hands against the wall as if that might make him feel better. He needed light.

Laila's trigger was an Eldrace word, but did it always have to be in Eldrace? If so, it'd be forever before he found his.

He thought to give Laila's a try. "*Vint*," he said quietly while opening his hand. The light appeared above his hand, just as Laila's had. It was blinding at first, but his eyes adjusted and he could see the way forward.

Whether the word triggered the light or if it worked just from his voice, he wasn't sure. But he'd controlled his magic and lessened his fear. He shuffled along sideways to catch up to the others.

Dimitri was waiting for him at the place where the walls spread apart. He smiled at Raidan's light and clapped a hand on his back. "Nice one."

Laila had gone too far ahead and was nowhere to be seen. Without her, they were completely lost. Raidan's light dimmed in his panic at the thought of her leaving them behind.

Her light came back into view and he relaxed a little. She waved for them to come. "This way."

The space was wide enough to walk side by side in these parts, so Raidan and Dimitri moved together to catch up with Laila. The tunnels had changed and were consistently the same height and width. Unlit torches lined one wall. Between Raidan's and Laila's light, they had all they needed to see the way.

A long time had passed and without seeing the sun, Raidan had no idea what time of day it was. He was getting hungry, but his desire to get out of these tunnels kept him going. Only briefly he stopped to retrieve an apple from their pack, offering one to Dimitri as well. He'd have offered one to Laila if she were ever close enough to ask. Dimitri accepted the apple, and they walked on. Raidan tried to cut slices of his apple using the knife Kameron had given him, all while attempting to keep his light up and stay close to Laila.

She always walked ahead, barely slowing down long enough for them to catch up to her. Her ability to navigate through this labyrinth of tunnels was impressive. But by the way her eyes flitted around, Raidan couldn't help but notice that she seemed nervous about something.

He raised his voice loud enough so she could hear, while at the same time, staying aware of his power. "Are we being followed?"

No ground trembling or earthquakes. But anytime that had happened, he'd been in a dire situation.

Laila stopped to let them catch up. She looked at Raidan, her eyes round. "No. Why? Did you hear something?"

Raidan shook his head. "You're hard to keep up with. Thought there might be something that got you spooked that you're walking so fast."

"No, nothing at all," she said a little too quickly. Then she added, "I just really hate it down here."

Raidan nodded. "I understand that." He and Dimitri caught up to Laila, and they continued to walk together—Laila slowing her pace enough to keep up with.

"Are the mines close to here?" Raidan asked, wondering how near they were to Cassian and Ida.

Laila shook her head. "We're heading in the opposite direction. The mines are west."

"They're the place where your people have hidden these past years?"

"Yes. They used to be abandoned. A hundred years ago, Landon tried to kill us all, but many of us took refuge there and have been there since. Until now, thanks to you."

Raidan looked at the ground ahead of him as he walked, keeping his hand up with his light hovering above it.

"I didn't do anything," he said. If he'd had his way, none of this would have happened at all. He'd have been back in Veryl fretting over Kingston's demand for men for his army. Or perhaps already been chosen and in the process of being beaten into submission.

He cleared his throat. "You said a hundred years? So you were born in the mines?"

Laila chuckled. "No. You'd be surprised how old I actually am."

Dimitri looked her over like he might take a guess. Raidan asked before he could. "How old?"

"A hundred and fourteen."

Raidan's eyebrows raised. "You look good for an old woman," he said, drawing a laugh out of Laila.

"What about your magic?" he asked. "In the war, why not use it to fend off the Valca Order?"

"We lost our magic when Litlen became cursed."

"And you got it back after I was bound to the stone?" Raidan asked, though he already knew. "But the curse is only half broken. Until Dimitri becomes bound, what does that mean for your magic?"

Laila looked over her shoulder. Her eyes caught on Raidan's light hovering above his palm. She lifted her hand and pushed her own light upward above her head, then rested her hand at her side and indicated with a nod that Raidan try it.

Raidan copied her motion, and his light floated up, stopping just above his head. He let his hand relax.

Laila smiled. "Our magic came from the Chronicle Storm. Centuries ago—nearly a full millennium—there was a great storm in Kartha. The heart of it took place over Litlen and the Teiry Mountains. In that storm, the rain in Litlen and the surrounding regions gave us our magic that coincided with the elements. Our people were also changed physically, in that our years of life extended well beyond that of the mayanon. When you broke half the curse in Litlen, you awakened the dormant waters of Azure Lake. After my people drank from there, our magic was restored to us."

"You didn't automatically get your magic back after the curse was gone?" Dimitri asked.

Laila shook her head. "No. Initially, we received our magic through the storm and as long as we had it, it was passed down from generation to generation. But after the curse, we lost our spark. All magic was gone. And, just like you didn't have magic by being the descendants of Sermarc, neither did we have it, though we were born with it. Something had to be done for us to get it back."

"But all you had to do was drink water?" Raidan said.

If that had been the case for him, would he have had magic all those years since his first time meeting Adrik? Or because he and Dimitri were mayanon, did it take binding their blood to the stone to give them magical abilities? Seeing as Dimitri had no magic, even though he drank from the Pool of Sovereignty, Raidan assumed it was the latter.

"Yes," Laila said. "The Pool of Sovereignty would have been better to drink from, but . . . well." Laila shrugged. "It was inaccessible. Azure Lake did the trick. That's where we're going now. This path will take us along until we get to the exit in the woods near there."

As if on cue, she picked up her pace to walk ahead of them again. Raidan and Dimitri speed-walked to keep up. They had to be getting close now.

Chapter 74

Laila made sure to stay close enough that Raidan and Dimitri could see where she was going. The familiar sense of Beiron's nearby presence overcame her, raising the hairs on her arms. Startled, she gasped. Raidan and Dimitri were not far behind.

"*Farino,*" she whispered.

Beiron's presence left. Her heart raced at the thought that he might have seen either of the brothers.

Raidan caught up. His light bobbed above his head, matching the rhythm of his movement. "Did you say something?"

"Hm? No," she said. She bit her lip. "I just . . . We're close now." She turned on her heel and walked away. They had to get to the cave and start on their way back. Then Beiron could show up all he liked, and she'd not have to worry about him learning anything important.

As she neared the exit of the tunnel, the warm red hues in the sky told of the setting sun. The light was a welcome sight. She took her first step on the grassy ground of the forest floor and closed her hand into a fist, extinguishing her light.

As she'd always done whenever she set foot outside, she drew in a deep breath. When she let it out, her muscles didn't relax all the way like they usually did. The exit of the tunnel they'd just come out of looked like a big hole in a cliff face.

"Laila," Raidan said. She turned to face him. "How far is it from here to the cave?"

"About two hours."

"Can we make the hike in the dark?"

Laila looked around at the fading light. The coverage of the surrounding evergreens already blocked much of what remained. "We could, but if we hurry, we can make it before then."

"Then I think we should wait until it's dark before we go from here." Dimitri nodded. "We'll have the cover of night."

"You want to wait until dark?" Laila asked. "What about seeing where we're going? We can't very well shine our lights around like a beacon." She pointed to Raidan's magic light, which glowed and hovered above his head. For herself, the darkness was of no concern. She'd lived in it for long enough that its presence made no difference to her.

Raidan looked up. "The sky's clear. The moon should be bright enough to see by for the most part. We're less likely to be seen by anyone if we wait. I'm also hungry and could use the rest."

"What about the Valca Order? They're marching now and could already be upon Litlen for all we know."

Raidan pursed his lips. "I know. But we take a risk being seen when we go from here."

"Ilan left his army in Veryl," Dimitri added. "We don't know if they're on the move to join Kingston or not. It's better to go in the dark and keep to the shadows."

It wasn't ideal, but Laila considered it. As nice as food sounded right now, she needed to keep herself away from the two of them as much as possible.

"All right," she said. "We'll take a break and rest, then leave as soon as the sun goes down. And Raidan, you don't need that anymore." She directed his attention to his light.

Raidan looked up at it. "I don't know how to make it go away."

Laila wasn't sure if he was kidding, and she almost laughed. But when he shrugged at her, she realized he was serious. She showed him how. "Do this." She opened her hand in front of herself, palm up, then closed her fingers, making a fist.

Raidan mimicked her and his light disappeared. "Thanks." He indicated the pack Dimitri carried. "Shall we?"

Dimitri set it down, and the two of them crouched over it. They removed the food contents, which were neatly wrapped in cloth.

Laila indicated a place by Azure lake that was away from them. "I'm not hungry," she lied. "I'll just be over this way, resting."

They both acknowledged her with a nod as they made themselves comfortable near a tree with their food. She left them to it and walked toward the lake. Checking that she was far enough away, she sat down. This way, if Beiron did show up, she'd still look like she was alone. She just had to hope he hadn't already seen them.

With her back to the brothers and her front to the lake, she lay down and looked up at the sunset. This would never get old. She ignored the delicious smell wafting from the pack and focused on the other smells of the forest. The fiery, piney scent of a feurcodix flower reached her nose. It gave the impression of burning wood in a campfire. She breathed it in deeply and closed her eyes, embracing the cool breeze that blew across her face.

The smell changed abruptly. What was that? Damp earth? She opened her eyes. Water dripped down from stalactites in what looked like a cave chamber. It trickled down the mountainous grey walls.

She quickly sat up from her laying position. Blue light illuminated the spacious room.

"*Veralnin tushov*," she heard Beiron say from behind her. Her muscles tensed.

"You've come to see me again, have you?" Beiron said.

Laila stood and turned to face him. "Not on purpose."

"But you were thinking of me?" he asked, though Laila didn't think it was really a question.

She ignored his comment and studied the wet rock walls. "What is this place?"

Beiron moved toward her, and she stepped back.

"I'll tell you what," Beiron said. "You tell me where you are, and I'll tell you where I am." He grinned.

That wasn't going to happen. She almost spoke the Eldrace word to go, then realized she was in his space now. Saying something else along the lines of leaving might work, just as telling him to go had, but since she was here now, she held off. There had to be something she could take from this to help Royl and the warriors find and catch him. He'd opened the invitation for her to ask him anything before. She wanted to know if he'd answer another question, yet she couldn't bring herself to ask. But as long as she was here, he couldn't be where she was.

"Is there something you want?" Beiron asked.

"Yes, actually. I've read your book—your father's book—many times. I want to know what's so important about it that you gave up Raidan's son for it. I can't recall anything that could be useful in getting the power of the stone."

"That's because I never journaled that information. I never got the chance." He smiled at her. It was a genuine smile, and while it made his face look less scary, it somehow made her more uncomfortable.

"I like that you're trying to understand things, Laila. You're willing to ask questions to get the answers." He stepped closer, and this time, she didn't step away.

"I don't need the book for anything at all," he said.

"What do you mean?"

"I just wanted to meet the thief who managed to take it in the first place."

Heat flushed her cheeks. She lowered her eyes and thought back to her first time meeting Beiron. "But you did meet me," she said. "Before we even made the deal to trade."

"Yes."

"So, why go through with the deal?"

395

He shrugged. "Infants are too much work. I have no use for caring for one when I have more important things to attend to. And despite your accusations, I am not the monster you think I am."

"You threatened to kill a baby."

"I did. And I've told you before, I'm a man of my word. I would have had to follow through had you not changed that by offering to make the deal."

That didn't make him any less of a monster. "So the book had nothing to do with it?" she asked. "Not even for sentiment?" She raised her pitch on the last word, thinking maybe he had some deeper attachment to it.

He shook his head. "My father gave it to me after my sister died. He'd written the first few pages, then told me the rest was mine to discover. And so I did. Everything that's written in there is in my mind." He pointed at his head. "And I don't forget so easily."

Laila glanced around the damp chamber, trying to understand what this place was. From afar she could hear a thunderous sound. Her gaze fell on a long wooden table set out with supplies. On it was a candle and hot plate, as well as a pestle and mortar. There were no plants or herbs laid out, which led her to believe he'd not been using them right at this moment. What *was* this place?

There, beside the candle, rested the book. Laila wanted to walk over and take it. She stared at it. Her own attachment to it was likely to be frowned upon by Royl. And everyone else for that matter, but she'd had a hard time parting with it. If Beiron didn't truly need it, what was the harm in her having it?

In her peripheral vision, she could see Beiron. His gaze followed hers. He went to the table and picked up the book, then returned to her.

Laila couldn't take her eyes off it.

Beiron grinned. "Do you want it?"

She wanted to say no, but that wasn't true.

Beiron held it out to her. "The knowledge is yours for the taking."

Blood Bound

*

Raidan woke with a start. He'd fallen asleep leaning against a tree. He stretched his tight muscles and looked over at Dimitri, standing by Azure lake with his hands on his hips. His body ached from the day's riding and travelling. The jitters he'd been getting used to came and went still, though they weren't as intense as they'd been at first.

Kingston's army approached nearer with every passing minute, and Raidan knew he didn't have the luxury of taking his time. The sooner he and Dimitri got this done, the sooner they could help the others. He hoped that waiting until dark was a good idea.

The sun was minutes from dipping below the western horizon. It shone low through the branches of trees. Dimitri gazed to the east, at the mountains ahead where it was darkest. Laila looked like she'd fallen asleep, lying in the grass farther away from the two of them.

Raidan stood and stretched again. He supposed it was time to go. Making his way to Dimitri, he tapped his shoulder as he passed him by.

"Let's get moving," he said, then went to wake Laila. Dimitri picked up their pack and followed. When they got to where she lay, Raidan jumped back and bumped into Dimitri.

"Ow!" Dimitri exclaimed, then gasped when he saw Laila.

Her eyes were open and pure white. There was no sign of her pupils and irises, nor that she registered Raidan and Dimitri standing in front of her.

Raidan put a hand to her shoulder and shook her. "Laila," he said. "Laila, wake up."

*

Laila couldn't tear her gaze from the cracked, faded leather and discoloured pages of Beiron's book. She almost reached for it, then stopped herself. "I shouldn't."

"Why not? You've already read it. And you've had it in your possession for a long time before, haven't you? Take it. I want you to have it." Beiron gave the book a little shake.

Laila looked at it, then at him. What could be the harm?

She extended her arm and wrapped her hand around the book. Beiron grabbed her wrist. She gasped, and her body seized up. A second later, he released her and stepped back. The book dropped from Laila's hand to the floor, and she staggered backward, away from Beiron.

He had a curious expression on his face. His lips turned up in a smirk. "Where could you possibly be going with those brothers?"

Panic swelled in her. He'd tricked her. How could she have been so stupid?

"You'll need to get back to them, I imagine. But don't worry, we'll see each other again soon," he said, then added with a wink, "*Farino.*"

And then she was back.

Chapter 75

LAILA'S WHITE EYES BLINKED AT RAIDAN AND CLEARED. HE REMOVED his hand from her shoulder and backed away. She focused on him and sprang to her feet. Her gaze darted around. She looked at Raidan, then at Dimitri, breathing hard.

"Are you all right?" Raidan said. He offered her water from the canteen, which she ignored.

"We have to turn back," she said. "We can't keep going. We have to go back." Her frantic eyes scanned all around the woods and across the lake. Whatever had just happened had clearly scared her.

Raidan sealed the top on the canteen and tucked it away. "What do you mean? What happened?"

"Because it's—I . . . We—" She stammered. "I have a bad feeling about this. What if this is a trap? What if we get there and someone's waiting?"

The thought had crossed Raidan's mind once or twice. But going back to Ida without completing his task wasn't an option. He needed to know he could protect her and Cass before returning to them. "What happened, Laila?" he asked.

"I just—" Laila stopped talking and breathed deeply. Her gaze veered past Raidan and Dimitri to the mountains and the dusky blues filling the sky. The sun had set, and the moon hadn't yet risen over the peaks.

Raidan closed the small space between himself and Laila. He gently took her hand, knowing all too well what it was like to experience horrifying nightmares. "Kingston is about to wage war on your people. I won't be much help to anyone until this is done. And I do want to help."

Laila said nothing. She groaned.

"Believe me, Laila. If I can't even convince myself to turn back, then nothing you say will make me change my mind." Raidan gave Dimitri a sideways glance. Dimitri smiled and clapped Raidan on the back.

Laila's shoulders drooped. "I saw him," she said. "I mean, I have been seeing him. In visions or dreams or . . . I don't know what they are. He's coming."

"Who's coming?" Raidan asked.

"Beiron. He knows where you're going, and he's on his way there now."

Raidan's stomach knotted. "How does he know where we're going?" he asked. "The last time I saw him was in the forest where we ran into Kingston's men, when Beiron was taking me to my son."

"Yes, but a lot of time has passed since then. He has ways of knowing things. . . ."

"What ways?" Raidan asked.

Laila pressed her lips closed and shook her head. "Ways I don't understand."

"I have a bit of an idea of his methods," Dimitri stated. "Trust me when I say you don't want to find out firsthand."

Raidan never did learn how Dimitri had wound up with Ilan and Beiron or what had happened to him in the time he'd gone to Altrow. He let go of Laila's hand. "How close is he?"

Laila looked again at the mountains. "I'm not sure. He was somewhere in a cave. I could hear the sea nearby. Maybe near the coast?"

Either they turned back to wait until things cooled down with Kingston and his army, then return when Kameron could spare some of his people to go along, or they could take a chance and hurry to the cave now, get this done with, and aid in the fight. If Laila's estimate was accurate, they could still have time to get there before Beiron. The coast was a ways from the delegates' cave. Also, something about the music night in the camp had opened his eyes. This was the only way forward.

He shook his head. "We have to try. I can't turn back now."

Laila's gaze shifted from him to Dimitri. Dimitri lifted his head high and gave a slight nod.

"Laila, you've been a tremendous help getting us here," Raidan said. "And I can't tell you how grateful I am. If you want to turn back, we shouldn't have a problem finding our own way from here. If Beiron is there, we won't lead you into danger."

Laila's smile was brief and didn't meet her eyes. "I'm not leaving you. You're the Guardians of the Weldafire Stone. It is up to me and my people to look out for you. And my people are a little preoccupied at the moment, so I'm all you've got."

Raidan may not have known Laila that well, but he felt a kinship with her—this woman who was a bit of an enigma to him, who was willing to help him and his family and wasn't going to back down at the prospect of danger.

He turned to face the mountains, then twisted his body to look back at Laila and Dimitri. "Well, we ready?" He cocked his head and indicated the way forward. His anxiety was mixed with an odd sense of eagerness. For the first time ever, he found himself wanting this, really, truly wanting to be able to reach the power within himself.

They just had to get there before Beiron did.

Chapter 76

THE LAKE IN THE MOUNTAINS LOOKED DIFFERENT AT NIGHT. NOTHING at all like the first night Raidan and Dimitri had stood atop this mountain looking down into it.

Raaaiiiidddannn.

Dimmiiittttrrii.

The hiss of Adrik's voice cut through the air. Raidan looked at Dimitri, once again confirming that he'd heard too.

Releaaassse meee. The voice resounded in a harsh whisper.

Raidan took slow steps forward, his feet angling on the decline as he walked down the slope and into the basin, toward the water's edge. He hadn't forgotten about the vine, but to allow himself to consider coming back here, he'd forced himself not to think of it. But now he was here. How was he to get through this without encountering the creature?

Dimitri and Laila hiked the short distance down with him. He stopped a few feet from the shore. The water was still and black. The high moon reflected off the lake's surface.

There was no sign of Beiron, but Laila's head swivelled from side to side constantly, checking around.

Break the barrier. Adrik's voice came more clearly now.

"How?" Raidan asked out loud.

Laila turned her attention to him. "How what?"

Raidan opened his mouth to respond, but before he made a sound, Adrik's voice spoke again.

Come.

Raidan stepped back, away from the lake. His chest constricted. Adrik's summoning was the same as the first night he had come here with Dimitri, when Adrik's voice carried to them from within the cave.

What was he doing here? He couldn't be doing this again.

Raidan closed his eyes, trying to shut out his doubts. This was where he needed to be. He opened his eyes, resolving to finish this. "Not until you call that thing off," he called to Adrik, assuming he could somehow hear him. If he was meant to go in the water, he didn't want to have to worry about a killer vine attacking him.

"It's the Anguivina," Laila said. "The protector of the Pool of Sovereignty. The delegates used to control the creature, but since they've been gone . . . I assumed a master no longer controlled it."

"Adrik controls it," Raidan said. His muscles tightened, remembering how Adrik had used it to restrain him. He couldn't help but wonder whether Adrik would take out his anger on Raidan for trapping him there. In his defence, Adrik had brought it upon himself. Body trembling, Raidan looked up at the peak of the mountain they'd just come down from.

Dimitri bent down and removed his boots. Raidan slipped his feet out of his own boots and kicked them aside, away from the edge of the water.

"What will you do?" he asked Laila, who was still eyeing their surroundings.

She slowly turned her face to Raidan, raising her eyebrows. "Hm?"

"While we're down there, what are you going to do?"

She watched Dimitri pick up his boots and arrange them next to a large boulder. "I'll find a place to hide until you're back and we can return together."

Raidan unstrapped Kameron's knife from around his waist. He handed his belt and scabbard to Laila. It would only restrict him when he went into the water.

"Keep this on you," he said. "I don't know what to expect when we're down there, nor do I know what things will be like when we're done. Stay alert, and if you see Beiron, don't stick around. Just get out of here."

Laila accepted the belt and didn't bother to remove the knife from the scabbard. The long string from the belt strap hung down and nearly touched the ground. She flashed Raidan a brief smile, then frowned as she looked between him and Dimitri. "Be careful."

Raidan hoped his own smile showed his appreciation for her concern. He turned to face the water, where Dimitri had already waded in up to his shins and was taking short quick breaths through clenched teeth. Raidan stepped into the water and immediately understood why. The water was cold. Cold enough to make him reconsider going in at all.

Dimitri dunked under the water, getting himself fully wet. Raidan held his breath as he waded further in, slowly blowing the air out of his mouth.

"Just get it over with," Dimitri coaxed. "Don't think about it."

Raidan took his advice and submerged himself. He gasped when he came back up, then swam to the middle, where Dimitri waited.

The tunnels leading to the room with the Pool of Sovereignty had contained multiple twists and bends. How long would it take to get there? Would they be swimming the whole time? Raidan didn't think he'd be able to hold his breath that long.

Laila stood at the edge of the lake, scanning its surface.

Raidan shivered in the cold water. "Do you remember how to get there?" he asked Dimitri.

"I do. I can get us there. Can you give us a light?"

Teeth chattering, Raidan looked at Laila. "What's the Eldrace word for light?"

"*Luzen,*" she replied. She drew her cloak closer to herself.

Raidan raised his hand, palm up and said, "*Luzen.*" The blue light hovered above his hand and brought a bit of warmth to his body. He was starting to get the hang of this. With a push of his hand, he nudged the light up. It moved above his head and hovered there. He hoped it would stay lit once he dove down.

"We'll go down and see what we're up against, then come back up to make a plan," Raidan said. "It might take some time to move those rocks that fell in front of the entrance."

Dimitri nodded. "Race you to the bottom." He smiled, but his voice lacked humour.

"Let's just get this done," Raidan said. He took a breath and dove down.

Chapter 77

By his light, Raidan could only see Dimitri swimming in front of him. At about seven feet down, they made it to the heap of rocks that had fallen in front of the cave entrance. Except for the lake, it was exactly how they'd left it the morning after he'd been bound to the stone. The boulders fully blocked the way in, leaving no room for passage.

Raidan began to swim to the surface, but something in the water shifted. All around them seemed to vibrate as the mountain rumbled. A cloud of underwater smoke made it impossible to see for a few seconds.

The cloud dissolved, leaving a clear opening into the cave. The rock pile no longer blocked the way. Dimitri swam into the opening without hesitating. Raidan would have liked to have gone up for a breath before continuing but didn't want to abandon Dimitri. He kicked his legs, propelling himself forward, though he didn't think they'd go very far before having to turn back for air.

Once they were surrounded by the mountainous walls, the rumbling returned, making Raidan's heart jump. He glanced behind. The rocks had moved back in place, trapping them inside the cave. Bubbles escaped from his nose in his panic. There was no going back now.

Suddenly, he was very aware of the pressure of the water in his ears and the lack of air. His lungs burned. Dimitri swam ahead, and Raidan stroked his arms and kicked his legs, thinking only about their destination.

He stayed close to the ceiling, hoping to come to an opening where he could breathe. Further into the mountain he swam, through tight winding passages. His light lit the darkness, and he was able to stay at Dimitri's heels. He reached up, desperate for a breath, and relief flooded him when his hand broke through a gap of air between the water and the ceiling.

He raised his face to the gap and took a few short breaths, revelling in the feeling of air filling his lungs. His light reflected blue off the water. Dimitri came up a second after him. He inhaled and blinked water from his eyes. "Not far to go," he said. His voice sounded condensed in the space. The water was up to Raidan's chin, and his head hit the ceiling.

"Ready?" Dimitri asked.

Raidan nodded. He sucked in another breath and slipped down, back into the water, keeping his hands up for anymore air pockets. His light directed his path, staying at just the right distance above and ahead. Dimitri led the way to the chamber where they'd left Adrik.

It was easier to glide through the water using the walls on either side to propel himself forward. A few bends later, Raidan's lungs were burning again. He drifted upward while kicking his legs and paddling forward.

Not panicking was getting harder now as his lungs craved air. He had a terrifying thought: What if the room were as flooded as the tunnels? Or what if Adrik were actually dead and this was all a mistake? What if Adrik's voice existed solely in his imagination?

He followed Dimitri around the last right turn and came across the threshold, where blue light flickered through the water on the other side. Dimitri drifted through the opening, and disappeared. Raidan treaded water at the threshold. Dark shapes moved in shadow through the dim blue glow.

He stuck his hand through first. Warm air touched his fingers on the other side. Somehow the water seemed to have been held back at this point rather than fill the room.

He pulled his body forward through the threshold and fell to the ground on his hands and knees when there was no water there to take his weight.

*

Bright moonlight reflected off the water. Laila watched for Raidan and Dimitri to re-emerge, but they weren't coming up. The rumbling beneath her feet indicated something had happened, but she had no way of knowing what. Whatever the case, she'd give them some time and, in the meantime, was going to hide.

All her fears about Beiron showing up came back to her in full force. She searched around for a place to conceal herself, expecting to see him at any moment. He seemed to pride himself on being a man of his word. If he said he was coming, there was a good chance he would follow through. She did not want to be here when he came.

There was nowhere to run or hide in the basin, so she tied the belt with the knife around her dress at the waist and hiked up the slope of the Hayat Point. At the top, she watched for movement in the dark, then made her way down toward the pass.

She stopped. The pass would be too obvious. If Beiron decided to show up and use her whereabouts to find them, she'd need a less distinguished hiding place. Instead of going left toward the pass, she went right, scanning the area as she walked.

The moonlight made it easy to see. She found a place where the shape of the mountain blocked where the light touched. It remained in shadow. Perfect. It was close to the Hayat Point and tucked away from obvious sight. If she listened hard enough, she should be able to hear talking or splashing—something to indicate that she could come out of hiding.

The rocks in her chosen hiding place were sharp, pointing up out of the mountain. She wedged herself into a dip that formed a hole and sat with her knees drawn close to her chest. The rocks jutting up hid her upper body and head from behind. She needed only remain still, and as far as she could tell, she would not be seen. Nothing hid her face, but she'd be able to see if someone was coming and duck down. Should Beiron's presence show up, it would be difficult for him to pinpoint her exact whereabouts. She hoped it was enough.

Shifting her backside to get settled for a long wait, she released a quiet sigh.

"Nice little place you've found yourself," Beiron's voice cut through the dark. Laila gasped and looked around for him. This connection of theirs was messing with her head. Was it just his presence there, or had he actually found her?

The moon cast its light on the figure coming her way. He couldn't see her. No way could he see her.

Unless he'd watched her enter the hiding place.

Laila closed her eyes, realizing how oblivious she'd been. He'd been here the whole time, observing her. She stood up and froze. He was looking right at her.

"Are you really here?" she asked, knowing the answer.

"I am," Beiron said. He walked over to her and extended his hand to help her up out of the hole.

Like she'd let him touch her again. She ignored his hand and stepped out on her own. Her body shook, and she hoped it wasn't obvious.

His face was in shadow, and his silhouette loomed before her. "Walk with me," he said. "There's something I want to talk to you about."

He touched the small of her back and guided her forward. Her feet moved, though she was hardly aware of them. He stayed at her side, his hand behind her, leading her back toward the lake.

Should she draw Raidan's knife and use it? Her heart raced as she contemplated her options.

Beiron led her over the Hayat Point and they descended together into the basin, stopping at the shore of the lake. He looked down at Raidan's boots, which had been tossed aside. He kicked one and smirked. "I'm sure they'll be a while. We have some time. Sit." He indicated the boulder nearby, where Dimitri had placed his boots.

Laila couldn't move. Here Dimitri and Raidan were—about to break the barrier and unwittingly allow Beiron entry into the delegates' cave and access to the Weldafire Stone—and she'd led him right to them. She had no way to warn them.

"I only want to talk, Laila. I promise."

Laila did as she was told. She went to the boulder and perched on the edge, ready to run at a moment's notice.

Chapter 78

Raidan gasped air into his lungs. When he caught his breath, he looked up and around the room. It was just as he'd remembered. The chairs encircling the Pool of Sovereignty. A gentle stream of water pouring from the stalactite in the ceiling into the pool. The tables to the left of each chair, and the incense, though it no longer burned. Even the bethrail flower was exactly where it had been before, but it had wilted and the edges were brown.

Adrik's blue light hovered in place above his head. He sat in the farthest chair from the threshold, facing the entry. On the ground, beside his chair, a mound of green plant lay coiled. It had no visible head or tail. The thing was all body. Was it creature or plant? Raidan stared. Its only movement was an up-and-down motion as though it were breathing.

"I was beginning to think you were not going to come," Adrik said. He sat in one of the unusually long-backed stone chairs. His fingers were steepled together, and he wore a grimace, as if he had a right to be annoyed.

Dimitri offered a hand to Raidan and helped him to his feet. Raidan looked at Adrik, trying very hard to see the man in a different light from the way he'd always viewed him.

"Yes, well, you weren't the only one," Raidan replied honestly.

"What made you change your mind?" Adrik asked.

"It wasn't you."

Like everything else in the room, Adrik looked the same—albeit a little more ragged than before. His deep red tunic, belted with a simple string, was dirty along with the rest of him. He appeared uninjured from the cave-in. His hair and beard, which had been trimmed the night of the cave-in, had grown. In his unkempt state, he looked again like the madman Raidan recalled from his nightmares. His appearance wasn't helping Raidan keep his emotions in check.

"Things not going so well out there?" Adrik said, rising to his feet.

Raidan clenched his hands into fists. Dimitri looked at him. He gave him a slight encouraging nod. How could one man make him so angry?

"You know it's not," Raidan said. "You did this. Had you left things well enough alone, Kingston wouldn't be about to march on Litlen."

In a matter-of-fact tone, Adrik said, "I had no intentions of letting you leave here without finishing the ceremony. If you had let me, things would have gone a lot smoother for everyone."

Raidan scoffed. His anger and frustration were wearing him down, threatening to become sadness, and ultimately defeat. He forced his tense muscles to relax. They'd journeyed here for a purpose. He'd come with a mind to move past all this. He just had to remind himself why he was here.

He sighed. "We didn't come here to fight. As I said, Kingston and the Valca Order are marching on Litlen as we speak. Dimitri and I want to help in whatever way we can, but . . ." He bit his lip. To admit he needed Adrik's help felt wrong. He rubbed the base of his neck. "I don't know how we can help."

"You must let me finish the ceremony," Adrik said. He approached the two of them and stood before Dimitri.

Raidan had seen for himself that having the stone's power was not a bad thing. Yes, it attracted unwanted attention, but the power itself did him no harm. What Adrik had done, though the way he'd done it was wrong—well, Raidan could understand his determination to bind the stone's power.

Raidan stole a glance at the coiled vine. Other than its slight breathing, it hadn't moved since they'd entered the room.

"One thing," he said to Adrik, eyes still on the vine. "You really need to work on your communication skills. Your choice of meeting place that night was a poor way to gain my trust."

"Yes, well. I needed you here," Adrik said. "Enough time had been wasted. And you are stubborn."

Raidan raised an eyebrow and cocked his head. Stubborn was one thing. Forcing someone into an unwanted role was entirely different. He let it go before it got to him.

"What do we have to do?" Dimitri asked.

Adrik drew his knife from his belt. He extracted the rough blue-green stone from a little leather pouch at his side. It appeared he had found the Weldafire Stone in the water after they'd left him there.

"Give me your hand," Adrik told Dimitri. Dimitri offered it, and Adrik put the blade to his palm and broke through the skin. He turned to Raidan. "First, the stone must be bound to you both." He looked at Dimitri and deposited the stone in his hand. Dimitri wrapped his fingers over it and closed his eyes.

The jitters Raidan had grown so accustomed to over the past weeks had ceased completely. He stood motionless, waiting for something to happen. Anything.

Dimitri's body slouched as he relaxed and opened his eyes. He uncurled his fingers, revealing the stone with his blood on it. Raidan couldn't tear his gaze from it. The blue light in the room emphasized its colour, making it glisten.

Adrik grasped the stone and dropped it back into the pouch. Dimitri held his hands out and examined them. The cut on his palm was gone. Not even a trace of it remained. He made a fist and released it. In his eye, Raidan could see that familiar sparkle of excitement, like he couldn't wait to try out his new power.

"Now," Adrik said before he could give it a go. "Come to the pool."

"Who?" Dimitri asked.

Adrik waved a flippant gesture. "Either of you. Since you are both bound now, you will both see."

Dimitri turned to Raidan. "You want me to do this?"

Raidan shook his head. "I should be the one. I don't want anything to hinder me in moving forward. And right now, I'm the only one doing the hindering."

"I agree," Adrik added, though Raidan didn't recall asking his opinion. "Come now," he said. "You must stand in the water."

"You want me to stand in the water?" Raidan asked. "Why?"

Adrik squinted at him. "You are bound to the stone, but you lack the knowledge that accompanies it. How could you be expected to act with such power when you do not understand it? I am going to give you that knowledge. Do as I have said." Adrik gestured to the Pool of Sovereignty.

The water pouring down from the ceiling made a wide spray. There would be no avoiding getting wet if Raidan stood where Adrik wanted him to stand. He wasn't completely dry from the swim down, but he'd managed to warm up some since then.

It took great willpower for him to move his feet to where Adrik motioned. Raidan braced himself for the cold and stepped into the water. It was warmer than the lake had been. The water went almost up to his knees, and he swayed to balance himself. The spray that came down splashed the top of his head and his face. It tickled the back of his neck.

Dimitri walked to one of the chairs and sat at the edge of the seat, leaning forward over his knees.

Being in the pool, Raidan stood a head shorter than Adrik, who looked down on him. Raidan didn't like this placement.

"Have you had any opportunities to learn about your power?" Adrik asked.

"You didn't think to ask me that before I got in here?" Raidan responded in a raised voice. Maybe his irritation had to do with the splashing water, or it might have been the fact that Adrik stood over him. The base of his neck ached from tension.

Adrik narrowed his eyes, and Raidan returned his stare with a glare of his own. Heat rose to his cheeks, and he balled his hands into fists. Really, he was trying.

He closed his eyes and bowed his head. After a deep breath, he opened his eyes and blinked from the splashes of water hitting his face. "No, Adrik," he said through clenched teeth. "I don't know anything. Please tell me more."

Adrik blew a puff of air from his nose. "The Pool of Sovereignty has healing waters. Provided they are protected and continue to flow, there will always be hope for our home. With these waters, life may be restored. Of course, the Weldafire Stone plays a part in the restoration of life as well. The waters and the pool go hand in hand. They are Kartha. When I give you the knowledge of the stone, it will seal the bond between yourselves and the stone. The healing power will flow in the land and through you, and the curse over Litlen will be fully lifted. Do you understand?"

Raidan nodded.

"Good." Adrik arched his eyebrows and dipped his chin. "Are you ready?"

Chapter 79

Laila couldn't speak. She was mute with fear as she sat numbly upon the boulder. She'd been able to say a whole lot of things to Beiron when she could make him go away. But this was for real, and nothing she could say would make him leave.

He sat down next to her on the boulder, saying nothing as he looked out at the lake.

Her eyes glossed over as she stared at the ominous black water gleaming in the moonlight. How might she reach for the knife without Beiron stopping her? He sat so near and could probably see the panic written on her face. He must know she was thinking of trying something.

"I knew your mother," he said. "We were close once." He paused and looked out at the lake before continuing. "She had just lost her husband and was going through a difficult time. I'd been going to see her. You weren't born. There was one night, she was having a bad day and she called on me. She opened up to me, fully trusting, and allowed me to comfort her."

Laila refrained from looking at him. It was hard to believe he'd ever been a friend to anyone, let alone her mother. Freya was not so naive as to let someone like Beiron get close to her. Yet Laila's gift for knowing truth from lies made it clear he was telling the truth.

He went on. "Not long after that, she just . . . shut me out. She'd heard some rumours, and she wouldn't allow me near her. It was quite out of character for her to not allow me a chance to explain myself."

Laila snuck a glance at him as he stared at the water. She wanted to reach for the knife, but he was too close to her. He'd stop her before she could use it. She averted her gaze, not wanting him to catch her looking over. In the dark, she inched her hand across her body toward the knife as slowly as she dared.

"And then," Beiron said. "When I first felt your presence in that dream, and then again when I saw you in her home—in Freya's home—it all made sense. I understood for the first time. It was why you were able to take my book when no one else should have been able to. And why she pushed me away. It's all so clear to me now." He stopped talking, and the air was still.

Laila touched the handle of the knife. She wrapped her fingers around it, then took a second to process what Beiron had said. What was so clear to him? As she thought it through, what he was saying sank in. His words from Azure Lake came to mind. *You're Freya's daughter?*

He'd mentioned Royl. He knew Royl. And Royl had been concerned because—

She shook her head fervently. As soon as the thought took form, she was on her feet, the knife completely gone from her mind. "No!" she said. "No, no! It's not—you're not . . ." She couldn't bring herself to say it. "No."

Beiron stood. "Laila—"

"No." It was all she could think to say. "You're wrong."

Beiron moved closer, taking one of her wrists when she tried to step away. "I'm not wrong," he said. "Our deal—when we shook on it—I felt the power. I know you did too. That was a shared blood bond."

Laila tugged her wrist, trying to break free from Beiron's grasp. This could not be happening. Her mother would have told her. Or Royl would have said something. . . .

She used her free hand to reach across her body for the knife. Beiron stopped her, grabbing her other wrist as her hand nearly touched the handle. He pulled it away from the knife and reeled her closer to him.

Laila shook her head. "Let go of me!" It came out weak. She raised her leg up to knee him but didn't have the space to lift it high enough. He drew her even closer to himself. So close that her hair stuck to his stubbly beard. He squeezed her wrists tighter, and her hands tingled as the circulation was cut off.

"Stop fighting, Laila," he said. "Relax. I don't want to hurt you."

"Let me go," she said again, trying to pull away.

"Not until you're calm."

His squeezing her wrists hurt. She stopped tugging. Her knees shook, and she could hardly breathe. It couldn't be true. But the more she thought about it, the less she doubted it. Royl's worry confirmed it the most. His concern about Beiron's return and the way he'd reacted in front of their mother. She could hardly let herself think it.

Releasing her tension made her stomach churn. She refused to look Beiron in the eye.

He released her wrists and made her jump when he spread his arms wide on either side of her, wrapping them around her. Her body tensed while he embraced her, and she held her arms protectively close in front of herself.

There was that smell on him. The flower and pine. She tried to stop her shaking.

"*Deihara,*" Beiron whispered in her ear. "There's so much I have to teach you."

Daughter? Laila's bottom lip trembled.

Beiron held onto her firmly. She struggled to move out of his arms, pushing her hands against his chest, but that only made him hold her tighter.

She was going to need something more than her physical strength to drive him away. Her elbows were bent, and her hands, stuck near her chin. She couldn't reach the knife like this. And he was too close for her to use her magic against him.

Except . . .

Laila's heart raced so fast, it hurt her chest. If she thought of her own body as though she were one of the elements, perhaps she could use blood magic, like Beiron's sister Gilia had done. How hard could it be? Using the forbidden magic frightened her, but not more than Beiron.

All her resisting ceased as she focused only on connecting her mind, soul, and body in unity, just as Beiron's book instructed. She reached down deep to the core of her very being. What she needed was the strength to push Beiron off her. The ability to move him. She flattened her hand against Beiron's chest and pushed him, willing the strength to come.

An energy surged through her veins. A power like no other, flowing from the top of her head to her toes. She raised her chest, confident that the strength was hers for the taking. But something was wrong.

Beiron's footing stumbled, and he loosened his hold on her. He was reacting to the effects of her magic as she'd intended. But what she felt in herself—what was supposed to be strength—was not working. As she held her hand in place, she did not feel powerful or strong. She felt weakened. A sharp pain pierced the area near her heart. She cried out and let go. It was as if her touch had somehow weakened them both.

Beiron fell to his knees and gasped while she managed to remain on her feet, though only just. She backed away, keeping her arms stretched out in front of her. Her strength all but gone, she stumbled and nearly fell. But she couldn't. Not now. She needed to run while she had the chance.

As long as Raidan and Dimitri remained in the cave, they were safe. She had to get away first, then come up with a plan.

She climbed up the slope, using her hands to assist. Beiron had recovered somewhat and was clasping his chest, breathing hard. "You have a knack for it," he said through laboured breaths. "Just like my sister did."

Laila could hear the smile in his voice. She stole a look behind her. He'd already gotten to his feet and was moving toward her.

The knife crossed her mind again. She fumbled for it but couldn't pull it out fast enough. There was no time for this. She needed to outrun him.

Ignoring the sharp pain in her chest, she gave up on the knife and moved quicker up the slope. It didn't take Beiron long to catch up to her. He grabbed her by the arm and threw it behind her back, twisting it upward so it hurt to resist. She hollered from the pain. He pushed her to start walking back to the boulder they'd been sitting on.

Her arm was pinned behind her, bent up from the elbow. Trying to break free only caused her pain, so she went where he prodded.

"You're going to be useful to me," he told her as they walked. "You see, blood relations can make you stronger. You've learned the hard way that the relation can also weaken you, but you'll soon find that when you help me become stronger, you, too, will benefit."

Laila tried once more to pull free, but he held on and the movement hurt her shoulder. She stopped fighting to allow the pain to subside. Beiron used that moment to bring her hands together behind her back. He took a long, thin rope from his pocket and wound it around her wrists, tying them tight.

After her hands were secured, he sat her down in front of the boulder. She landed on Dimitri's boots and shifted uncomfortably to get off them.

Beiron crouched down to her level and rested an elbow on his knee. The boulder at her back, Laila had nowhere to go.

"You're out of your mind if you think I'm going to help you," she spat.

"You will. You're blood of my blood. Maybe you won't help me for your own sake, but your brother is not my blood, and I'll do what I must if it means you do as I say."

"This is how you treat your blood?" she shouted, ignoring his threats. Royl was far away from this place, thankfully. "And you wonder why my mother shut you out. What would Gilia think of this treatment toward your blood?" Laila herself didn't know what Gilia would think, but she hoped speaking his sister's name would stir some remorse in him.

"You don't know the half of it," Beiron said without a hint of regret. "And neither did Gilia, because she's dead."

Struggling did nothing but cause Laila pain. Beiron watched her with no sympathy in his face. She stopped trying to free her hands, but continued to squirm. "Just let me go," she said. "I'll stay out of your way; you don't need me."

"I need you to learn."

Until now, she'd managed to hold back her tears, but she could no longer stop them from coming. "Why?" she asked.

"Because you're my daughter, and a father must teach his children the hard lessons. This is the hardest lesson of all. The sooner you learn, the better off you'll be. Caring makes you weak. The more you care, the more power someone has over you. Your mother taught me that."

Laila's breathing was shaky. Was this some twisted form of vengeance on her mother for cutting him out of her life? "My mother did what she did to protect us. And it's no wonder."

Beiron glanced at the lake, then back at Laila. "Those brothers are down there," he said. "Soon, the barrier will be broken, and you're going to go to them and do exactly as I say. Do you understand?"

Laila shook her head. No way would she help Beiron accomplish his goals.

He shifted his weight to his other side. "I know what you're thinking. You think I can't make you do anything, and when I can't convince you to help me, I'll have no choice but to leave you here, where you'll escape and run back to your brother to protect you. Am I right?"

Her thoughts were not far off.

"That's not going to happen. Do you want to know why?" he asked. "First off, I think when you know what's at stake, you'll help me willingly. But if not, then I have a way to keep you close. That book—my book that you took from my home—had a sort of spell over it. No one could remove it from its place except me or my blood. It's what led me to first suspect our relation. I will tie you to this rock and use that same method to ensure that you won't be able to leave this spot until I remove you from it. By then, I'll have made my point clear and the lesson will be complete."

Laila couldn't stop the flow of tears as she tried hopelessly to free her hands. Beiron hadn't once lied to her. She doubted he was bluffing. Still, she would not be used by him. "I refuse to help you," she told him.

Beiron drew Raidan's knife from the belt at her waist. He raised the tip of the blade to her upper arm and cut quickly, ripping the fabric of her sleeve and breaking the skin. She winced and bit down on her tongue to keep from making a sound. Beiron put his hand over her arm where she bled. "Royl Madx. *Adilfim. Bludevint ti bludevint. Thei tsim sustixtinen.*"

He removed his hand from her arm and further ripped her sleeve to show that the cut was gone. Laila's jaw dropped. She blinked twice at her arm.

Beiron again placed the blade to her skin. "Shall we go deeper this time?" He didn't give her a chance to protest as he pressed the blade down and cut her arm in the same place.

She gasped. Beiron covered the cut with his hand and repeated the phrase. *Royl Madx. Brother. Blood to blood. The price is his to bear.*

He took his hand away and again the cut miraculously disappeared. Somewhere out there, Royl would have a fresh cut on his arm. For all she knew, he was in the midst of battle at that very moment. Even a scratch could jeopardize his focus.

Beiron readied the knife a third time in the same place.

"No, stop!" Laila shouted. "Don't do it again."

"Are you ready to hear what you're going to do?" Beiron said.

She bowed her head. Somehow she would find a way out of this, but for the time being, all she could do was go along. Appease him in the moment. The right opportunity would present itself soon enough. It had to. Until then, she would make Beiron believe she was willing to help.

"Laila," he said. "Are you listening carefully?"

Fresh tears ran down her cheeks. She nodded.

"That's better," he said. "Here's what you're going to do."

Chapter 80

ALL CIVILIZATION WAS BEHIND HIM NOW, AS WERE ILAN'S PURSUERS.

Ilan walked through the Forest of Litlen alone. What an odd thing to be left alone. He was no stranger to loneliness, but to be physically alone was something he'd never known in his life. He didn't know who would stand by him, or who of his men would turn on him and drag him back to his father if given the chance. He could trust no one. That knowledge left an empty ache in his gut.

Ahead, creeping vines climbed the stone chairs of the Chronicle Monument. The small white flowers along the vine shone brightly in the night. He was nearly to Litlen and still hadn't planned how to approach the people there. He first had to find them. Surely someone had to be about. If they didn't already know of his father's approaching army, they soon would. Then he'd offer his sword to fight alongside them.

Kingston had done enough to try to steer him away from the Elderace. After all his efforts, Ilan would not give up, especially knowing they lived after all this time! He could hardly believe that after his father, grandfather, *and* great-grandfather put their best efforts into wiping them out, the Elderace still prevailed. He grinned to himself and realized how silly his face must look if someone were watching.

The thought of someone watching made him stop to look around. If there were eyes on him now, he'd likely know. He had a good sense of these things.

The forest was quiet and bright. No moving shadows caught his eye nor any unnatural sounds. He walked on. When he came upon the Chronicle Monument, he stopped to pick a flower off the vine. These hadn't been there the last time he came to this place, when he'd first picked up Raidan and his family. The flower continued to glow even as he held it between his thumb and forefinger.

As he crossed the line between the forest and the open plain into Litlen, a tangible change filled the air. The whole place seemed . . . fuller. More life grew here than when he'd first come through the day Litlen awoke. The grass was taller, and a haze in the air drifted upward. Ilan squinted through the floral-scented purple mist.

He turned his attention to the Teiry Mountains. Something had happened again. He suspected it was related to the Pool of Sovereignty. Beiron, whom he'd lost track of long ago, likely had something to do with this new change. Yes, that made the most sense.

Not knowing what to do now, he groaned. His father was coming. If Ilan had any hope of earning the trust of the Elderace, staying in Litlen to fight would be the way to do it. But what of the Pool of Sovereignty?

As if he didn't already feel pressured to decide, a sound blasted through the air, making him jump. It had come from the west, near where Litlen bordered the Bludesel Mountains. The cannon's blast set a new kind of tension in the night air. The booming sound carried all the way to where he stood. It resonated like a battle cry for the fighting to begin.

Ilan bounced on his toes. Should he go left or right? West, where the battle was about to commence, or east, where he may or may not find Beiron and claim magic for himself?

He closed his eyes. Indecision would get him nowhere. When he opened his eyes, his choice was clear.

Chapter 81

Raidan blinked rapidly as the water sprayed his face. He wiped his eyes and stepped forward to avoid the worst of the drizzle. Adrik still had the higher ground while Raidan teetered in the water. In trying not to let it bother him, he dug his nails into his palms.

"Close your eyes," Adrik said.

For a crazy second, Raidan debated refusing. It was difficult to obey Adrik. Overlooking their past was no easy task.

Let it go, he told himself. He closed his eyes.

"Be calm, Raidan," Adrik said. "I am going to place my hands on your head. Do not fight it."

Raidan's eyes opened. Fear tugged at his heart. "Fight what?"

"You must relax. Put everything from your mind."

"Fight what?" he repeated.

Adrik sighed. "I am going to give you memories. Elderace history and knowledge. It is only for the Guardians and the delegates to know and pass down. But this will not work unless you put everything from your mind."

So simple, yet so difficult. "You sound like Kameron."

"A wise man, he is. Now, close your eyes."

Raidan complied and tried to clear his mind as he'd done on music night. And just like then, it was not easy.

Adrik reached for Raidan's temples. The instant he made contact, Raidan's knees buckled. His blood streamed through his veins, up his arms, down his spine. Its distinct, rapid pulsing was loud in his ears. The power in him swelled, and he thought he might implode. Colours streamed behind his closed eyes in a swirling jumble of chaos. His breath left him, and a heaviness came over him. A high-pitched ringing made him cringe, and he was aware his body was convulsing.

Adrik let go and Raidan lost his balance. Breathless, he stumbled about in the pool and nearly fell. He shuffled his feet and steadied himself.

Adrik scowled. "You are not relaxing. You are fighting."

Raidan didn't think he'd been. "I'm trying."

"You are trying too hard. Do not think, just be. Again." Adrik put his hands back to Raidan's temples before he'd even fully recovered. It took less time than before for him to start convulsing. Still Adrik held on, telling him to relax and be calm.

"Stop!" Raidan pushed Adrik away. His head throbbed as he stepped out of the pool and sat on the chair next to Dimitri. "You're not helping," he told Adrik.

"What is the problem?" Adrik threw his hands up. "Why is this so difficult for you?"

Somehow, Kameron had made it easier. Adrik's voice telling him to be calm and relax had the opposite effect.

"Is this really necessary?" Dimitri asked Adrik. "This could take too long. Couldn't we continue after we've helped in the fight?"

Adrik heaved a sigh. "No one can leave here until the barrier is broken. Not even you two. Until you have the knowledge of the stone, your power will not work as needed when you go up against Kingston's army."

Dimitri ran his hands through his hair. "How do we break the barrier?"

"By receiving the knowledge of the stone."

The aching in Raidan's head grew as his shoulders tensed. He spoke, raising his voice. "You should have explained all this to us before you performed the ceremony in the first place!"

Dimitri touched his arm as if to remind him to stay calm. Not wanting to start another incident like the last time, Raidan took the cue. He leaned forward and buried his face in his hands. This was necessary, he knew. He just didn't understand why.

The water pouring from the ceiling into the pool echoed in the cave room. Adrik perched on the ledge of the pool. "Before he died, my father passed on to me the honour of becoming a delegate. The trace of element in my blood allows me the ability to sense the stone's power. That's how I identified you as Sermarc's heir when we first met, though I did not recognize it until we had physical contact. But now you are resisting me and not allowing my trace of element to flow through you."

Raidan remembered the way Adrik's body had gone rigid and convulsed the night they'd met. "Why Sermarc?" Raidan asked. "The Elderace and the mayanon don't get along, so why give something so important to a mayanon?"

Adrik slouched as he relented to taking a brief rest. "Originally the delegates intended to bind it to either myself or Beiron, but Beiron's experimentation in blood magic and methods of education led him down a dark path. He crossed lines that disqualified him for the candidacy. As for me, it had always been my desire to take after my father and become a delegate—to protect the stone and the Guardian bound to it.

"When Landon Valca established the Valca Order, he sought to rule the country, just as Kingston does today. He instigated war with my people. When he'd learned of the Weldafire Stone, he became intent on acquiring it. Marc Dairner was the son of Anwyll and Adira. They had led the revolution and nearly succeeded against Landon. The people of Kartha—Elderace and mayanon alike—viewed them as heroes. If anyone could truly unite our two peoples, my father believed it would be a mayanon. And if any mayanon was going to be accepted by the Elderace, who better than the son of Anwyll and Adira Dairner? The heroes who were not afraid to challenge The Order?"

Raidan leaned back. The throbbing in his head had subsided. He'd always known his family name stirred strong feelings in some. Ida's cousin Esef was one such person. But Raidan had never heard the details.

The blue light glowed above them and reflected in Dimitri's eyes, which focused intently on Adrik. "If they were such heroes, why does no one know their names now?"

Adrik set his hands on the pool's ledge on either side of him. "Because the Valca Order won the war. Landon saw to it that they were not remembered. He was betrothed to the woman Marc loved, whom Marc married in secret. After the curse destroyed Litlen and Marc was killed, he'd spent years searching for Marvelle. I thought she'd died in the fight, just as everyone else I cared for had. But I suppose she'd laid low and took precautions to ensure Landon would not find her, especially considering we now know she carried Marc's child. Or else you two would not be here today." He stood up and brushed grit from his hands. "Now, we do need to finish this. If there is to be war, you have much to learn." He motioned for Raidan to stand.

Raidan blinked. What he and Dimitri were doing—taking a stand against The Order, defying Kingston, and protecting the Elderace—this was the Dairner legacy. He glanced around the room as if seeing it for the first time, then walked to the Pool of Sovereignty. He stepped in and didn't mind so much that he was getting wet. Adrik took his place standing over him.

"Remember what I said. Clear your mind and your thoughts. Think of nothing except that which I am going to show you. It is our history and our heritage, and I am entrusting it to you—the Guardians of the Weldafire Stone."

Raidan nodded. He closed his eyes in anticipation of what came next.

Chapter 82

THE MOMENT ADRIK PUT HIS HANDS TO RAIDAN'S TEMPLES, THE awareness returned, as did the pulse of blood in his ears and the power threatening to burst from the walls keeping it at bay. He squeezed his closed eyes tighter.

The chaos of colourful light swirled around in his mind's eye. The sound of blood swishing through his body became muffled, and a baby's cry pierced through his awareness. He gasped.

Cassian!

The thought of his son took over all else. Even through the dull ache at the base of his neck. His heart beat fast and loud. He hadn't started convulsing yet. That was a start.

Ida's laughter overpowered Cassian's cries. Raidan relaxed at the sound of her playful voice. Releasing the tension eased the ache in his head.

His family was safe. But they needed him. A strong desire came over him to protect them, to protect his home and country. As his mind let go of all he'd been holding onto, he found he wasn't so afraid. All that he'd feared didn't seem so frightening anymore. The Valca Order. Magic. Adrik.

Adrik was no enemy to him. And the Valca Order: they were no match for this magic he possessed, the magic that begged to be set free in him. It was a part of who he was, bound to him by blood. And it was powerful. It boiled up from his core. He allowed it to move, summoning it to the surface.

All the anger and hate that had built up—they only caused him pain. They were a cage, keeping him locked up for far too long, holding him back from fulfilling his destiny.

He opened his mind to receive the knowledge—surrendering himself to it. He let everything go. Time seemed to freeze in the moment. Every sound that filled his ears stopped, and all that remained was the steady rhythm of his heart.

Images took shape in his head. Raidan relaxed completely and allowed the visions to come.

Dark, heavy clouds loomed over the land, over all of Kartha. Raidan stood at the top of a hill with Dimitri. Black clouds covered the sky. Lightning struck, and in its flash, six figures appeared around them in a circle.

The storm overhead darkened the land and the hill. The men and women surrounding them had their hands raised, and their blank eyes, to the heavens. Raidan shared a look with Dimitri before returning his attention to the six men and women.

They chanted in Eldrace. Somehow, Raidan understood their words and knew these six had summoned the storm.

Protect our land, protect our people, the Six chanted in unison.

The ground shook. From beneath Raidan's feet, through mounds of earth, green-blue crystals ripped through the hills. Thousands of shards of the crystals lifted into the air and whirled in the winds of the growing storm.

Another flash of lightning, and he and Dimitri were transported elsewhere. They stood at the entrance to the sacred room of the delegates' cave. It looked the same, except that the six men and women sat in the six stone chairs that encircled the Pool of Sovereignty. The Weldafire Stone rested on the ledge of the pool. Another man stood in the room next to Adrik. The man had brown eyes like Raidan's and

Dimitri's. Although he looked quite young, Raidan knew this man to be his ancestor, Marc Dairner.

In another instant, they stood again in the same room, but the Six were gone. In their places were Sermarc—as that was now his name—Beiron and a man who resembled Adrik but was not him: Norick. His face and name came unbidden to Raidan.

The storm resumed within the sacred room. The stone shook on the ledge of the pool, and a blinding light filled the room. Raidan shielded his eyes, but the light was gone in a split second. He blinked, and when he refocused, Adrik stood before him, hands at his sides.

He had finished. The knowledge of the Weldafire Stone was theirs.

It wasn't just visions Raidan had seen, but the knowledge associated with each. The visions were clear as day. He understood their meaning. The names and faces of the Six. Adrik. Sermarc. Even Beiron's part in it all. His spirit filled with a longing to protect the Weldafire Stone. It was all too clear now what would happen if it fell into Beiron's hands.

Water trickling drew Raidan's attention to the threshold. The wall of water that was magically held back between the tunnels and the sacred room receded.

The barrier was broken.

Chapter 83

Every once in a while, Laila lost feeling in her fingers and had to shift around to regain circulation. Her hands were like ice. She leant forward, wriggling her wrists. Using her discomfort as an excuse to move, she stretched her fingers toward the rope.

Beiron stood at the edge of the water, peering into the black lake. She doubted he could see anything beneath the surface. He turned his head slightly but didn't look back at her. She knew he could hear her squirming about.

Her tears had stopped flowing. The sky was lightening in the early morning hours. Not long ago, the breeze had shifted. She didn't know if she'd be able to tell when Raidan and Dimitri broke what remained of the curse, but she sensed a change. An air of revival. That should have brought her joy, but she was far from it. How could Beiron be her father?

And how could her mother not have told her? Or Royl. He had to have known. Why wouldn't he have said anything?

She pressed her fingers as close to the rope as she could. In her quietest whisper, she said, "*Vint.*"

Without seeing her hands, she felt the power go from her and knew she'd sparked a flame into existence at her fingertips. Now came the tricky part of aiming her little fire to burn just through the rope and not her skin. Her shoulders twisted. The heat seared her wrist, and the flame touched her. She made a small sound, then quickly closed her hands to extinguish the fire.

Laila glanced up to see if Beiron had heard. His face was turned her way. She glared at him. He rubbed his own wrist, stepped away from the lake, and approached her. Had he felt her burn?

He sat down beside her so their shoulders were touching. "Your trigger is *vint*?" he asked. "You know it's common for children to inherit the triggers of their parents. Have you ever tried *bludevint*?"

Laila ignored him. In truth, she'd never tried his suggestion as a trigger word before. *Vint* came naturally, and that was always what she'd said.

Beiron patted his pockets on either side of his long black coat, then his trouser pockets. He reached into his right pocket and extracted a small glass vial. Raidan's knife was stowed in his own waistband, and he now withdrew it from its scabbard. There was nothing special about the knife. It had a plain wooden handle, and the blade was only sharp on one side.

"I wish I could trust you, Laila," Beiron said as he twirled the knife in his hand. "But we're not there yet."

Laila tried not to look at the knife.

He stopped twirling it and examined the blade. "As you've probably already noticed, my book didn't include everything I've ever discovered. I chose to record only that which I was willing to share for the benefit of others. The book itself was not something I planned on sharing, but I do intend to educate you in many things, *deihara*. Consider yourself lucky to have such a teacher as myself. For this lesson, I am sorry I will have to teach you in this way."

He moved away from her just enough so that he could put the blade to her shoulder, and then he cut her. A whimper escaped her throat. She gaped at the red flow of blood. It trailed down her arm beneath her already torn and bloodied shirtsleeve.

Beiron opened the vial and set it against her arm to collect her blood. "I need you to take this seriously," he said while it filled. "You're not always going to be within my reach." He gave the filled vial a little shake and sealed it. "This will give me access to you, whether you're near or not. With this, there are many things I can do to get to Royl. I don't think I need to explain myself to make my point clear. Please don't make me hurt him, Laila. I am fond of the boy."

He stowed the vial in his pocket, rummaged around for a handkerchief, and pressed the cloth onto the cut to stop the bleeding.

Laila's mind was reeling. How could she refuse him now? Or ever for that matter? All the progress she'd made toward living in freedom was gone. Was this to be her fate? To be Beiron's minion, doing his bidding—or else?

The ground trembled, and water lapped the shore. It receded, leaving the rocks beneath wet and shiny, glistening in the early light of dawn. The water continued to go down until it revealed the hole in the mountain face—the cave entrance.

She held her breath. It was time.

Beiron put away the handkerchief and pushed her forward so he could untie her wrists. The rope snapped when he cut it, and blood rushed back into her fingers.

Beiron stood and offered a hand to help her up. She let him stand there, not accepting his hand nor making any effort to get up on her own. A willful defiance took root in her, and she wished so badly to run from this place.

Beiron looked from the entrance of the cave to Laila. "Let's go."

Laila's nostrils flared. Defying him while he had the power to force her along would only waste her strength—strength she'd need when the time came to fight.

Her time would come. She just needed the right moment. She would find a way out of this as soon as she got that vial.

She rose on shaky legs. Beiron put his hand to her back and nudged her forward. She moved her feet slowly. They descended the remainder of the slope together, into the basin and into the opening in the mountain. Moving from the fresh outside air into a tunnel in the earth was all too familiar.

Beiron lit his light and led Laila under the arching ceiling of grey rock. Water dripped down the walls. The ceiling was high enough for them to stand and with little room to spare. They took the first left turn and continued through a course of tight turns and bends. Voices echoed ahead. Laila couldn't understand what was being said but knew Raidan and Dimitri's voices well enough to recognize them.

Beiron slowed. He thrust a hand out in front of Laila, stopping her, and directed her attention to the floor. Pressed up against the wall was a long, thick green vine.

The Anguivina.

Laila put her hands to her heart and stepped back, but Beiron took her by the elbow. "You know what has to be done."

She did. She thought of the little vial of her blood in Beiron's pocket. The time would come, but this wasn't it.

She gave Beiron her hand, and he used the knife to cut a small slit into her palm and draw blood once again. He gestured to the Anguivina. "Go on. I can't do the next part for you."

Laila looked at the blood oozing from the fresh cut by her thumb. She crouched down and resisted the urge to wipe it away.

"We haven't got all day," Beiron said, keeping his voice low.

Little fuzzy hairs rose along the creature's long body, which extended in either direction of the tunnel path. Laila pressed her hand to its skin. It was warm to the touch. She took a deep breath and spoke the words she'd been instructed to say. "*In ceptrin mandonr du thei Anguivina.*"

The creature writhed and shivered, almost as if it were purring. The power of the beast moved through her.

It was hers to control now.

Chapter 84

Morning dawned, and Ilan hadn't yet reached the battlegrounds. A hush came over the land as if the animals and critters knew what was coming. As the sun rose, the haze lifted. A puff of black smoke dissipated in the sky above Litlen ahead. Ilan grimaced. The land had been devoid of life for so long and had only recently been restored. He shuddered at what would come of it after his father stormed through.

He'd not seen any sign of the Elderace, but he didn't expect to come across anyone this far outside the city.

Disorderly marching in the distance broke the silence. Ilan turned to the sound.

Far off, approaching from the Teiry Mountains, he could make out a cloud of shape that was the troop. The soldiers were here. This was sure to interfere with his plan. What Elderace man or woman was going to receive him with an army advancing at his heels. His army.

Ilan glanced around. Should he hide? Where would he go? What did it matter? If his father was victorious, there would be no where Ilan could go to escape him. And no more Elderace or magic.

Ilan raised his chin. Something had to be done. He strode toward the approaching army. Now was the time to see where these men's loyalties lied—with him or his father.

Upon spotting Ilan, the men at the front of the line altered course to march toward him. A familiar face commanded the ranks. Miles raised a fist and the soldiers came to a stop. He had a new ring in his nose to replace the one Dimitri had ripped out.

On second thought, would Miles be keen to fight for the Elderace? Maybe not, if he held a grudge. Ilan almost turned around. He slowed his pace, allowing the battalion to close the distance.

Miles stepped forward from his troop. "Was wondering where you'd gotten to," Miles said. "Your father ordered the men in Veryl to march on Litlen and join ranks."

Ilan licked his lips. "About that, I could use your help, Miles."

Miles was silent, and Ilan took that to mean that he was willing to listen.

Ilan went on. "I don't want to fight the Elderace. My father is trying to ensure their extinction. Help me to defend them and those who fight alongside them." He wiped his sweaty hands on his trousers. Holding his breath, he waited for a reaction before saying anymore.

Miles adjusted his nose ring. He sniffed. His silence was making Ilan think he'd made a mistake. Was he his man or his father's?

After an agonizing minute, Miles nodded. "I did think this was a bit overkill. I'll talk to some of the men and see where they stand. Many will not likely choose to fight their fellow soldiers, but I might be able to convince some to defend the opposition. It might be the best we can do. Do you have a plan?"

Ilan nodded, uncertain. "I might have something to make my father give this up." It was Kingston who'd put things into motion. It seemed Ilan would have to take matters into his own hands to make his father end this war, even if he had to marry some woman from Tsein and live there for the remainder of his life.

From behind, cannon-fire split the air, resonating from afar. Ilan looked past Miles to the combat-ready men. If Miles could sway them, the Elderace stood a better chance. It was possible that Ilan wouldn't be able to persuade Kingston to let this fight go.

"Where is my father?" Ilan asked.

Miles gestured in the direction he faced. "He's setting up camp at the edge of the Forest of Litlen, near the city boundary, on the road out from the Bludesel Mountains."

"I'll speak to him." Though, the idea made Ilan's stomach turn. "In the meantime, see who will fight for me and defend the Elderace."

Miles nodded. "Oh, and Ilan, you should know, some time after you left Veryl, Perry was approached by your father's men. I don't know what was discussed."

Ilan pressed his lips together. Perry had always been close to Ilan. As captain of his own portion of the army, they'd spent a great deal of time training together. Still, he might be swayed by Kingston if offered the right motivation. It was a question he would ponder later. But Perry hadn't returned after he was meant to retrieve Raidan from that camp in the mountains. That meant he was either dead, captured, or had deserted.

Ilan stepped aside while Miles passed, leading his company. With him recruiting for Ilan, they could tip the scales in favour of the Elderace. Some would accept and join him, and some would not. But some was better than none.

Chapter 85

WAS THIS REALLY ALL THAT REMAINED OF THE ELDERACE PEOPLE? Throughout the abandoned region of Litlen, from one end of the derelict city to the other, stood a force of men and women. They were more than Kingston expected, but no match for his great forces.

With the tall grass, scattered trees, and strewn rubble of the broken stone buildings all over the cobbled streets, it was difficult to clearly identify their number. Kingston guessed they were in the thousands—an impressive turnout for a bunch of nobodies.

Surely they were not only Elderace. Somehow, the survivors must have enlisted the help of others. Had the people of Kartha really learned nothing since the Great Battle at Reen?

Many of the opposition were armed with swords, clubs, axes, or other miscellaneous weapons. Some dressed for battle in mail and helmets. Others looked bulky in thick, layered clothing, and some wore common garb.

Kingston scoffed at the sight. Owen sat atop his horse, keeping close to his master. Even the weaselly man didn't appear afraid of the Elderace and their motley army.

Kingston's rank of ten thousand men lined up along the tree line of the edge of the forest and spread out throughout the forest and along the city's limits. They faced the battle-ready resistance. His captain,

Mason, was leading another ten thousand through the Gap, with the three cannons in tow. It was the only road wide enough for the weapons to pass through. And still another rank of soldiers marched from the east, through the Teiry Mountain pass, and would join them shortly.

Soon, all of Kingston's forces would be together. He wouldn't have to lift a finger in this fight.

Completing his grandfather's work would be a pleasure. This fight would be over within the first hour and victory would be his. When all was said and done, the people of Kartha would come to regret this day.

The men were taking a long time to spread out, and Kingston couldn't wait for everyone to line up to begin. He raised his sword and screamed. His men—those who were lined up—returned his scream with their own shouting. They waved their swords and beat their chests.

This battle wasn't going to take long. He could wrap this up and return home in time for supper.

Chapter 86

RAIDAN STEPPED OUT OF THE POOL OF SOVEREIGNTY. AFTER ALL THAT he'd just seen and felt, he expected to have been exhausted, but instead, he felt fresh and new.

"Strange," Dimitri said as he stood. "I thought I'd know everything there is to know about how to use magic, but I don't think I do."

Adrik smiled, showing his teeth. It was the first time his smile didn't seem malicious to Raidan. From the very first night they'd met, Raidan had never noticed the gentleness in his eyes. They carried a hurt, but beneath their jading, they were kind.

Raidan understood what Dimitri meant about magic. The knowledge Adrik gave them was only knowledge of the Weldafire Stone's capabilities and the history of where it'd come from. How it was formed from the Vastgerdite crystal in the hills and mountains around Litlen in a time when the surrounding countries were converging on the land to take claim to the healing rock. The knowledge didn't provide them with a full understanding of exactly how to control their power.

But whatever magic was at work in what Adrik had just done, the invisible barricade blocking Raidan from using his power was gone. The magic that sparked like lighting in him was attainable. He had it—he'd had it all along.

The three of them stood next to the pool, the six chairs surrounding them. The chair nearest to Raidan was only three paces away, but he remained on his feet. He couldn't sit now. His excitement about this newfound knowledge made him want to find Ida at last and tell her everything.

Adrik plucked the Weldafire Stone from the leather pouch and handed it to Raidan, who accepted it. When he turned it around in his hand, it changed from glimmering blue to green and somewhere in between.

"Your power is something you must discover on your own," Adrik said. "Both of you will be able to manipulate the elements: light, darkness, water, earth, air, and fire. What sets the power of the stone apart is its unity with the land. With the stone's power, you possess the ability to move your magic throughout the land itself. That, and you have the power to heal.

"As I have said before, the Weldafire Stone and the Pool of Sovereignty coincide with one another. The pool offers healing, therefore, you can too."

"How do we manipulate the elements?" Raidan asked. He'd only ever been able to make the ground shake and produce a little blue light. His control over fire needed work, and he'd not even tried the other elements. Knowing a little more before heading into battle would be useful.

"Find your trigger." Adrik raised his hands up and out. "*Luzen.*"

White light outshone the blue and filled the room. Raidan lowered his gaze and allowed his eyes to readjust.

"Triggers are words, sometimes objects or particular actions or movements," Adrik explained. "Once you find your trigger, you will have an easier time controlling your power."

"But we don't speak Eldrace," Dimitri said.

"Magic does not work like that. It is a part of *you.*" Adrik poked his finger at Dimitri's chest. "It does not know language. It responds to you alone. Take time to listen within yourself. You will know your trigger when you are one with your power."

Kingston was commencing battle against the Elderace perhaps at that very moment. There was no time to sit around and figure out their triggers. Raidan knew his voice was effective. He thought of something to try, just to see that he had control of his magic to some extent.

Dimitri beat him to it. He extended his arms high and said, "*Kartha.*" He looked like he'd tried to mimic Adrik's action from a moment ago, except he over exaggerated the movement. A gust of wind swept across the room and made the water in the pool ripple.

Raidan brushed his hair aside and narrowed one eye at his brother. Dimitri smirked, then burst out laughing. He was like a child. Raidan's smile grew wide, but before he could try his own magic, footsteps sounded near the threshold of the room.

Laila entered, looking pale and grim. Dimitri dropped his hands and stepped past the chairs to go to her. Movement came from the farthest chair, where the mound of green vines lay coiled. The hairs on the back of Raidan's neck rose and sent a chill down his spine.

"Laila, are you all right?" Dimitri asked, sounding far away. Raidan's attention was hyper focused on the vinelike creature as it uncurled itself. He stepped back.

"Adrik—" Raidan stopped short when the vine slithered straight for him. He backed up and bumped into the chair, his backside landing in the seat. The vine looped around his ankles, and he pushed himself upward with his arms.

He was about to speak to use his magic when Dimitri shouted his name. Raidan turned toward him just as something fuzzy and soft whacked the back of his head. It wound itself around and covered his mouth.

More vines crept up from the ground, seemingly coming from everywhere. They twirled around Raidan's waist and wrists. He was so focused on the vines looping around his body that he barely noticed Adrik's pained yelp.

Dimitri ran over to Raidan. His gaze darted to the many branches weaving their way up his body.

"*Karth*—" Dimitri started, but a branch of vine fell from the ceiling and prevented him from finishing, as it covered his mouth. Multiple thick branches crawled up Dimitri's body and dragged him back.

Vines wrenched Raidan down, pinning him to the chair. The back of his head bumped against its tall backing. The creature continued to twist around his legs and arms, tying him in place. He screamed, willing his magic to work even as he was unable to speak.

Adrik lay on the ground next to the Pool of Sovereignty. Vines wrapped themselves around his ankles, and he looked like he might have hit his head on the pool during his fall. A gash cut across his forehead above his brow. His body was still.

Laila walked through the chaos of vines and stepped into the centre, where Adrik lay and where Dimitri and Raidan sat, both bound to a chair. She moved her hands this way and that, as though she were conducting the movements of the vines. She cried while she manipulated them to do her bidding. Raidan's chest tightened. Why was she doing this? What had happened in the time since they'd left her until now?

There were much more vines now than there had been a minute ago. They were all over the floor, walls, and ceiling.

To Raidan's left, Dimitri's state matched his own. Tied, gagged, and struggling to break free. Raidan pulled against the restraints, but they squeezed back when he resisted.

Laila's hands shook as she motioned them downward. The vines followed her direction and slackened, except for those doing the restraining. The floor was covered by the thick green plant. They looked like balls of snakes piled on top of one another. Hundreds of them, joined somehow as if they were all one, connected from multiple branches sticking out in all directions.

Laila looked at Raidan. "I'm so sorry," she whispered. She closed her eyes and tears streamed down her cheeks.

Slow clapping echoed throughout the room, coming from behind Raidan. He couldn't see past the high back of the chair, but then Beiron's voice spoke over his applause. "Well done, Laila." He walked between the chairs that Raidan and Dimitri were tied to, taking wide steps over the vines. "I couldn't have done this better myself."

Beiron grinned. "Your son was returned to you, as promised," he said to Raidan. He leaned over and cupped Raidan's cheek in his hand. "We're almost done. Just a little longer, and we'll be through with each other."

Raidan couldn't do much more than narrow his eyes at him. Adrik stirred, which drew Beiron's attention. He stepped over the vines toward him, then bent down and hauled him up upright, leaning his back against the pool's ledge. Laila hugged her arms across her body, keeping her eyes down.

Beiron withdrew a knife—Raidan's knife—or . . . technically Kameron's. He crouched low to Adrik's level. "Adrik." Beiron slapped his face lightly to wake him.

Adrik's eyes fluttered, then widened when they landed on Beiron crouched down in his face. The corner of Beiron's mouth curled up. "Long time, old friend." He thrust the knife into Adrik's abdomen. Adrik stiffened, gasping in a breath.

"What you and your father did," Beiron said. "That was clever. Norick giving you his trace of element behind my back." He tutted. "And now he's dead, as is Marc. And here I am, about to get exactly what I've always wanted, despite your best efforts to stop me." He patted down the pockets of Adrik's tunic. He'd not find the stone there.

"You'll destroy Kartha," Adrik said through laboured breaths. His hand compressed his stomach, near where the knife stuck out of him. "It won't just be Litlen this time." He coughed. "But all of Kartha. You will be the ruin of us all."

Beiron pulled the knife out of him and Adrik howled. Laila looked on with wide, frightened eyes.

Blood spurted from Adrik's wound. Adrik's body slouched a little lower, and his hands fell to his sides. He was not dead yet, but it wouldn't take long at the rate at which he was losing blood. Beiron allowed some of Adrik's blood to flow into the bowl shape his hands made.

Raidan didn't like where this was going. The history of the stone was written in the walls of his mind. Litlen's curse was Beiron's doing, and if Norick hadn't given up his trace of element to Adrik first, all of Kartha would have been cursed. Not getting Norick's trace of element was the only reason he'd not succeeded in cursing the whole country. But now that he had Adrik's blood, he could set in motion the downfall of their homeland.

Raidan strained against the vines. Beside him, Dimitri didn't seem to be faring any better. Laila kept her gaze averted from everyone.

Beiron lifted his cupped hands to his lips and drank. When he finished, he spilled out the remaining blood in his hands and wiped them on Adrik's already deep red tunic. He wiped his mouth, using his own sleeve, and stood to his full height. His appearance seemed bigger than before he'd taken the trace of element. Beastly, even. He puffed out his chest, and a wicked smile spread across his face.

"And now we begin."

Chapter 87

Raidan tugged at his arms, one at a time. He tried his legs next, testing the strength of the vines that kept him in the chair. Dimitri fought hard. The vines visibly tightened as he thrashed, and Raidan wished he would calm down. It was going to take more than muscle to get out of this. The ground trembled a little from Dimitri's muffled yelling. His voice, though he could make a sound, was not powerful enough to help them to get out of this.

Beiron stepped over Adrik's legs and approached Raidan. He leaned over and reached toward Raidan's pockets, where vines clustered, blocking him. He turned toward Laila and raised an eyebrow.

Laila stiffened. "What?"

"You know." Beiron's gaze fixed on her, he motioned with his head toward Raidan.

"I'm doing what you told me."

"I need to check his pockets."

Laila met Raidan's eyes for a second before looking away. The cluster of vine crept off Raidan's lap, allowing Beiron access.

Beiron searched both of Raidan's pockets and found the Weldafire Stone. He dug it out and transferred it to his own pocket, then walked back over to the pool in the centre.

Adrik's white light flickered and dimmed. Blood pooled around his abdomen.

Beiron faced the Pool of Sovereignty, Adrik at his feet. He held his arms out wide and low over the water, palms to the ground, and spoke quietly in Eldrace. *"In vocanin nar thei eirta ten em podin."* At his words, dirt from the cave floor hovered over the ground and swirled in small circles that expanded slowly.

Raidan had learned a lot recently, but another language was not among his newfound knowledge. He could guess the gist of Beiron's meaning as each word caused a reaction.

"Ay thei eir in apthnin."

A breeze blew and picked up the dirt. It swept it in gusts around the room, whipping across Raidan's face.

"Unthatnen apt luzen."

The dimming white light brightened, and Raidan had to shut his eyes. It illuminated the room like a flash of lighting. Raidan opened his eyes to slits so he could still see Beiron.

Beiron called out, louder now as the wind blowing around the room grew stronger. *"Ay shaydenev!"* The room plunged into utter darkness. Every sound intensified: the sweeping dirt in the wind; the water falling from the stalactite in the ceiling and into the Pool of Sovereignty.

Beiron said nothing. The darkness enveloped the room. Every once in a while, a piece of rock hit Raidan in the face or arm as the dirt swirled around, seemingly faster each time it circled the chairs and pool.

"Feury!" Beiron shouted. Fire erupted from the ground. It lit in a ring around the chairs and extended as high as the ceiling. The wind blew louder and faster. Flames licked close enough that Raidan felt its heat on his cheeks.

Dimitri attempted to yell through the gag, Adrik lay still, and Laila's forehead creased. Her eyes glistened in the flickering firelight, now the only source of light in the room.

Beiron continued to wave his arms as he conjured his magic. He bent down low over the Pool of Sovereignty. The noise from the wind and fire in the small space was loud enough now that he had to shout. "*Acuoda ceptnen ix thei Sovrn Vassul!*" He swept his arms upward. Water from the Pool of Sovereignty swooped up and joined the circulating storm.

"And now," Beiron roared, "with each trace, I will take the Weldafire Stone from the bloodline of Dairner and bind it to that of Cailt." He withdrew the stone from his pocket and placed it on the ledge of the Pool of Sovereignty next to Adrik's head. Adrik's finger twitched by his side.

Beiron grabbed the knife that he'd left on the ground and used Adrik's shoulder to wipe off the blood. He cut his own hand, then let his blood drip onto the stone.

Laila held her hair out of her face as the wind buffeted it about. She looked at Raidan and bit her bottom lip.

The storm that swirled around them intensified. The fierce wind whipped Raidan's hair across his forehead and against the back of his neck.

Beiron picked up the stone, which now had his blood on it. He turned to Raidan and Dimitri. "All that's needed is the blood of the sons of Sermarc."

If Raidan didn't do something now, it would be too late. He didn't dare close his eyes, but he needed to reach into himself and find a way to use his power without his voice. Clearing his head was not something he did well, as he'd recently learned. He focused on the ground. He needed to become one with the land. With Kartha.

Raidan searched around the room for something—inspiration of any kind. He wished he knew more about what he was supposed to do.

Beiron gripped the knife and went first to Dimitri. He held the blade to Dimitri's arm and cut a long line into his bare skin. Dimitri panted hard through his nostrils and screamed a muffled scream at

Beiron. Raidan suspected it wasn't because of the sting of the cut. Dimitri tried to kick his legs, but the vines wound tighter.

Beiron put the stone to Dimitri's arm, where his blood dripped onto it. He took the stone away and squinted at it. His eyes focused past the stone and on Raidan. He was next.

Raidan's thoughts raced. His heart raced. Time was running out and he couldn't concentrate.

Beiron took a step toward him.

"Stop!" Laila shouted over the noise of the wind.

*

This had gone far enough. Laila stood near to Adrik, who's breaths were slow and raspy. The wind circling the room was strong. Her hair was all over the place, and she fought to hold it back.

She'd waited and hoped for the right moment to steal the vial of her blood from Beiron and run, but Beiron would have his way by the time that moment could come. And now, hearing that Litlen's curse was *his* doing?

She could not let him succeed. Not at the expense of all of Kartha. She loved Royl and would do anything to protect him, but right now, it was within her power to save Kartha from becoming cursed as Litlen had been.

Dimitri stopped squirming. Raidan watched Laila intently as she pointed a finger at Beiron. "You were the one who cursed my home?"

To make the Anguivina do her bidding, all she need do was think for the creature to move and behave the way she wanted it to. She allowed the vines around Raidan and Dimitri to slacken.

She cast a quick glance at Raidan. He had to know this wasn't what she'd wanted. She directed her accusations at Beiron. "It was you?" Tears flowed freely from her eyes. "You were the reason I've had to live in the mines for the past hundred years?"

"Laila," Beiron said, lowering his voice to speak like a father reprimanding his daughter, which she supposed was exactly what he was.

He cocked his head and spoke loud enough that she could hear him over the wind. "You know what's at stake. Stand back while I finish this. We'll speak after."

"You're right!" Laila shouted. "I do know what's at stake." She held her hand to her heart. "I don't understand it," she said. "But I'm willing to bet you will feel this." He'd felt it when she'd burned her wrist earlier, she was sure of it. And she had a hunch this would hurt him too. If only she could hurt him enough, and then get to the vial. . . .

Beiron pressed his lips together into a thin line. He transferred the stone to his hand with the knife and reached his free hand into his pocket. He held the vial near his lips and opened his mouth to speak. Before he could get a word out, Laila closed her eyes. She drew from the power within her, unifying body, mind, and spirit, just as she'd done earlier. Except now she knew it was going to hurt, as that was her intention.

The pain was instant. A constricting sensation pressed against her ribs and heart. She closed her eyes and focused on her reasons for doing this. This was for Kartha. For her people. And if this was what it took to ensure Beiron failed, then so be it.

Chapter 88

THE VINES LOOSENED, AND RAIDAN WAS ABLE TO WRIGGLE HIS ARMS. Whatever magic Laila was using against herself was affecting Beiron. Her hand clutched her chest, her shoulders curled into her body, and her face was all scrunched up. She fell to her knees and Beiron stumbled backward at the same time. He wavered on his feet, and the back of his knee hit against the pool, opposite to where Adrik rested against it.

Whatever was happening, it seemed Laila had bought Raidan some time, though he didn't think much.

The vine around his mouth was as thick as his wrist. He turned his head and shrugged his shoulder to get it down. After a few shrugs, the vine moved to his chin, then his neck.

The wind blew in his face, and the noise of it was deafening in the small room. Blazing behind him, the fire roared around all six chairs, lighting the room.

Beiron grasped at his chest and bared his teeth at Raidan, who thrust himself against the bonds. They were loose enough to slip out of, but it would take time to free his limbs and body completely. Dimitri also struggled against the loosened vines.

There wasn't time for this. With another strong pull of his arms and legs, Raidan yelled. The vines broke off. The tremble that followed shook Beiron off balance, and he stumbled back. His nails dug into his chest. In his loss of balance, everything he'd had in his hands fell to the ground—the knife, the vial of blood, and the Weldafire Stone. As long as Laila was doing whatever it was she was doing, Beiron stumbled around like a drunk, barely able to stay upright.

A few small stones fell from the ceiling and joined in the mist and wind that swirled around the perimeter of the room.

Laila collapsed to the ground. From the way she fell, it was hard to know if she was breathing. Half her body was hidden by the pool. Raidan could only see her head and shoulders behind Adrik. Beiron remained on his feet.

Raidan leapt from the chair and lunged toward him. Beiron flung his hands out, sending a ball of electric blue light directly at Raidan.

Dimitri yelled as he dove in front and took the hit. The trembling floor shook Beiron, causing him to fall, while the force of his attack threw Dimitri onto Raidan, knocking them to the ground. In a tangle, Raidan scrambled to get out from under Dimitri. He scooted his legs out and got to his feet just as Beiron lifted himself onto his hands and knees.

Without warning, the ring of fire encompassing the chairs diminished like a lantern's wick being shortened. The tall flames dropped low to the floor, and the room darkened. An oily black liquid beneath the flicker of flame glided along the floor, moving toward Beiron's hand. It flowed smooth as it went to where Beiron summoned it. When it surrounded him in a full circle, the flames grew high again—as tall as the ceiling. They sheltered Beiron and gave him his own encircling infernal wall. Raidan faced the fire and searched for a way through to Beiron.

The storm was less of a storm now and more of a swirling breeze. Tiny rocks and dust hit Raidan's cheeks and stuck to his skin in the clammy air. Heaps of vines coated the floor where he stood. They covered the two chairs where he and Dimitri had been tied and were

Blood Bound

now motionless with no one to command them. Laila's prone body lay on the other side of the pool.

Adrik made a small sound. His eyelids fluttered. Dimitri crawled across the floor toward him, and Raidan shuffled closer, glancing from the fire to Adrik to the fire again. Dimitri checked Adrik's stomach where the knife had pierced him. Adrik's lips moved, but he was barely audible. Raidan cocked his ear down to try and discern what he was saying.

"Water," Adrik said with the little breath he had. "Use . . . water."

Raidan wiped sweat from his brow. The fire blazed and grew wider. He took a step back, nearly falling into the Pool of Sovereignty, and peered into the dark water. The water in the pool was shallower after Beiron had swooped some out to join the swirling storm. Where it used to sit level with the top of the ledge, it was now only about half filled.

Dimitri must have taken Adrik's meaning differently from Raidan because he reached into the pool and collected water into his cupped hands.

Supposedly, they could manipulate the elements. That was exactly what Beiron had done here in this sacred room. All Raidan had to do was figure out how to make the elements do what he wanted.

He gazed at the towering fire and raised his hands. The fire popped sparks out and grew wider. Raidan dropped his hands and swept his foot back before the flames could touch him. They inched dangerously close to Adrik and Dimitri.

Raising his hands again, he imagined the millions of water particles floating around the room. He saw them in his thoughts and said, "Come." It was the best he could come up with without knowing what specific word to use.

Tiny water droplets stopped circling and hovered between Raidan's outstretched hands. More joined, and soon a few water droplets multiplied into hundreds until he had one large water-ball. It continued to grow bigger as more droplets joined.

Raidan's jaw fell, and he smiled. He looked down at Dimitri to share in his excitement. His smile dropped. Adrik drank water from Dimitri's hands, and Laila hadn't moved. This was no time to get excited.

When the top of the ball of water touched the ceiling, Raidan thrust it into the fire. The room darkened once again as a plume of smoke billowed upward, causing Raidan's eyes to burn. He squinted and covered his mouth and nose with his elbow.

Beiron leapt out at him like a shadow in the smoke, knife up and aimed at Raidan's face. Raidan threw his arms out and caught Beiron's knife hand. He strained as he kept the knife from coming any closer.

Beiron planted his free hand against Raidan's chest. The shock of his magic took Raidan's breath away. He sucked in air through constricted lungs, clenching his teeth through the pain. A moan came from Dimitri, who was bent over Adrik.

Beiron pointed the knife toward Raidan's face, forcing it forward. Raidan grasped Beiron's wrist with both hands and focused all his strength on keeping the knife from cutting him. All Beiron needed to finish the transference was his blood.

The tip of the blade was nearly to Raidan's eye. He couldn't hold on much longer. His ribs felt like they were crushing him and pressing against his heart. Every bit of his focus was trained on keeping the knife away. He had no breath to scream or yell.

Beiron smiled, teeth bared and his eyebrows slanted downward. He appeared demonic.

The fire flickered low. The black smoke had joined in the wind and was spinning about the room slowly. Piles of thick green vines were scattered about, easy to trip over with one wrong step.

"The stone's power belongs to me," Beiron said. "It's mine."

Raidan's arm shook. He locked eyes with Beiron, wanting to tell him that the stone was right where it was meant to be. All he managed was a grunt.

Beiron seemed to grow stronger the longer he held onto Raidan. And as Raidan grew weak, feeling like this was it, like he might not make it, he could think only of how he was going to be the cause of Kartha's destruction.

He stepped backward, and Beiron matched his step, holding the knife inches from his face. Raidan bumped into a chair and had no more room to back up. He needed his strength back. No—he needed more than that.

He turned his thoughts inward to focus on the pain in his chest. Though it seemed counterintuitive, he leaned into the pain of Beiron's magic, accepting it rather than fighting it. He stopped resisting and surrendered his body to the feeling. Amazingly, the constricting in his chest released. He could breathe again.

Taking it one step further, he welcomed Beiron's magic to move through him. The pain left him, and a tingling sensation started from his heart and extended in warm pulses throughout his body. Magic coursed in him, more powerful than he'd ever felt before, and his strength returned. It took little effort to stop Beiron from stabbing him now.

Beiron's grin faded, and fear flashed in his eyes. Raidan removed one hand from Beiron's wrist and pushed him. His light touch threw Beiron back onto the floor, where he landed on top of a pile of vines between two chairs.

Chapter 89

The power emanating throughout Raidan was like a surging fire in him, ready to explode. He stood tall, embracing this new peace that settled in his core. He spread his arms out wide, palms up.

"*Luzen*," he called in a strong voice. The room lit with white light even brighter than Adrik's had been. It illuminated the entire room, revealing Beiron shielding his eyes from the light, Dimitri stooped over Laila's still body, and Adrik shifting onto his side, looking like he had some life back in him.

The wind died down into barely a breeze. The fire was gone. The shine off the Weldafire Stone on the floor caught Raidan's eye.

Beiron lifted his arms from where he sat, tangled in the vines. "*Bludevint!*" he yelled. A chunk of the ceiling cracked above Dimitri's head. Raidan shouted as it came down and fell on Dimitri, who cried out. Together their voices created a quake so powerful that the whole mountain rumbled and shook around them. The half-filled water in the Pool of Sovereignty bubbled.

Dimitri groaned under the weight of the rock that crushed his torso. He'd landed on Adrik, pinning him down while he himself was pinned by the boulder. Laila did not wake.

Beiron waved his hands. There was another loud crunching of rock against rock. From ahead and behind Beiron, a giant chunk of the wall hurtled toward Raidan. It knocked him down, and the back of his head hit the floor. Dark spots danced around the edges of his vision.

Beiron pounced and knelt on top of him. He clamped a hand over Raidan's mouth, pressing down hard. Again, he tried to bring the knife down on Raidan. Raidan flung his hands up and caught Beiron's wrist before the point could touch his skin. He kept a tight grip using both hands, unwilling to let go. Kicking his legs did nothing to get Beiron off him. He shouted into Beiron's hand and tried to shake his head free.

The low rumbling in the mountain vibrated the floor and ceiling. Beiron's eyes shifted up and around. He grinned. "Pretty soon, we'll have all the time we need." His demonic appearance was even worse with him mounted on top of Raidan, looking down the edge of the knife.

Rocks fell from the ceiling. Water rose and spilled from the pool. The rumbling grew louder.

The back of Raidan's head dug into the gritty floor. He arched his back and squirmed. Beiron sunk his weight onto Raidan's hips and drove the knife closer to his throat. If Raidan let go, he'd not be able to get out of the way in time. His muscles shook with effort. Breathing hard, he tried to keep his panicking mind under control.

Water trickled under him as it seeped across the floor. It soaked under his head, quiet as a whisper.

Raidan let the hushed voice of the water calm his thoughts. It was as though it were trying to speak to him. He attuned his thoughts to the whispering water. Although he couldn't make out any actual words, he had a deep sense of being connected to it. And to the earth and the land. The water, the ground, the rocks and plants. He looked past Beiron to the ceiling, where roots and vines clung and trembled.

Come, he told them in his head. They moved along the cave ceiling. The thin tendrils lowered, lengthening as they swung.

Raidan turned his eyes back to the tip of the blade pointed at him. Beiron's hand still pressed against his mouth, he pushed the knife down with the other, and Raidan resisted. One vine dropped from the ceiling, landing on Beiron's shoulder. He startled, and another vine fell on his head.

Rocks fell from above. Most of them missed Raidan and struck Beiron's exposed back.

Another few vines descended onto Beiron, twisting around the base of his neck. He shrugged them away, releasing some of the force on the knife. Another vine dropped down on his other side. Roots fell and coiled around Beiron's arms.

While Beiron's sweaty hand covered Raidan's mouth, Raidan relied on his thoughts to communicate with the plants. Beiron looked from side to side and up. He turned his gaze on Raidan and narrowed his eyes.

In a rage, he drove the knife down again. Raidan wasn't unprepared. He resisted with an extra force of strength.

The water on the floor was nearly up to Raidan's ears. Dimitri groaned as if he were lifting something heavy. His groan turned into a pained cry and was followed by a heavy splash.

The rumbling turned into shaking, and more rocks plummeted from the ceiling.

Raidan's eyes followed a long vine as he commanded it. It wound slowly around Beiron's body and tugged some of his weight off Raidan's hips. Beiron growled, his eyes manic. He removed his hand from Raidan's mouth and threw his knife aside. With his hands raised, he shouted at the ceiling. "*Bludevint!*"

The vines wrapping around him snapped and fell. Raidan wasted no time. With his mouth free, he roared and shoved Beiron aside. Beiron fell sideways, and Raidan rolled the opposite direction. A few rocks fell from the ceiling and splashed into the water in front of him. He lifted himself off his stomach and out of the water. The Weldafire Stone was right there in front of him, beneath the shallow depth. He grabbed it and stuffed it in his pocket, then scrambled to his feet.

Raidan extended his arms wide. Without a word, he commanded all the plant life within these walls to break loose. The walls were already crumbling, as was the ceiling. New roots and plants burst from all directions and converged on Beiron. They wound around him, pinning his hands to his sides and binding him from top to bottom, covering his mouth, and ceasing his shouts. Off balance, he fell onto his side, wriggling like a worm in the water within the circle of chairs.

Dimitri made his way over to Raidan. He looked like he'd regained some strength, seeing as he held Laila in his arms. Adrik was on his feet and had some colour back in his dark cheeks.

"We need to get out!" Dimitri shouted over the noise of the collapsing cave. The water on the floor was at their ankles now. The tunnels would be filling with water and would soon leave them trapped there if they didn't go now.

"The Weldafire Stone!" Adrik shouted. "Do you—"

"I've got it," Raidan said.

Something floated by on top of the water near Beiron. It was the vial he'd waved at Laila. Raidan didn't know what it contained, but it seemed important to Beiron. Anything that was important to him, Raidan didn't want him to have. He took a long step forward and snatched the vial, making direct eye contact with Beiron as he took it.

His pity for the man came as a surprise. Beiron huffed from his nose like a bull ready to charge.

A rock glanced off Raidan's head. It stung where it'd hit him. It was time to get out of there.

The room shook, the water rose, the rumbling intensified, and the falling rocks grew larger. Raidan quickly joined Dimitri and Adrik. Together, they left behind the bright light of the sacred room, this time for good.

Chapter 90

Colours swam in Laila's vision, and everything was tilting around her. She focused on a single point in the overcast sky until everything levelled off.

The smell of burning sulphur filled the air. From somewhere in the distance, a series of blasts resonated throughout the land. Laila cringed at each boom. The reminder of the war brought a sinking feeling to her stomach.

Lying on the ground, she looked up at the faces gazing down on her. Adrik, on his knees, had his head bowed and eyes closed. He held her hand and mumbled under his breath. Raidan and Dimitri stared with concern. Laila slipped her hand free from Adrik's and sat up. She swayed. Raidan reached for her and steadied her. Adrik blinked his eyes open slowly but not fully. His eyelids drooped when he looked at her.

"Take it easy, Laila," Raidan said. "It'll take some time to regain your strength."

"Where are we?" Her mind couldn't register their surroundings or understand why they were idling between two houses. This was Litlen, but she couldn't figure where exactly. She squeezed her eyes shut, then opened them again. She thought of Beiron and shot up abruptly, throwing her hands to her head, partly to balance herself and because she just remembered.

"The cave... the vial..." Breathing heavy, she glanced from Raidan to Dimitri. It only occurred to her now that Adrik was here, not lying dead in the cave.

Raidan raised his hands to calm her. "Beiron's gone. We fled the cave." He retrieved the vial with her blood. "I grabbed this on the way out." He approached and gave it to her. "It seemed important to you."

Tears streamed down Laila's cheeks. She looked fixedly at the vial, disbelieving. "But I aided Beiron in subduing you. Why would you help me?"

"We weren't just going to leave you there," Raidan said.

Dimitri assisted Adrik to his feet. Adrik stabilized himself using the wall of the nearest house. Laila searched for the wound in his abdomen.

"You were dead. How are you here?"

"The Pool of Sovereignty is powerful," Adrik said. "If I'd been in that condition for much longer, I wouldn't be here. There is an amount of time when it is too late to heal. Nonetheless, the pool provided healing for me. The same kind of healing as is available to the Guardians." He nodded at the brothers, then pointed at Laila.

"As for you, miss, the Pool of Sovereignty has limitations. Your use of blood magic interfered with the pool's healing ability in you. Blood magic is forbidden for a reason." He gave her a stern look.

Did he realize her relationship with Beiron? She supposed he'd know that for her to use blood magic against herself and for it to have affected Beiron, there'd have to be a relation.

Raidan cocked his head at Adrik. "Forbidden? But isn't that the kind of magic you just used on Laila to bring her back?"

Adrik bowed his head. "I am weakened because of it. It takes a toll."

Adrik had used blood magic on her? Laila gazed down at the vial. She closed her hand around it and slammed it to the ground, then stomped on it, smashing it. Her blood spilled out of it, no longer contained to be used against her. She caught Adrik's eye and detected the slightest nod.

A loud *boom* pulsed in her throat.

Clanking swords and battle cries sounded from faraway. Her mind thinking more clearly now, she recognized where they were. Just within the boundary of Litlen region, concealed between houses in a neighbourhood that looked similar to hers.

Her head throbbed. With everything going on, she couldn't think about blood magic. Royl was out there somewhere fighting for their people. For their land. Anxious as she was to learn more and hear about what happened after she'd passed out in the cave, more than anything she wanted to lay eyes upon her brother and see that he was safe. That Beiron hadn't somehow gotten to him after she'd done what she did.

She wrapped her arms around herself and suppressed the urge to wretch. She'd never forgive herself.

Dimitri peered out behind the houses, then faced them. "Let's get moving. It's time we made some use of this magic." He turned toward Laila. "You and Adrik should lay low in one of these houses. You'll be—"

"Lie low?" Laila cut him off. "This is my home; these are my people!"

"You've not recovered. You're in no state to blaze into battle. You could die."

"Then I'll die." Laila pinched the bridge of her nose. A hundred years living in hiding, only to re-emerge and be caught up in another war. She'd waited long enough for a chance to live free. No way was she going to allow things to go back to how they were. She had to fight.

She set her feet. "I'm not sitting this out." If she died, then so be it. At least she'd have tried.

The late afternoon sun disappeared behind dark, ominous clouds, heavy with rain.

Adrik carried his own weight, pushing off from the wall. "I, too, will fight. It is my duty to protect the Guardians of the Weldafire Stone. I failed once, and it will not happen again."

Another *boom*.

Raidan raised his hands. He focused on them, his forehead creasing in concentration. "*Luzen.*" Light erupted between his hands. It flickered, then maintained a bright burn. He shook his head. "Let's hope I can get a grasp on this quickly."

"You're thinking too hard," Laila said. "Allow the elements to move though your spirit. Or better yet, be the spirit. The *spiertra* of Kartha."

"*Spiertra,*" Raidan whispered on his breath. A breeze from behind swept past Laila, pushing her forward. The vine-infested wall of the houses on either side sprouted blossoms.

Dimitri grinned. "Looks like you might have found your trigger."

"It looks that way." Raidan clapped Dimitri on the shoulder. "We'll be a stronger force if we stick together." He turned toward Laila. "Dimitri and I are not familiar with Litlen well enough to navigate our way. Do you know where we might find your brother?"

Among the best of the warriors, Royl would be where most of the fighting was. Which meant if Laila was going to get to him, she'd have to fight her way past hundreds of Valca soldiers first.

"He'll be in the heart of the battle. From the sounds of those cannons, I'd say within Litlen's centre, where the courtyard and the Abberbrat tree are. That's where we'll find Royl."

"Right. We'll find Royl and see about destroying those cannons." Raidan looked at each of them, raising his chin, assuring they all understood.

Laila understood. "Is that all?"

"That's it," Raidan said. "Oh, and don't die."

Laila rubbed her hands together, preparing to put them to use on the battlefield. "I don't intend to." She bounced on her feet, adrenaline pumping. Litlen's freedom hung in the balance of this battle. It was time to claim it, and take Litlen back.

Chapter 91

THE LAND GREW DARK AS THE SUN SET BEHIND THE CLOUDS. WITH the curse fully broken, plants thrived and glowed brighter than before. But what should have been beautiful was marred by blood and bodies.

Flashes of blue light shot in all directions. Rocks flew every which way. Even the wind seemed to defend the Elderace, lashing through the broken streets of Litlen in vigorous squalls, pounding against soldiers garbed in tan and red leather armour.

Raidan's legs trembled. Swords clanked where men and women fought. There were more opposing The Order than Raidan could have imagined, but the soldiers still outnumbered them ten to one.

A swarm of soldiers had spotted them storming toward Litlen's centre. A dozen at least. They lined up in front of Raidan and the others, swords raised.

Raidan dug his heels into the ground and came to a halt. He turned. More soldiers obstructed the road they'd just come from. They moved to close the open space between. There was nowhere to go. They were surrounded. Raidan's heart raced.

The rubble, overgrowth, and bodies forced the soldiers to slow their sprint, but there were still too many of them to fend off at once. Raidan scanned the area for something he could use, some element he could manipulate. Adrik stood poised to fight, hands raised, palms out.

Ruins of the old city lay scattered where they'd fallen many years ago. At Raidan's feet were earth and dirt and a whole lot of green, breaking through the cracks in the cobblestone. He crouched low and put his hand flat to the ground. He would need help if he was going to pull off what he had in mind.

Dimitri eyed the approaching soldiers.

Raidan yelled his brother's name and got his attention. Dimitri glanced at him. He paused for only a second before he crouched down and placed his hand against the ground, mimicking Raidan. His expression asked the question: *what now?*

"Give it your all," Raidan said. He closed his eyes and reached inward for his magic, then let out a roar. Dimitri's voice joined with his own.

The dirt rose in a lump where Raidan's hand touched. As a raised mound, the earth rippled, extending in every direction from where he and Dimitri crouched. Adrik and Laila pressed in closer and were unaffected. Raidan ran out of breath and he breathed hard. A few soldiers lay flat on their backs; some had fallen on their backside. None remained on their feet.

Before the soldiers had a chance to orient themselves, Raidan leapt up and sprinted past, trusting that Dimitri, Laila, and Adrik would keep up.

A cannon blasted and was followed shortly after by multiple smaller explosions. A smoke trail blazed across the sky. The clouds grew darker and made it even more difficult to see in the growing night.

Raidan headed toward a tree visible through the streets ahead. Beneath its branches glowed a subtle red-orange hue, flickering like fire. Within the courtyard in the middle, hordes of people clustered in close battle. One of the cannons stood beside the tree, guarded by soldiers maintaining a shield wall on all sides.

Raidan stopped to assess a way to it. Dimitri stole a sword off a fallen soldier. Raidan didn't blame him. If he'd felt competent with a weapon, he might have done the same.

Royl was in this mayhem somewhere. Raidan moved from the street onto grass and made his way into the courtyard, his senses on high alert. Dimitri, Laila, and Adrik joined him, angling themselves to form a protective circle.

Red shades and black clouds gave a hell-like impression of the courtyard. Voices hollered and grunted. Smoke polluted the air. A foul smell like excrement lingered in the humid air, overpowering the fragrance of rain. Raidan tried not to breathe it in, but it was impossible to avoid.

A soldier ran at them, his sword pointed at Raidan. Dimitri bound in front and blocked the strike with his sword. Another two soldiers came at once from another angle. Adrik raised his hands. "*Luzen.*"

Blinded by Adrik's light, the soldiers shielded their eyes as another four soldiers ran toward them, then three more from behind. Laila waved her hands about and the grass swayed and danced. Tall as it was, it grew taller still, and wove between a soldier's legs, tripping him. Raidan raised his hands and pressed them forward while yelling, "*Spiertra*!"

Clouds cumulated directly overhead, causing all eyes to gaze up. The earth trembled, redirecting attention to the ground. A soldier shouted and charged Raidan, who hardly had time to react. Raidan thrust his hands out toward the charging soldier, and the trembling ground shook hard enough to throw the man off balance.

The growing crowd stumbled into each other, losing their footing. Raidan lost sight of the others in the chaos. The soldiers who were undeterred by the ground shakes closed in on Raidan. Acting on instinct, he ducked low to the ground and rested his hand flat to the earth. His touch calmed its quaking. But he wasn't finished.

With one hand to the ground, he raised the other above his head, reaching for the sky. Whispering this time, he spoke his new trigger word. The gathering clouds above descended as if reaching for Raidan's hand. A fierce wind picked up, and Raidan made a fist, slamming it into the earth, bringing with it a gale and flashes of lightning. The power of it dispersed the men, exposing Raidan, crouched in the middle of scattered soldiers. He glanced at the faces of those fallen, searching for Adrik, Dimitri, or Laila.

A soldier atop a horse stood tall above the strewn men. He steered his horse toward Raidan and leaned forward.

Raidan rose too fast and the world spun. That last burst of power took much from him. He set his feet and raised his hands.

The horse leapt, its feet landing almost on top of Raidan. It clipped him, knocking him to the ground flat on his back, breathless. Two cannons fired at the same time, sounding muffled through the ringing in his ears. He blinked fast, willing himself to see clearly. And breathe. No air would come.

A shape appeared in his line of vision, unclear through his blurred sight.

At last, his reflex kicked in and he sucked in a harsh breath. The soldier kicked him in the stomach, and Raidan gasped, clutching an arm around his torso. A hand seized around his waistband and collar of his tunic, hauling him up and draping him over the horse's neck like a dead man.

Then the rider was back atop his horse and riding away with Raidan, leaving the heart of the city behind.

Chapter 92

With every bump and jostle of the horse's hooves against the ground, a sharp object pricked Raidan's back.

"Make a sound and I'll sink this knife into your flesh," the soldier said over the sounds of screams, sword clatter, and men grunting.

Raidan twisted his neck back to get a glimpse of his captor. He recognized the tattoo of a dragon wrapped around his neck. Ilan's man? The one who'd attacked at the Elefthan camp?

The horseman rode away from the courtyard, through the grounds and past the fighting. The intensity of the battle lessened the farther they went.

Was he to be brought to Ilan? What use could he have for Raidan at a time like this?

They slowed to a trot at the edge of the Forest of Litlen, on the trail leading toward the Bludesel Mountains. They came to a halt, and Ilan's man threw Raidan down off the horse. Raidan landed on his side, hard, at the feet of a blond man. But not the one he'd expected to see.

"Delivered, as promised," the soldier said. "You keep him quiet and he shouldn't give you any trouble."

"Thank you, Perry, you have done well," Kingston said. "Find my son and you'll be doubly rewarded."

Perry rode off.

A figure approached from behind Raidan and wrapped a burly arm around his neck. He squeezed, lifting Raidan to his feet. Raidan clawed at the hairy arm. He panicked as his air was cut off. He thrust his body back, trying to trip up the man so that he'd let go. The man didn't budge.

Kingston lifted a finger for his man to stop. The pressure let up around Raidan's neck, but the hairy man kept Raidan's head locked in his arm, just enough so Raidan could breathe. Raidan gasped and sucked in a breath, then succumbed to a fit of coughing.

"You." Kingston pointed at Raidan and grinned. "That was impressive back in the dungeon, I'll admit. But it won't happen again."

Standing torches lit the area around a tent pitched in a clearing at the edge of the forest. Flickering firelight came from within the tent, making it look warm and welcoming. Only Valca soldiers were here in these parts. Most of them watched Raidan and Kingston, appearing relaxed with no one to oppose them. Some even passed a smoking pipe among each other. The smell of tobacco reached Raidan.

"I like to consider myself a fair man," Kingston said. "You've shown you have some power, yes, but that's not real skill." He withdrew his sword, then addressed a guard at his side. "Get this man a sword." He looked at Raidan. "We'll see what kind of real skills you have. We're going to fight. Just you and me. And to make things fun, let's do this: if by some miracle you happen to win, you'll be allowed to live, but my men will cut out your tongue and you'll be my son's personal servant for the rest of your life. But don't get your hopes up. There will be no magic allowed in this duel."

Kingston waved a hand at the soldier restraining Raidan. "Gag him. No voice, no magic. Or so I'm told."

The soldier squeezed Raidan's neck, then let go. Raidan breathed hard while the soldier snatched the filthy rag at his waist—which he'd used to clean his sword—and tied it tight around Raidan's mouth. It tasted of blood and salt. Raidan gagged as the man tightened it around the back of his head.

Kingston pointed his sword at Raidan's neck. The tip touched his skin.

"You remove that or attempt to use magic—you forfeit, you die." He lowered his weapon. One of his men handed Raidan a sword. The men within the light of the torches created a perimeter around Raidan and Kingston, blocking any escape.

Raidan gripped the sword with two hands. Sword fighting was not his strength. He may not have use of his voice, but he'd accomplished great power without it. So long as he could focus.

Kingston's teeth glowed in the firelight as he flashed Raidan a wide grin.

A cannon blasted in the distance, and clouds that had threatened heavy rain since they'd left the cave let loose at last. The giant raindrops were cold on Raidan's arm. He took up a sword stance he'd seen others use: legs apart and staggered, both hands on the sword in front of him, and shoulders back.

His mouth was dry and he tried to swallow past the gag, resisting the urge to remove it. The rain picked up and poured down in heavy droplets. He breathed in through his nostrils and narrowed his eyes at Kingston.

He was ready.

Chapter 93

Despite Ilan's reputation, he did not like the sight of blood. In single combat and training, it never bothered him so much. But this—the red-stained cobblestone streets of Litlen—this was too much. His father took things too far.

The Elderace were easy to tell apart from the others in the fight, as they used magic. He'd also spotted people from that awful barbarian prison he'd been held captive in with Raidan. He'd been shocked to learn they too had magic. All that time, and he'd never figured it out. If he'd known, he might not have been so eager to leave. It didn't matter now. If Kingston wasn't stopped, they were all going to die anyway.

The firelight coming from the north at the edge of the forest had to be his father's camp. The rain made the flames of the torches flicker and darken. A large tent was erected right in the middle of the road. It was so like Kingston to stand in the way of anyone and everyone.

The ruins and rubble were less this way. Along with the driving rain, the ups and downs in the hilly terrain sometimes obscured Ilan's view. The luminous overgrown plants offered light on the dirt road.

Ilan looked ahead to the rectangle of torches posted around the entrance to his father's tent. He could glimpse a large crowd near the perimeter of the torch posts. Shielding his eyes, he squinted through the rain as he approached the encampment. Kingston stood within the lit area. He faced a man whose back was to Ilan. They both stood poised, swords in hand. From what Ilan could tell, at least fifty men gathered around to watch. Only a sliver of the army currently battling in Litlen.

As Ilan descended from the higher ground, his view became obscured by the men crowded around. He hurried, making his way to his father. Whatever was going on couldn't be good. Anything his father did these days seemed to be solely to crush Ilan's desires.

At the back of the crowd now, he couldn't see past the many heads. His feet sloshed in the soaking mud as he squeezed past a few soldiers and found a gap. In the opening ahead, everyone's attention was drawn to a duel—one that didn't look like it would last long. The man opposing his father had poor form. His counterattacks were all wrong, and his strikes were sloppy.

Owen stood by the entrance to the tent, wearing a pleased smirk. Ilan had already had the privilege of wiping it off his face once. He looked forward to getting another chance to do so again.

It was too difficult to see who his father fought. Ilan squeezed past more men. Soldiers parted for him and his distinguishable blond hair. He turned his body sideways to slip past others who were too focused on the fight to notice him. The swords clashed. Ilan glanced up, and his heart jumped when he saw who opposed his father.

Raidan swung his sword in what Ilan thought was meant to be a cross strike. It was sloppy, and Kingston only had to step back to get out of the way of the swing. Kingston let his sword fall to one hand.

"Is this really all you've got?" Kingston taunted. He laughed. He could have done any number of moves to maim Raidan or kill him, but it seemed he was purposely dragging it out, mocking Raidan.

Raidan was gagged, his eyes full of determination. But his skill was lacking. Though he was brave to keep trying, it would do him no good. Ilan had to do something. Somehow, he didn't think talking would be of much use right now. His last encounter with his father and Raidan hadn't gone so well.

Raidan swung again, starting with the sword raised above his head and hammering it down. Kingston's blade made contact in his cross counter. He let Raidan's sword follow through with its momentum, nearly disarming Raidan. Kingston's footwork was precise, even though the ground was slick. He glided his sword forward while Raidan's sword was still falling, then cut across Raidan's shoulder with the sharp edge of his own blade.

Raidan's teeth clenched over the gag. He put a hand to the cut on his arm, where blood seeped through the fabric of his already tattered shirt.

This was painful to watch. His father's toying with Raidan would only last so long. He'd grow bored soon and then that would be it. Ilan moved through the crowd.

*

Raidan's arm stung where Kingston cut him. Breathing hard through his nose, his throat was dry. He raised a hand toward his face and stopped halfway there, remembering Kingston's threat. He lowered his hand and gripped the sword again.

By now, it had become clear that he had no chance at beating Kingston in a sword fight, unless Kingston got cocky and let down his guard. It was not such an impossibility, but then there were the soldiers gathered around watching. His magic would do the trick.

Kingston strutted in a circle, arms out, encouraging his men to cheer him on. They hollered and whistled. Raidan drowned out their noises to tune in to his senses. The word *spiertra* on his tongue, he thought it as if speaking. The torch's flames flickered brighter in a flash, even through the driving rain. Wind picked up, battering raindrops hard against Raidan's cheek. Kingston's sword glinted in the light. He raised it in a strike, and Raidan flung his arm up, blocking the blow with his own sword. The firelight flickered back to normal, and the wind died down.

Kingston lowered his weapon. "What did I tell you about using magic?" He growled.

With his concentration limited, the magic was too weak. Raidan wanted so badly to remove the gag. He tried to recall his minimal knowledge of sword fighting. The strikes, the guards, and counter-moves—all things he'd learned in passing and not through any actual training.

Eyes on the sternum. He knew that. He set his stance, staggering his legs, preparing to defend himself once again. His feet slipped in the wet mud. It was difficult to look straight on while the rain pelted his face.

One of the cannons in the distance fired. The sound, though far away, echoed in the air.

The corner of Kingston's mouth raised up. "If your serving skills are anything like your swordplay, you'll make a terrible servant to Ilan. On second thought, he'll will be better off without you."

He came straight on with his blade pointed at Raidan's chest. Raidan jumped sideways. He skidded in the mud and quickly regained his balance, swinging his sword at the same time. His swing was met with resistance. Kingston had turned up on his heel and clanked his sword against Raidan's. Kingston leaned into the force of the two swords pushing against one another. He extended his foot behind Raidan's leg, and Raidan tripped and fell on his backside. His sword fell, and he scrambled backward on his hands and feet away from Kingston, closer to the crowd of soldiers.

Kingston took two long strides and stepped on Raidan's hand. He pressed his foot down, crushing his fingers. Raidan groaned through the gag.

With both hands gripping his sword, Kingston pointed it at Raidan. Raidan blinked through the rain and didn't dare look away. Kingston pressed the tip of his sword to Raidan's heart. "You should have died in the dungeon."

Raidan's heart beat against his ribs as Kingston's sword pressed slowly into his flesh. He bit down on the gag. Then the pressure on his chest let up. Kingston gasped. He coughed and blood spewed from his mouth.

Raidan held his breath. The blade of a sword stuck out through Kingston's body, and his sword dropped from his hand. Silence fell among the soldiers. Only the sound of rain pattering leaves filled the air.

The sword that pierced Kingston's chest was withdrawn, and he fell to his knees, nearly landing on top of Raidan. Ilan stood behind him, shoulders heaving. Kingston crumpled forward, facedown. His eyes were wide in shock, lifeless, looking at Raidan. Ilan's own eyes were just as wide.

Raidan shimmied himself out from under Kingston's body. He pulled the gag down, away from his mouth, and thrust a hand out toward the soldiers who'd begun to approach him and Ilan. "Don't!" he shouted. The earth trembled. The soldiers stopped, wide eyed, searching around.

"Stay back!" Raidan called to them. He scanned the faces of The Order, prepared to use his magic. None of the soldiers came forward. At least not yet. The sudden turn of events was still sinking in.

Kingston's face was half sunk in the wet mud, blood beginning to pool under his body.

Raidan shielded his eyes from the rain. "Ilan," he said, then hesitated. He didn't know what to say. What Ilan had done . . . He'd saved his life, but how would he deal with the implications of his action?

"Ilan, you need to end this. You have to call off the army."

*

His hands. He'd done this. Ilan stared at his hands and the sword, still covered in his father's blood.

He shifted his gaze past it to watch the warm blood pulse out from his father's back. Ilan's breath shuddered.

He'd done this.

In the moment, he'd known what he was doing. "It was the only way," he whispered.

Raidan sat on the ground, his hand up toward the crowd gathered around, as if that would keep them back. Maybe not his hand, but his magic certainly would. Many soldiers stared at Kingston's body. Others stared at Ilan, probably wondering what he would do next. What *should* he do next?

"Ilan, it's not over yet," Raidan said. "They'll listen to you."

Ilan snapped out of his stupor. The Order watched him, waiting.

"Fall back," Ilan said. Then he cleared his throat and raised his voice. "It's over. This war ends now. Valca Order, fall back!"

No one moved. The rain slowed its driving force. Droplets plopped in puddles.

Did they not hear him? Had he not been clear?

He spoke even louder now. "This war was driven by my father's need for control. I refused to be controlled by him, and this is how he responded. Is that a reason to keep fighting? Stand down, Valca Order, and return to Valmain. The Elderace are now under my protection."

No one moved.

Raidan kept his hand raised. Ilan tightened his grip on his sword.

Now would come the true test of loyalties.

Chapter 94

Slowly, the crowd surrounding Raidan and Ilan dispersed. A horn blew nearby, and a member of The Order called for soldiers to withdraw. The rain had let up and was only a light drizzle. Clouds parted and the moon poked through.

Raidan sat, drenched, on the soaking wet earth. He'd not yet gotten up from his fallen position. He held a hand over his heart as if that might slow its racing.

Ilan stood over him, gripping the hilt of his sword as it dripped his father's blood. He pointed it at a soldier. "You!" he shouted. "Ride into the city and announce our withdrawal." The man's gaze fell to the bloody sword pointed at him. He nodded, turned, and disappeared into the crowd of soldiers.

While most of them were meandering to gather belongings and pack up to leave, some stayed where they were and glared at Ilan. A few glanced at Raidan, looking uncertain about him. Raidan kept his guard up, ready to use his magic should he need it.

A group of soldiers parted abruptly as someone forced his way to the front of the crowd. The man with the dragon tattoo broke through and raised his arm to throw a knife.

"No!" Raidan shouted as he extended his hand out toward Perry. His voice stirred up a wind. Perry threw the knife just as the wind knocked into him. The knife missed Ilan and stuck in the ground by his feet. Then Perry made a gurgling sound and clutched his throat. Raidan wiped rain from his face using his shirt sleeve. Behind Perry, the soldier with the nose ring stood, holding a bloodied dagger, having just used it to slice Perry's neck. Blood spurted from a thin red line where Perry tried to stop the flow. His eyes bulged and he fell, hitting the ground with a solid *thud*. The mud squelched under his weight.

The septum-soldier wiped his dagger with a rag. He sheathed it and addressed those who stood by staring. "What are you all still doing here? You heard the man. Disperse."

The crowd went back to packing up.

The soldier stepped over Raidan's legs to approach Ilan. Ilan wiped his own sword, sheathed it, and extended a hand to his man. "Miles, I owe you one." His shoulders fell, looking at Perry's still body.

Miles shook his hand. "I'll take you up on that some day. Until then, what do you need?"

"Pack up camp and round up the men."

Miles nodded. He glanced down at Raidan, who hadn't recovered from the shock of almost dying. Ilan lightly smacked Miles's chest. "I'll handle this, then find you later." He reached a hand to Raidan, who accepted and got to his feet. Miles joined the busyness of decamping.

Ilan cleared his throat. "I suppose I owe you thanks as well."

Raidan shrugged. "Call it even."

"Right." Ilan's gaze reverted to his father, then to Perry. He sighed. "I need to put an end to this. It's time I made peace with the Elderace. Take me to them and introduce me as a friend. After that, you're free to go on your way."

For once, Raidan had no objections.

Chapter 95

LAILA SHIELDED HER EYES IN THE RAIN. THE DARKNESS WAS COMPLETE, leaving only the soft glow of Litlen and the Abberbrat to light the battlegrounds. Her body weary, she forced herself to stay alert. She'd lost Raidan, Dimitri, and Adrik a while ago and fended for herself while keeping a lookout for Royl.

The cannon-fire sounded like it came from multiple places, but now fired with longer gaps between each blast. She hoped that meant one or more had been destroyed.

A few feet ahead, a Valca soldier whose face was black with grime pulled his sword from the chest of a man Laila didn't know. The man fell, and the soldier turned toward her. Laila raised her shoulders and faced him. Tired as she was, she had to keep fighting.

The soldier raised his sword and smirked. His confidence was misplaced. He'd soon find Laila would not go down easy. The rubble-strewn streets, overgrown with roots and vines, gave her plenty of ammunition. A second soldier appeared beside her, but rather than attack her, he raised his sword toward the grimy soldier.

"Stand down," the newcomer said. "We have no quarrel with the Elderace."

The grimy soldier took up a guard and planted his feet. "Traitor. You'll die alongside them."

Laila jutted her chin. "Wrong choice." She extended her hand. "*Bludevint!*" The word rolled off her tongue before she realized what she was saying. But the force of power that emanated from her was greater than anything she'd ever experienced. The long grass twisted around the soldier's ankles and tripped him. He fell forward but kept his grip on his sword as he growled up at her. Laila focused on what she wanted the grass to do. She wrapped it around his torso and rolled him onto his back. With her magic, she layered the grass flat on top of his body, burying him so only his face was visible and he couldn't move. He gasped and turned his head sideways as rain battered his face. The man who'd come to her aid watched wide-eyed.

The Abberbrat was alive and glowing, even as the fighting took place beside it. A cannon sat next to the tree, crushing the beautiful garden.

Laila faced the traitor-soldier. "The weapons, how many are there?"

The man nodded at the one near the tree. "There were three, but only one remains. But now that the other two have been eliminated, men have reenforced the guard around the last one."

The cannon fired, blasting a black ball into the air. The *boom* that rang out caused mostly everyone pause as they gazed up to watch its trajectory. Laila imagined an invisible line, determining where it might come down. But the ball didn't come down. It shattered in the air and multiple plum-sized pellets rained down.

Royl fought in a line, alongside Zulu, Stefan, and Bailey—each of them bloody and drenched from the rain. They fought against The Order as a unit, alternating between swords and magic, depending on proximity of the soldiers. The pellets hurtled down right above where they fought. Laila's heart jolted. She'd seen what happens when they were near to the ground.

She raced across the battlefield, shouting Royl's name, which was useless with all the noise.

The pellets drew many eyes to the sky. Those fighting beneath their path scattered in every direction. Laila raced past soldiers and felt her dress tug a little when one tried to grab her as she ran. She scooted out of the way. Almost everyone she passed was distracted, looking up or fleeing. She used that to get through the people without having to fight. She clutched at her heart, breathing through the pain of the stitch in her side as she kept going.

Her mouth was dry, but still she yelled. "Get back!"

She wasn't going to make it to Royl in time. She stopped in her tracks, raised her hands, and focused her power on the pellets hurtling toward the ground above Royl. "*Bludevint!*"

Wind gusted from behind, making her stumble. She dug her heels and held her ground, pouring her heart into her magic. The wind intensified. She directed it up toward the many balls, slowing their descent.

Determined to save her brother, she thrust her hands forward. The wind flung her hair everywhere and lashed rain against her cheeks. Some of the pellets flew higher and changed course; Laila didn't see where to, just as long as they weren't over Royl. She grit her teeth and ignored the pounding in her head, not daring to let up. The gust nearly knocked her off her feet. It whooshed upward where she directed it, toward the remaining pellets before they reached an altitude where they could really do damage. The last of them flung up in the air again, their trajectory altered.

Laila lowered her hands and the wind stopped abruptly. Her knees wobbled. Explosions went off from where she'd relaunched the pellets. Somewhere near the tree maybe. She fell onto her knees, eyelids drooping.

Movement caught her attention above. A missed pellet sped toward where she had collapsed. She gasped, jumped to her feet, and ran.

Twelve feet above and behind, the piece exploded. A wave of heat smacked into her back and threw her forward onto the ground. She flung her hands out to catch her fall and landed hard, elbows bending under her. Her ears rang. Black smoke engulfed her and made her eyes burn. She choked and tried to see through the suffocating smoke.

Sounding far away, someone called her name. Laila glanced up. "Royl?" A man's shape blurred in her vision. He put an arm around her.

"I've got you, Laila." The voice didn't sound like Royl's. "You did it," he said. "You destroyed it."

Destroyed what? She wanted to ask, but her voice wouldn't work.

"I've got you," the voice said again. She knew that voice. Blinking in the smoke, her eyes watered. Dimitri grasped her shoulders and turned her face to his. Or was it Raidan? They looked so alike.

He grinned. "It's over. The Valca Order are leaving."

Chapter 96

THE CLOUDS DISSIPATED, AND THE SKY LIGHTENED WITH THE DAWN. There was no designated building for the infirmary. The people were camped out in a wide-open space, with one large tent pitched in the middle. The river looped around the north side of the field, separating it from the rest of Litlen and offering protection from attacks. No attacks could come from the coastal cliffs to the south, and all other angles were guarded.

The long grass here was flattened and looked like it had been woven together into a thick vibrant-green carpet.

The tent overflowed with people in need of attention. The wounded were grouped together outside and around the tent. Small groups of two or three people were huddled around friends who'd been hurt or killed in battle and likely died here. Those who tended to the injured were hastening from one patient to the next, trying to get to them all. The open tent revealed cots crammed inside with little space for the healers to walk.

Raidan looked for anyone he knew as he led Ilan toward the tent. What had become of Dimitri, Adrik, and Laila?

A woman stood at the front of a line of people waiting to have their injuries tended to. Her back to them, she wrapped gauze around a gash on a man's forearm. Her light curls fell down her back, tied with a loose string. Raidan stared. His heart beat faster. Without a second thought, he strode over to his wife, not knowing or caring if Ilan followed.

Ida finished what she was doing and turned before Raidan reached her. She dropped the cloth she had been wiping her hands with, closed the distance between them, and threw her arms around Raidan's neck. Raidan took her around the waist and held her tight. Her damp hair stuck to his face, which he had buried in her neck. Ida's shoulders shook as she sobbed into him. Neither of them spoke.

Raidan was aware of Ilan standing behind him, a silent shadow. To his credit, he didn't interrupt.

When Ida settled, Raidan reluctantly pulled out of her embrace. "Cassian?"

She nodded, allowing tears to flow freely. "Safe."

Raidan kissed her deeply, and she leaned into his kiss. Then he rested his forehead against hers and spoke softly. "I have so much to tell you, Ida, but there's still work to be done." He indicated Ilan. "I'll come find you after."

Ida's lip trembled. Eyes wet, she nodded. "I'll be here."

He kissed her again. She returned the kiss, then gently wiped the moisture from under his eyes. Raidan cupped her chin with both hands.

Ilan tugged Raidan's sleeve. Walking away from Ida was not easy. But with so many hurt and dying, this new healing power strained within him, bursting to be released. He and Dimitri would have their work cut out for them.

Raidan didn't know who spoke for the Elderace, but Royl carried himself like a leader. He would take Ilan to him, but Adrik crossed paths with them first, scuttling through a narrow aisle clear of people beside the tent. He weaved around the wounded, studying their faces, bending over prone bodies, turning faces to look his way, and whipping his head back and forth between rows of the injured. Heads, arms, torsos, legs. Each injury varied in severity, and each would require Raidan's and Dimitri's attention.

Adrik glanced up, and his eyes widened when he saw Raidan. There was a time when Adrik had instilled fear and anxiety in Raidan, but now the sight of him brought a strange sense of joy.

"Where did you go?" Adrik called to Raidan, eyebrows furrowed. "I turned around, and you disappeared? I looked everywhere."

Raidan glanced at Ilan. "I got picked up by Kingston's man. And actually, it's because of Ilan that I'm not dead."

Adrik looked Ilan up and down with no expression. Ilan returned his look, but no recognition filled his face.

"Ilan," Raidan said. "This is Adrik."

Ilan's face lit up. "Adrik? But I thought you were dead."

"Why?" Adrik said. "Because Raidan dropped a cave on my head? It will take a lot more than that to kill me." He turned to Raidan. "You have work to do. Where is your brother?"

"Raidan and I have an arrangement first," Ilan said. "He's with me until I say we're through."

"I'll get to that," Raidan said. He turned toward Adrik. "As for Dimitri, I was hoping you could tell me."

Adrik looked around at the hundreds of bodies on cots and bedrolls. The line of those waiting to have minor injuries tended to wound around the tent and into the field, where the grass hadn't been groomed. Adrik shook his head. "I have not seen him."

As if hearing his name, Dimitri came out from within the tent. He raised a hand in greeting and jogged toward Raidan. Raidan couldn't keep the smile off his face at the sight of his brother safe.

Ten feet away, Dimitri stopped short and his face dropped. Then he stormed at them with a fierce scowl and an accusatory finger pointed at Ilan. "What is he doing here?"

"Before you get all worked up," Raidan said quickly, "you should know that Ilan is the reason we're not still fighting."

Dimitri practically growled at Ilan.

Raidan continued, "He ended the war and is here to make peace. Where's Royl?"

Dimitri's eyes continued to bore into Ilan. Raidan would talk to him later, but right now was not the time for a heart-to-heart. Raidan had been able to forgive Adrik's wrongdoing in his own life, so whatever Ilan had done to Dimitri, Raidan was sure he could learn to let it go.

Dimitri jabbed a thumb behind his head. "With Laila in the tent."

Raidan moved past him. Adrik, Ilan, and Dimitri followed.

Inside, Laila's bright red hair was visible in the middle of the room, sitting up on a cot while Royl hovered over her, examining her head.

Eli bandaged a woman's neck in the far left corner, while another man and four women saw to others' injuries. In one corner were those that looked close to death. Those outside didn't seem to be in as poor condition as these inside the tent.

The cots were lined up in neat rows, spaced so close that barely one person could walk between them. Raidan shuffled sideways through the maze of cots to get to Royl.

"You're not dead?" Laila said when Raidan was nearly to her. She brushed Royl's hand away and stood up.

"Neither are you." Raidan smiled at her. "Are you hurt?"

Laila shook her head. "Royl's worrying about nothing." She and Royl shifted their glances at Ilan, who stood behind Raidan.

"Royl," Raidan said. "This is Ilan Valca."

Royl eyed Ilan. He rubbed his chin.

Raidan put his hand on Ilan's shoulder. "None of us would be having this conversation right now if not for him."

Royl took longer to consider this. Then he extended his hand. "If that's true, I suppose we owe you thanks."

Ilan shook Royl's hand. His eyes shone, and his smile came slow at first, then filled his face.

His promise fulfilled, Raidan left them to talk, and prompted Dimitri to join him at the corner, where those there appeared to have the most severe injuries.

They approached a man who moaned and clutched his stomach. Blood seeped through his bandaged abdomen. Raidan sat on his knees on the floor and put his hand over the man's wound.

Dimitri remained standing. "What do we do?"

Raidan gave him a sideways look. How could he explain? When he had spoken to Kartha on a deeper level, he'd understood his power in a whole new way. But how to put it into words?

"Here." He indicated his hand that rested on the man's chest and encouraged Dimitri to do the same. "You feel it from the heart." With his free hand, he pointed to Dimitri's heart. "Draw from here and allow it to move through the ground beneath you. It's alive and in you."

Dimitri stared.

Raidan knew how it must look, of him telling Dimitri how to use his magic. After everything that had happened, Raidan wouldn't have believed it himself.

"Focus," Raidan told him. He closed his eyes, then reached within himself and grabbed hold of the power of the Weldafire Stone—that healing power that drew from the land itself.

Raidan listened to the beat of his own heart and became hypnotized by its steady rhythm. The magic moved through his body, coursed through his blood. Its warmth flowed through his veins, to his fingertips, spreading into the man's body.

He held on until the work was done, then opened his eyes. Dimitri's were still closed. The wounded man blinked. He patted his stomach where the blood stained through the bandaging. Ripping away the bandage, he sat upright, searching his body for the injury. There was none.

Dimitri opened his eyes. He gaped at the man and his healed abdomen. A crowd of spectators had gathered: those seeing to the wounded, visitors comforting friends and family, even some of the injured themselves. Hushed awe spread through the brothers' corner of the tent.

Raidan stood. The eyes of all nearby followed his every move.

A woman lay a hand on Raidan's arm. "Please. My father." Tear stains lined her pale face as she pointed at an unconscious man who was so covered in blood, it was difficult to know which of his multiple wounds were more pressing.

Raidan looked at Dimitri. They had a long way to go.

Chapter 97

Six Weeks Later

Life at the Keep was different without Kingston around. The tense atmosphere Ilan had grown accustomed to all his life was gone, although not at first. When Ilan had originally arrived back in Valmain, servants had skirted around him in the halls, keeping their heads low. People had bowed, but their eyes never met his. They'd treated him like Kingston.

Ilan had detested it.

He walked the gardens around the Keep, circling the round fountain spraying water from five spouts. This had become a regular routine he'd established in hopes of altering the people's view of him. It was early in the morning still, and he was expecting visitors that afternoon. A letter had arrived by a vohrsit carrier two days ago, requesting he accept guests for a few days. Ilan hadn't received many letters by the carrier birds. His father had always insisted letters be handed directly into the hands of the recipient. The bird showing up with a letter for him came as a surprise.

A woman walked by with her baby in a pram. She glanced at Ilan and recognition flashed in her eyes. Ilan smiled and greeted her with a nod, something he'd been intentional about doing during his walks. The woman gave a hesitant smile in return and passed him by.

Townsfolk as well as the workers in the Keep were finally beginning to see that he was not his father. A few times, he'd received a hello in return, or a smile. Little by little, they would come to realize they need not fear him.

He approached the door of the main entry to the Keep. Miles met him there. Ilan had promoted him to his right-hand man. He'd proved his loyalty to Ilan by making the decision to defend the Elderace. That meant more to Ilan than he could say, especially after Perry's betrayal.

Kingston still had a large following, even now. Ilan was conscious of that and was sure to watch his back. Killing his own father had been a decision made in the heat of the moment. He hadn't been able to let Raidan die. And his father had been beyond reasoning.

Ilan mentally justified his actions for the hundredth time. At the door, Miles jutted his chin at Ilan. He'd traded his Valca Order uniform for a dark green tunic, black trousers, and knee-high boots. Kingston had been particular about soldiers staying in uniform anytime they were in public. Ilan would have liked to burn all the uniforms, but he didn't push it one way or another. Control was Kingston's thing.

"They've arrived," Miles informed him.

Ilan's stomach churned. They were early. His legs wobbled a little.

He went inside and walked through the narrow, carpeted hallways and into the grand room, where Kameron, Royl, and Zulu—an elder whom Ilan had met briefly after the battle—awaited his arrival. Ilan knew they'd already been invited to sit and offered drinks as soon as they'd arrived. His staff was hospitable—always had been. It was his father who was not.

Kameron was not Ilan's favourite choice of guest, but as a result of Raidan's introducing him to the Elderace, Ilan hoped things would go well between them all. Taking over the Valca Order hadn't been his plan, but until the people of Kartha figured something else out, he intended to temporarily make good use of his position in power. This was the meeting he'd been waiting for—the one that would relieve him of his role.

The couch by the window was big enough for three, but with Kameron and Zulu on either end, there wasn't much space left for anyone to comfortably sit between them. Royl stood by the window, looking out at the grounds. With his arms crossed, he leaned back in a casual stance.

The chaise lounge was unoccupied, as was the armchair. Ilan sank into the armchair. His hands trembled slightly. He clenched them into fists and relaxed them to try to stop the trembling.

"Thank you for coming to see me," he said. "I hope the journey was not too difficult."

"On the contrary," Kameron responded in his thick accent. "It was quite pleasant. And better still to not pay the Valca Order tolls."

Ilan had seen an end to that. Just as he'd put a stop to many systems his father had put in place upon the people of Kartha. Kingston had believed that the less they had, the more they relied on him.

"Yes, I hope to make a true difference in Kartha," Ilan said.

Royl left his place at the window and sat on the edge of the chaise. Zulu's dark skin was a shade lighter than Kameron's.

"We are pleased to see you taking this responsibility and doing something for the better with it," Zulu said. His own accent indicated he had not been born in Kartha. Reij, perhaps. His odd fluctuations were similar to Adrik's but more predominant. "It is what we have come to speak to you about."

Ilan straightened. He maintained eye contact as he dipped his chin, encouraging Zulu to go on.

"The people of Kartha do not wish for the Valca Order to continue its reign. We are here to discuss a new system. One in which we hope you might consider becoming a part of, in that you would represent the people of your region or domain. Valmain, that is."

Heat flushed Ilan's face. He'd expected to be approached about the end of the Valca Order. Looked forward to it even. But to be asked to continue to have a place in a council and to represent the people . . . He was burning up. Why wasn't the window open in this sweltering room?

"I . . . um . . . I'm not—I don't think I'm the right one for the position." He cleared his throat. "It was never my wish to rule. That was always something my father wanted for me, which only made me want it less. The only reason I came back was to clean up after my father. He was planning to take Tsein and had arranged for my marriage to their princess. I ended the arrangement."

Royl clasped his hands before him. "What will you do then?"

Ilan's only desire was to live among the Elderace—to be seen not as the tyrant ruler his father was but simply as himself. "I'd like to move south, closer to Litlen and, well . . . live as a friend and fellow Karthan." It sounded pathetic out loud.

No one replied right away, and the seconds of silence were agonizing. He shouldn't have said it. He could have agreed and been done with it, then left Valmain without a word. He could disappear and none would be the wiser.

Kameron broke the silence. "You have done well in your father's place, and we wish for you to consider our offer at the very least. You could accomplish great things. But, if you decline, there is a place for you in Elefthan, if you wish to take it."

Ilan cocked his head.

"As a welcome guest," Kameron clarified. "But we encourage you to think about what we are offering. You have an opportunity to make changes for the better in our country." He stood, as did Zulu.

Ilan remained seated. Was that it? Was their meeting finished?

"Can you stay for a meal this afternoon?" Ilan asked. "I've asked the kitchen staff to prepare for guests."

Royl stood too. "Thank you, we accept your invitation. We, too, wish to extend an invitation to you. It's been a long time since our people have been able to set foot in our homeland safely. We're planning a celebration in Litlen three days from now and would like you to join us. It will be a time to proclaim a new beginning and acknowledge the sacrifice others have made. Will you come?"

Ilan smiled. He nodded, a little too eagerly. "I'll be there."

"Good," Kameron said. "Then for now, our business is done. Take time to consider our offer, and we will reconvene to hear your answer one day soon. There is still much to organize before we are established."

A weight lifted from Ilan's chest. He'd been accepted by the Elderace and was on his way to building a future alongside them.

He directed them from the grand hall, thinking to offer them a tour around the Keep before food was served. He had a big decision to make, but he would take the time to ponder it later. Each day, the future of Kartha was looking brighter.

Chapter 98

LAILA SAVOURED THE FRESH AIR. WITHIN A FEW WEEKS, THE FRAgrance of Litlen had overpowered any lingering smells from the war.

She faced the warm breeze over the cliffs. The wind kept her hair off her face, blowing past her. Even though she'd done this a million times in all her years living underground, none of those times felt as good as this one.

A few days after the battle, she'd sat down with Raidan, Dimitri, and Adrik and listened to the events that had played out after she'd lost consciousness. Beiron was alive but trapped. And if Adrik couldn't escape the curse in the cave, Beiron certainly shouldn't be able to. Laila kept the information about her relation to Beiron to herself, but she worried about her connection with him. She hadn't felt his presence in all of six weeks. Once, just to see if she could, she made a few attempts to connect with him, but nothing happened. It was too soon to hope he was gone from her life completely.

She sat on a stone bench overlooking the cliffs to the south. This spot was so perfect.

While Litlen had been abandoned, she'd had the city to herself. Now it bustled with people all the time. She could never get a moment of privacy in any of her favourite places anymore. Which was another reason to explore beyond Kartha's borders. Her encounter with Beiron and learning he was her father made her question everything she knew about herself. Everything about her mother, her people, Royl.

The way Beiron spoke about the elders and the system—she hated to admit it, but he made some good points. They really weren't teaching anyone to their full potential. Laila was certain that Beiron's intentions had always been to gain more power so he could rule over the mayanon, but Laila would love to know more for the purpose of fulfillment. What were her own limitations? And what was it about the blood magic that made the elders so afraid? Would they feel the same if they could grasp a better understanding of it?

Laila brushed off the cover of the book in her lap. Royl was meeting her here soon. He'd just returned yesterday from Valmain after visiting Ilan Valca. The war had taken an interesting turn, and Laila did wonder what the future had in store for Kartha. She would stick around a little longer, but ultimately, she needed to get out of here and see the world for herself. There was so much to discover and learn. Staying here would only hold her back.

"I see you've found a nice little place to make your perch, *tsarioc*," Royl said from behind. He approached in his casual gait that Laila knew so well, then lowered himself onto the stone bench beside her. "How are you coping?"

Laila thought for a moment. The images of blood and war haunted her every night. Beiron's voice echoed in her head often, and she feared he was spying on her constantly.

"I'm getting there," she said. She hadn't asked him to come here so she could delve into all the things keeping her up at night. As soon as she had this conversation off her chest, she'd feel a whole lot better. Or worse.

"Royl, what do you remember about Father?"

Royl's quick intake of breath through his nose was subtle. Laila heard it all the same. "I was so young when he died. Why? What's on your mind?"

Laila turned her head from the sea and locked eyes with her brother. He ought to know she could see right through him. It was, after all, her gift to be able to tell when one was not being truthful. "I learned something recently," she said. "Something about Beiron."

"Laila, that doesn't matter. It was—"

"You knew?" She stood up and faced him, her book dropping to the ground. Her voice came out louder than she'd intended. "How could you not have told me? All this time? You kept this secret from me!"

It had not been her plan to get upset. She thought she'd be able to control her emotions when the time came. Apparently she was wrong. And so the tears began. "Why didn't you tell me?"

Royl stood up. He made no move to reach for her. Not yet anyway. "I knew, yes. I wanted to tell you. So many times. But Mum insisted I didn't. I'm sorry, Laila. I didn't mean to hurt you."

Laila hugged herself. She watched the sun set over the sea, something she didn't get to see very often because of hills surrounding Litlen.

Royl extended his hand, hesitated, and dropped it to his side. He shook his head. "I remember Beiron coming around a few times. I told Mum he was bad news, but she saw something in him that no one else did. Don't ask me what. Then I think, one day, she saw what everyone else saw. So she stopped seeing him and decided not to tell him about you or you about him. She thought she was protecting you, Laila." He scratched his head. "You really should be talking to her about this, not me."

Laila tucked her arms closer to herself. The wind felt cool against her skin. She turned to Royl, remembering all too well the cut on his upper arm that was there because of her. She looked away. She wasn't mad at him. How could she be mad at him about this?

"He used me to hurt you," Laila said. She nodded at his arm. "In case you were wondering how you got that cut."

Royl reached his arm across his body and rubbed the place she'd indicated. "I did wonder, actually." He sighed and rested a hand on her shoulder. "He's gone now anyway. You got your wish, and we're living aboveground finally. The city is looking more and more habitable each day. You've even got your own place. Things are changing for the better in Kartha. I think that's a win, don't you?"

Laila gave Royl a weak smile.

Royl gestured to the book that had fallen on the ground during her outburst. "What's that?"

Laila picked it up and brushed off the dirt. She suspected he already had a pretty good idea what it was. Rather than directly answer the question, she answered around it. "I don't agree with the way he made discoveries," she said. "But some of what he learned is incredible and—"

"Laila, stop. You can't keep that. Why would you want to hold onto a piece of him like that?"

"It's not a piece of him. This is my own writing. If you knew what was in here—"

"I don't want to know. And I suggest you get rid of it."

Laila shook her head. "No." She hugged the book close. "I plan on bringing some of the ideas to the elders to take into consideration for regular use. If you read about the plants in here and their cures, you'd not be able to deny the good they could do. There are ointments for your muscles, salves, potions for all kinds of things, like your eyes or ears. These remedies should be common knowledge."

Royl's steady gaze fixed on her with his usual concern. Even now, he still viewed her as irresponsible. "If you bring that to the elders," he said, "they'll know where it came from and they'll turn down anything you have to say because of that alone."

"Who says they have to know where it came from?"

Royl rubbed the back of his neck. His eyes looked tired. "They will. Or they'll ask, and do you plan on lying about it?"

Laila would have thought that after everything they had gone through, her people would be able to let go of their old ways and try something new. She felt trapped all over again. So much for freedom.

She paced back and forth in front of the bench. Royl reached for her. "Laila, stop. Just—let it go for now. The celebration is in a couple of days. Let's go and enjoy ourselves. Our people need a reminder of what it's like to have fun again. We can talk about this another time, when everything is not so fresh. For now, let's just breathe."

Laila took his suggestion literally. She took a calming breath.

"There's something I want to tell you," Royl said. His face lit up. "The elders are going to name me an official elder at the celebration. Since more jobs are being delegated throughout the city, I finally get the title. I'll continue my usual duties but will focus more on training warriors."

Laila had no appreciation for the elders just now. She was happy for him, but she lacked his enthusiasm. She smiled anyway. "That's great. Congratulations. You've earned it."

Royl faced her straight on. He hugged her. "You know I'm right here, *tsarioc*. I always will be."

Laila's eyes filled with tears again. She hugged him back. The world could fall apart around them, but Royl would always be there. The world *did* fall apart around them, and he *was* there. Knowing now what she knew, she understood his protectiveness for her, even if she didn't always appreciate his idea of protection. She knew his love was real. Not forced or manipulated.

She cried into his shoulder. Here she was, fully prepared to leave Kartha, realizing her going would break his heart. She would tell him her plan eventually. But for now, she enjoyed the warmth of his embrace for as long as it lasted.

Chapter 99

THE CENTRE OF LITLEN WAS TRULY A SIGHT TO BEHOLD WHEN IT WAS not a war zone. Raidan sat shoulder to shoulder with Ida on a blanket, Cassian in his arms. His son giggled at the swaying tree, and Raidan's face relaxed in a smile.

The tree at the centre of this place looked like it had long silver hair draped over its trunk. The Elderace called it the Abberbrat—bright tree, aptly named for its glowing fruit at night.

The battle felt like a lifetime ago, though there was still a mourning in his heart. The celebration tonight was meant to be joyous, yet he was filled with a deep sense of loss. So much blood had been spilled. Those who'd sacrificed their lives for this would never reap the benefits of their country's freedom.

The festivities were set to begin when the sun went down, which it was about to now. The band from Elefthan had hauled their instruments here to play music in the middle of the city. The spiral garden had recovered after being trampled on by so many. With the help of Elderace magic, it flourished. The band set up next to the tree where the cannon had been during the battle; Raidan put the image from his mind.

In the past weeks, he and Ida had discussed moving to Litlen when the homes were ready. In the meantime, they'd been helping to restore the city to its former glory. Raidan had finally managed to finish the cabinet for Rees, who had been understanding and appreciative.

Across the courtyard from where Raidan and Ida sat, Eli stood with Adrik behind a row of seats. Since Adrik had been back, Eli had become as eager as a child to show everyone the new light tricks he'd learned from him. Adrik created his light-ball, then reformed it to take the shape of a bird. The light bird swooped over the heads of the hundreds of people gathered.

The band was about to play. All around, people sat in rows of chairs or on blankets. Ilan had been invited, but Raidan hadn't seen him yet, nor Laila. He searched the crowd. Andrei had joined Eli and Adrik, half hidden by the mass of people. He was with a man and woman. The woman's belly swelled as a new life took form inside her womb. Her face glowed. Raidan had never seen so many joyful people gathered in all his life.

Adrik, having been made the delegate of light, had never lost his light magic. Had the other delegates lived, they, too, would have had the magic of their element through the cursed years.

With nearly a full millennia of history in Raidan's mind—since the time of the Chronicle Storm that shattered the crystals to the time when Beiron cursed all of Litlen—came an overwhelming need to protect the stone. He and Dimitri would fulfill their duty and, eventually, pass down the responsibility to their heirs.

Raidan looked at his boy, who was all smiles. Cassian reached for Ida. She lifted him from under his arms, taking him from Raidan. She rubbed her nose to his and set him on her lap.

Dimitri came over from behind and found a seat on the blanket next to Ida. He'd been busy in Veryl these past weeks, getting things back in order there, where he'd been greatly missed. Many from home would be joining the evening celebration. Their old friend and Dimitri's mentor Lothaire had travelled through the mountain pass from Veryl with Dimitri.

Dimitri tickled Cassian's belly with his finger and Cassian squealed. The top of his single tooth that poked through his gums was visible as he laughed.

"Where's Lothaire?" Raidan asked.

Dimitri shrugged. "The old man made friends and wanted to sit with them."

Raidan chuckled. It was no wonder Dimitri and Lothaire got along so well.

Near the tree, Royl sat with the four elders who governed the Elderace. Raidan had met the elders a few days after the battle was over. Initially, he'd assumed the delegates governed the Elderace, but he'd later learned they only guarded the Weldafire Stone—and then, when it was bound—the Guardians of the Weldafire Stone. It looked like he and Dimitri were going to be stuck with Adrik for a long time. Raidan didn't mind so much, though.

Kameron crossed over to them from where the band was about to start playing. Raidan had learned that Kameron and his people were responsible for disabling two of the three cannons in an ambush at the Gap, where the weapons had been towed into Litlen. The destruction of the third was Laila's doing, according to Dimitri, who'd found her.

Kameron crouched down at the edge of the blanket, half in the grass, and squeezed Raidan's shoulder. "He has your eyes," he said as he nodded at Cassian.

Raidan smiled. Yes, he did.

"Enjoy the music," Kameron said, then stood. "And remember to listen," he added with a wink as he walked off toward Keshlyn.

The fruit of the tree glowed now that the sun had gone down. The stars were out. It was bright in the courtyard and hard to see a lot of them in the sky, but Raidan knew they were there. The moon was only a thin crescent tonight.

He leaned back, hands in the grass behind him, and closed his eyes. The first chord of the music struck, followed by a few minor chords as the band played a tune of mourning. A lament for those who'd died in battle.

Cassian quieted. Raidan opened his eyes and peeked over at his son, who'd become captivated with the music. His eyes, wide and watching, soon glazed over, and he swayed. His fingers slowly moved toward his half-open mouth.

Ida stared at the tree and the ember-like glow of its fruit. Her eyes shone in its light.

Keshlyn stepped in front of the musicians and she sang. Her voice was a gentle river flowing around them, and her words seemed to echo everywhere. Raidan thought they could be heard—or felt, rather—by every person in Kartha. In his heart, he believed it to be the song that had echoed throughout Kartha after Litlen was awakened. And although it had initially been sung in Eldrace, or so he'd been told, this time, it was sung for all to understand.

> *Light turned to dark,*
> *in our hearts, in our spirits.*
> *In our hearts, there was no song,*
> *no song.*

> *Fire raining down, pouring down;*
> *blood flowing through the streets.*
> *In our hearts, devastation,*
> *devastation.*

> *Shadows, though dark, grew darker still;*
> *enemies surround.*
> *Where to run, to flee, to hide?*
> *War! War!*

As Keshlyn sang, others joined in. Their voices reached deep to Raidan's core, and tears rolled down his cheeks. The steady rhythm of the bass instrument pulsed in his throat, as it had done the last time he'd heard the music of the people of Elefthan. He'd had much on his mind then. Now he had nothing holding him back from truly hearing it. The musician playing the djembe rubbed his hands across the surface of the skin, creating a sound that flowed rather than bopped, like a gentle breeze.

As if the idea brought it on, a breeze hit Raidan's face and he breathed in the fresh scent of the sea, coming off the coast. Flowers carried their scent in the air as well. Lavenders and lilacs, roses and lilies and the unfamiliar fragrances of flowers Raidan had never heard of or seen before coming to Litlen.

But we will see the day,
the day will come that we will sing again.

Rejoice! Take heart!

Rejoice! The day will come
when we will have peace.

The songs in our hearts will come alive;
the music in our spirits, move;
and the spirit of the land will be restored.

The music carried out its tune while Keshlyn bowed her head. Cassian had fallen asleep. Ida cradled him in her crossed legs, her own eyes closed and lips turned up in a subtle smile.

Raidan took the Weldafire Stone from his pocket and twirled it in his hand. It was the size of a strawberry, and its colour was a vibrant blue-green turquoise that seemed to change when he turned it. From one angle, it looked blue, and from another, green. Straight on, it was a solid turquoise. He closed his fist around its rough surface.

This new power and knowledge he had attained equipped him with the ability to protect those around him: his family, Litlen, Kartha. It opened his eyes to a world of magic and new life.

The delegates' goal in making Sermarc the Guardian of the Weldafire Stone was to bring peace to the land—to bring the peoples together as one. One Kartha.

Raidan listened as the melody drew him in. He caught Kameron's eye, and peace overwhelmed his heart.

What Raidan held in his hand was much more than just a stone. Yes, it had a unique power, but it was also a symbol to the people of something that could bring them together. The day would come when there would be no distinction between Elderace and mayanon. The people would stand as one. With The Order gone, they had a second chance to do things better. And although the road ahead was long and there was still much to learn, Raidan accepted his responsibility. He intended to uphold the task given him—to him and Dimitri both. Together, they would help to keep this peace. Together, as the Guardians of the Weldafire Stone.

About the Author

From a young age, Trinity Cunningham began storytelling and writing. She dabbled in screenwriting and song writing before moving to novels and short stories. Often caught up in far-off worlds, with characters that have only ever existed in her imagination, she's excited to see them come to life and share her stories, while hopefully leaving readers impacted emotionally. Besides writing, Trinity enjoys reading, watching films, photography, and spending time with friends and family. She lives in Canada, with her husband and their three children.

Printed in Canada